Absolution

BOB RIEPE

Gotham Books
30 N Gould St.
Ste. 20820, Sheridan, WY 82801
https://gothambooksinc.com/
Phone: 1 (307) 464-7800

ISBN: 978-1-956349-30-6 P
ISBN: 978-1-956349-31-3 E

DEB GUTHMAN TERNUS **ON**

ABSOLUTION
BOOK REVIEW

bsolution

keeps the reader on the edge of their seat unravelling many dark secrets and twists and turns along the way. The protagonist, Quinn, embarks on a journey of self-discovery, which evolves throughout the book as he comes to terms with demons in his personal, professional and spiritual life.

The author paints a picture so vivid, you can imagine being at the very location where many exhilarating & haunting events take place.

Riepe uses recognizable Minnesota landmarks and effectively mixes historic truths with fiction and successfully brings to life the era he is writing about.

Using symbolism and metaphors, the author provides the reader with insightful observations and the ability to relate to many of the lessons learned by the key characters. Despite his flaws, it is inspiring to accompany Quinn on his physical and emotional journey.

BOB RIEPE

"**B**ITTERNESS MAY LEAD TO DENIAL,

while

FORGIVENESS CAN LEAD TO ACCEPTANCE."

BOB RIEPE

"THE UNEXPECTED ENGAGEMENT"

APRIL 1883

NEVER TAKE YOUR LOVED ONES FOR GRANTED. With fire and ice in his veins, a satchel of wounds clinging to his back, and a heavy dose of April snow filling the air, young Dr. Quinn Shanahan was thinking about that statement, as he directed his carriage down the snow-covered, Lincoln Avenue, in Fergus Falls, Minnesota. He was heading for a Party of Engagement at the House of Wiggins, with his 19-year old brother, Braden, sitting next to him. Both were dressed in a dazzling tuxedo with a black tophat and matching coat.

With nerves frazzled and confusion on display, Quinn was in deep thought. He kept thinking about that quote of never taking your loved ones for granted. Am I doing the right thing? He asked himself. Was Harriet the right person? Maybe I deserve more. Can I afford her? Will it change her? Or, better yet, will it change me? Will it affect Braden? These were questions that kept jumping out at him as the blond-haired Irishman glanced over at the young man sitting beside him. Ah, my dear little brother. So helpful, yet so helpless! What's going to happen to him? What will Harriet think? Will she accept him as part of the family? He was 19 but sometimes acted like 10. He didn't care what he looked like in public, just as long as he could be with me.

"Dilodaffs!" shouted Braden, as he smiled and pointed to the flowers alongside the road.

"Means spring is here."

"I see them," replied Quinn as he laughed. "Daffodils! Beautiful?"

"Yes, yes. Beau, beautiful. Yellow. You sing?"

The Unexpected Engagement

"Sing? You want meeee to sing in the dark?" Quinn cleared his voice as Braden began to rock back and forth with a big smile.

"Oh, I wandered lonely as a cloud that floats on high o'er vales and hills, When all at once I saw a crowd, a host of golden daffodils,

Beside the l ake, beneath the trees, fluttering and dancing in the breeze.

Continuous as the star that shines and twinkles on the Milky Way.

They stretched in a never-ending line. Along the margin of a bay;

Ten thousand I s aw at a glance. Tossing their heads in sprightly dance.

The waves beside them danced, but they out-did the sparking waves in play,

A poet could not but be gay, in such a jocund company;

I gazed and gazed but little thought what wealth the show to me had brought;

For oft, when on my couch I lie, in vacant or pensive mood.

They flash upon that inward eye, which is the bliss of solitude,

And then my heart with pleasure fills and dances with the daffodils."

"Good! Good!" shouted Braden as he clapped his approval. "Daff,

Daffodils! My favorite!"

"Courtesy of Mr. William Wordsworth," added Quinn.

"It's so calm and peaceful, Braden. The light snow coming down is so relaxing. That's a good sign that our evening is going to be one to remember. Braden. Thank-you for being you. I am so proud to say you are my brother. If Harriet agrees to marry me, I'd like you to be my Best Man."

"What's that?"

"It means that I'd like you to stand up next to me when I get married."
"Me get married too?"
"Ah, no. Not quite," laughed Quinn. "You'll be my right-hand man."
"Me, your right-hand man always," offered Braden as he displayed a huge smile.

"Yes, but this will be a special day for Harriet, and me, and you."
"Shhhhh! What was that?" cautioned the startled Quinn as he looked down the side street. He squinted, in search of a source, but all he noticed was the putrid aura of the neighborhood vaults. No movement! No sounds! Nothing, he told himself. Just my imagination.

"Look!" commanded Braden. "What is that?"
Quinn stopped the wagon and looked over to where Braden was pointing. "That's the 'Well of Despondency'. A water well. My wishing well."

"It's high."

"Yes, Braden. Probably the first well dug in this town. Back at the beginning when there was a hill right here that was about 15-20 feet taller than it is now."

"That looks scary."

More noise. It was coming from the same area. He put a toothpick in his mouth and pulled on his right ear and glanced over at the unfazed Braden. There he was, rocking forward and back with nothing but smiles. Innocent as ever. Nineteen years old and clutching his favorite family item, a dirty old yellow ribbon that had been a part of his toy box ever since Mum left this world oh so long ago. The little guy could care less as long as he could ride in the buggy and play with that memory.

5

The Unexpected Engagement

With toothpick in mouth, Quinn directed his attention back to where the sound was coming from. Still nothing. Nothing but darkness---an eerie darkness, ominous and sinister. But then it happened. A buckboard with six men in masks and hooded buffalo robes, came rumbling down the street directly towards Quinn. With guns in h and, the marauders disembarked and surrounded the Shanahan wagon.

"What do you want?" yelled Quinn as he placed his arm around Braden.
-"Going to a party?" laughed the leader.
"Who are you?" asked Quinn as excessive saliva oozed from his mouth.
"Never mind. Get down from there. Both of you!"
The odds a ren't that good but I'll be danged if I'm going to just stand and let them do harm to Braden, thought Quinn, as he pondered his plan of attack. He stared at one of the attackers. Those eyes? There's something about those eyes, he thought as a sheen of sweat appeared on his cheeks and forehead.

As Quinn helped Braden down, they were jumped by the thugs, pummeling and battering and thrashing, with reckless abandon. Quinn tried to protect Braden as best he could. Knocked down to the icy street they went, desperately trying to evade the flailing arms of the intruders.

"Bad!" cried out Braden.

"Don't worry, Braden. We'll survive. We'll get to our destination. We have to. I need it."

"Give me your money," yelled the tall, lanky leader as he ripped open Quinn's pockets.

"You can't stop us," blurted Quinn as two men held his arms and a third cut open Quinn's shirt with a knife. "You do as you're told," he shouted as he placed the knife up to Quinn's neck. Quinn kicked him in the stomach, knocking the knife away, and the attacker, to the ground. The attacker arose and rushed Quinn, pulverizing him in the face and stomach.

The Unexpected
Engagement

Blood squirted from Quinn's nose, mouth, and arms. He fell to his knees, trying to protect his little brother. He picked up the knife, swung around, and slashed the attacker across the face, ripping the mask partially off. Screams ensued as the attacker covered his face and ran off into the darkness.

Quinn's top coat and hat were torn off and two ruffians fought over ownership. His blood-stained, white shirt was ripped to shreds. His long blond hair was a mess. His left eye was swollen, yet he would not give up. He glanced over towards Braden. "Leave him alone!" he snapped. "He's harmless."

Two took turns punching the defenseless Braden. They drug him across the fresh snow, all the while laughing, as his coat was torn off and his shirt shredded to pieces. They pulled back his hair and slapped his face with reckless abandon, till blood appeared from his mouth. Still, he resisted. He fell to his knees, wavering forward, then back. He looked up. "Never!" he yelled as he held back his tears. He tried to return the punches but there was no match. "Quinn!" he blurted. "I love you." And he fell to the ground.

The two men switched their attention to Quinn. One attacking the top half and the other, the bottom. While one held him down, the other obliterated the defenseless Quinn, ripping at his face and gouging at his eyes.

"That's enough!" commanded the leader. "Take their carriage. Throw the kid in our wagon and leave the other."

As the attackers departed, the snow stopped. A brown rabbit bounced slowly past the lifeless Quinn, while a German shepherd approached from two blocks away. The dog sniffed the boots, and then his coat, and then his face. He licked the face. He stepped back and barked.

Quinn squinted at the dog. "Voyance? Is that you? You're a sight for sore eyes. How did you get way over here, so far from the Wiggins house?"
 Voyance barked and put his tail in motion, and barked again.
 Quinn glanced around. Nothing but snow and darkness. "Braden?" he cried out. "Braden? Where are you?"

No reply, just the excited display of Voyance acting as if he had just found his best friend.

Quinn sat up. Pain was everywhere. He rubbed his eyes and then the back of his neck. Both arms were cut and bruised. He felt his face, all puffed and bloody. A front tooth was chipped out. A knife cut across his chest. With aching head and wounded ego, he stood up. "This had to have been the work of that Bannister! That judge has been a thorn in my side ever since I came out here," he shouted as he continued to look around. "Oh Braden! I'm so sorry. I feel so bad. I failed you. There's no way they're going to get away with this," he yelled in a gruff voice. "I can't help but wonder why these kinds of things always happen to me. At least we weren't by the water. I'll find you, Braden. Just give me a little time."

He tried standing up, but his left leg could not hold him. He fell down on his knees and began the slow journey to the House of Wiggins, three blocks away, all the while on constant alert, shivering, and looking to his left, and then to his right, and then behind him, and even ahead of him. Darkness was fast approaching. A cold, northerly breeze penetrated, as he crawled onward. Blood oozed from his knees and fingers. Eyes, puffed and closing. Nose, running and sore. Toes and fingers, numb, and aching teeth. A lonesome train whistle, off in the distant, permeated the air, with competition coming from a band of howling coyotes, out by Fish Lake, as the smell of oysters arose from the Silver Moon restaurant. He tried to think of Braden, but the sympathy kept coming back to him.

With Voyance leading the way, the House of Wiggins came into view. High on the hilltop overlooking the pristine Lake Alice, Quinn stopped limping and glued his eyes on the magnificent edifice in front of him. The massive, brown and tan mansion stood out amongst the neighboring shanties and hovels. Three stories reaching above the tree line, high enough to keep an eye on the surroundings below. It was a modern example of family snobbery. With its Queen Anne towers on each side and a hip roof covering a balcony on t he second floor, it provided an ideal welcome mat for visitors and occupants. A spindled hand railing ran around the front, on both the main floor and the balcony. Four wooden columns supported an entry porch wher e Quinn and Voyance approached. They were greeted by lady of the house, Clare. Mrs. Wiggins, with her slender body and short, black hair, was the overseer, the farmer's wife, in charge of the musical exploits of her three daughters.

The Unexpected Engagement

"Voyance! Where have you been?" she angrily shook her finger at the scared German shepherd. "Mr. Shanahan! Whatever happened to you?" gasped Clare. "Please, come in. The girls are upstairs getting ready. It looks like just about everyone is prepared except for you. Do you care to explain?" she continued as she led him into the castle.

"They took Braden. I don't know what to do? We, we were attacked. They beat us up. My God! I'll never be able to forgive myself. I was responsible for him. I let them take him. Where's Stanley? Where's Stanley? We have to find Braden." "Now, slow down, Quinn. Catch your breath. Here. Sit down."
Clare was the matriarch, the glue that held the family together. She was slender, yet full. She was domineering, yet submissive. More than six inches taller than her husband, Stanley. She wore nothing but the best, but wasn't afraid to get her hands dirty. She was wearing a red and white, cotton scarf wrapped around her head, with long, gold earrings dangling down her sides, and she topped it off with a red Victorian day dress. She was the prognosticator, the clairvoyant of the family. " I told Stanley just yesterday that something didn't seem right about having this party tonight."

"We were hoodwinked down the road not far from here. Braden was with. They stopped us and roughed us up. They took off with Braden and left me lying in the street."
"Oh my!" continued Clare, as she checked over Quinn's bruises. "Stanley!" she yelled. "Stanley! Get out here!"
"Here," lie down," continued Clare. "Deborah! Bring me a bowl of warm water and a wash cloth. We need to get our doctor cleaned up."
"Yes, Mother," replied the young spitfire of a teenager, as she turned around and headed back up the stairs.

"We were on our way over. Got bushwhacked by a group of thumpers. They didn't find much on me, so they decided to take it out on us. I'm not much of a fighter when it comes to the knuckles, but I got a couple of good ones in. I sort of recognized one of them, but can't put my finger on exactly who he is. They took my carriage. The one with the two golden spokes. The seat on their buckboard seemed to be quite torn up, especially on the back base."

The Unexpected Engagement

"Stanley!" again shouted Clare, as he appeared from a back room. "Can you help Dr. Shanahan? We're going to have to cancel the dinner. When you're upstairs, find some clothes that he can wear, and tell the girls to stop what they're doing. We'll change the date till next Saturday evening. The cake will have to be done over, and we haven't shucked the oysters yet, so they should be fine. Now, go get some clothes for him."

"Yes, dear."

Quinn kept his eyes locked in on Clare as she kept babbling on, but inside he was thinking differently. Old Clare, he thought. She could be the sweetest person in the world unless she felt that you crossed her, or that she had been taken advantage of. Then revenge would come into play, and she could dish that out with the best of them. She had a good thing going with the girls. Her three daughters were the talk of the town and of Minnesota for that matter. All three were expert concert pianists and they had sweet voices that went with it. It was her girls that were going to be her savior. She pushed them to be their best with the piano and their talented voices. Hours upon hours of practice. Every day, no matter. She pushed and pushed, all with the hope of one day being repaid for all the time spent.

"Here's the water, Mother," noted Deborah as she set the bowl down beside Quinn.

"Go get him something to eat and drink," commanded Clare. "I could use a few extra towels too. We have a lot of cleaning up to do. He's a mess."

"Never mind that," interrupted Quinn, with a wince. "We need to go find my brother."

"That can wait," insisted Clare, as she began wiping the blood away.

Stanley came down with an arm full of clothes. He was a short and heavyset man in a lightweight suit. He was a farmer by trade, with his rough, sunburnt complexion and gnarled hands. He had a full beard of brown, sprinkled with a tint of gray, and he carried a shiny ear trumpet in his coat pocket. "Not sure if they'll fit you, or not."

10

The Unexpected Engagement

Might be a little short and baggy, but it should work so that you can get back to the Occidental. You can change in my room. I'll go out and hitch up the team. I still don't understand why anyone would want to hurt Braden. I need to get over and catch Reverend Martin and we better stop and talk to Chief Sullivan. Then, I'll get you home."

Quinn glanced up to the top of the stairs. Ah, the pride and joy of the Wiggins hierarchy was standing at the top, waiting to be noticed. Harriet, the eldest of the three performers and the future bride of Quinn, maybe. The young damsel fit the definition of beauty, yet she showed her utter dismay. With her sapphire eyes and auburn hair and a pocket mirror in hand, she looked down upon her minions. "Mother! This will not do! Cancel the event! Change it to next week. Perhaps by then, he will be able to explain this absurdity."

"Oh child! We can't do that."
 Harriet came down the stairs, dressed in a stunning, white evening gown, with an overload of pearls and diamonds. She was the first to master the piano and the rest of the family. She was the leader of the "Wiggin's Trio. With guidance supplied by Clare, Harriet was well on her way to becoming one of the top concert pianists, not only in the United States, but was renowned all over the world.

Like her two sisters, she was in the market for marriage, but that didn't mean Quinn was the answer. She had many unanswered questions, just like Quinn. She had plenty of young men courting her in the past, especially when she lived in Northfield, but now that would have to change, or would it? She loved to dance and she didn't care who she danced with, but now that would have to change, or would it?

She stared at Quinn as she came down the stairs. "Quinn! What in the world?"
 "You look absolutely marvelous," observed Quinn as he took her hand. "I feel so lucky to have this chance. I thought we'd get here early, before the guests arrived. They kidnapped Braden. There were six of them."

"I can't understand anyone doing such a thing. I'm sure I'll never hear the end of it from Mother. She mentioned it several days ago about problems, and sure enough, her prediction came true. If we wait till tomorrow evening, will this affect your plans?"
 "No. I'll go into work in the morning and meet Gavin in the afternoon."

"SHANAHAN AND OGLESBY"

The medical office of Shanahan and Oglesby was situated on Lincoln Avenue, the busiest street in Fergus Falls. It was on the second floor of the McKnight Drug store, right next to the Occidental Hotel, the temporary home of Quinn.

Quinn sat in his office chair, nursing his wounds. They were everywhere---on his arms, legs, face, chest---everywhere. Cuts above his eyes and across his breast and down his legs. Anguish showed as the tender spots were cleansed and the battle scars gave their proper display. "I still can't believe what Sullivan told me," he disgustedly noted. "He said it couldn't be Bannister because he was down in Minneapolis. He'll be there for another three weeks, he said. That doesn't prove anything. It could very well be his hired hands. If I'm not going to get any help from the law I'll do it myself. I know it's that so-called judge. I'll find poor Braden, if it's the last thing I do."

Quinn paused to listen to screams coming from Oglesby's operating room, while a young lady, short and stout, and with hazel eyes and long, blonde hair, cautiously entered. Dressed in a lady's black, ottoman, silk cape, with black knit, fascinator, head wrap, she was greeted by the smell of over-cooked coffee, mixed with an aura of ether, competing with a rotten egg odor, all hovering over the poorly lit office.

"Ah, Maggie! Nice to see you. Please, come in. I understand you had been in to see my partner a while back?"

"Yes sir."
"I take it that it didn't go so well?"
"I got out of there before he could do anymore damage. Now, it sounds like he's doing it to another girl."

Shanahan
and Oglesby

"Remy is from the Baker Brother's school. He feels the best way to cure female hysteria is by this process. Many medical books recommend that excision, but I do not."

Quinn turned toward the entrance where a big man, about 6'5" and 240 lbs, with small eyes and big ears came bursting into the room. "Doc! Doc!" he shouted. "You gotta help me."

"Now, hold on there. Wait your turn! Can't you see I'm busy?"
"Don't you know who I am?"
"No Sir. Can't say that I do."
"I'm the new judge in town. Franklin Bannister."
"Well Mr. Bannister. Please take a seat and I'll be right with you after I finish with this patient."

"Maggie! Come into my operating room."
Maggie followed Quinn, while the judge sat there and turned beet red. "Have a seat," offered Quinn.

"I'm sorry to bother you, Quinn. I only have a few minutes so I'll try and make this fast," she noted as she entered, wearing her working uniform of a white blouse and a black skirt. "Have you found out anything on Braden? It's the talk of the town. I've heard so many rumors from that he was floating in the Red, to being shot in the head. I just had to find out the truth."
"Not a word. Sullivan said he was going out first thing this morning. I'm heading over to Remy's in a bit. Then I'm going to look for myself."
"Have you received a note, or anything?"

"Nothing."
"Quinn! I want to leave town. Back to Minneapolis. I want to be a

13

writer, an author, a somebody. I could do it right here but I need to be where there's lots of people, where I can become famous. Where I can become rich and find myself a lucky man, a man that will appreciate me for what I am."

"That's where Spat comes in, right?"
"I'm not sure. He treats me well, but I want more. I want adoration. I want equality."
"Oh, don't we all?"

"Here I am just a poor little slave, a victim of the time, an unfortunate, unlucky maid, wasting away an empty life. Some people say I'm beautiful, but it's the inside that I have the problems. People usually judge a person by what they see on the outside, but it's more difficult to understand the person on the inside. People look at me and think slut, whore, prostitute, just by my looks. They don't understand me. Understanding requires compassion, patience, and a willingness to believe that good hearts sometimes choose poor methods. To understand a person one must be able to know what's going on in the inside." "That's very true, Maggie."

"I try to write. I want to do a novel, but I still have a lot to learn. I don't know if I'll ever finish it, but I like to dream."
Quinn paused and sniffed. "Is that cinnamon I smell? Are you on laudanum, by any chance?"

"Why, ah, yes. It helps me write. There's times I get so caught up in what I'm plotting out I get confused and forget my line of thought. It settles me down."
"You don't need that. That's addictive. Before you know it'll gobble you up."

"Shanahan!" came the shout from Bannister. "What's taking so long?"
"Never mind him," noted Quinn. "Sit down here on the edge of the table. We're going to try something new. You have many of the symptoms of the 'wandering of the womb' disease. It's usually found in the upper classes, caused by stress. Much of the problem seems to be based on the restrictive view of female sexuality.

14

Shanahan and Oglesby

It's almost as if it's forbidden to talk about it. The stress associated with this has made women more susceptible to nervous disorders and to develop faulty reproductive tracts. There are several ways to deal with this problem."

"But, Doc."
"One way is with a vibrator, and the other way is massage," continued Quinn, as he raised her cape.

Quiet reigned over both operating tables. They were both dimly lit and murky. The fishy smell was overwhelming, but the screams and tears disappeared. One patient was in ecstasy while the other was asleep in a blood-soaked bed.
"Hey, Remy!" yelled Quinn as he came out of his operating room. "Are you about done in there?"
"In a minute."
"About time," shouted Bannister, as he coughed and wiped his runny nose.
"I can't believe it took you so long. A man could die waiting for you."
"Alright, Mr. What can I do for you?"

"You see this?" asked Bannister as he pointed to the red rash on his face and neck.
"I see. Yes. I, I believe you have the measles."
"You're not telling me anything new. What do I do to get rid of them?"
"Let it run its course," suggested Quinn, as he took Bannister's temp. "I see you're running a fever."
"Tell me something I don't already know. I feel miserable. From head to toe. I have aches and pains all over."
"Normally, the rash will last for about five days and then fade away. The fever, cough, watery eyes, and runny nose will disappear also, but before that all goes away expect that rash to become more solid and spread to the arms. Let me see the inside of your mouth."

Bannister opened up and Quinn peaked in. 'Oh your breath is terrible,' mentioned Quinn as he turned away for a moment to gather his composure. "Oh, ah, yes, I see white spots.

Shanahan and Oglesby

They too will disappear. What you need is plenty of rest and take daily sponge baths with luke-warm water. Drink plenty of liquids, like water and milk and eat plenty of fruits."

"I didn't need to come and listen to what I already knew. Tell me something new."

"Well, I didn't ask you to come. I'm telling you like it is. You have the measles, just like thousands of others. If you do as I tell you, it'll go away in five or six days. If not, there could be complications.
Bannister slapped the table as he arose and left. "You can expect to hear a lot from me in the future. No one treats me like that and gets away with it. Mark my words. I've been seeing that Harriet Wiggins and I plan on seeing more of her."

Quinn watched him leave. "What a character!" he murmured. "How dare he talk like that about Harriet!"
Maggie appeared from the operating room, still in a sweat. "I want to thank you, Quinn. "I've never felt better. I am so relieved. I can't wait to tell Deborah."

"Deborah?"
"Yes. Wiggins. She's in Oglesby's room right now."

"Really? That's who was screaming?"

"Yes. I can't believe you're still a partner. He just drags your business down."
"If it weren't for him there wouldn't be an office. When I first got here, after getting robbed twice on the way from Pennsylvania, he was a lifesaver. He's been a classmate of mine, all through Medical school back in New York. I'll always be indebted to him. He had the money when I needed it."

"It seems like he takes advantage of you at every chance he gets."
"I have a couple of projects started and have my fingers crossed that they come through.

16

Shanahan and Oglesby

I have this idea of a Family Medical Kit that should be a part of every family's cupboard of necessities. The other idea is real estate. I've met with my brother-in-law, Gavin Delaney, and with Ellsworth Montgomery III. They both suggested that I get into that business while it is a hot item. There's a lot money to be made. Maybe by the time I get those two projects off the ground I'll be able to afford a wife."

"Yes, speaking of that. I was all ready to head over to the Wiggins last night and then Naddy told me what happened. Have you heard any more on your brother? I just couldn't believe anyone would be mean enough to go stealing that poor boy. I sure do hope you find him."

"We will. By the way, how's your writing coming along?"

"It's not as easy as I thought it would be. I can't seem to get much done where I'm working now. Spending entirely too much time cleaning at the Occidental. I need a place where there's peace and quiet, where I can hear Mother Nature, where I can put my creative juices to work."

"I know the perfect place. Out at Fish Lake. When I first got out here, coming over from Perham by stage, we stopped by a lake about seven miles, or so, from Fergus. I fell in love with it. All I could think about for weeks was if only I could afford to build a resort out there. That idea is still in the back of my head, but reality is winning out for now, but some day, Maggie. Some day. Maybe when Harriet makes up her mind, maybe then I'll be able to afford it."

"Oh, Maggie. Those hazel eyes have such a magnificent and refreshing glow. It compliments your long, light brown hair. Your body deserves to wear more elegance. Your soft, glistening skin is the perfect medicine I need for my tired eyes. If I wasn't courting Harriet, I'd love nothing better than to kiss those tempting lips."

Maggie stepped closer, while adjusting her blouse and licking her lips. "There's no law against it," she whispered as their lips drew closer and closer, and Quinn ran his fingers through her hair, and their lips met. With their eyes closed, they enjoyed the moment.

17

Shanahan
and Oglesby

Maggie pulled back. "Oh my, Quinn. That was wonderful! But, I really must get back to work. Thank-you for making my morning and I hope everything turns out well with Braden," she noted as she headed out the door.

Quinn put on a jacket and cap, put a toothpick in his mouth and headed out, with the Oglesby household the next stop. "Remy! I'm heading over to check out your new home. How long before you get there?"
"Tell her I'll be home in about an hour. I still have some work to do on my patient."

The Remington Oglesby manor was a monster on the midway at its veritable crossroads of life. It was located near Lake Alice, but quite a distance from the Wiggins. It was away from the affluent part of town down on the west end. It sat alone, mired in mud, hidden among the dying balsam firs and withering elms. Like a wounded warship in the middle of the Pacific, she begged for recognition. Its terms of entrapment were set. Patches of poison ivy dotted along the wooden path, leading up to the gated façade. Beehive armies, under the unpainted eaves, lie in wait for their next victim. The stench of horse manure competed with the nearby, run-down vault. The lonesome bleating of several goats was the only sound heard by Quinn as he approached. The walls of unpainted granite were covered with barnacles and lichen. Tall, narrow windows draped the sides, all shuddered and cold. "Wow!" gasped Quinn. This has Remy written all over it."

The main entrance was enamored with signage: NO ONE HOME, BEWARE OF DOG, and GONE FISHING. On the left side of the entrance hung a huge portrait of "Remington Oglesby, Doctor of Medicine", and on the right, a faded picture of " Caitlin Oglesby, Connoisseur of Revenge".
The house was an embodiment of Victorian, Tudor, and American. With its tall stacks of soot shooting up from the roof that had missing shingles. She wore an armament of mystery in a field of enmity.

Quinn knocked and waited. He was pleasantly greeted by Lin. She was dressed in black. She was strong and domineering. Her curly black hair was out of place. Her face was stern and devoid. Her calloused hands, withdrawn. Her palms, worn from too much of something. Her hazel eyes darted back and forth as if wary of her surroundings. "Quinn! What a nice surprise! Please come in. How are you doing after last night? Did you find Braden?"

Shanahan
and Oglesby

"No. I haven't heard a word."

"Remy said he'd be here within an hour. I have an appointment at one. This would give me time to take a tour of your new residence, plus he mentioned beef stew."

"He did, huh? I'd be glad to show you. It's nice to see you. I know you both have been quite busy with the new business, but it gets very lonely in this big house. I haven't made many friends since we got here. I suppose it's my fault but I prefer to keep a low profile. That doesn't mean we can't spend time together," she continued as she stepped right up next to Quinn and looked him straight in the eye, and smiled. "I can always get another deck of cards, or maybe an extra pillow."

Quinn stood there in amazement. I can't believe I heard that, he thought to himself as he smiled and glanced around the room. The furniture was fragile and showed an agenda of aggravation. Sparse and liked to their way of thinking. A modest credenza here, a superfluous lounge chair there. A table of warped oak here, a night stand of maple there. A conglomeration of mix and match throughout, with no rhyme or reason. Confusion run rampant, organization, absent. An open invitation to hell lie at the bottom of the stairwell to their bedroom. An enticement to subjugation. He followed the quiet Lin up the creaking stairs that had several missing spindles. "This isn't what I was expecting. Knowing Remy, I could believe this, but I always thought you were so much different."

"You have to excuse the mess. I haven't been feeling well, plus it is very difficult to keep a house in order with someone like Remy always messing things up."

At the top of the steps there was a door to the left and one to the right. They entered the one on the left. It was Remy's room. It was dark and dreary, with austerity throughout. A pair of binoculars set on a window sill, primed and ready. Above a granite fireplace hung a compass, night light, and a ships' anchor. In front, a captain's chair. Another wall contained a plethora of portraits---all of the doctor, all begging for congratulations and notice. Off to the side was a small table and chair, both in dire need of a paint job. It was piled high with what looked like un-read medical journals. A six-foot mirror was on the wall in front of the table. "As you can tell," continued Lin. "He spends a lot of time in this room. You can follow me to my room."

19

Shanahan and Oglesby

Upon entry, she lit a kerosene lantern. "This is my favorite chair," she exclaimed. "It was my mother's rocking chair. I spend much of my day right in that spot, either playing solitaire or thinking of what might have been."

There were three pictures on the wall in front of the chair. The one on the left was that of a large eye. The one on her right, another large eye. The one in the middle, a large number four. There were two huge windows on one side, both with steel bars from top to bottom. There was a pink bassinet with a life-size doll setting next to the rocking chair. On the table sat a music box. Lin picked it up and gave it a crank and it began playing 'Lullaby Baby'. Beside the music box was a deck of used playing cards. The smell of tincture of iodine filled the room. A flower vase, filled with dandelions, set off in a corner next to an empty pedestal. "As you can see, I spend a lot of time in here. We each have our own single bed. Remy has a habit of moving all over the place every night and I couldn't get any sleep."

"Lin!" came the shout from downstairs. "I'm home."
"Oh my! We better get down there. He probably won't like the idea of us being upstairs in my bedroom. Although, I rather liked the idea."
Ignoring what she had just said, Quinn headed for the exit.
Downstairs, stood Remy. He was very short and heavyset. He had a pudgy nose with long nostril hairs and he wore mutton chop sideburns. He looked around for his meal. "You don't have everything ready," he shouted.

"I just got done showing Quinn our home. Give me a few minutes," she quipped as she rushed off into the kitchen.
"Very nice home," offered Quinn. "And your wife looks as lovely as ever."
"Who are you kidding?" shot back Remy. "She's a mess. I know it. You know it. She's had a lot to adjust to and isn't taking to this town very well. I'm sure you must be wondering about the bassinet? She can't have babies. It's not because of me. She has something wrong with her. Ever since we got married she has talked every day about raising a family. I wish there was something I could do for her."

"How about adoption?"

"I've thought about that, but that would mean more responsibility for me."

Shanahan and Oglesby

"There's nothing wrong with having some responsibility when it comes to family manners. I have heard there are many orphanages in this country overflowing with young children that would love to be part of a family."

"I barely make enough to support a wife, let alone children. I've heard about those places. Breeding grounds for crime. Not enough discipline. The boys end up getting into trouble. Turn into runaways. That sounds like more trouble than it's worth."

"I know it's none of my business, but that is something you two should really think about."

"Come and get it!" commanded Lin as she placed a kettle of beef stew on the kitchen table.

"Ah, it smells delicious, L in," complimented Quinn. "I absolutely love your cooking. Remy! You should feel very lucky to have a wife like her." Remy nodded his head as he filled his plate and began to eat. "So, how's that kit coming along?"

"That's been on my mind a lot also, but that takes money. If I can get in good standing with Montgomery that sure would make things a lot easier, not only for me, but for him, plus if Harriet could see what my potential would be maybe she would pick a wedding date. I'm the first to admit that, as it stands now, my chances aren't that great, but you know my history, all the problems I had back in Pennsylvania. How my father was, how much he despised me. He's the reason why I limp."

"You know everything about my childhood. All that has given me the willpower to be a success in life. Failure is simply out of the question. I am determined that I would make him eat his words. He was bad for the whole family. He tried forcing me to learn to swim and all it did was make me afraid of water. He sent me into the mines during that accident and the sights I saw in there will be forever etched on my mind. Then Mum died and I swear it was because of him. Then he leaves me with Braden, and he hightails back to Ireland.

Shanahan and Oglesby

God, I love my little brother, and I wish he were here right now eating with us. I made a promise to myself to take care of little Braden, and look at it now. I let them have him and I have no idea where he is."

"Oh Quinn, I've told you many a time that you can't keep beating yourself up because of your father. He tried to support his family as best he could."

"There's where your wrong, Remy. He used to beat Mum up. Maybe not in front of the children, but there was many a night when I'd be lying in bed and I'd hear him come home from the pub all full of whisky, or beer, and he'd take it out on Mum. I could hear him hitting her and cussing at her and blaming her for all of his problems. I wanted so much to jump out of bed and go out there and beat the ever-living crap out of him, but I was too scared. I prayed every night that he would change his ways, but it didn't seem to do any good, so I started praying less and less until it got to the point I quit altogether. Oh Remy. Don't let me go rattling off my past. Tell me to shut up."

"We're having that dinner on Saturday. That has to be something special for you. That means Harriet's father approves of you. He likes you, otherwise why would he give you his permission? Now it'll be up to you to prove to Harriet that you are a worthy Irishman who will adore and spoil her and love her and raise a family with her."

"But Remy, don't you see. My first wife was Harriet, too. Remember? I was the doctor that helped her give birth to our first child. She had problems at childbirth. I couldn't fix it. I saved the child, but let my poor Harriet down. It was shortly after I graduated from medical school with you. That was ten years ago and I still have nightmares about that day, and about giving William away to my brother, knowing full well that I could not take care of him and be the best possible doctor. God! Remy! Don't you see how can I expect Harriet to become my wife when I don't have a thing to be proud of?"

"That's not true, Quinn. You have so much going for you. You were first in our class. Voted most likely to succeed, while I was almost last in our class."

22

"But you have Lin!"

"It may seem like it, Quinn, but we have our problems too."

Quinn pushed his bowl towards the center of the table. "That was excellent, Lin. Thank-you very much, but I must be leaving," offered Quinn.

"I'll see you tomorrow," noted Remy as he got up and walked Quinn to the door. "I'm sure everything will work out for the best."

When Quinn got out to his buckboard he noticed a slip of paper attached to his seat. His face reddened. "Never!" he shouted.

Chapter 3

"PARTY OF ENGAGEMENT"

NEXT EVENING.
The party of engagement time arrived. The short list of guests mingled and small talk was running rampant. The ladies were decked out in their finest evening gowns, while the men, with their tuxedos, were imbibing. Little did they know what, and who, lay off in the background!

Harriet was upstairs in her bedroom, preparing for the grand entry. She was staring into her floor-length mirror. The day has come, she mused, when I will accept the challenge of being the wife of a doctor. Am I doing the right thing? Maybe I deserve more. Maybe he's not the one for me. I know he has a lot of selfish beliefs, but I suppose I do too. Is he too much like me? They say opposites attract. What about two people who have a lot of the same thought processes? Oh, I'll go ahead and face the challenges ahead. I'll straighten him out. He is handsome, and he is a doctor. Those are good qualities. His weaknesses could be a challenge for me, but I'm strong enough to fix him. I've learned a lot from my mother. She showed me how she handles father. I can do the same with Quinn.

She glanced around the overly-large room. It needed to be, with a monstrous black Steinway piano taking up an entire corner. This is my key to notoriety and success. Nothing but the best for this talented musician extraordinaire. The walls were covered with self-portraits. Paintings of her as a baby, then as a young lady, and then several of her playing the piano.

There was a queen-sized canopy bed on the other side of the room, all dressed out in beautiful, state of the art silks.

24

Party
OF
Engagement

Beside the bed was a large dresser, overflowing with new clothes. Harriet's eyes returned to the mirror.

What am I getting into? She asked herself. Is he the right man? Does he deserve me? Maybe I should give the others more of a chance. Yes, maybe a little competition between two. Oh, I absolutely love the idea of two men fighting over me. There's no way I lose. I'll lead them both on, but only until I decide who wins. I'll be in control of both. Yes, that's the perfect way. I deserve nothing but the best.

She looked out of her doorway and could see the gathering below. Deborah was lighting the many candles situated on the walls. She's the baby at 20. She's the soldier, the protector, the brains behind our trio. Always in the background in person, yet at the forefront in battle. A general in action, a private in private. She could handle losing a battle but was terrified of losing the war. Her intense eyes were deep and cold. Her complexion was cratered from acne and combat. Her hair, like her passion, was fiery red and vibrant. The spotlight was her favorite, living in a small town, her least. She was a spitfire and always seemed to have a box of matches nearby. Her temper was quick, but her decisions, quicker. She had obsessions but tried to keep them under check. She put her trust in everyone, but if she ever was misled, she never forgot. Her demeanor on the outside was calm and collected, but inside was entirely the opposite. Her first appearance was quietude, but she ends up going out in a blaze of glory.

Harriet noticed her father talking to her mother. Father spoiled me. He made it easy for me to get what I wanted. I didn't even have to ask. I'd throw little hints and before I knew it my requests were answered. I think he felt sorry for me for having to put up with such a nagging dictator. Mother didn't think too kindly of the manipulating, nor to the fact that he made it look like he was just following her orders. He had a way of doing that with all of us, mostly for spite, for he had each of us as the main ingredient in the family hierarchy.

Party
OF
Engagement

She returned to the mirror. Quinn should feel so lucky to have a wife like me. Sure, he's a doctor. There is status. I'll be bringing in the money. I'm the one taking all the chances. I could stay single and all the money I make would be mine and mine alone.

She placed facial powder over her cheeks, around her lips, on her forehead and neck, as she continued to adore her body. She walked over to her bed and picked up a small package, wrapped in white paper, with a red ribbon on it. My dowry. My father provided. I'm not sure if Quinn deserves it. Her younger sister, Naddy, knocked on the door and entered. She was a short, blue-eyed snot. She thinks she is the prettiest of the three. She is Mother's favorite and we all knew it. Her short, blond hair made her different than the rest of us, yet she displayed her fiercely independent demeanor with a continuous somber look that poured forth her bitterness towards the frontier.

"They're ready downstairs. Are you?"

"I think so."
"I mean to marry him," shot back Naddy.
"Oh Sis. Until today I wasn't sure. Why would I accept the hand of a man who has so many faults? Why would I put myself in such a situation? But, I'm ready now." (pause) "I think."

Harriet picked up the package and led Naddy down the stairs and into the music room, where they were greeted by Clare.

"He hasn't arrived yet," noted Clare. "Naddy! Start playing. Do some entertaining while we wait for the main guest."

As piano music filled the air, Quinn arrived on the scene. Harriet watched as Quinn, with bruises and black eyes, entered. He was dressed in a gray, silk suit. Their eyes met. Harriet smiled. She'd been looking forward to this evening for quite some time. Ever since the last time the two had met.

26

Party
OF
Engagement

Harriet turned to Naddy. "We spent the evening talking about oysters. How he absolutely loved them and I despised them. Ah those beautiful oysters, he'd say. These little bivalve mollusks are like people. All are unique. Some are stimulating, some not. Some have colorful stories, some not. They can be pleasing or hard to please. They can be fresh, clean, and sweet, or they can be bitter. They will lead to discussion, then to contemplation, and finally to sensual delight. His real life story is following that path. He was trapped out in Pennsylvania, spending much of his time dreaming and hoping that someone would rescue him. He was so lonely after his wife died. He was so bitter and then we met in Fergus Falls. His chance for a new beginning, a new purpose in life, and a world of contentment was promised. He called me stimulating. He said I had such a colorful story, and was so pleasant. That I was fresh, clean, and sweet. I was all he could think about. Yet, he also said that oysters alone will not do the trick. They need help. Man can accomplish by adding and subtracting. Add the right ingredient, subtract the desired target.

That's when oysters are at their best. Can you imagine? He was comparing me to an oyster! That alone should tell me to look elsewhere."

"He said, that not all oysters are created equal. He says there are those that are edible and succulent and then there are the ones that are gem producing. Pearls! Yes, my favorite. The lustrous gems with their radiance and natural beauty. Objects of desire in the eyes of every female alive, especially in mine. The most opulent reminder that oysters are exceptional. Pearls, the only precious stone produced by living creatures. I have a string. Got them from Quinn. Yes, he's the one for me, even though he has shortcomings. I can overlook them. I can use him to my advantage. He says that his knees have been inactive on Sundays, that his nails are jagged, his eyes, searching; and his heart, noble. He's a builder of dreams. He wants success. So do I."

"My God! An oyster?"
Quinn wore a serious look of question marks, of disappointment. As he entered, the piano music stopped, as did most of the conversations. Most eyes were pointed in his direction.

27

"Sorry for being late," noted Quinn as he took a seat at the head of the table. "I just had a long meeting with Chief Sullivan and the Sheriff. They have search parties out but as of yet haven't had any breaks. Unfortunately, I don't have anything to report. I've started to do some praying and would like it if you all did the same. I did receive a note and I passed that onto the authorities. I guess we'll just have to be patient. If anyone notices anything out of the ordinary please contact Sullivan, even if you don't think it has much meaning. I just don't know what to do with myself."

"We'll find the culprits," assured Father. "I can't for the life of me imagine anyone wanting to harm poor Braden. Do you have any suspects?"
"To be honest with you, Mr. Wiggins. Yes, I can think of several people that would want to get even with me."
"Can you name names?" queried Harriet.

"No. I better not. I'll let Sullivan and the sheriff figure it out. How have you been, Harriet?"

"I've been very worried about you two. Now I see why. It's going to take some time for you to get back to your old self."

"I'm not sure if I ever will," bluntly answered Quinn. "The chicken smells absolutely marvelous."

"I know you were expecting oysters. It's not that I didn't try. There just wasn't any fresh ones to be had. So, you'll have to settle for chicken."
"That's fine. Thank-you."

The small group prepared to sit for the evening feast. The dining table was set. Naddy had everything in the perfect spot. Each setting was precisely placed.

Name cards were situated according to her discretion. Napkins, bread knife, butter knife, salad fork, regular fork, dessert fork, soup spoon, regular spoon, plate, coffee cup and saucer. Wine glass and water glass. Flower vases filled with lilacs. Her father was at the head of the table and her mother at the opposite end. From Stanley's left side and going clockwise, was Harriet, Naddy, Remy, Lin, Spat, two empty seats, Reverend Martin, Clare, another empty seat, Maggie, Deborah, and Quinn. Out came the evening feast. Southern fried chicken, with all the trimmings. The serving was being done by the good ladies from the Occidental hotel. Refreshments were in everyone's hands as Deborah returned from her piano. Conversational chatter was at the forefront as verbal shots were fired across the bow and rebuttals were supplied. The hallowed confines of Wiggins World were on fire and it was still early in the evening.

Naddy, with her strategic position on the battlefield, was able to direct Quinn's attention towards her at the most effective times while Harriet was kept busy fielding shots from my father. The little crowd was hungry and she felt sorry and gave them what they were looking for and Deborah razed the temperament of many a poor soul with her scorching admonitions and fiery dialogue.

Mother tapped on her wine glass, as everyone else lifted their glasses. "As you can see, we have several empty chairs. The seat beside Quinn was reserved for Braden. We were hoping that he would be back with us by now, so we must continue to pray for his return. The two chairs next to Spat were for Gavin and a surprise guest. Gavin had a meeting so he won't be here. The empty chair beside Maggie is reserved for the honorable judge. Not sure why he hasn't arrived. Hopefully, he'll get here before it's over."

Harriet could see that Quinn was in complete dismay as he stared down at the empty chair beside Maggie and she watched his eyes move to his right and come in contact with Naddy, as he smiled and winked and Naddy did likewise, as she arose and went over to perform. Oh, what nerve!

Party
OF
Engagement

"Can I have everyone's attention?" begged Father as he stood up and pounded on the table. "I want to welcome you all to my humble home and thank-you for taking part in this little celebration for the soon-to-be married couple. Enjoy the meal being prepared for you and enjoy your friends. The wine that is being served to you as we speak comes all the way from the Napa Valley vineyards. Rather expensive yet the best I've ever tested, so be careful with the wine glass. Sip, rather than gulp. I don't want to run out too soon. Now, Naddy, you may begin."

Within seconds, the music started and then stopped. All eyes turned to the main entrance. Anticipation grew as silence overtook the room. The guests looked at each other in wonder. Harriet had her fingers crossed. Could this be Mr. Bannister? She couldn't help but rub her tongue on her upper lip, in anticipation. What was happening? Who was preparing to enter? A special guest? A surprise? So quiet! So tense!

The door opened and in came Chief Sullivan. The handsome and debonair chief of the Fergus Falls police department walked over to Father. A hush fell over the entire room. Everyone turned their ears to what he had to say.

"I'm sorry for interrupting your party, but I came to tell you that the judge has taken very sick and won't be able to attend this evening." Harriet's hopes had faded. She felt like a dagger had just tore into her heart. This was going to be his chance to meet the cream of Fergus Falls society. This was to be the warning bell for Quinn to pay attention. "What happened?"

"I stopped over to ask him a few questions. I had heard he was back from Minneapolis, so I knocked on the door and could barely hear someone saying to come in. He was in his bed and he didn't look good at all. White as a sheet. Sweat rolling down his forehead. Trouble breathing. Looked like he had been puking and you all know I have a weak stomach when it comes to things like that. I tried wiping him down. Tried to relax him. Tried to make him feel important. You know what he's like. Attention! He'll never pass it up. I finally got him calmed down and he looked like he was falling back to sleep. All he kept saying was to get a doctor, get a doctor."

30

Party
OF
Engagement

"Why didn't you?" queried Clare.

"I knew he had the measles and I didn't think anyone died from the measles."

"That sounds pretty inconsiderate and selfish. Don't you think?"

"What were you doing over there, in the first place?" interjected Quinn.

"After I heard that he had the measles I decided to pay a visit and make sure he wasn't going to miss this party. I didn't think he needed a doctor so I convinced him that I'd have you come over tomorrow and get him back on his feet."

"I can't understand why you didn't tell me sooner."

"I wasn't sure what he was going to do. He was so delirious before I got him relaxed. I figure he was going to go to sleep and everything would be much better tomorrow."

Oh, how stupid that sounded, thought Harriet. That poor man could be dying right now and it would all be my fault. I have to make it sound like I was comforting him the best that I know how. One part of me said that he didn't look well at all. Another part said to leave it for Quinn to take care of.

I finally convinced him to wait till Quinn got over there and that he'd fix everything.

"So, the judge is all by himself?"

"As far as I know. He had mentioned something about another woman coming by, so I figured whoever that was would take care of him."

"I told him that measles would disappear after a while, but that he had to be careful not to catch pneumonia, which I'm thinking he has right now."

"Pneumonia? That doesn't sound good."

"Yes, Harriet. That doesn't. I'll go over and see him in the morning. Just tell me where he lives."

"He has a house over on Vine. Near the Grand Hotel site. Near the river. It's relatively small. One story. Nothing that you would suspect a judge would be living in. He said that it was just temporary until he could get a new home built."

31

Party
OF
Engagement

"I still can't believe you went over there and didn't tell me," stated Quinn, as his face reddened.

"Sure, and then you'd get jealous and mad. You must understand that I barely know the man."

While this conversation was going on Harriet noticed that everyone, even her parents, were listening with interest to the present conversation. Some positively, some not so positively.

"Alright. Let's change the subject," demanded Quinn. "I don't want this to ruin the evening."

Harriet shifted her attention to Naddy. Younger by one year, yet more mature than most her age. She was strong on the outside, but stronger yet on the inside. Packed with energy and ideas. The perfect example of temperance. Conservative in thought, discretionary in finance, prohibitionist with alcohol, and prudent in judgement. Her main problem was she liked to stick her nose into other people's business. Always looking for fun but sometimes finding turmoil. Rimless glasses surrounded her eyes of hazel. Her forever cheeks of rose provided the perfect detail of innocence, but I can't trust her. She could be a snake in the grass. Self-confidence showed on the outside but I'm not so sure about the inside. Her intense manipulation of the keyboard and her fervent desire for perfection made those cheeks even rosier. Liberated and resilient, she represented 'smooth' with each of the keys, as perspiration flowed down her face and neck. Down to the top of her gown and even further. She was in her own world and was very comfortable. She was performing and she was content. She loved the piano and her fingers proved it.

But, she didn't understand men. I can't trust her. I know she would prefer to be in my shoes. I know she gets excited thinking about Quinn. She's mentioned to me several times Quinn this and Quinn that. You could see her eyes light up every time she'd mention his name. She liked to ask me questions about him. What it felt like to kiss him, or when he kissed me. What silly questions to ask, or were they? Maybe she used that to carry on a conversation, or maybe she was planning to take him away from me. I better pay closer attention to what she's up to.

Party
OF
Engagement

"Naddy's my piano prodigy," proudly whispered Clare to the Reverend Martin. "All of my girls spend countless hours every day, seven days a week on their piano lessons. I can proudly say that they are all reaching new heights, but Naddy is so much further along.

"Now, we have a surprise for you, Mr. Shanahan," continued Mother as she and Father disappeared into an adjoining room.

Bagpipes arrived. The powerful sound of bagpipes filling the air. Coming from the back room. Louder and louder, they roared. Out came Father, dressed in full garb with kilt and all. Harriet accompanied him on the piano as they played 'Amazing Grace'.

Quinn sat with eyes closed and a smile on his face. Ah, this is Braden's favorite song. My poor Braden!

Upon completion of Father's song, Mother came out playing the violin. The sweet, romantic sound of heavenly flavor, sending tears of joy and love to all at the table. Powerful music created by a powerful musician. The pleasure showed all over Quinn's body. "Amazing family!"

Everyone seemed to be enjoying the Wiggins feast. Food everywhere! Chicken, potatoes, home-made dressing, salads, and desserts. Nothing held back. Mother knew it was time to impress and she accomplished that.

Another clanging of the glass. "May I have your attention," shouted Remy. "Cheers to my good friend, Quinn. May everything go right for him and his brother! May Harriet and he have a joyous and everlasting marriage! It couldn't happen to a nicer couple."

Everyone drank to the toast and then went back to eating and gossiping.

"Excuse me," noted Harriet, as she arose. "I must freshen up. I'll be right back."

"What do you have to say for yourself on what has been happening here?" enquired Father, as he looked straight into Quinn's eyes.

"I feel I'm walking in a dream, sir. Everything is falling into place. I couldn't be more pleased on her decision."

"You do know that you have a lot to prove to my wife. I don't think she was none too happy when Harriet told her."

33

Party
OF
Engagement

Harriet returned to the table. "Getting a little cold outside," she stated as she looked at Quinn.

"I want to take you out to Fish Lake in the morning. Would you accept my request? There's some property that I'd like to get your opinion on. I saw that lake when I came out here. I fell in love with it. Spat and Maggie are coming along."

"Why Spat and Maggie?"

"Spat would be my partner."

"I have my lessons from 7-11 in the morning. Mother would never allow me to miss those."

"Good. That will give me time to see that dang judge. I'll pick you up at eleven. Maybe we could even have a picnic?"

"I'd love to and thank-you for thinking of asking me."

Chapter 4

"BANNISTER"

Judge Franklin Bannister lay in his bed half awake, coughing and moaning moaning as he looked out the cracked window and watched a pair of mallards floating down the rushing waters of the Red River. Spring was in the morning air as he made a futile attempt to get comfortable. His small residence was in a shambles. Dirty dishes were spread throughout. The bedroom smelled of vomit. The kitchen, like rotten eggs, the refuse, like stale bread. The walls were unpainted and void of any pictures, while the floors were covered in filth. Garbage everywhere. Several rats partaking in a pile of stink. Dust, throughout. Living conditions were to the point of almost unbearable, especially for a man that had caught the measles and had let it digress to pneumonia.

Not sure of his future, he was watching the river, yet he was thinking of how he could get his health back. Where is that dang doctor? Surely he knows the situation by now! It's been four days. Not one single soul has been here. If he doesn't start feeling better he might as well call it quits. But, he can't. He has too many unfinished plans. New house being built. Too many cases to hear in court. He can't pass up that money. Still has bills to pay from law school.

He leaned over the side of his bed and began to vomit. Oh that pain! It's constant. How to stop it? What else is there to do? Can't eat! Can't sleep! Such misery! No one deserves to have to go through this. It would be better to give in. It's as if someone was paying him back for previous misdeeds, but who could do such a thing?

Bannister was in complete denial. It's been thirteen years since my life changed. My marriage was a total failure. Had one daughter but after the wife left I had to give my 3 year old baby to the orphanage. What a time! Found out my best friend had been a 'secret friend' of my wife. Had to confront her. She denied it, but it was true. She was pregnant and it wasn't mine. Things had to change. My colt 45 took care of the problem. It was all his fault. He shouldn't have done what he did, and to think he was supposedly my best friend.

35

Bannister

There was a knock at the door, and then another knock. Still no answer. The door slowly opened and Quinn entered. "Hello! Anybody here?"
"In here," came the weak reply from a dark room in the back of the house. Quinn made his way into the room, with the help of a lantern. It was the bedroom. "Mr. Bannister! It's me, Doc Shanahan."

"Oh, ah, what took you so long?" said the man with bedraggled, dark brown hair and an uneven and small pointed, paintbrush mustache.
"I didn't find out till last night about your condition. Let me take a look," suggested Quinn as he set his bag down on the bed. He listened as Bannister began to cough, a hard cough, a cough that anyone could see was tearing the patient apart. He grabbed a towel and wiped Bannister's forehead. "Why didn't you let me know that you weren't getting any better?"

"How? Did you expect me to get in my buggy and ride over to your office? Can't you see? I can't move around. I'm lucky to still be alive. My breathing leaves a lot to be desired. When I cough I spit up so much phlegm, and then I vomit till I have nothing more to vomit. The pain in my chest is almost unbearable. I just wish I could end it all. What good am I, lying in this bed completely helpless and pathetic?"

"Now, you quit talking like that. People survive this. It's called pneumonia. It's not the end of the world. You'll be back to normal in no time. First thing, I'm going to take some blood from you. They say when your lungs are not performing like they should, prick one of your main arteries and draw some blood. That'll give your lungs a chance to get back the way they should be. Now, let's find that vein," continued Quinn as he reached in his bag and pulled out a syringe.

"You're not going to poke me with that," weakly commanded Bannister.
"Why didn't you send someone to get me before it got this bad?"
"Nobody stopped here since I came back from your office."
"No friends? No neighbors? Surely, someone must have noticed the lack of activity?"

Bannister

"Friends? I have no real friends. Oh, they act like it when I have my robes on, but they don't come by the house. I'm all alone, but that's alright. I like it that way. I have enough problems of my own. I don't need to listen to the woes of others. I hear enough of that in court."

"Let me see your right arm," requested Quinn as he prepared his syringe.

"I told you that I don't want you poking me."

"If you want to get through this you'll listen to what I have to say and what I ask you to do. If we don't try to help your lungs out there's no way you'll be able to get out of that bed, other than by the coroner putting you in a wooden coffin and hauling you off to the cemetery."

Bannister lifted his right arm. Quinn searched for and found a vein and proceeded to withdraw blood. "There. That should help. I'm going to heat up a pail of water and give you a nice, warm sponge bath. I'm assuming you have a bucket?"

"Over by the pump," replied Bannister.

"I don't know why you're going through the bother. I really don't like the idea of getting a bath, especially from you. Besides, I can't see how that's going to help me get over this malaise."

"You'll be surprised," continued Quinn as he filled the pail with water and poured it into a kettle over the fireplace. "Once I get this fire going we'll be in business. You don't have to worry about me seeing your private parts. I'm a doctor."

After lighting the fire he returned to Bannister's bedside. "Now let's get you on this chair and get you undressed. You don't have to take off the bottom half of your long johns."

Bannister continued to cough, while Quinn found a washcloth and walked back over to the fireplace. "Just about ready. Is this your beautiful cane?" asked Quinn as he picked up the shiny, crooked, mahogany piece of wood.

"What a stupid question?" shot back Bannister. "Of course it is."

"Looks quite expensive."

"It was, but money is no problem."

37

Bannister

"How did you end up in Fergus?"

"I was appointed by the governor. He was looking for a man who was an expert in law and it didn't take him long to find me. I enjoy the work very much. I like the control aspect and the power that goes with it. I thrive in that kind of atmosphere."

"Where you from?"

"Pennsylvania. Just like you."

"You weren't entertaining the notion of spending time with Harriet by any chance?"

"Now why would you ask such a question?"

"You missed the party last night. Lots of people were talking about you and some of them weren't very nice. I asked Harriet about you and she seemed to dodge the question. I had a feeling that she was hiding something, but I'm hoping I'm completely wrong."

"I did see her about a week before I came to your office. I congratulated her on her decision to marry you and that's as far as it went."

"Word has it that you are callous with a complete lack of remorse. That empathy is not in your vocabulary. They say you trust no one, sometimes not even yourself. Some people say they have never seen you smile. They also say you show no mercy. What do you have to say to that?"

"You're talking to the wrong people. I get along with most everyone that I come in contact with. I have a bit of a problem with you but I'm starting to clear that perception."

"We were well off in London until my father overstepped his bounds and ot in trouble with the law. That's about the time we headed for America. That was the worst trip I've ever taken. Seasick all the way. Up and down. Up and down, with no end in sight. I still haven't forgiven my father for what he did to cause us to pull up roots and head for the wilds of America, near Philadelphia. It was there that I met my wife, Barbara. I thought she was the perfect match. Little did I know that was just the beginning of my problems! We got married and lo and behold she got pregnant. Had the most beautiful baby girl I had ever seen. My wife had a terrible experience with childbirth.

I could tell her heart and mind weren't into it. She became lackadaisical and lazy. It seemed like she didn't care, while I was so excited about what was to happen. She laid back and put on lots of weight.

38

I warned her but she was one not to argue with. She wasn't ready for married life. When I'd stay at home for the evening, she would go out and I had a hunch she was up to no good, but it didn't do any good to complain. I knew what she was doing, but by then I was in law school and really didn't have time to pamper her. I tried to help but to no avail. You couldn't tell her. She'd get mad and storm out of the room. When it came time for delivery I was too busy in school. Her mother stayed with her and helped with the delivery. It was a bad experience for all. The baby made it but the wife died during childbirth. I didn't know what to do. I was going to law school at the time and couldn't take care of the baby, so I gave her to an orphanage and that's the last time I saw her."

"Here we are," continued Quinn as he set the pail of hot water down next to Bannister. He took the towel and dipped it in the water. "Oh my! It's probably too hot. Better let it cool a bit. Meanwhile, I'm going to go get my carriage hitched up. I've got an important date with Harriet and Spat and Maggie. We're going out to Fish Lake."

"You going to leave me here all alone? What happens if I need something? If I need to go to the john? Before you leave, could you change the sheets? I've had a minor problem of keeping them dry."

"Yes, of course. I'll leave you high and dry. I'll stop by when we get back. It shouldn't be long. Maybe a couple of hours."

As Bannister struggled to watch Quinn leave he couldn't help but think about the nerve of that guy. Comes out here to see me, talks a bit, and then plans on leaving for Fish Lake. What to do for me? Leave me here to rot, or even die? The more I see this man the more I despise him. He's all in it for himself. He's no doctor. All he's thinking about is being with that Harriet. Of course, who could blame him? She is quite the specimen. A pretty nice fish to catch. I wouldn't mind having something like that in my bed. She has a lot to offer. A concert pianist, with a beautiful singing voice. From a family of positives, well-to-do parents, with lots of farmland and bulging bank accounts. You'd have to be crazy not to try to get some of that for yourself. Harriet was the main prize for gentlemen looking for attachment in the entire Fergus Falls area. Why not give it a shot. Surely, I would have just as much of a chance at getting her hand as Shanahan has. Maybe, even more of a chance. I have more to offer, especially when my new home is completed. Yes, I think I shall. Maybe, I'll even check to see if there are any resorts to be had out there.

The judge couldn't believe the fact that he told such a huge whopper of a lie, but what else could he do? He couldn't let anyone know the truth. If that ever happened it would be his own demise.

39

Chapter 5
"FiSH LAKE"

uinn got into his carriage and headed for the Wiggins house. All he could think about was what Bannister was spewing. Was it the truth? He didn't know. Gonna have to do some checking. It sounds almost unbelievable what he was saying about his wife and child. Wouldn't be the first time that he lied. He's my biggest competition. I just know he had something to do with the abduction. If I could only prove it.

Spat was sitting in the veranda area with Maggie, while both waited for Quinn's arrival and for Harriet to make her appearance, which only took a few minutes and in no time the foursome was on their way to Fish Lake. Harriet sat beside him and was in a very talkative mood, with Spat and Maggie sitting in the back seat. "Any word on Braden?"

"Nothing," calmly replied Quinn. It's going to be a beautiful day, my friends. I can't wait till we get out by the lake," noted Quinn as he put a toothpick in his mouth. "It's only a seven mile ride, so sit back and enjoy the beautiful spring weather with the trees in blossom and the daffodils and tulips in full bloom, and the farmers preparing the soil for their summer crops, and all the birds and animals active in their spring rituals. Isn't it a wonderful time to be alive?"

"So, just what are we going to be looking at?" inquired Harriet. "Birds and animals don't really get me excited."

"Going to meet Gavin. He's going to make a sales pitch. There's a piece of shoreline on the north side of the lake where a certain Mr. Walters started a resort and he has quite a clientele built up, but due to health reasons he needs to sell and move south. He owns all along this shoreline, plus that one island, Pinafore Island. The main lake is about three miles long by about two miles wide. It has four islands. The water is generally deep, pure, and abounds with plenty of fish."

Fish Lake

"Over there to the east, and connected with this lake, is a torturous narrows, with a strong current flowing into the l arger lake which is another charming body of water about half the size. That's Pleasant Lake. This small lake is entirely in Sverdrup town, while Fish is in Aurdal, and has its outlet into the Red from its northeastern extremity, which lies in the southern part of Maine town."

"AJ Charles has a claim on the west end and is creating a resort. He, too, has an island. He's been talking with that Bannister about him buying it, but I keep my fingers crossed that he doesn't."

"You talk to any of the settlers out here and they'll tell you that they aren't satisfied with the name of 'Fish Lake'. Too common, they say. Last week there was a group of campers on Walter's Island. They suggested it either should be named 'Laurie Lee' or Pinafore. Don't ask me how they came up with that name. It's in the dictionary as an apron, but you go down to the Boston Hair Emporium, on Lincoln, and they have a hair style called the 'Pinafore'. Anyway, Mrs. Laura Thickston, suggested 'Laurie Lee', while Old Lady Gould suggested 'Pinafore'. As the lake gets more and more developed, it'll be harder and harder to change the name, so I'm thinking it'll forever be called 'Fish Lake'."

"It strikes me as a little odd that for being afraid of water that you would end up buying a resort," snidely noted Harriet.
"It's a sign of the future. I want to get in on the action."

The wagon creaked along the Red river, right past where Quinn had a few problems when he first came out here. He looked at a certain spot in the river and began to shiver and shake and yet said not a word.
"I would love nothing better than to be a part of this beautiful lake. It would be ideal for Braden. Oh God! Yes, my little brother. They tell me they're still looking but have no clues. We don't know if he's in Fergus. He could be in New York for all we know."
Quinn took out a hanky and wiped his eyes. "If only! I just don't understand it. I've received that one note asking for a thousand as ransom. I refused and haven't heard a word since. Every night when I go to bed I've been asking for His help."

41

Fish Lake

"Your prayers will be answered," consoled Harriet. "We must be patient."

"I was reading a while back in the 'Advocate', that this lake is fast becoming known as the "Long Branch" of Otter Tail County," chimed in Spat.

"What does that mean?" asked Harriet.

"That's a reference to the bustling town of Long Branch, New Jersey. It's a summer resort, a place where people can gamble. Maybe we could get something l ike that started around here. There's getting to be lots of 'competition' what with all the lakes in the area. Already seeing resorts on some of the neighboring lakes that are becoming popular. Over by Southwick, there's the Maplewood Resort, an island on the west end of South Turtle Lake, and then there's McFarland's Resort, on Ten Mile Lake. There might be a lot of lakes and a lot of competition but I think there's enough interest for a lot more resorts to start up and make a profitable endeavor."

"But they'll only be good for like four or five months a year."

"If one plays their cards right one could make enough to cover the whole year. Besides, if I got involved, it would only be a part time scenario."

"I have a surprise for you," anxiously suggested Spat. "I wanted to come out here with you to see for myself what the prospects were for such a worthwhile possibility. Well, I've seen enough. If we can get it for a reasonable price I'm with you. I had a meeting earlier this morning with Corliss. It seems that I've inherited over $25,000. It's been killing me not to be able t o let the whole world know. My luck is changing. No more being the poor man on the block. Those days are all gone. Gonna find me a new house and get me a wife to take care of it. I might even have to quit my painting business. Can you imagine that? Right on my birthday. Couldn't ask for no better present."

"That is good news," chimed in Quinn. "I'm happy for you, but I need to spread a little caution. You need to be careful. I wouldn't go shooting this around so loud. You never know who might be listening. Make sure you put most of it in a bank that you can trust. You should probably talk to Compton and get his advice."

"I already did. He will take good care of me."

"Maggie!" continued Spat. "Aren't you excited for me?"

"That sounds wonderful."

Fish Lake

"My parents got a divorce when I was only ten. I had no one to teach me about life. No one to confide in. No one to show me how courting was being done. Now, Now I have money. Now things are going to change. I'm not going to be that dunce that spends his time painting barns and sheds. I'm going to build them and find someone else to paint them. I'm going to show those people with all the wealth and power just what this old Irishman, Spat O'Malley, can do with money when given the chance."

"We're almost there. If you look to your right you can see some of the lake."

"Up till now," continued Spat. "I've been running in place. I run and run and yet, get nowhere. I run uphill and I run downhill, but always end up in the same place. I run towards and I run away, with the only accomplishment being fatigue. I run in the woods and I run on the prairie. I run alone and I run with Quinn, and yet I remain by myself. I create facades with my paint brush, often unable to accept reality, yet I continue to run. I admit my weakness only to myself while carrying the hope of change in the background. I know where I want to go but have been unable to find the right trail. I'm looking for the path of least resistance, yet I always end up on the wrong trail, coming to a dead end, or returning to the starting line. I keep trying to find the easy way, yet only to meet up with roadblocks."

"My feet are tired and sore. Tired from repetition and failure, sore from colliding with obstacles. I hunt, but I cannot shoot. I plant, but I'm not a farmer. I learn, but I'm not educated. I love, but I'm not a lover. I float, but I cannot swim. I preach, but I'm not a preacher. I'm dressed in pride, but I'm ashamed on the inside. I wear beautiful clothes, yet I feel naked. I command empathy, y et only receive sympathy. This is all going to change. No more running. No more chasing. No more painting. My time has come. Just you wait and see."

"That's enough," ordered Harriet. "Who cares about your running?" Maggie ignored Harriet and looked straight at Spat. "Take me with," she pleaded. "Let me help."

"We'll see."

"Look! There's Gavin," pointed Quinn, as he guided the wagon over to where the bald-headed Gavin Delaney was awaiting their arrival.

43

Fish Lake

Gavin was short and thin, with freckles everywhere and a huge mole on his forehead. He waved to the arrivals. "Welcome! Welcome to the choicest sight on this beautiful lake."

"Hello Mouser," returned Quinn.

"Isn't this just the most beautiful piece of property you've ever seen? It runs all along this shoreline. There are more than a dozen boats that are part of the deal. You'll need to use those to get out to that Pinafore Island, the most beautiful part of the whole resort."

"Yes, I've been checking it out."

"I understand you're going into the real estate business. I tell you, Quinn, it's a dog eat dog world out there, but the rewards can be gratifying. First off, you have to sell yourself. Make them believe in you, and then make them want to buy. Cast your net out and bring in the prize. Sink your teeth into their pocketbook. Use your imagination to bait them. Paint a picture of profit, but beware, there are plenty of sharks out there lying in the weeds. Don't be one of them. Stay on top of your game and you will succeed. Any questions?"

"Where's the owner?" asked Quinn.

"He's down in Minneapolis, setting up his new living quarters. I have all the details listed in this paper. I'm not charging any fees."

Quinn glanced over the paper. "It looks real good. Spat! Take a look at this."

While Spat perused the paper, Gavin continued. "I have a boat ready to go do some fishing. I brought two rods. How would you like to spend an hour or so on the high seas and try your luck?"

"But I brought Harriet and Spat and Maggie out here."

"That's fine," interrupted Harriet. "We can take a boat and go out to that island. But, only be out there for an hour."

"Looks fine," noted Spat as he handed the paper back to Quinn.

The little red boat lie in wait, biding its time before heading out into the deep, clear waters, expecting to show the rookie fishermen where to catch the big one.

44

Fish Lake

Into this buoyant vessel the daring adventurers entered. Quinn sat in the middle and grabbed the oars. Gavin followed and sat in the front, prepared to shout instructions on which direction the mighty little boat should go.

Teamwork was involved. Gavin with the mental, Quinn with the muscle.
"Lovely day," mused Gavin. "Should be excellent fishing. Heard this is the best time of the day to catch those bass. Mara says she'll clean them for a fish fry around the campfire, so we have to do our part. Head left."
"Just tell me how much."
"You see that island to the south? Point the boat right at it. Has a date been set?"
"The last thing I need right now is a wife. I need to get my medicine chest out into the market. I'm convinced it will be a big hit. It's something every household will want. I need to spend most of my free time promoting, Gavin, but I realize I can't do it all by myself. I need sales reps. People who can devote the time and energy to get this ball rolling."
"It sounds like a difficult task."

"I know, but I believe in it. That's half the battle."
"You can stop rowing. I think we're about at the right spot," ordered Gavin as he threw the anchor overboard. "Should be in about fifteen feet."
"I'll be alright, as long as I don't think about it."
"I tell you what, there's a lot more spots deeper than that. I could take you over to the eastern side. There's some holes forty to forty five feet deep."

"That's fine. I don't need to know that," noted Quinn as he baited his hook.
"Go ahead and throw her out," suggested Gavin. "You use the left side and

I'll use the right. Let the contest begin."
Anxiety was on full display as the two pretenders showed their ignorance when it came to fishing. Nothing seemed to be working. Maybe it was the bait. Maybe it was the wrong depth. Maybe it was the impatience. Trying too hard. Yes, that's it.

Fish Lake

"I didn't realize it was going to be so difficult. Don't know what I was thinking. I figured those little fish would just be down there waiting to chomp on the hook as we lowered it to them. We'll probably have to go to school to catch the school."

"No, Quinn. It takes skill and expertise. We'll get the hang of it if we do it enough."

The fishermen were still sitting in their boat with an empty fish basket. "Nothing to show how great we are," stated Quinn. "Maybe we should give up and go back to the island."

"We can't. What kind of fish story do we have? Not too impressive! One of the keys to being a good fisherman is patience. We have to have patience."

"I could possibly have better luck being a fisher of men rather than a fisherman. People have told me that I lack patience, and I agree with them. I never could reach my goals as quick as I wanted. Haven't changed a bit. Probably never will. I can't even catch a mermaid, but you know what? Isn't a big part of fishing the fact you can get away from everything and everybody and go into a world of your own? Just relax and forget all about the hustle and bustle of everyday life. It's so peaceful out here. Gives one a chance to recollect, to put everything into a proper perspective, and make adjustments wherever needed. Don't have to put up a front. Don't have to feel guilty about offending someone. Don't have to worry. You can catch a parasite, but you can also scrub them off. It's not like when you're in town. They're not as easy to get rid of."

"You mean like Spat?"

"He's one of them right at the top of the list."

"One other comes to mind. Oglesby. He's been getting under my skin ever since we started sharing an office. I've regretted going into a partnership right off the bat. He can get on my nerves so easy, but of course, he probably says the same thing about me. You know me. My determination for success runs very deep. I've always said, even back to my younger days in Ireland, when I didn't know where my next meal was going to come from, that I'd set a goal and, no matter what, I'd reach it. I have never taken failure as a final outcome. I never wanted anyone to see me fail, especially me. I plan on getting some nice sales in real estate, thanks to Montgomery.

46

Fish Lake

That'll keep my medical practice afloat. Oops! I think I got a bite. Ah it feels like a good one. Come on, baby. Come on home. Ahhk! I lost him. Just a weed! All I can catch is a dang weed."

"Supposedly, there are plenty of fish in the sea, so you don't necessarily have to settle on one certain type. Who knows? You might catch one that you didn't even think existed."

"Oh, I don't know. I have my net out pretty far right now and can't seem to make up my mind which one is the right one. I want one that I can control, that'll bow to my every command."

"You'll know when the right one comes along. They'll grab on to your net and melt your heart and you'll want to celebrate on high. Just you wait."

"I dated women back in Pennsylvania but wasn't very good at it. They all seemed to be such snobs and it seemed like they wanted to control me. I'd have none of that. The thought of my first wife kept coming into the picture."

"First wife?"

"Yes. Her name was Harriet, too. I called her Hattie. We were only married for a couple of years. She died while giving birth. I'll never forget that day. I was delivering and failed to save her. She was the most beautiful woman I've ever known. Not a bad bone in her entire body. She was the perfect example of a wife."

"Mara never told me that. When was this?"

"When I was doctoring out in Bloomsburg. People never said anything to my face, but I could tell what they were thinking. They blamed me for her death and I guess maybe they were right because I've gone over and over that scenario. To this day I still do not know what I could have done differently. She basically died of a heart attack."

"And the baby?"

"A little boy. That was ten years ago, so he'd be around ten now."

"What happened to him?"

"I gave him to my brother. I haven't seen them since."

"Look!" gasped Gavin, as he jumped towards the front of the boat.

47

Fish Lake

"Water coming in! This darn boat is leaking. Bring in your line! Get to the oars!" he continued to bark as he tried getting rid of the invading water.

Quinn got the oars moving as fast as he could, all the while with visions of water flowing over his head. "Gavin! I've never told you, but I can't swim."

"You what? Can't swim? You graduated from medical school and you never learned how to swim?"

"I know it's terrible. You're the second person I told today. I am so embarrassed. I almost drowned when I was four, back in Ireland. Thank God my uncle was nearby and heard me screaming. He pulled me out. I'll never forget that scene. I tell you, Gavin, that trip over to America was one of my biggest challenges. Seeing all that water as I got aboard the Orinoco, made my stomach churn to the point where I almost heaved my morning breakfast. I found a dark space as far down as I could go and spent the next week weaving up and down far away from the water, yet close, but out of sight. We came from Ireland and arrived in Philadelphia harbor on 13 October 1857, without a penny in my pocket, nor idea of where me and my brother, Jim, and sister, Mary, God rest her soul, were going to go. My older brother, John and older sister, Katie, came over on the Joseph Jones. There were to land a day before us three. Well, we got there and, sure enough, there was not one of the Shanahan clan to save us."

"Mara never told me about that, either," chimed in Gavin, as the water kept invading.

"No. I made it rough on her, I was never so scared. To this day, I can't stand being engulfed and swallowed up by the mysterious sea."

The boat was taking on water faster than Quinn could row. With Gavin scooping and Quinn rowing, their journey back to Walter's was becoming an exercise of futility. "I don't know how much more of this I can handle," gasped Quinn as he shook his arms and went back to rowing.

"My God! We're going to sink," shouted Gavin, while wiping his forehead.

48

Fish Lake

"Can't let that happen," shot back Quinn. "Keep working!"

"Here! Let me row and you scoop," suggested Gavin. "Pinafore is straight ahead."

"We can do this," stated Quinn.

"I should have known better than to lease one of Walter's boats. This one is certainly not seaworthy."

Harriet was watching from shore. "Listen! It's Quinn. He's in trouble." She ran to the top of the hill and caught sight of the boat in distress. She ran down and got into one of the nearby boats and headed out to the two men.

"I think we're going to have to swim for it," suggested Gavin, as more and more water entered the boat.

"I told you, I can't."

Into the water they plunged. Gavin was the first to reappear. He looked around for Quinn. "Come on, get up here," he shouted as Quinn burst out, gasping for air. "Grab the boat," he commanded as he helped him to the side of the sinking boat.

"I didn't realize the water was so, so cold," noted Quinn, between gasps of air. "There's not much time before it disappears."

"Just hang on. They'll see what's happening. They'll come out and save us."

"Listen, Mouser! If we should end up going down, don't worry about me. Save yourself first."

"Stop talking like that."

Quinn was in panic mode. He could see his hands and arms turning blue. With chest pains on the rise and a shortness of breath, he knew he was in deep trouble. He glanced over at Gavin. "I've known you for quite some time. You've been a true friend. A friend that I could trust completely."

"Don't Quinn. Save your breath. Looks like you'll need it. It it's our mea culpa time, so be it."

"Look!" weakly yelled Quinn. "They see us. Somebody is coming in a boat. We're going to make it. It's hard to tell, but I think it's Harriet."

49

Fish Lake

"Would you look at that? And you're swimming."
"You're right. I am."

Desperation continued to show its ugly face as the two fishermen bobbed up and down. Fear of the unknown and fear of the known clouded their minds as they clung to the boat. But alas, the boat was inching closer and closer to its demise and Quinn knew it, but was unable to do anything about it. The cold, wet, chilling water was trying to pull them down into the abyss, but Quinn would have none of it. I'm not ready to give up. I've got too many tasks that are undone. I can't die. I'm too important to me, to Harriet, to Fergus Falls, to the world.
"Hang on, Quinn. She'll be here soon."
"I'm trying."

"Here," continued Gavin as he tore off his shirt and made a primitive life jacket by inflating it after he tied the end of the arms together. "It's an old sailor's trick. This'll give you a few more minutes." He placed the shirt under Quinn's arms. "Hold it right here," he commanded, and then he grabbed at his chest. "No. It can't be happening!" He began grunting and gasping as he held his right hand over his heart.
"Don't go pulling a stunt," commanded Quinn. "We don't have the time or place."

"Help me! Help me! Sa, save me, Quinn."
"What can I do? You're the one that should be saving me. Harriet! Hurry! We're both going down."

"It's my heart, Quinn," shouted Gavin as he let go of Quinn and was headed downward.

"Stay up here," commanded Quinn as he grabbed him by the arm and held on. "You're not going down there if I can help it."

Harriet pulled up next to the struggling fishermen. "I tried getting here as fast as I could," she gasped.

With difficulty, the two drowned urchins made their way over to the rescue craft.

Fish Lake

While swimming, Quinn pushed Gavin up and over the side of Harriet's boat, to safety, then he followed. "My new heroine. You're a goddess," praised Quinn, as he hugged her and watched the wooden boat sink into its grave. "Just in time."

"It's Gavin! He's having a heart attack," continued Quinn. "Hurry! We need to get to shore as soon as possible. We need blankets!" He began giving mouth to mouth until Gavin started to breathe on his own. Noticing the improvement, he grabbed the oars and furiously began to row.

Gavin continued to have minor breathing problems as he lie curled up in the boat. He moaned. Looking over at Quinn and then at Harriet, he tightened up and stopped breathing.

"Quinn! He needs you," shouted Harriet as she returned to the oars while Quinn went back to mouth to mouth.

They arrived back on the island. Quinn took off most of his wet clothes and wrapped himself up in a blanket. Then he returned to tending Gavin. "I'm losing him! I'm losing him!" he shouted in desperation. "Damn it, Harriet. I'm a doctor and I'm helpless. Spat! Get the wagon and horses ready. We got to get to town as fast as we can."

The trip back to Fergus Falls was somber. Reality was beginning to set in as Quinn watched Gavin's life gradually disappear.

"You've been pretty quiet," noted Quinn as he looked over at Harriet. "I am quite surprised. You do know about the schedule of our upcoming concerts? That's going to keep my whole family very busy for quite a bit of the summer. That cuts down the choices of dates for the wedding. By the way, how did Keegan get the nickname of Spat? I've never heard of that word before. It's rather intriguing."

"That's a good question. He loves oysters and their history. "Spat" is the name given to the beginning oyster.

51

Fish Lake

The offspring, you might say, who are shot out by the thousands over the water and these little 'spats' gently fall into the water and settle down on the floor of the ocean and it is there that spat creates his new home, a home that he will live in either forever or until someone comes along and moves him. It's kind of the way his lifestyle is. He's a free-wheeler.

He hasn't had much success with his barn painting. Very few of the hundreds of new settlers can afford him. They build their own barns and just never paint them, but Spat is a good painter with a lot of patience. By his finished work he is proving to be one of the best in his field. It's just that it doesn't pay well. Spat wants to change that."

"You just figure out when we can fit it in according to your schedule. I'm rather flexible. It'll probably take me more than this summer to get this all put together. Spat and I are going down to the bank in the morning and we should get started on creating our dream resort, our Hotel LePette."

"LePette?"
"That was my first wife's favorite word. I think it means 'favorite'. I want to name the hotel as a reminder of my first wife."
Harriet looked surprised. She snickered, but said nothing.

Quinn stopped the wagon. "Spat! You and Maggie switch with us. I have some important things to say to Harriet."

After the switch, Harriet spoke up. "Tell me, Quinn. What will you expect of me after we get married?"

Quinn was a bit stunned at the question. "Ah, I, ah, I expect you to be my wife forever. To be there when I need comforting. To stand beside me when I'm in danger. To share everything we have together. How about you?"
"I expect you to be my knight in shining armor, my admirer, my lover, my provider, and my listening post. I want you to be my confidant, a person I can trust with my deepest and darkest secrets. In return, I shall be at your every beck and call, at your mercy when I'm home, and I shall be your lover."

"Have you ever had any boyfriends?"

52

Fish Lake

"Oh yes! Yes, I did. There was one. His name was Jasper. It was quite serious. I actually thought I was in love with him, but one day he up and left without saying a word. Nobody knew what happened to him. I just thought that he ran off with some other woman."

"Jasper, you say?" queried Quinn with curiosity. "A while back I was told by Maggie that she had been married to a Jasper, and that he had run off and was never heard from again."

"Quinn!" weakly gasped Gavin.
Quinn turned around and grabbed Gavin's hand. "Yes, my friend?"
"I, I can't see you."

"I'm right here. We're almost back to town. Just hold on. We'll get you taken care of."

"Mara! Where's Mara?"

"We'll get you to your wife as soon as possible. Just try and relax."
"I, I can't breathe! Help me! Get Father Boever!" commanded Gavin. "I need. I need. Oh God! Our Father who art in Heaven, hallowed be thy name (mumbles). And it was 4:10.

Quinn handed the reins to Harriet and gave Gavin a big hug while tears formed. My best friend, he thought. My only real friend. My brother-in-law. He was always willing to help. Never put himself first. I couldn't have asked for a better friend. My best man. Same age as me. Way too young to die. Way too young.

Gavin perked up and reached out to Quinn. "Pray for me, Quinn. Pray for..."

A silence swarmed the wagon, and it was 4:15. A feeling of nothingness reached deep into Quinn's gut and stabbed and stabbed some more. He made the horses stop and Harriet wrapped her arms tightly around her husband. Squeezing and calming the runaway nerves of her man in need and soon she joined in making it a duet of daunting upheaval, both ranting into a tirade of futility, breaking down all barriers of normality, and it was 4:19, in the afternoon.

53

Fish Lake

The anticipation of death entered Quinn's mind as he desperately tried to gather his wits, but to no avail. Cry like a baby he did, and it was 4:20 and unfettered gloom showed up with its sad disposition and Harriet joined in, devouring common sense and disrupting the composure of all sensibility, discarding all anticipation of comfort and instinctive spontaneity. They became involved in a tirade of turbulence, hectic confusion, and tumultuous discombobulation.

The horses remained at a standstill as they watched Quinn and Harriet share the time of incoherence and gibberish, with visions of Purgatory flowing across their paths.

Then calm returned. Tears were wiped away and it was 4:30.
"Yes. We must pray," suggested Quinn. "Pray for his soul. Pray that he has a smooth flight and that his days of clemency and purification will be short and he'll be able to join his babies, Annie and Leah, and the rest of his family, and then they can wait for you and I."

"Revelations 21-27 says: but nothing unclean will ever enter Heaven, nor anyone who does what is detestable or false, but only those who are written in the Lamb's book of life." And it was 4:34.

The wagon made its way into Fergus Falls and stopped at Quinn's office, where Mara happened to be. "I already know," sobbed Mara, as she looked at Gavin. "I already know. Gavin wanted to be buried back in Pennsylvania, when he died. Would you take him and me to the undertaker so I can take care of his wishes?

"Of course," noted Quinn. And it was 4:50.

Chapter 6
"BRADEN'S BASTILLE"

The room was cold and dark. The air, musty and putrid. It was 12'x12' with frosted rock walls and a frozen dirt floor. The only access in and out was a door at one end of the room. Braden lie on a makeshift bed of straw, waiting for food. His right ankle was in shackles and connected to a two-foot chain which in turn was hooked to a pin in the far corner of the room, opposite the entrance. A 3'x3" rag strip covered his mouth and another 3'x3" strip covered his eyes. A thick rope tied his hands behind his back. He was growling and he wanted to cry.

Where was she, he asked himself. It was way past her time. Surely, she wouldn't forget about me! He heard a noise from above. Someone had a pitchfork and was spreading hay. He could hear several horses battling for best position, while in the backdrop a cow was bellowing and a calf was bleating. "What's keeping her? I'm starving," he noted as he began to cry.

Footsteps were descending the stairs. Braden listened as the door creaked open. Light! He could see light through his mask.

"Here you are," exclaimed a small wisp of a girl as she set a tray down beside him. She untied the rag covering his eyes. He squinted and blinked and adjusted his sight. There she was. First time he saw her since he was put in this prison. He figured she must be around 14, or 15. She had long, straggly, brown hair down past her shoulders.

She took off the second rag rope that covered his mouth. He wiggled his jaw and wetted his lips with his tongue. She looked like a young farm girl, dressed in a simple brown dress and bonnet, and wearing a pair or worn cowboy boots.

55

Braden's
Bastille

She had freckles on her nose. Pretty red freckles. Her teeth were glistening white with a tinge of brown. Her lips were chapped and rough, but inviting. Her eyes were intriguing. He glanced around the room. Just as he thought. No windows. One door. Nothing else but bare rock walls, damp and coated in moss, and a small makeshift bed of straw with one wool blanket. Beside it lie the tray with the bowl and glass. "Whose maid are you?" he asked.

"Never mind!" she shot back as she picked up the eye mask and headed for the exit. "I'll be back."

"Why don't you untie my hands? My arms are killing me and it sure would be a whole lot easier if I could eat with my hands."

Molly stared back at the poor Braden. "Alright. It's against my better judgement, but I do feel sorry for you," she noted as she untied his hands.
"What is it? Looks like the same thing I had last night. Always the same. Where's Quinn?"

"I don't know. You keep asking me the same question and I give you the same answer."
"I need Quinn. He's my brother. He take care of Braden. Wha, what's your name?"
"Molly. I'm not supposed to talk to you. My job is to feed you and the animals, and milk the cow".
"My hand," objected Braden. "Not good. Broken. You need to fix."
She gently held his hand and smiled. She covered his eyes. "I have to leave. I'll be back to cover your mouth," she added as she closed the door and made her way up the steps.

Back into darkness he went. He took off the eye mask and felt his way down to the food bowl and began eating. He heard a noise coming from near the door. Some kind of animal. Something was coming toward him. He could hear the tiny footsteps. Slowly, it came closer and closer. Braden stopped eating and turned his attention toward the door. It was a twitching sound. A squeaking sound. He squinted harder. There it was. A big fat rat with a tail a mile long. He was trying to get closer to the tray. "So you're the culprit. You think this mush is for you?"

56

Braden's Bastille

The rat stared at Braden and Braden stared at the rat. Both were scared. Braden reached down and grabbed at the ankle cuff. He pulled and tugged without any result. He couldn't move and the rat knew it.

"Mordecai! That's a good name for you," whispered Braden.
Mordecai sniffed at the mush and moved closer. His sharp, pointed nose, his beady eyes, his oversized ears, his front paws with elongated nails. Inch by inch, he came closer as Braden wet his pants. He moved away from the tray and allowed Mordecai to have all he wanted. He watched as Mordecai licked the bowl clean, glanced at Braden and returned to the hole in the wall.

"Ah, my escape route," noted Braden as he grabbed the tray and began scratching the frozen floor. Bit by bit, piece by piece, he began to collect a small pile of loose dirt. The only problem was that the hole was still too far away. How much time did he have before she'd be back? Got to get closer! He searched around where the tray had been and found the two rag ropes. He unraveled both and tore an inch off all along. He now had three four foot ropes, two were 3'x2" and two were 3'x1". He twisted the two inch ropes like they had been and set them aside, and then twisted the two 3'x1" and tied them together, making one 6'x1" rope, which he hid in his pants. As he was finishing his task he heard footsteps. He laid down beside his tray and put his eye mask on, sat down on his bed of straw, and waited for her return.

"All done?"
"Yes," calmly replied Braden.
"You need to appreciate what you get. We could starve you."
"That's about what you're doing now."
"How would you know, you, you simpleton."
"Me no simpleton. Me good. You bad."
"We'll see about that," she noted as she picked up the tray. "I can be nice you know. You treat Molly like a lady, I treat you like a man."
"Make sure you clean that bucket out tomorrow. I don't know where to put it."

Braden's Bastille

"I'll take care of it in the morning," she noted as she headed for the door.
"Wait!" begged Braden. "What did you mean if I treat you like a lady?"
"I kinda like you, Braden. I feel sorry for the condition that you have to put up with. I'd like it very much if I could make life better for you," she acknowledged as she closed the door and headed back upstairs.

Braden smiled as he took out the six foot rope and put it in a pile, urinated on it and stretched it out as far as he could along the frozen wall. He laid back down on his straw and continued to think about Molly. I have to make up a plan. I have to get her to cooperate. I have to figure her out. So unpredictable! Wow! She just like me.

"THE PINAFORE INN"

For the next several weeks change was the name of the game out at Fish Lake. Construction was going full bore. With a lot of help from Spat and a little from Remy, the modernized campsite was taking shape. Johnny Fisher, the old foreman, was given control of day to day operations. New buildings, although rather primitive, took the place of the old primitive buildings. Hammers were hammering and saws were sawing. Magic was occurring. As each day passed, buildings were born. Board by board, the hotel was taking on the looks of a destination point. 50'x50' was the size. Enough for four rooms, plus the office and storeroom. It stood tall and proud, even with the constant disruption from above. Yes, the spring rains had arrived and the skies refused to shut off. The boathouse was the nicest on the lake, albeit the only one. The billiard hall was started but had to be put on hold. There were ten wooden fishing boats ready for service, but now were being used as storage containers.

The island was calling. Pinafore Island, the final destiny for some, especially among the partygoers, lie in wait with open arms to all those desiring fun and frivolity. Her arms were open, but not seen. Her calls were put out, but not heard. Her cottonwoods were being decimated one by one. Her beauty had been on display until the hail made its grand entrance. Now it was beginning to look like a war-torn site from the Civil War. It was showing battle scars, and no one wanted a thing to do with it under those conditions.

Plans for the first building to be erected on Pinafore Island were coming to fruition. Construction was begun. Quinn had the tools. Building materials had arrived. All that was left was to put it all together. With plans in hand, he jumped in with both feet while his help built a large boathouse. "Gonna be the best darn vault ever in the whole county.

59

The
Pinafore Inn

People from all around will be talking about the future edifice. It'll be known all over Minnesota and beyond," he noted as he pounded nails and sawed cottonwoods, with the sun providing warmth to an otherwise cool spring morning while the northwest breeze continued to sting.

"Need some help?" queried Remy as he arrived on Pinafore, in a row boat. "Not sure if I'll be that much help when it comes to building something. I may be more of a hindrance than a help. This site would be a perfect placed for a house," continued Remy. "Why are you wasting all this beautiful lumber on a vault?"

"This isn't going to be your ordinary outhouse. This is going to be the pinnacle of Pinafore, to be seen afar as the House of Quinn on Fish Lake. It'll be my talking point for my Hotel LePette set-up. Everybody will be talking about that beautiful structure high on the hill. When the weather cooperates, these gently rolling hills with these gorgeous 75 foot cottonwoods will be a spectacle to behold. Can't you just picture where tents can be placed and fireplaces built and entertainment can thrive?"

"I don't see the reasoning behind spending so much time and money on something so unnecessary. I would think a man of your character would be spending more time looking for a friend, a companion, a lover, a wife. I thought you were headed in that direction with Harriet."

"That's what I thought too, but it only took me a week to start doubting. After that trip we had out here a few days back we moved further and further apart. Of course, since she's gone on her trip to Fargo, I keep thinking that I don't have much free time left, so why don't I make the best of it. I like her very much, but I'm not ready yet. My job at the office comes first, and then there's real estate. Someday I'll be ready for her. There's no single area of marriage that affects the rest of marriage as much as meeting the emotional needs for love. It seems impossible for me, but I think the stress has a lot to do with it. Once I can get a handle on that I'll look at marriage."

"I still think she's too good for you."
"I may not show it now, but I have a feeling of contentment. I try to believe that the things of this world can't really satisfy me.

60

The
Pinafore Inn

When I think of that and live for Him, it brings true satisfaction and I acknowledge that my relationships need to be prioritized.

"It sounds like you've been doing a lot of finding. Way too much for me to comprehend," noted Remy as he snapped his fingers.

"You have to come out of your shell, Remy. You and Lin aren't exactly setting the world on fire. I know you've been setting your sights on someone else. Harriet has told me. We are nothing more than jars of clay, desiring only to attract people to the incomparable treasure we hold inside. We are to seek to showcase the brilliance of the One who lives within."

"I really don't need no preaching from you today. Let's talk about this project."

"This will be my most gratifying attempt at creating," noted Quinn as he continued to hammer away. "Best material I could find. I want this to be a beacon, a haven for concealment, a landmark of sophistry. I want it to be big enough where the occupants can relax and enjoy. My main goal, besides providing for customer relief, is to give a pleasant experience for each of the senses."

"Come now," shot back Remy. "It's just a john!"
"Oh no. No. It's so much more. You don't understand. Here! Help me raise this wall."

By evening the construction project had been completed. A temple on the hill, reaching out far and wide, with an open invitation to all to come visit and enjoy. Satisfaction showed on Quinn's face as he stepped back and admired his work. Two spacious rooms, one for the men, one for the women, and an empty room in the middle. "Ready for use," exclaimed Quinn. 12'x40'. Made of logs and with a touch of love. Quinn's pride and joy. No more hiding in the bushes. No more public outcries. Completion was complete once Quinn put up the welcome sign and the sign that stood up on the roof, 'THE PINAFORE INN'.

The Pinafore Inn

The first of the month was fast approaching. Deadlines to be met, but broken. The weather was not cooperating. Rain in the morning, rain in the evening, rain during the night. With more rain came more of a mess on the dirt trails leading to the Promised Land. Question marks appeared on Quinn's face, as the end of May had arrived. Requests for rooms, or for camping sites on Pinafore Island were phenomenal.

Visions of overflow filled Quinn's mind. Smiles flowed as he looked at the guest list. Everyone of importance from Fergus Falls planned on being there. Everyone that had a name for themselves, or everyone that thought they were the cream of the crop was planning to attend. The only problem was the weather. The dark clouds didn't want to leave. They were content with destruction. More pressure felt by Quinn, as if it wasn't enough of a problem, or lack thereof, in the medical field.

With the arrival of the First, that was about the only thing that arrived, beside the rain, and the wind, and the hail. Quinn stood in his brand new, rough smelling, untreated lumber complex of a hotel, looking out and wanting to cry. The rains were at a downpour stage, along with strong northwest winds, and carp in the turbulent waters of Fish Lake. The Cottonwoods were crashing, trying desperately to hide from the ferocious breath of Mother Nature. Now came the hail. Pounding! Pulverizing! Anything in its way. Death knell for the new crops, as well as the new boathouse at the Hotel LePette, and even for Dr. Quinn Shanahan, while a man dressed in black, and wearing a shiny rain coat, watched in disbelief.

Quinn was beside himself. No one in their right mind will come out here with this weather. Why would they leave the comforting confines of their own abode? Fishing? No one can go fishing anytime. Swimming? Nobody will enter these mad waters. Besides, even if they wanted to come, the roads have to be absolutely impassable. "Why God? Why do you have it in for me? Can't I ever get a break?" he shouted as he looked up at the brutal onslaught. "If only I could be with Braden!"

62

"BRADEN TRANSFER"

Darkness remained as Braden was lying near his straw bed. He had no masks over his eyes and mouth. His hands were untied and his shackle was gone. A small table stood where the old tray used to be. Life was a whole lot easier for him, yet he still yearned for Quinn.

Molly unlocked the main entrance and brought a basket of food in for her favorite prisoner. "Good morning, Braden," she noted as she set the basket down. "I have more surprises for you today. We are moving."
"Moving? To where?"

"Out to the farm. Boss is thinking that your brother is going to figure out where we've been hiding out. We have to keep you on the move until he pays up. The wagon should be here any moment now. You'll like it there. I think I hear him out there right now. I'm going to have to cover your eyes while we're on this long trip. Don't worry. As soon as we get there I'll take it off. Oh, by the way, I'm not quite sure what that rope you put together that led to the doorway was all about, but I picked it up and threw it away."

"I was after Mordecai."
"Who's that?"
"Some rat. He shared my food. He came out of that hole dang near every night at suppertime and he visited me. I was going to block it so he'd leave me alone."
"I never heard of such stupidity! Why didn't you just ask me? I would have filled the hole. You know you can trust me."
Molly went outside and greeted a man driving a buggy with two gold spokes. With eyes covered and mind wondering, Braden was given something, some drug, something that made him incapacitated, and was asleep within minutes. Molly sat in the back of the buggy with Braden on her lap.

63

Braden
Transfer

She kept looking at her prized prisoner, while the man with the peculiar-looking eyes directed the horses to trails that went in all directions.

Braden began to wake up. He observed his present situation. What's going on? He asked himself. Something was up. It had been weeks since he had heard anything about Quinn. It was as if his brother had disappeared from the face of the Earth. Or was he dead? Braden asked himself as a tear came to his eye. Why won't anyone tell me what's going on?

He was in a new place, an unfamiliar location. He had no eye cover, nor mouth cover. His hands were not tied. He had fresh new clothes. He was in a farm house, with windows and doors. There were dishes on the table, clothes hanging on pegs, a fireplace still smoldering from a night's work. "Where am I?" he murmured as he fell back to sleep.

Outside, the sun was beginning its daily ritual, as a rooster crowed and Molly was walking in from the nearby barn, having finished her morning chores. She was in a good mood. She was smiling. She was frolicking along the path as if she had not a worry in the world.

Something strange, thought Braden. Something was up. Her purplish-blue passionflower eyes were so evident and her crimson cheeks overwhelmed her acne and pimples, erasing her normal weather-beaten skin.
"You smell real good! New?"
"No, Braden. Just used some soap."
"I like. How old?"

"17."
"Almost like me. Me, 19. There's something different. I like your laugh. Makes me feel good."

"Oh Braden. Come! Let me show you your room," she suggested as she took his hand and led him to one of the rooms in the back. "This will be yours."

64

Transfer

Braden looked around. A real bed! A bed with a real mattress, and blankets and sheets. There are two windows. One showing nothing but woods while the other, water. Lots of water.

"I will be staying out here with you," noted Molly as she fluffed up Braden's pillow, but you will be responsible for keeping this room clean. My room is right beside yours, however, your room will be locked up each night."

"How long will this go on?"
"That's entirely up to your brother. I told you. My boss thinks you're worth quite a bit."

"KISS OF BETRAYAL"

Lawrence Aune's Grocery, on the northwest side of Lincoln and Mill, was extra busy on this particularly gorgeous day in Fergus. Naddy was on a mission. Shopping was at the top of her list and fresh off a tour of monumental proportions with the Asa Hutchinson troupe.

"Good morning, Miss Naddy," offered Mr. Aune. "I was just reading an outstanding article in the 'Journal' on you and your sisters. So, when will you be going on a national tour?"

"Oh my! I have no answer for you," replied Naddy. "I'm lucky to remember what I came here to get. Could you tell me where I can find some of that 'Rough On Rats'?"

"Of course! Right over here, Ma'am."
"Hey Naddy," interrupted Quinn as he entered the store. "How's Harriet? I haven't seen her since you left for Fargo."

"She's fine," replied Naddy as she picked up a box of 'Rough On Rats'."

"How's it coming along with that new horse?"
"Fire Cracker? I get out to ride him every chance I can. I plan on going out as soon as I get done here."

"How would you like company?"
"You? You would like to go riding with me?"

"Sure. I have a new horse also. His name is 'Pistol'. I'd like to go out riding, but I don't care to go out by myself."

Kiss Of Betrayal

"I didn't know you liked horseback riding. Sure. I'd love it. Let me finish up here and I'll get Firecracker and we can meet wherever you want."

"Good. Give me an hour. I have a few things I need to finish at the office. I'll meet you out by the river. By the Northern Pacific tracks, just past the Mill. Then we can decide where to go."

Naddy paid for her supplies and headed out, with an extra bounce in her step and an extra special smile on her face as she got in her buggy while Quinn continued to look out the store window. She was baffled at the thought of Quinn Shanahan wanting to ride with her. Maybe this would be her chance to make a good impression and lean him towards her.

Upon arrival at home, Naddy put the old plug out to the paddock and brought her riding, a beautiful sorrel, quarter horse gelding, with a flaxen mane, and a white star on its forehead, up to the hitching post in front of the house. She went inside and changed into her riding outfit. When she came back down, Clare was standing by the door. "I thought I heard someone come in."

"Hello, Mother. I'm going to go for a short ride. I shall return in time for my piano lesson."

"Good. I was hoping you wouldn't forget. I wouldn't go out too far. It looks like dark clouds are banking up in the west."

"I got the rat poison Father wanted. I shouldn't be gone no more than an hour," continued Naddy as she put on her horse riding cap and headed out the door. Dressed in her knee-high riding britches and wearing a pair of tall brown English boots, she went straight for the stable and proceeded to saddle Firecracker.

Naddy headed for the river where, to her surprise, Quinn was already waiting, standing beside his shiny stallion.

Kiss
Of Betrayal

"What took you so long?" he laughed. "Actually, I just got here."

"You're just too fast for me. I had to change horses, change clothes, and change me. The easiest part was me. My old 'Nellie' doesn't like to be put out to pasture. She fights it all the way, and my 'Firecracker' is going to be the same way. Where should we go?"

"How about if we just follow the river and see where it takes us?"
"I don't know. I've heard some ghastly stories about going along this river."

"You don't have to worry none. I'm here to protect you. That's a very pretty horse you have there. The rider matches perfectly."

"Oh Quinn! That is so nice of you to say."

They headed down river ever so slowly, with each quietly looking the other over. "Beautiful day for a ride. Do you do much riding?"

"I try to go out every day, but there are days that it's impossible. I've been training with 'Firecracker'. I have him entered in a show jumping contest next week, in Fargo. Was gone on that tour out west and that has set me back. This'll be my first contest and I'm really nervous."

"I'm sure you'll do just fine. Do you get any help from your sisters?"

"Not really. Harriet is the only one that really cares about horses. Deb could care less. She'd rather spend her time in the house."

"Does Harriet have a horse?"
"Yes. One like mine, only more of a chestnut."
"Is Harriet your favorite?"

68

Kiss
Of Betrayal

"Most of the time. There's been times where I get a little jealous of what she's doing. She's very competitive, like me. She's probably too much like me. You know, Quinn. There are three girls in our family and none of us are married. Mother doesn't want us to break up our group and neither does Deb, but Harriet and I want to do something about that. We both believe that we can be married and still play music. Mother thinks that once we get married, we'll stop playing and go raise a family. What do you think?"

"I'd love nothing better than to get involved and be a part of the Wiggin's monopoly. How about this spot? Perfect location for a picnic," noted Quinn as he pointed to an open area right next to the river.

"Sure. That'll be fine."
Quinn spread out a blanket and placed the picnic basket in the middle. He sat down and listened to the river babble on its way westward. Not sure if I should be doing this, but, dang it, he thought. I need something of a life too. She's gallivanting around the country while I'm stuck here. It's a perfect time to spend with Naddy. What harm is that? She's her sister. Oh, she's so much different than Harriet.

The robins were chirping and the doves were cooing as Naddy and Quinn began to relax.

"What do you think of me, Quinn? I love my family. My most favorite person in the whole world is my mother. She has taught me everything I know about life and living it to the fullest. If I had my way, I'd never grow up. Life is so much simpler in your younger years. Riding horses is my escape. Out into the countryside, along the Red, where it's so peaceful, so thought provoking. A perfect time to learn and to forget, to dream and to plot. A perfect place to enjoy the open space and let my hair down, with not a worry in the world."

"Well, Naddy. I actually know very little about you. Perhaps, you should fill me in."

69

Kiss
Of Betrayal

"I think I'm a mess. My eyes are open, but I cannot see. I can read, but I do not understand the words. I can talk, yet I cannot speak. My ears can hear, but they do not listen. My fingers can touch, yet I do not feel. My mind is clear, yet I live in fog. I carry opinions, but can't express. I am afraid of nothing, yet scared of everything. I am innocent of guilt, yet am guilty of innocence. In other words, I'm messed up."

"Not really, Naddy. You sound like a lot of people I know, and even a lot like me. You make a lot of sense."

Naddy stepped closer and put her left hand on his right shoulder. Quinn shivered as he turned to her and smiled. "You do know that I'm going with your sister?"

"I do, Quinn. I do. May the strongest survive," she continued as she bent over and kissed him. A simple little kiss. Quinn felt an urge to resist, but his weakness won out. He returned the kiss and added another. They both stood up and held each other tightly, as true feelings appeared. For Naddy, success. For Quinn, guilt. The plans for both have changed. Naddy was flying high and Quinn was shaking. Both were confused. Both questioning each other. Naddy, in delight. Quinn, in consternation. Sweat rolled down their faces. They joined together in ecstasy. And then it was done.

"We better get back to town," suggested Quinn. "Must check up on a patient. It looks like rain coming."

"But we haven't been gone that long!"
"Another time and another place, Naddy. I need to do some soul searching."

Naddy smiled a smile of conquest while Quinn put his tail between his legs.

"BANNISTER, THE UNKNOWN"

Judge Bannister, with umbrella in hand, walked up to a dilapidated hovel situated on the west end of Lincoln Avenue. It was dark and cold, just like the inclement rain. A lone red light brightened up the entrance to the small one-story shack, but Bannister made his way to the back, where it was really dark. He knocked and nervously waited, while he shifted his eyes to the left and then to the right. The door opened. He was greeted by a short, disheveled lady with long reddish-gray hair flowing down to her waist. She was a specimen of her trade, compact and belittled, blemished beyond hope, sloven and reckless, fragile in mind and body. Her scarlet hair gave off a sheen like the guiding red light at the entrance. Her shark-like eyes of jade, cold and indifferent, gave her away. Her pallid lips cried out for help due to neglect, yet it seemed no one came to the rescue. Likewise, her body, abused, malnourished, and forsaken, begged for sustenance to no avail. Her best years, if that were ever possible, were behind her. "Mr. Bannister," she roughly acknowledged. "Come in."

"Nelda! Do you have it ready?"

She handed him a leather pouch, which Bannister immediately opened and checked its contents. "I've been meaning to tell you that I believe you have not been placing the correct amount of proceeds in the past few weeks."

"What are you implying? We're new to the area. It will take my girls some time to develop a clientele base."

"Come now, Nelda. I know that you are a cauldron of contempt to your underlings. Your rasping voice haunts me to no end. You must change. You were perfect for the job down in the Cities. Whatever happened to that lady in charge? She never came up to Fergus with the others.

71

Bannister,
The Unknown

I'm implying that you are skimming, Miss Nelda. You have three working and according to the collections they are barely working."

"You'll find everything in the ledger, Mr. Bannister. Why on Earth would I ever try to cheat you, of all people? You need to take my word as the truth.

Expenses seem to be increasing at an alarming rate and the girls can only do so much. They need to survive too. Besides, Anna hasn't been in the picture.

She's just coming back today, and Maggie? You never know when she's going to show up."

"I'll send you Molly. She should make a big difference. By the way, how is
Anna doing?"

"She's clean."

"That was a rather expensive ordeal. I believe Shanahan overcharged. We have to find a cheaper alternative. Now, getting back to the problem at hand. I'm keeping an eye on what's going on out here. Don't ever let me catch you taking advantage."

"WEDDING BELLS"

The days of being single were quickly disappearing for Quinn. He realized that his days of testing the market were soon to be history. More time to be spent with the love of his life. More time to be with her at least when she wasn't on some tour somewhere miles and miles away. This gave him plenty of time to his doctoring and to his realty business, and to the promotion of his Family Medical Kit, and plenty of time to try to figure out where Braden was. All roads led to nowhere. Whenever a clue arose, it didn't take long for failure to return.

July 18th arrived. The day of the wedding of Dr. Quinn Shanahan and Harriet Wiggins. The stage was set. To be held in the Wiggins house in the evening. Just for a small group of guests. Only the close friends of the bride and groom. Only people who mattered to Quinn and Harriet.

Wedding cake, refreshments, food, and more refreshments were supplied. Decorations were minimal. Brides dress, groom's tuxedo, flowers, guest book, candles, and more refreshments, appeared. Flowers were on display all along the projected path of the wedding marchers. Hydrangeas, Callalilies, and Clematis, were ready on the main floor.

Everything seemed ready but, alas, not all was right in the Wiggins world. The house was full with tables and chairs and all of the bare necessities, yet the house was empty. The organ lie in wait for the 'key' players, while the neighborhood kept their eyes open for the latest gossip's sake, by looking around for the orange blossoms. Where were the orange blossoms? Every wedding had orange blossoms sprinkled along the path of the wedding march. They were an important part of the symbolism for they represented purity. Were they forgotten? I don't think so, and neither did the guests.

Wedding
Bells

The house that Wiggins built was being overtaken for a minimum time by Quinn and Harriet. Cursed by the ominous prognostication of Clare and the crossed fingers of Stanley, and damned by the enemies of Quinn, the plans, nevertheless, appeared in readiness. Doubts remained, yet all moved forward. Someone left the door open and a battalion of mosquitoes found their way in. The upstairs was buzzing with bride and her honorable maid in one room, groom and his best man in another, and the doubters still in yet another, while the Wiggin's piano player sat by her piano, with eyes of jealousy and remorse, surveyed the scene.

The future bride was in a tizzy, with sister Naddy, by her side, making sure their collection was complete. Dressed only in corsets of discomfort and classic white cotton bloomers, and their hair of communication, shorn and pulled back at the sides, with bangs of femininity at the forefront and clusters of ringlets flowing down the sides, decisions were made. Something old, something new, something borrowed, something blue, and a lucky sixpence in the shoe. Oh, what to put in that shoe? What's a sixpence? They asked. No one knew. "I believe it's a half shilling," noted Naddy, "but what's a shilling?"

"Just put six pennies in there. No one will know anyway," shot back Harriet. "Who cares?"

Something old, a rusted brooch from the Clare Collection. Something new, a family Bible, with mountains of unknown. Something borrowed, a list of fantasies from sister, Naddy. Something blue, a dried-up morning glory, begging for riddance. The list was complete and quickly forgotten.

Now to matters of more importance. In the background a masterpiece of chiffon was lying in wait to be filled. The stunning white chiffon dress, embellished with little nuggets of diamonds and pearls, and coordinated with a white veil, connected to a long, full court train of splendor would surely put the element of surprise and jealousy in the minds of the observers.

Wedding
Bells

Harriet sat back and stared out the window. From under the watchful eye of her parents she was about to enter a world of unknown. Experienced in the life of a married woman she was void. Her world would be changed forever. She was about to enter a world of subjugation, a world where her tired fingers from needlework would be intermingled with flour and water, and dust clothes, and diapers, and providing relief to Quinn's back in the evenings, and to still be strong enough for the hours of piano practice. Her knees had been very active on Sundays, but now they would be in use seven days a week, making connections with the floors. Her heart was of gold, but would soon change to one of anxiety. Her body, shielded with pride, would put her back into reality, a reality of magnanimous servitude to not only the man above, but also to the man beside.

With shoulders full of chips and a mind tough as nails she smiled at the thought of putting her life, and even her very soul, into the hands of a doctor. Her desire to share was tantamount to success. Her pampered lifestyle may take a hit, but she was prepared. At least she thought she was.

Naddy was a bundle of nerves as she stepped forward to assist in the task at hand. With a heart of jealousy, and a mind of resentment, she toiled in a contrived state, vowed and determined, to make this Harriet's day, regardless of what her thoughts may assume. With a valiant effort she assisted in fitting her sister into her heavenly garb. With moments of dreaming that she was Harriet, she allowed herself to covet with guilt.

With dress and train on board, next came the long-sleeved, white gloves and a pair of white, soft, flat shoes, with bows. Her final piece of the puzzle was the beautiful bouquet of white roses.

She was a beautiful bride. She would be the talk of the town. Everyone would be contributing their two cents worth, regardless of what they saw, even if most were jealous, or really didn't know what they were talking about, and even if their pockets were empty.

Wedding Bells

With the nervous Harriet all set, Naddy prepared herself. Adjusting her corset by putting more on display, she then climbed into her dress of white, fingered her hair, and placed a string of pearls around her neck.
 In the room next door, Quinn and his best man, Spat, were in a frenzy to see who could get dressed the fastest. Each were similarly dressed. White shirts; a white waistcoat; dark gray trousers; with a button fly and suspender rivets; thin, high-heeled gray shoes; and a white tailcoat, lavender gloves and a black top hat.

Quinn looked in the mirror, somber and remorseful. "If only Braden were here," he mused. "My poor little brother. If only I knew."

Downstairs, the guests were arriving, gathering around to mix. All waiting for the arrival of Reverend Martin and the wedding party.
 The Wiggins family sat in wait in their own private room. Clare, all dressed in her finest satins and silks, stood with swatter in hand, awaiting for an unsuspecting mosquito. Right beside her sat 'Voyance'. "Ah, I remember my wedding day. The best day of my life. I just knew you were the one for me. It wasn't like this one. Back then pomp and pageantry and excess were not even listed in Webster's. Everything was so simple. Oh yes, simple, but not welcomed. I felt like a used piano key. Constantly being pounded but still making beautiful music. I wanted to be a pianist in my younger years. You didn't think much of the idea. See what is happening because of my determination? All our girls are years ahead of everyone else. They have musical talents that many would love to have. They are going to go places and they are going to make us rich, Stanley. Just wait and see."

Stanley, the protector, wore his coat of velvet and top hat. With cane in one hand and ear trumpet in the other, he stoically stood by the window in deep thought, stating "Yes Dear" whenever necessary. "Well, the Reverend can show up any time."

 "He probably knows this marriage isn't going to work."
 "Don't talk so," shot back Stanley.

Wedding Bells

"You know, as well as I, Stanley, she's a lot younger. I've heard some stories about Quinn that I'm not sure if I want his kind taking my Harriet away from me. I don't give them a year."

"What are you talking about? He's a doctor!"

"He's more than a doctor. I tell you, Stanley. Something doesn't smell right about that man. When I first met him I thought what a pleasant upstanding person that was. Well, the more I hear about him, the less there is to like about him. I tried telling Harriet, but she has her mind set."

"Reverend Martin is here," observed Stanley. "I'll go let him in. I'll be out in a minute."

With Deborah playing the organ and Reverend Martin, with prayer book in hand, now at his command post, the wedding hour had arrived. The guests settled in their observation posts and the wedding participants made their appearance. First through the doorway was Quinn and Spat. They made their way to the side of the Reverend. Now, all were waiting for the main attraction.

The music stopped while the crowd whispered and looked at their watches and Remy was on the move. He made his way over to where Maggie was seated. He talked with her for a few minutes and they departed, quietly sneaking out the back door, as Lin watched. Everyone else directed their attention towards Reverend Martin. As the March music began, Naddy approached from one side and Spat from the other. Then came the main attraction---Harriet.

Quinn watched her every move, as she slowly made her way up to the makeshift altar, one step at a time. Once to the left, pause, and then the right. Beauty on display. What a catch! The fisherman thought. My plan is working to perfection. Bannister can go to hell!

The Reverend Herald Martin, tall, stout, and dedicated, stood waltzing back and forth, as he smiled upon the wedding party. Adroit in his responsibilities and in his field of expertise he had become a favorite of Quinn's realm in just a matter of several meetings.

77

Wedding Bells

He was a sage of prudence and foresight, somewhat of an adversary to Clare. His bushy gotee and long black hair gave a perception of neglect, however he was far from that. There was an aura of simplicity and divine cognizance that was so very noticeable in his actions and his demeanor.

"Dearly beloved," addressed the preacher. "We are gathered here together on this fine evening to join together Harriet Marie Wiggins and Dr. Quinn Michael Shanahan, in matrimony. If there be anyone in the audience that objects to this union, let them speak now, or forever hold their peace."

Outside, things were heating up between Remy and Maggie. "You can't do this to me," shouted Remy. "I have a reputation to uphold." "You should have thought about that when you started this."

"I didn't start anything. It was you. You're the one that set me up, led me along, kept stringing me out, and now, now you want money, or else?"

"It's only a thousand dollars."

"You know I don't have that kind of money. For God's sake, I'm only a doctor."

"Ah, but your partner can."
"Who? Quinn? He's got problems of his own, plus now he's going to be tied in with the Wiggins."

"That's what I mean. They're the ones with the money. Somehow you must get their money through Quinn."

"That's utter nonsense! You'll just have to ask Lin if she believes you, or me."

"The only other choice you have is if you talk to your secret partner. I'll give you one more week. Either make payment or I will make life miserable for you."

Wedding Bells

"We'll see," shot back Remy, as he headed back into the house.

"I now pronounce you, man and wife," noted Reverend Martin. "You may kiss the bride."

Quinn lifted the veil and the new couple kissed, to the approval of the onlookers. Clare showed her approval with a huge smile and was the first to get in the reception line to shower a congratulatory paragraph upon the new Shanahan family. Stanley followed and gave his daughter a little kiss on the forehead. "You looked absolutely stunning. I am a proud father today."

"Oh, thank-you, Father."
Without saying a word, he shook hands with his new son-in-law and moved on into the reception area, followed closely by Clare.

As the line for chow filled up so too did the gift table. There were large gifts and small gifts---all a part of the bare necessities for a new beginning. Several of the young ladies were observing the haul. Maggie stopped while others continued on. She picked up a gold-lined toothpick holder. After close examination she placed it off to the side and directed her attention to a solid silver napkin ring, while others in line had to go around her.

"Aren't these just absolutely wonderful gifts?" inquired Mara.
"Why, yes, of course," answered Maggie. "But I have a weakness for cultivated society. These things are way out of my line, but, perhaps someday that'll be different."

Meanwhile, the wedding party headed over to their designated table and sat down. "So, where do you plan on going on your honeymoon?" asked Spat.

"Down to Lake Minnetonka and then over to White Bear Lake. Two weeks. Catching the morning train first thing."

Wedding Bells

"Oglesby covering for you?"

"No. I don't trust him. There's a new doctor in town. Doc Jackson. He's going to see my patients."

"I heard your partner may be in trouble."

"I don't know anything about that. I heard the same story but I have no idea if it's true, or not."

"Well, someone told me that he is doing illegal abortions."

"I have nothing to do with him. I've been doing a lot of real estate sales when I'm not practicing medicine, so we haven't been talking much."

Quinn glanced over to where Maggie was standing. He watched as she put something into her handbag.

"So," continued Spat. "Do you have your new home ready?"

"I do. Stanley took care of everything. It hasn't cost me a cent. I didn't have much say in any of the procedures but it looks like it's turning out to be fine. Most of our possessions are in there already. I'm hoping Mara will have everything in perfect shape by the time we get back from our little trip down to the Cities."

"Is there anything I can do to help?" interrupted Naddy.

"Yes," shouted Mara. "You can meet me over there tomorrow morning. I'm heading over there now. Going to give them a little surprise."

The new, never-been-lived in house of Shanahan was the talk of the town. Ridiculous, some said; others, unimpressed; still others, show-off. It was situated on Cavour Avenue, just a few blocks from downtown and a short distance from the Catholic Church. The neighborhood was considered to be upper class, perfect for Quinn. From outside it looked stunning----a magnificent edifice for a doctor and his new bride. A three story affair, with a Witches Hat turret on the left side, as you approach on the straight and narrow, mud-filled path, to the main entrance. A white porch awaited the visitors. It was matched on the second floor by a dazzling balcony of epic proportions. The brilliant white siding put a magic luster on the entire villa. An off-white balustrade blended in perfectly with the wood siding. The entire plot was surrounded by a five foot, black, metal fence, built to keep intruders, or maybe to keep people in.

Wedding Bells

Upon entry, the visitor is greeted by an inviting Victorian coat rack, a sparkling oak floor and trim, and a warmth like sunshine. The smell of lavender poured out to capture relaxation of all who partook. The rooms were awe-inspiring, even though most were empty. Two bedrooms on the main floor and three upstairs. Indoor plumbing included bucket cupboards, downstairs and upstairs. Chain-pulled showers downstairs and toilet, outside. The bedrooms were fantastic. Top of the line, freshly produced at the factories in Minneapolis. Over-sized oak beds with feather-filled mattresses and silk sheets and luxurious quilts painted a picture of wealth, another favorite of Quinn. Matching vanities and chests of drawers filled the rooms.

Back down the creaking stairs we find a library, with empty shelves, and a smoking parlor, with a no smoking sign. A dining room with the long table and eight chairs, was beside the small kitchen and adjoining empty pantry.

As evening arrived, rain gently fell on the new House of Shanahan outside, and inside the newlyweds were almost ready to call it a day. By now the heat had been turned up. Neither could wait to rush off to their virgin night home. The first day in the lives of the Quinn Shanahan couple was coming to an end. It was to be the beginning of the end, a smudge in the lives of two interesting characters on two different paths. "Oh, if only Sarah could have been here," moaned Harriet. "Oh, if only Braden could have been here," suggested Quinn.

It was off to the luxury bedroom. Full of excitement and hungry for companionship, the two joined forces. Gentle hugs and little kisses grew into a period of enrapture. Enchanting moments of pleasure engulfed the setting. Temperatures elevated to record heights as Harriet melted in the arms of Quinn. Breaking in a new bedroom seemed to be the big thing to do, as they wondered what type of history this room would have.

"HONEYMOONING"

The next morning, off to the train station the newlyweds hurried. Honeymoon time. Time to head for Lake Minnetonka and White Bear Lake, two of the most attractive bodies of water in Minnesota. Two places where newlyweds could let it all down and relax, even though the problem with the missing Braden had not been taken care of. The St. Paul, Minneapolis & Manitoba Railroad was the designated carrier, bringing the newlyweds down to Wayzata, on the shores of Lake Minnetonka. The site where they were connected with the 'City of St. Louis' steamer, the pride of the Lake Minnetonka Navigation Company. Only in its' second year of duty, the vessel flaunted itself with space for a thousand customers, with three decks of viewing area. Its' sides glittered with fresh white paint. Each side of the paddle box, located towards the stern of the ship, was painted with a scene of a famous bridge, one side, the Ft. Snelling Bridge, the other, a St. Louis bridge. The newness was evident, as the Shanahan's made their way through the crowded deck, past the mahogany walls, to the stairwell.

They were awed at the beauty of such a large mass of water and awesome wooded shoreline, and the air, redolent with the perfume of all types of wild flowers, dotting the countryside. They made their way to the hurricane deck and found vacant seats in the bow of the open-aired promenade, close to the two slender and tall smokestacks right in front of the pilothouse.

"On behalf of Captain Telfer," noted the ship's greeter, who was standing in front of the crowd on the upper deck, "I would like to welcome you on our first excursion of the summer season around the beautiful Lake Minnetonka.

Honeymooning

Our round trip will total 36 miles. We will have several short stops on the way to our destination of Chapman's, where we will have a lunch, and then we'll have several stops on the way around the lake and end up back here in Wayzata. Our first stop will be at the Hotel St. Louis, which is about three miles from here. We do have a band that will soon be playing for your pleasure. So, sit back and relax. Enjoy the beautiful scenery and your trip on the 'City of St. Louis'".

The views were of brilliant colors of blues in the water and greens on the shore, and whites, reds, and yellows on the steamer. No mosquitoes here. It was a time for relaxation and invigoration for the passengers. A time for Quinn and Harriet to enjoy each other's company. A time to learn more about each other, their likenesses and their differences; their good habits and bad; their strengths and their weaknesses.

 Not a cloud in the sky and a light northwesterly breeze was ideal for the tourists on Lake Minnetonka. "Couldn't ask for any better weather,"noted Quinn. "Especially for this time of year."

 "We'll be making a quick stop up ahead, on your left, at the 'Hotel St. Louis'. Long enough for those that need to depart and those that will be boarding," stated the ship's greeter.

"This is where we'll be staying for the next four days," suggested Quinn.

 "Darling, have you noticed how these so-called tourists are dressed? I think we're associating ourselves with an elite group of people. Most of them sound like they have a southern drawl and the women look like they're going to a ball."

"Yes. I have. Isn't that great? It feels good to be tied in with the upper class, for once. After all, Harriet, you did marry a doctor."

 "Really? You're starting to be full of all kinds of surprises," replied Harriet as she winced and put her hand on her stomach.

83

Honeymooning

"There! Look at that building," suggested Quinn as the 'Hotel St. Louis' came into view. The long, gray, wooden building, trimmed in green, majestically lie in wait amidst a grove of cottonwoods. "They should have our honeymoon suite ready by the time we get back. Just look at all the verandas. What a beautiful building! From the brochure I got, it said that some lawyer, from St. Louis, a Sir Charles Gibson, was mainly responsible."

In a matter of minutes the steamer was headed off to its next destination, the Excelsior Hotel, down the shoreline in a southwesterly direction, about three miles away. "Such a fantastic scene," acknowledged Harriet. "So beautiful! Thank-you for being so thoughtful on making our honeymoon so memorable."

Gradually, the steamer puffed along towards its destination of Chapman's House, located towards the western end of the entangled Lake Minnetonka. Across the bay from the Excelsior came the Lake Park Hotel. Known as the 'veranda crazy' hotel, it stood on high ground overlooking Gideon's Bay. Each room had a veranda which was a drawing point for many vacationers.

"It's becoming known as a health resort. We'll be coming back to this one," commented Quinn.

Onward the steamer continued, heading for the all new Hotel LaFayette. "It's just opening up," continued Quinn. "Brand new. James J. Hill, the head man of the St. Paul, Minneapolis, and Manitoba line is responsible for getting this built."

"I've never seen such a large building," gasped Harriet. "Unbelievable."

"He's got his railroad tracks going right by the hotel. Four stories high, room for a thousand plus. Extravagant! Money was no problem. I've heard stories about that man. Always has to one-up his competition. He has a very big ego. His appetite for extravagance has no bounds. This is one of the places I've secured for you to play piano, this coming Saturday evening."

84

Honeymooning

"You what?"

"Yea. I figured you could get a lot of exposure while we're down here. A good time to boost your musical career."

"Why didn't you ask me?"

"It was a spur of the moment thing. Besides, that'll help pay for this trip. You're set for an appearance at the Lake Park on the day before this one."

"Oh, Quinn. I don't want to hear any more. I need time to prepare. What am I going to play?"

"I have it all worked out. You'll play whatever songs you love to play. There will be no objections from anyone."

For the next couple of hours Harriet was silent, but that didn't mean she wasn't thinking. Her face was red. It was boiling inside and Quinn noticed. She looked to the left and then to the right as the sound of the sloshing waves met the hull of the floating behemoth.

I can't believe that man, she thought. Setting up engagements and not even asking me. What kind of nerve does that take? I know he does a lot of self-satisfaction moves, but this is going too far. I can't let him control me like that. Some changes are going to have to take place, or I'm not going to put up with his ways. I've heard lots of stories about how he is rather unthoughtful when it comes to some of his actions. I figure I can change his ways, but maybe I might have to straighten him out.

The steamer headed into the Narrows, where thousands of fragrant water lilies were floating along the way. Quinn went down to the main deck, got on his knees, and bent over the side and grabbed a water lily. He brought it back up to Harriet, but still no change. Harriet watched his every move. That was very thoughtful. Maybe I should just play along and see what happens. No, that would mean that I'm a lot like him and I don't think I am.

85

Honeymooning

Once free of the Narrows, the steamer went past the Spring Park peninsula and several small islands, the Spray, the Shady, the Enchanted, and the Crane. The Crane was an uninhabited island, the nesting home to thousands of blue herons. As they became disturbed, these long-necked and long-legged birds, with enormously slow wings from which floated long pendent plumes, took to the skies. The island boasted of a colony of black cormorants, where they nested on the cliffs, while the blue herons nested in the tree tops. Going past all this shrill music, the steamer made its' way into Cook Bay, and landed at the Chapman House.

This hotel was no more than an oversized, three-storied, L-shaped farmhouse, set on a high bluff, fifty feet above the waterline, where visitors could come and rent a room, or enjoy their favorite meal in the popular lunch room, or partake of a picnic in the wooded grove, surrounding the house. Freshly-washed linen, fluttering in the breeze, was competing with the backyard cesspool for the visitor's nostrils, while the gulls screeched and the cockroaches lied in wait. On s hore was a fleet of row boats, waiting to be put to use. "Nothing like a little bit of heaven," noted Quinn as he languished in the moment. "Life is good! Married life is agreeing with me."

Rather than go into the dining area, the newlyweds chose to go behind the building and into the grove area, where there was a trail that contained several benches on the sides, where they could have lunch served. During this layover the clear skies gave way to dark, heavy storm clouds. The gentle northwesterly breeze was gaining in intensity, causing a commotion in the grove where Quinn and Harriet were having a picnic lunch, with some newfound friends, Frank Carman and his wife, Adella. Frank was a friendly chap, middle-aged and well-rounded. Always with a smile, he enjoyed conversing with strangers to the area. He was part-owner of the Chapman House and loved the Lake Minnetonka area with a passion. He owned a general store and ran a post office in the nearby township of Minnetrista.

Honeymooning

He ran a freight boat from Mound City to Wayzata, and knew every nook and cranny of the lake. "If you have any questions about this area concerning hunting, or fishing, feel free to ask," noted Frank. "But, be careful," interrupted Adella. "You'll get paragraphs for a reply."

"Ahk, woman," shot back Frank. "You're one to talk. I tell ya, Quinn. If you ask her a question of how's she doing, she'll give you a spiel of a half hour of what's all wrong with her. She'd fill you in on all the pills and elixirs, and megrims, and vaporings she takes. Why, I don't think there's a healthy bone in her body if you listened to her."

"I did notice quite a few boats out there fishing."
"This bay is one of the most productive fishing holes in the entire lake. Why, you could catch a decent mess within an hour. Enough for you and your wife to have a meal. You go take your wife out in one of those boats. I'll get set up. Show you what you need for tackle, and I'll even take you out, so all you'll have to do is put the line in the water and start hauling them in."

As Quinn was about to agree with Frank the ship's greeter was out letting everybody know that the 'City of St. Louis' was ready for departure. "Please, come back to the ship. We will be pulling out in five minutes."

"I guess we better get moving," suggested Quinn. "We don't want to be stranded out here. So much for the fishing idea."

"Oh, Quinn," noted Harriet as she held her stomach. "Something's not right." She turned away and began to vomit. "I think, I think I'm pregnant," she proudly announced.

"No! It's too early! You can't be. I don't believe you."
"I didn't want to say anything until I was sure, but I missed my last blood. Now this. I'm positive that I'm going to have a baby."

"C'mon! Let's get on the steamer, before he takes off without us. It was nice talking to you folks," he offered as he waved at the Carman's.

Honeymooning

With thunder and lightning as a backdrop, the steamer headed out
and went full bore towards its' home port, with several quick stops
along the way. As the rain turned to a downpour, the winds picked up
to gale force. The passengers were trying to find any cover they could.
The Shanahan's were no exception. T hey were finally successful in
finding a little space in the Captain's office. Along with a dozen, or so,
fellow passengers, they watched as the onslaught continued to unfold.
The steamer was up to the task, as it rolled with the punches. Powerful
waves splashed up over the bow, as the mighty 'City of St. Louis' put
up a valiant fight. The steamer was huffing and puffing, taking every
charge that Mother Nature threw at her. "This storm is bad enough,"
shouted Quinn. "Now, I have to put up with your doings. I can't have
children yet. It's too early! I don't think I'm ready for this married life."

The captain, drenched to the hilt, pushed the steamer onward, passed
the hermitage, and into uncharted territory. Blinding and haunting,
the winds and rain continued unabated and everyone was waiting to
hear the intimidating bark of a German shepherd. Up and down went
the steamer. It was bad enough to traverse the open waters when it
was pleasant, but when the wrath of Mother Nature opened up, he
wanted nothing to do with her. Hundreds of souls getting baptized.
Hundreds of souls, scared. Going down with the steamer was a scary
 thought, yet the travelers kept their fingers crossed, while holding on
for dear life and talking to the Man above.

"Oh, where is that hotel?" asked Quinn. "Oh, where is my father?"
queried Harriet. The storm seemed to worsen. Strong winds pushing
the raindrops into the sides of everyone unprotected, piercing and
punching, tormenting and wounding. Waves rocking the boat, sending
warning signs to the weary travelers. And then everything was over.
The storm ceased as fast as it had started. The sun appeared, as the
skies cleared. A rainbow crossed the bow. Prayers were answered as
the Shanahan's stepped on terra firma at the 'Hotel St. Louis', and
into their new quarters they arrived. The walk up to the main entry
was long and trying. Mosquito patrols were everywhere, attacking the
vulnerable as they trudged through the puddles and mud.

Honeymooning

The four-story structure was on raised ground with the main entry in the front middle. The first three floors were entirely wrapped around with spacious verandas, while the upper floor had dormers along the front. Situated on the east side of Carson Bay, it commanded an excellent view of the bay.

The 'Hotel St. Louis' welcomed them with open arms. Their room was waiting. It was a large room, with a king-sized brass bed, adorned with red satin sheets and red, white, and blue cotton bed spread. Beside the bed was a beautiful marble-topped, oak table. Each wall had a huge picture of a wild animal, one a deer, another a bear, and another a raccoon, while the windows wore velvet curtains. The floor was covered with a gorgeous brown carpet, with several Smyrna rugs scattered about. The air was a combination of cigars and fish. The two windows were cracked, both searching for fresh air. Their luggage was waiting for them, setting beside the elegant writing table. The only other item in the room was a chamber pot.

"Listen! I'm sorry for not asking you before I set up those appearances, but I really thought you would love to have a chance to show off your talents to people who have never heard your voice, or your piano playing," offered Quinn as he took off his wet clothes.

"Oh Quinn. Yes, I do appreciate what you did," replied Harriet as she began to disrobe. "I forgive you."

NEXT MORNING.

The sun peeked through the curtain as Quinn lie on his back with Harriet snuggled up in his arms. The birds were chirping and the train whistle was blowing as life was awakening on this beautiful day on Lake Minnetonka. "Good morning," noted Quinn as he gave her a little kiss on the forehead.

"Good morning," softly replied Harriet. "That was a wonderful night! I still haven't come back down to Earth. Thank-you."

"Perfect way to end a not so perfect day. Today is a new day. What better way to spend it than going horseback riding with my beautiful bride, but first, I'll go find that bath."

Honeymooning

There was a knock at the door. "Oh my God!" exclaimed Quinn as he jumped out of bed and put some clothes on. "Just a minute."

"Room service," came the voice from out in the hall.

"Stay under the blankets," suggested Quinn as he looked over at Harriet, and then went to answer the door. "Come in! Come in!" he ordered. "I wasn't expecting you for another half hour."

"Breakfast for two! Just as you ordered," noted the black waiter as he placed the large silver tray on the writing table.

"What a surprise!" softly noted Harriet as she arose. "You are full of surprises."

"Breakfast for a queen," noted Quinn as he took the lid off of the silver platter and showed it to her. "Bacon and eggs and potatoes. Just like you like them. I left a note for the clerk. I figured after last night you'd have worked up a hunger. I know I sure did. I also requested that they have two horses ready for us to ride at ten. We have about half an hour."

"We don't get to pick out our own horse? Doesn't it make more sense that I might like a slower, older mare than a fast stallion?" asked Harriet as she took out a piece of paper and a quill and sat down by the writing table. She dipped the quill and began to write.

"What are you doing? Your breakfast will get cold."

"This'll only take a minute. Just a short note to Maggie. I want to tell her the good news and that we're going horseback riding together.

All's I ask is that you take it to the hotel desk and have them post it. Hopefully, she'll receive it before we get back home."

Activity on the grounds was picking up. Carriages were departing and arriving as new guests came in and old guests were moving on. Many were scurrying about, like squirrels out collecting.

Honeymooning

After delivering Harriet's letter, the Shanahans headed to where the stable was located, in the back of the hotel.

"Isn't it just gorgeous out here?" observed Harriet. "I could really get used to this place."

In the back side of the hotel was a long row of individual white houses. "These are the living quarters for the employees," noted Quinn as they arrived at the stable.

"Ah, Mr. Shanahan," shouted the stable master. "Your horses are ready. Bring out Shanahan's," he yelled into the stable. "There are 12 in your group. I'll be leading. My name is Roberto. The horses are well-trained to follow, so you shouldn't have to worry about runaways, or going too fast. Your horse is "Pepper". Mrs. Shanahan, yours is "Salt"."

As the vacationers were mounting their rides a young servant came running out of the hotel. "Telegram for Mrs. Shanahan!" he yelled.
"Over here," pointed out Harriet as she raised her left arm.
"Special delivery, Ma'am."

Harriet opened the letter and silently read. "Yes! Yes!" she shouted as she looked over at Quinn. "They want me, Quinn. They want me in Chicago. To play for the President when he comes to town. The end of this month. In three weeks, Quinn. Do you realize what that means? My dreams are turning to reality. This is my chance. My time to shine. Oh, I can hardly wait. I wish I were back in Fergus Falls right now."

"That's wonderful, dear. Do I need to send a telegram back?"
"Yes. Tell them I accept. I'm honored."
After Quinn disappeared into the building, the leader walked over to Harriet, as she was dismounting. "Your husband didn't seem too excited about you telegram? All I know is that if you were my wife and got a telegram like that I'd be celebrating. That's for sure. What's your talent?"

"I play the piano and I sing."
As the riders were waiting for Quinn to return, a tiny elderly lady walked up to Harriet.

91

Honeymooning

She was a wisp of a lady, no more than four feet tall, and maybe 90 pounds. She looked like a piece of china, so fragile and meek. She had chestnut hair, center parted, and put in a bun in the back, and a pair of enormous blue eyes. "Care for any strawberries, ma'am?" she asked.
"Oh, I'd love some but my husband has all the money."

"Are you from around here?"
"No Ma'am. I'm from Fergus Falls."
"Is that in Missouri?"
"No. Minnesota. Up north. You live nearby?"

"Yes. Real close. Through the woods, on the lake," she pointed outward. "I can see the Big Island in front of my place. Been here since '54. Long before the tourists started coming. Most of 'em come from down south, down by St. Louis and Kansas City. That's why I thought maybe you were from there, but you don't dress like a lot of them. You look young and pretty. That's how I looked once upon a time. My husband brought me out here. I had a foreboding about this place. Yes, Ma'am. A foreboding. It's that water. Every time the wind came up I was afraid someone was going to drown. Well, the wind didn't come up but he still up and drowned a while back. He always said that he wished we would have come out here ten years too soon. Had another feller come take care of the place. After the war was done he came back and pretty soon he ended up dying of tuberculosis, and I'm stuck out here all by myself. Yes sir, a premonition, that's what I had."

"What's your name?"
"Lydia. Lydia Ferguson."
"Glad to meet you, Lydia. My name is Harriet. Harriet Shanahan."
"When I arrived, my husband said that he couldn't get my beautiful rosewood, stand-up piano out here. Do I ever miss it! That was part of my soul. I never forgave him for not bringing it."

"I'm so sorry, Lydia. I love the piano. I'm going to be playing over at the Hotel LaFayette on Saturday. I'd be honored if you could be there. I'll see what my husband can do about it. Do you have any children?"

92

Honeymooning

"I have a son and a daughter. They both had scarlet fever back awhile. They survived, but Willie, something happened to his head. He grew up physically, but not mentally, and Alice, she done run off when she was 14. Headed for the city life in Minneapolis. She's married now and comes out during the summer for visits, with her daughter. My granddaughter. If it weren't for her I'd a been gone a long time ago. She keeps me going."

Quinn returned from the hotel. "Who do we have here?"
"This is Lydia Ferguson. She's one of the earliest settlers in these parts and she loves piano music. I mentioned to her about the LaFayette, on Saturday. Do you think we could take her there?"

"I don't see why not."
"She has some strawberries for sale. Would you buy some for me?"
"What are we going to do with strawberries when we're riding horse?"
"I can drop them off in the office," quietly suggested Lydia.
"How much?"

"Whatever you think they're worth," she replied as she showed the basket to him.

"Very well. Here's three. That should be more than enough. Tell the desk to keep them for Dr. Quinn Shanahan, and I'll stop by your place on Saturday to pick you up."

The riding party headed into the lonely, quiet woods, down a dark and wet trail. Quinn, on an overweight, black mare, and Harriet, on a little white stallion. Quinn was following Harriet. He shook his head in disgust. "Mighty poor timing," he whispered. "Now I know why there were no orange blossoms at the wedding. Dang. A baby. What's it going to do for my career?"

Harriet was happy. Out in the fresh air, riding a horse, feeling the warm southerly breeze. Life was good, and besides, she was pregnant, even though it meant a change in plans with her career, maybe.

93

Honeymooning

Ah yes, she thought. I can't hear what he was mumbling about, but he doesn't exactly seem very excited about the idea of me being pregnant. I am only kidding myself if I think this isn't going to affect my professional career. It could actually ruin it. Who's going to take care of the baby when I have to go on tour? Surely, Quinn can't. Maybe mother? No, she'd never be able to handle it. Oh, I sure can put myself in some challenging situations. Maybe I need to talk with Remy, without Quinn knowing about it.

There was a young lady, about the same age as Quinn, riding in front of Harriet. She was short, muscular, and very beautiful, with long blond hair and a shimmering suntan. She was having difficulty with her means of transportation. "Dang you, you old nag. Why do you keep stopping?" she yelled in disgust as she kept hitting the horse with her right hand.

"Maybe if you stopped hitting her she'd keep going," suggested Harriet.
 Quinn sat back and noticed the girl. "I've seen her before," he mused. "But where?"

 "Oh, and you're a specialist when it comes to riding horses?" shot back the girl.

 "No. I didn't say that. I just made a suggestion. When your horse does something you don't want it to do, you have to show him who's the boss, in a nice way. Treat him with respect and he'll listen to you."

`"I really don't need to take any advice from some know it all," noted the girl as she hit her horse again.

"Katie!" shouted the young man who was riding in front of the girl. "Do what she says. Don't be so stubborn."
 "Oh Ralph. Whose side are you on?"

"I'm not on either side. It just makes sense what she's saying."
 "If you would turn to your right," noted the tour guide, "you'll be able to see the 'Big Island'. We will be coming out by the coastline in a few minutes and you'll get a better idea of how close we are actually to the main body of Lake Minnetonka."

94

Honeymooning

The excursion down the coastline continued onward. Upon arrival at Ferguson's Point, the man in charge stopped the caravan. "We'll take a little break here and have a bite to eat."

Everyone dismounted. Quinn and Harriet walked over to Ralph and Katie. "We're from Fergus Falls, a little town about 200 miles north of here," noted Quinn. "How about you?"

"St. Peter, Missouri. Close to St. Louis," answered Ralph. "I'm a doctor. We take a two week vacation up here each year about this time. We love coming to this hotel. They treat us well and we love the climate. We're scheduled to leave next Tuesday. Wish I could stay longer, but reality says I need to get back to work. If the winters weren't so ungodly cold and snowy I'd really think about moving up here, but until that changes I'll have to settle for a couple of weeks a year."

"Listen! My wife is going to be playing out at the Hotel Lafayette, Saturday evening. She's a very good concert pianist. I'd love to have you and your wife as guests. They will be sending a boat over at 6 in the evening. She will be playing first. It starts at 7:30, so we could be coming back by 8."

"Yes," interrupted Katie. "I'd love to go."

"Good," noted Quinn as he smiled at Harriet and looked back over at Katie. "Katie?" he mused as he took his toothpick out of his mouth. "Katie, who? Have you ever lived in Pennsylvania?"

"I was wondering when you'd notice," replied Katie. "How are you?"
"You are who I think you are?"
"Yes, I am. How long has it been? Twelve years?"
"Katie Thompson? Well, I'll be darned. Katie Thompson."

Harriet watched and listened to what had just transpired, while glancing over at Katie and then at Quinn. Back to the horses they went. Back into the woods, and back to the hotel.

95

Honeymooning

A morning of sunshine, fun, and intrigue was enjoyed by most, and a time of wonderment for a few. Smiles on all the faces, except for one. Several days later, preparations were underway for the late afternoon excursion over to the Hotel LaFayette. Quinn and Harriet were awaiting the arrival of the special boat from the LaFayette, as Mrs. Ferguson, and Ralph and Katie sat off to the side, in the front parlor of the Hotel St. Louis. "I wish they'd hurry up and get here," noted the nervous Harriet. "I don't even know what kind of piano I'm going to be working with."

"I told them what you play with back home, and they said they had the same thing, so you don't need to worry about that," he noted as he turned and looked out into the bay. "There it is," he shouted. "Let's go." The group headed down to the wharf and was soon situated in the little boat and heading for the Hotel. "Isn't this exciting?" asked Quinn as he glanced over at Harriet.

"Nerve racking, Quinn. My nerves are shot."
"By the time we get there you should be all settled down," comforted Quinn as he turned and listened to the soothing sounds of Lake Minnetonka;

the gentle waves lapping up against the side of the boat; the screeching calls of a large group of sea gulls', the constant thug of the boat's engine; all part of the experience of traveling on the mighty Lake Minnetonka. The Hotel could be seen from a mile out. As the boat approached, the hotel grew bigger and bigger. Hordes of people arriving from all directions, via train, boat, and buggy. All heading for an evening of music in the Big Hall, in the big Hotel LaFayette.

Harriet, decked out in a festive white gown, laced with pearls, nervously waited for the boat to reach dockside. She perused the area in search of someone who would show her where to go, someone to guide her to her piano and show her what music she was to play. All this going on while Quinn conversed with Ralph in an attempt to talk him into moving to Fergus.

96

Honeymooning

With pearls dangling and lips quivering, Harriet focused her attention on an elderly man in a gray suit, as he came onto the dock and was watching Harriet's arrival very closely. "Ahh! Mrs. Shanahan, I presume?"

"Why, ah, yes. And you may be?"

"I'm in charge of the entertainment this evening. John Herrman. Welcome! I've heard nothing but good words about you and your piano play. I'm looking forward to being entertained by you. You will get two songs out of the gate. Chopin's Ballad #1 in C minor, and Beethoven's Moonlight Sonata. I talked with your husband and he mentioned those two songs and said you have played them before. Is that correct?"

"Why, ah, yes," replied Harriet as the group followed John into the large dance hall and directly to the baby grand piano. Harriet sat down by the piano and touched the keys. "What a beautiful piano."

"You can make it even more beautiful by playing," suggested John. "I don't know what your husband explained to you about who some of the people that will be in attendance this evening, but I'll fill you in a little. We have representatives from New York City, Chicago, Detroit, and Washington, DC. These are music people.

Representatives from various Opera houses and Entertainment facilities around the country. Not to make you nervous, but they will be watching you very closely. I'll leave you alone now. I will be introducing you in about 15 minutes. They are just opening the doors, so we should be ready to go in about 15 minutes. We are expecting a packed house of roughly 2,000, so you'll have a nice audience to serenade. Good luck!"

Harriet sat there in awe. "2000? Oh my. I'm used to 300. What am I going to do with 2000?" she gasped as she covered herself with goosebumps.

97

Honeymooning

Every chair was taken. Standing room only! Men, dressed in their finest and women all dolled up in their latest fashions. Anxiety everywhere, as people were waiting to hear from that 'new sensation from west central Minnesota'.

John came out from behind the curtain, in his tuxedo and top hat. "May I have your attention!" he begged. "Your attention, please!" The crowd began to quiet down. "I am honored to introduce to you a new pianist, from up north, by Fergus Falls. She is down here with her husband, on their honeymoon, and we were able to talk them into coming over and participating in our Grand Opening. Ladies and Gentlemen! Won't you please join with me in welcoming Mrs. Harriet Shanahan?"

The crowd gave their approval and sat down to listen. Harriet gazed around at the crowd. Never played in front of so many people in my life! She thought. Don't mess up! Whatever you do. Silence came over the entire audience. Harriet placed her delicate fingers on the keys. She looked over at Quinn. Then she made eye contact with Mrs. Ferguson. She smiled. This is for you! She thought, as she took her left hand and placed it on her lips and waved a kiss to her. Then, she looked back at Quinn. He shook his head in approval, and she began to perform.

Oh what a performance it was! Chopin would have been proud! The crowd dropped their jaws, in silence, with bodies swaying to the music. She had them eating out of her hand. She was in complete control. She was the lady of the hour, the maestro of the moment, the piano queen, and the ultimate concert pianist. Her value was rising with every hit of the keys. The accolades would be pouring forth. Success was in her grasp. Self-satisfaction was attained and she felt so good as she ended the first song.

The crowd rose to their feet, yelling their approval of what just occurred. Bravo! White carnations were thrown upon the piano. Chairs were rattling.

Honeymooning

The roof was shaking, for there was so much joy at the LaFayette. Harriet raised her arm. The crowd became silent and sat down, in anticipation. Harriet began playing the 'Moonlight Sonata', by Beethoven. The orchestra joined in. The crowd was mesmerized. With eyes closed, they wavered back and forth.

"Absolutely amazing," exclaimed Katie. "Outstanding!" offered Ralph.

When all was said and done and the crowd was heading back to their rooms, Harriet rushed up to Quinn. "I've done it! I've done it!"

"Yes, I know. You were superb."

"No, no," shouted Harriet. "I'm going to New York. They want me to perform in New York. Next week. They're lining up my transportation as we speak."

"Next week? What about White Bear Lake?"

"That'll have to wait. This trip to New York is what my goal has been. A chance of a lifetime. A dream come true. I've signed a contract. $5000 for one appearance. Aren't you excited for me?"
"Of course I am. It's a bit of a surprise."

"SHANAHAN SHENANAGANS"

Two weeks later.

Mother Nature was busy watering the crops and washing the trash off the streets of Fergus Falls on this humid summer evening, as Dr. Quinn was seated at a side table at the Silver Moon restaurant. A short distance away sat Lin, all decked out in her Sunday best, and with one of her most exquisite red hats. She was sipping on a glass of Merlot. Quinn noticed and motioned for her to come over. She obliged.

"It's a shame that such a beautiful lady should be sitting alone on such a dreary evening," noted Quinn as he stood up and moved a chair out for her to sit down. "What kind of wine are you dealing with?"

"Merlot."
"Ah yes. The little Blackbird. An elegant wine, just like the one I'm testing."
"Have you heard from Harriet?"

"Got a message this morning. She's on her way home. Should be back by tomorrow night. How about Remy?"

"He's enjoying Chicago. He says the classes are awfully hard. He figures on being home by Sunday."

"Gets pretty quiet when you're the only one in a big house, doesn't it?"

"That's part of the reason why I'm down here."

"Me too!" laughed Quinn. "Plus, I don't really care to drink by myself. Seems like there's been a lot of that 'by myself' lately. Have you eaten?"

"Yes. I've been sitting here doing a lot of thinking, waiting for the rain to stop."

"May I suggest," offered the waiter. "We just received several bushel of oysters off the train. Just picked out of Duxbury Bay. They are among the best oysters out East. We probably will only have them for a few days. I've been told that these are exceptional."

"My dear fellow, oysters are always exceptional. They are like a fine woman. They are a delicacy to be cherished. She can convey her life experiences directly to one's senses. She has a sense of purpose. Like a fine wine, oysters mirror their natural environment and draw their overall flavor from the waters in which they occupy. Duxbury Bay has the perfect water condition that determine the flavor and the character of the oysters. It's called merrier. Someone famous, I don't recall his name at the moment, said that oysters were a self-swallowing provocative. They are an aphrodisiac."
"And you believe that?"

"Of course. But No. Wait. I have a better idea, Lin," interrupted Quinn. "How about we go to my place and have a night cap?"

"Your place?"
"Sure. Why not? We can talk just as well there as here."
"But you haven't eaten?"

"That's alright. I'd rather just spend a little private time with you. We'll finish our wine and I'll get my carriage out of the stable and we'll be on our way. I have Merlot at home also."
"I'm not sure I need any more of that," objected Lin.

On their way to Quinn's the twosome showed apprehension, both uncomfortable and unsure of what was happening. "So, how's married life?" she asked.

"Seems to be fine. She's gone an awful lot, doing concerts. Some by herself, some with her sisters. She's making a good name for herself, but it does have its' drawbacks. She has lots of followers.

101

Shanahan
Shenanagans

Lots of admirers, yet lots of hustlers. Men looking for a good time at her expense."
 "Really? She told you that?"
 "No, but I believe it's true."

As the black carriage pulled up in front of the Shanahan domain, signs of anxiety remained on Lin's face. Was this really happening? She asked herself. Was this me, or the Merlot talking? Almost ten and I'm at a married man's house, alone. How did I get talked into this? Oh, maybe it was what I really wanted? Maybe, it's my fault, but this is the first chance I've ever had of being alone with him. My whole body is shaking. Is it the wine, or is it my desire?

"Here you are, ma'am," offered Quinn as he dismounted and held out his hand to her.

 She was shaking more than ever, but determined. She got down and held on tightly to his arm, as they made their way to the front entry. Everything was still wet from the rain---the grass, the trees, the flowers. Even the sidewalk boards and the minds of two wandering souls. They entered the confines of Quinn's world. He lit a lantern and then the fireplace, and then he turned to Lin.

Lin could feel her presence. The smell of her lavender perfume was everywhere. Harriet was everywhere. Nothing was hidden. Pictures of her on the walls---looking and watching, and following her every move.

"Give it a few minutes and I'll have this place nice and warm. Please, have a seat by the fireplace. I'll find us a little Merlot and then we can talk."

 As Quinn disappeared into the kitchen, Lin took a seat right in front of the burning fire. "I'm not sure which one, the fire or me," she murmured. Yet, there was the lavender.

 "Here you are," stated Quinn as he handed her a glass of wine. "Direct from the Napa Valley."

102

Shanahan
Shenanagans

"Oh Quinn. I don't know if I'll be able to take care of that," she noted as she accepted and sipped.

Quinn sat down next to her. He sipped and moved closer, and sipped some more, while Lin sipped a little and then sipped some more. They both stared at the fire. "Oh, my head!" she gasped.

"Just close your eyes and float." Quinn put his arms around her. "I'll be your protector. Don't you worry none! We are here together only for companionship. It does no one any good to be lonely, especially on a cool, wet evening."

She smiled as she wavered back and forth on the chair. She looked at the wall clock. 10:15 and still the smell of lavender, but oh how true what he says about loneliness, and she took another sip. Can I trust him? I've always thought that he had more positives than Remy.

Quinn had all the energy and desire to lift himself up and push himself forward. Harriet is a very person to have a man like him. He looks like he's had several glasses already. Maybe, this is the time to test the waters. Would I be taking advantage of him? No, maybe he wants to take advantage of me. He always has struck me as the kind of person who always gets what he wants. Should I tease? Should I try? What could it hurt? No one needs to know. Just him and me. Oh, I'm feeling something that I haven't felt in oh so long. What should I do? A little more Merlot won't hurt. Oh, he has a way of getting my juices going. I know he is a handful, but that's Harriet's problem. I could probably handle him for one night, or maybe two.

The fireplace crackled and glowed as the two bodies became entangled in fantasies and intertwined in profundities. It was 10:30 and no one cared.

"THE FIRST JUDGEMENT DAY"

Two weeks later.

The medical office of Shanahan and Oglesby was open for business. Located on Lincoln Avenue, the busiest street in town. It was situated on the second floor of the McKnight Drug Store, next to the Occidental Hotel. Quinn was sitting at his desk, doing paperwork, while Remy was in his operation room creating havoc. Quinn looked up and listened to the screaming of Remy's patient. He shook his head in the negative. "Not again!" he mused. "I can't believe I'm letting him do that."

In walked the tall, dark, and handsome Chief Sullivan. "Ah, Mr. Shanahan. Do you have a minute?"

Quinn stood up and took notice. "Mr. Sullivan. What can I do for you?"
"I'm sorry to inform you but I have a direct order to place you under arrest for grand larceny."

"What? And who did I rob?"
"A Miss Nelda Atkins."

"There must be a mistake. I have no idea who that is."

"Sorry, sir. Come with me. We'll let the judge decide."

"Bannister? This can't be. I'm being set up."

"Please, Mr. Shanahan. Don't give me any problems."

"At least let me tell Remy," insisted Quinn as he went in to inform his partner.

The first
Judgement Day

Remy! I'm sorry to interrupt but I've been arrested. Would you tell my wife? She'll be on the Manitoba train this evening."

The City Jail was small and uninviting. A little cot, a side table, and a tiny pot in the corner. The room was damp and musty; desolate and murky. Not a place for a human occupation. The walls were covered with peeling white paint. The wooden floor was covered with dirt and garbage. The only light was provided by a small window in the back. Into this environment Quinn was exposed. He sat down on the cot, once the Chief closed and locked the cell door. He could feel the dirt in the blanket and smell remnants of human defecation. Cobwebs filled the ceiling corners, with big black spiders working in each.

There was another adjoining cell and that had the s ame attributes, except that there was a young female occupant lying asleep in the bed. She seemed so innocent to Quinn, a picture of serenity but she was snoring so loud it disturbed the rats and mice that were in the vicinity. She was awakened by her own noise. She rubbed her eyes, yawned, and glanced over at Quinn. "My, my! Welcome to Hell. What are you in for?" she asked with a southern drawl.

"Grand Larceny. I've supposedly stole from a Nelda Atkins. I don't know what I stole or who this Nelda even is. How about you?"

"Oh, I had a few too many last night and got myself in trouble by starting a fight and doing a whole bunch of damage to O'Brien's, and now I'm paying for it."

"I didn't know O'Brien had any girls at his place."
"That was the problem. I tried to change that and I got some of the customers all excited and Mr. Reilly, the bartender, got mad and tried to kick me out and the boys objected and started fighting, so here I am."

The first
Judgement Day

"And the boys?"

"Oh, I imagine they're at home sleeping it off."

"This is the first time I've ever been in a jail."

"So! What do you want me to do about it?"

"Nothing. Just saying. You don't have to get all excited. What's your name?"

"Jessie. Just came over here from Perham. Got myself a job at a millinery store, down the block. Was scheduled to start tomorrow. Don't look too promising now. How about you?"

"I'm Dr. Quinn Shanahan."

"I thought so. You're a doctor and you're in jail?" laughed Jessie.

Chief Sullivan came in and interrupted the chit chat. "Hey, Shanahan. Just got word that the judge will be seeing you in court tomorrow morning."

The unsuspecting doctor slid further back in his chair as he went unnoticed by all concerned until Remy made an appearance. "I tried to get bail for you, but was denied."

"Can you do something for me?" queried Quinn. "I need to do a little research and find out who this Nelda Atkins is."

"I don't have to do any research. I know who you're talking about," noted Remy. She was a patient of mine a while back. She came into the office one day when you were out dealing with that Sundberg family. She was in a real bad situation. As a matter of fact, I wasn't sure if I'd be able to help her. She did an overdose and was about to cash in when she came staggering in, all out of whack. Very unstable.

The first
Judgement Day

Wasn't quite sure what was wrong with her. Thought for a minute she was cracking up. Then it dawned on me that she had taken something that she shouldn't have, so I pumped her out and saved her life! Last time I saw her, come to find out she run a little shack for chippies on the west end. It's the last house on Lincoln. On the left side. She didn't use her real name. As a matter of fact, maybe this isn't her real name either. Those girls usually make up a name to protect their relatives. Never did get paid."

"Can you see if you can tie this lady to Judge Bannister?"
Remy acted surprised. " I reckon I can try, but can't guarantee anything."

"I have a funny feeling that he's the one behind this. And there's one other thing. Can you find Corliss? Have him come here as soon as possible. Also, my wife is on tonight's train. Could you tell her where I am?"

"I'll go see what I can do," continued Remy as he headed out, followed closely by Quinn and the Chief.

An hour later.

Remy was with a patient in his office when in walked Bannister. "Got a minute?"
"Why, ah yes."
"Have you been doing your research?"

"Of course. I believe we have a case. I'm waiting for a reply. Will get it to you as soon as I receive it. From what I've been able to surmise, he has performed this operation four times over the past two months. They are totally illegal and we should be able to get some negative action out of the State Medical Board."

"Good. That is exactly what I wanted to hear. Maybe, this'll finally put him where he belongs."

107

The first
Judgement Day

"I have to admit that he is very good at that procedure, but, nevertheless, it is illegal, so they should suspend his license. I don't know how long but with four offenses it could be for years."

"Very good. If it turns out the way you think it will make it worth your while."

Harriet was all riled up as she made her way upstairs to the city jail house. "What on Earth are you doing in here?" she asked Quinn.

"Harriet! I was wondering when you were going to get here. Didn't Remy tell you what happened?"

"Remy? No, he didn't. I haven't seen Remy. My mother informed me of your whereabouts. I don't know how she found out and I don't care. It seems that I have to do everything, and then here you are in jail."

"Remy tried to get bail but it was refused."

"Isn't there anything I can do?"

"Go see Corliss. I asked Remy but I'm not so sure he's doing anything about it. Maybe Corliss can get me out of here? I go before the judge in the morning, so I don't have much time. I haven't done anything wrong. This all goes back to that Bannister fellow. He's out to get me."

"Oh, I find that hard to believe. He seems like such a nice fellow."

"You have no idea, Harriet. No idea whatsoever."

The courtroom was packed with people waiting for the arrival of Judge Bannister, as well as two people waiting to catch a glimpse of Quinn. Harriet and Naddy were sitting in the rear, situated so that they would be the first to see Quinn come through the door. Both had apprehension covering their faces. Their nerves were on edge, their doubts, overwhelming. "Don't be so high strung," suggested Naddy.

"We both know he's innocent."

The first
Judgement Day

"Yes, but we don't really know how fair that judge will be. When I visited Quinn yesterday he seemed so bitter. He thinks the judge has him right where he wants him. What if, Naddy? What if he's found guilty?"

"For heaven's sake, Harriet. That lady has no real proof. It's all he said /she said. That lady has no credibility. The judge will find that out. The people know. They won't stand for it. There's no way that he'll find Quinn guilty."

"You think so? Frank seems to have everybody wrapped around his little finger."

"You worry too much! Besides, what good does that do? Absolutely nothing. Worrying doesn't take away tomorrow's trouble. It takes away todays peace. If you wouldn't have given Bannister the idea of having some feelings for him none of this would have ever happened."

"Don't go blaming me. I could see the jealousy all over Quinn when he saw me with the judge. It made me feel good. The idea of two men fighting over me. Very entertaining to a point. I didn't realize it was going to lead to this. I thought I made it clear to both, but it looks like I was wrong.

This might be nothing but I heard that the State Medical Board has been looking into some accusations of malpractice against Quinn. I hope it's only rumor, but you never know. If he is found guilty by that board, they will probably pass that information on to Frank. I have no idea if there is any surprises out there, or not."

The heavily bearded Eb Corliss was sitting at the Defendant's table, also patiently waiting Quinn's arrival, while Quinn sat in his cell listening to the noisy crowd next door.

"Alright Shanahan," shouted the police chief. "Up and at'em. Time to meet your Waterloo."

The first
Judgement Day

"Waterloo? You know as well as I that I'm innocent. This thing is nothing more than a total sham. Corliss will get me off. I'm not worried about that. It's the fact that you two attempted to ruin my reputation. That's what I'll never forget. You and the judge both seem to think you're high and mighty. I'm just a country doctor trying to make a living and hoping to find some prosperity. Once again you people have to try and ruin it for me."

"Let's go!" clamored the Chief as he unlocked the cell and put handcuffs on Quinn. Down the stairs they went and over to the courtroom next door. As Quinn sat down in the defendant's chair the bailiff yelled: "Hear ye!

Hear ye! Order in the court. Please stand for the Honorable Judge Franklin Bannister."

Everyone arose, as quiet swept over the room and in came the judge, all decked out in his wardrobe of black. He wore this coat of honor with a comforting burst of pride, yet he had several others that clashed. It all depended on who he was dealing with. The latest in a line of aristocratic nobility to arrive on the scene. Today was to be his first as the presiding judge in the City Court. Having just arrived from the halls of Tammany. A fervent follower of the New York City establishment, he was already making his mark felt on the streets of Fergus Falls, as a man of Power.

Secrecy was his middle name. No one really knew much about his background and no one really cared, except for one person. He was tall at 6'5" and heavy-set at 240, and was Irish, born and bred. Like his dark, long, black hair that desperately tried to cover his overgrown ears, he was as smooth as the waters of Fish Lake on a quiet morning. He had a pair of tiny eyes, almost hidden by heavy cheeks, but they were very deceptive and made anyone who looked at them very inquisitive.

The courtroom was very quiet as the ruler situated himself on the bench. He looked into a special mirror located on his bench that made him feel secure and looking at his best, as he adjusted several out of place hairs on his head.

110

The first
Judgement Day

He decorated his face with a small, pointed, paint brush beard of black to match up with his mirthful smile. Setting next to him was his favorite catty walking stick.

His eyes took a trip around the room, searching for anyone, or anything, out of the ordinary. So crowded, he thought. Why would so many people come to watch a boring day in court? With his pompous elitism on full display, he kept his normal cynicism well off in the background.

This would be the day he'd finally get even with Shanahan. This was going to be fun running him down in the mud and making him look like the two-faced doctor that he surely must be. He may still be getting Harriet, but that's going to change if he had anything to say about it.
This was his court and no one was going to come in and take control. No one would be allowed to even think of taking him down and making him look bad.

"Order in the court!" shouted the judge as he pounded his gavel. "Let us begin! Bailiff! Who do we have up first?"

The short, balding, old codger stood up. "Shanahan vs. Nelda Atkins. A crime of Grand Larceny."

"Defense! How do you plead?"

"Not guilty. Your Honor," answered Corliss.

"Very well," noted Bannister. "I've been reviewing this case very seriously, Mr. Shanahan and I have come up with several comments and one verdict. Rather than drag you and your name through the mud I have decided to drop all charges against you for the lack of evidence. It looks like there was an attempt by someone to blackmail you and you didn't take the bait, so you are free to go on that account. However, there is one other issue that we must take care of. I have received a judgement from the Minnesota State Medical Board," he continued as he picked up a piece of paper and handed it to Quinn.

111

The first
Judgement Day

Q uinn took the paper and began to silently read: To whom it may concern, We, the below signed members in good standing of the Minnesota State Board of Medicine do find the defendant, Dr. Quinn Shanahan, guilty of the following malpractice of four times doing an illegal operation of abortion and do hereby rescind his medical license for the period of four months, to begin on the day of the official reading of this notification."

Quinn sat dumbfounded while Harriet looked over at Naddy, unsure of what to do next. Tears flowed from both girls as they rushed over to Quinn.

Chapter 15

"SUSTENANCE"

The chickens were hard at work scratching the soil for their daily sustenance as the sun gradually fell from the sky, while Molly was milking the cow and Braden sat nearby with his dirty old yellow ribbon.

Off in the distance a band of coyotes were serenading the neighborhood in a masquerade of survival. What sounded like a pack of twenty was only five, for the coyotes were using a strategy of combining wavering howls with a rapid changes in pitch. Their yipping and woofing were a series of deceptions to fool anyone nearby.

"They seem to be out and about earlier tonight," observed Molly. "It's not even dark yet."

"Me no like," moaned Braden.

"Been up in that woods since we've been out here. Probably got their dens up there. Raising their families. Alright, Braden. I'm all done here," she continued as she picked up the pail of milk. "Let's go back inside."

"What's the name of that lake over there?" he asked.
"I'm not sposta to tell you anything."
"I think I've seen it before."

As they walked back to the little white house Braden paid close attention to the surroundings. He couldn't help but think about that large body of water off in the distance. And all those trees! Giant cottonwoods, in their full regal splendor and majestic decorum, shooting high above the maples and elms. "Pretty!" he commented. "But they get messy!"

113

Sustenance

"So true," agreed Molly. "You continue to amaze me, Braden. You have such a good memory. You are very smart."

"A a a a are you from around here?"
Yes. Born and raised near Elizabeth."
"You ever get to see your parents?"

"No. They are both gone. Had a bad time with typhoid. I was too young. They died when I was only two."

"Let's go see if we can find those coyotes."

"No. It's getting too late. Going to be dark soon. We best get inside. We're going to have company in the morning. Best get some sleep."

"Quinn coming?"
"No. Just my boss."

As they walked into Braden's room, Braden stopped and turned towards Molly. "Tell me about you. You mentioned about your folks but I want to know about you. What do you want in life?"

"I don't know Braden. I feel so empty. I have so little to offer."

"Nonsense. You have lots more than you think. You very pretty. You are smart. You think how to fix a problem and then go out and do it. You are so lucky to be alive and have such a wonderful mind. Quinn would like you."

"You haven't said much about Quinn other than asking when he's coming."

"He's probably married by now. He loves Harriet, I think. You know, the piano player."
"Yes. I know who she is."

"AGONY IN THE GARDEN"

Over at the Shanahan residence things were a bit shaky. They were arriving home on Cavour, but something didn't seem right. Both were silent. Both seemed on edge. "I don't think you had to act that way," finally suggested Harriet. "You embarrassed me in public. I don't know if I can ever forgive you."

"But darling! You know how I get when someone gets too close to you. I can't stand the invasion."

"Don't be so stupid! It was no such thing. All he was doing was trying to carry on a polite conversation."

"You're my wife and I'll always stand up for you. I am your protector, your provider."

"I still think you should buy that boat from him. We could take it out to Fish Lake. You know how much we made off of that other one. Let it pay for itself. We could show everyone what we're made of. Why, no one could come close to what we'd have."

"But I still don't think we can afford it. The seeds are planted, but the crop's not ready. Maybe someday it will be, but for now, we have to accept reality, accept the fact that there is very little money to be made in this profession."

But you didn't have to point that out to him. He didn't need to know. Oh, sometimes I wonder about you getting upset because I was telling him how empty our house is. Why would you ever do such a thing?"

115

Agony in THE GARDEN

"*I* don't want people thinking that I'm not a good provider."
"But I need things. I want to have more things, more trophies, more respect."

"That will all come in due time. You keep doing your piano playing, and working with your sisters. Everything will fall in place. Things will get you very little in this life. It's the self-respect and respect from your fellow Americans. That will earn you a valued place in society and a virtual guarantee upstairs when the time comes."

"I'm not happy, Quinn. This pregnancy is taking its toll on my body and mind. I haven't felt good since I don't know how long. Upset stomach, sharp headaches, gaining such ungodly weight. I'm not satisfied with how this is turning out. My father has always told me to fight for what I want in life. Quinn! I want more. More love. More understanding. More recognition. More worthiness. More compliments. I need these things. I love music. I'm good at it. It puts me in another world. I'd love to be able to travel around the country and just sing and play piano. I'm not cut out to be tied down. There's so much of the world I can only dream of ever seeing."

"It's not my fault. Things just seem to go from bad to worse. My so-called friends are out to get me. At every turn there seems to be roadblocks set up by someone that is jealous of what I've been able to do in a short period of time. I know who these people are, and when they least expect it I will get even."

"Oh Quinn! Take some responsibility for your weaknesses."
"Give me time, Harriet. My real estate business is getting better and better. I promise to give you those things. I, too, want love and understanding."

"My patience has worn thin," continued Harriet as she paced back and forth in front of Quinn. "My father warned me that I didn't know what I was doing, getting involved with you.

Agony in
THE GARDEN

Of course, I disagreed with him, and now I'm paying for it. My dream has always been to find the right man who would take care of me; who would love me with all his heart and soul; who would cherish me, no matter the circumstances, no matter the pitfalls and human weaknesses you may find."

"I am changing, Quinn. After all of what I've been through I realized that I was blaming everybody else for my problems, rather than taking responsibility. That's what you need to do. Take responsibility for your actions. You see my body, while I see your soul. You want to control while I want to trust. You want me to make you happy, while I want you to be happy. You still see darkness, while I see sunshine. You say who's right, while I say what's right. You harden the heart while I'm trying to s often it. You pick the daffodil out of the ground while I water it. Don't you see, Quinn? There's so much difference between you and me. I want to love you and you want to possess me."

Harriet arose and scurried into her bedroom, shutting the door behind her, while Quinn sat by the table and stared out the window. "Lord!

What am I to do?"

Harriet laid on her single bed, with tears flowing and heart aching. Indecision was apparent. She wiped her eyes and went over to her floor-length mirror.

"What should I do?" she asked herself. "Am I being selfish? Maybe I'm too hard on him. Maybe if I tried to change. Maybe if I thought less of me, and more of him."

While staring into the mirror she began to undress. With a smile of smugness, she evolved. "No one can tell me what to do. Yes. I need to teach him a lesson," she murmured as she put her clothes back on. She rose and headed back out to her awaiting husband.

THE GARDEN

"You come to your senses?"
"I sure have. I'm leaving you. I'm moving back home."
"Don't be so silly."

"Silly? I'll show you. You don't, you don't know everything. You know nothing about Spat and Remington. They lived with us back in '80. Spat worked on the farm and Remy was a boarder."

"I know that."

"But, you didn't know them. My father had them in for a birthday party. After the meal all of us went outside and walked along the river. There was Spat, Naddy, Deborah, Remy, and myself. Father called us in when it was getting dark. My sisters hurried in. Spat said to tell their folks that us three would be in shortly. After they were gone Spat grabbed my hand and said: come on. I want to show you something. So, I followed him, and Remy came along. When we got in the woods Spat turned. He had been drinking earlier in the day and he was acting more different than usual. He grabbed my hand and pulled me up to his side. No, don't," I yelled. "Come on, Harriet," he insisted. "I know you want this. I could see in your eyes. Let's do a little exploring. Remy! Help me out."

"No, no," I screamed, but it didn't help. Spat put his left hand on my breast and then he started to unbutton my top, while Remy came closer. I resisted but I couldn't stop them. They took turns. We're going swimming, noted Spat. In the Red. You come and join us. Now, I was not only nervous, but I was scared. I objected. Don't, I said. Don't do something you'll be sorry for. Oh, come now, pretty girl, Spat said.

The water is warm. I can't swim, I said, but they knew I was lying."

"What?" gasped Quinn.

"They tried to rape me."

"Spat and Remy?"

Agony in
THE GARDEN

"Yes, but then we heard Father calling us, so we stopped."
"Why are you telling me this now?"

"I thought it would be better if you heard it from me before someone else. Spat insisted that I come with him. He grabbed my arm and pulled me into the bushes along the river. He told Remy to stand guard, and he took his boots off."

"Please, I begged. You don't realize what you're doing. You're too drunk. He replied that he'd be the judge of that, as he pulled me to the ground."

"That's enough! I don't want to hear anymore," he yelled as he went into his bedroom, only to reappear moments later with his Smith and Wesson 38 caliber, seven shooter in hand.

"Where are you going?" asked Harriet as she grabbed his right arm.
"Got some unfinished business."
"It happened a long time before I ever met you."
"That doesn't make any difference. I thought they were my friends," he continued as he rushed out the door.

"Don't do anything foolish!"

"That's what you should have told them."

He hopped in his buggy and headed down the street to Remy's house. The streets were dark and quiet as he pulled up in front. After dismounting, he cocked his revolver and went up to the entrance.

"Remy!" he shouted. "You get your tail out here. You have some explaining to do. You hear me?"

A lantern came on in the house and moments later the door opened. "What do you want at this time of night?"

Agony in
THE GARDEN

With his Smith & Wesson pointed right at Remy, Quinn yelled. "You son of a . You have 24 hours to get up and get out of Otter Tail County."
"Have you been drinking?"

"Haven't touched a drop. You know me, but I thought I knew you. You were my best friend once. How could you? Mess around with my wife."

"Sparking? What are you talking about?"

"Harriet told me all about it. How you and Spat took her out in the woods."

"What? That happened years ago. Long before you two got married."
"Heed my words," yelled Quinn as he got back in his buggy and left. Onward he went over to Spat's house. Again, he dismounted.

"Quinn, my friend. What brings you over here?"
"Time to pack up, Spat, and get your body out of here. I heard about what you did to my wife. I'll never be able to face you again."

"You expect me to up and leave because of what she claims I did? It'll be a cold day in hell before I follow through with such an outlandish request."

"If you know what's good for you, you will leave," ordered Quinn as he left. "I'll be waiting to see if you follow through."

Harriet sat by her table, rocking forward and back. "If only I could figure out what makes him like that," she whispered as she wiped tears away. There was a knock at the door. "Come in."

"Maggie! Come in. Where have you been?"

"Oh Harriet. I heard a rumor and just had to come to see for myself. I've been spending a lot of time out at the Pinafore Inn.

Agony in THE GARDEN

I came in this morning to get some more supplies. I was getting ready to head back out this evening and heard about you. It is a known fact that he has not been himself lately. It is a crying shame with what you have to put up with in that evil man. Is there anything I can do?"

But, Maggie. He is not evil, just misunderstood."

"Wake up, my dear. You have a problem on your hands. If you're not careful he'll have you chewed up and spit out before you know what hit you. He'll destroy your very soul. He'll destroy your family, your thought process, your religious beliefs."

"Oh Maggie! You're so wrong. All he needs is a little instruction, a little forgiveness, a little love."

"You cannot love a man like that. It is impossible. He is too far gone. He will never change for the better. I should have warned you before you got involved. I learned at an early stage of what kind of man he was and is. It didn't take him long after we dated to change me from easy-going and cheerful to bitter and reserved. Harriet! As a friend I would love nothing better than to assist you in ridding yourself from the clutches of that Satan. Your husband seems to have split personalities. When it comes to me he lets me do whatever I want out at the Inn. It is the perfect setup for me and he lets me do whatever I want with the rooms, but I have seen him in a different frame several times lately."

There was another knock on the door. "Yes?"
It was Chief Sullivan. "Ma'am. Is your husband home? We received a report that he has been harassing people and threatening them with a gun."

Quinn arrived back at his house.
"Mr. Shanahan. I am here to put you under arrest. Charges have been filed against you by two gentlemen who swear that you terrorized and threatened them with bodily harm. Please put your horse away and come with me."

Agony in
THE GARDEN

"Are you serious?"

"Sorry, Quinn, but I have orders to bring you in. You'll have your day in court in the morning."

Next morning.

Harriet was looking out her window, watching a little sparrow, all by himself, pecking on some roses. He looked lonely and sad. No one to share. No one to eat with. No one to hop around and play with. He paused and looked into the window. He pecked at it, and stared. He looked at Harriet as if she understood. So nice of her to provide. She looked so sad and lonely. No one to share with. No one to eat with. No one to play with. Like the Slough of Despond on the east side, his problems ran deep, mired in some imaginary, and some real, obstacles.

Quinn entered. He looked tired and disgusted. He walked into Harriet's room. He stared at her. "The judge released me. The charges were dropped. I didn't get a wink of sleep last night. I tried, but I just couldn't believe what I heard. This is going to ruin me and my profession."

"But it wasn't my fault."

"Liar! You let them. People will find out about this little episode of yours. What are they going to say? What will they think? My God! I have no choice. You must leave this house, immediately."

"No Quinn. The baby? I wanted to leave but all I could think of was the baby."

"To hell with the baby. I want nothing to do with it. Go back home to your daddy, like you mentioned earlier."

The house of Quinn was evolving from a position of strength to a ramshackle existence. The exterior was deceptive while the interior, morose.

122

Agony in
THE GARDEN

The exterior was glossed over with a coat of black, while the interior walls were peeling in shame. Harriet's room became a scene of victory. Her wall had a new addition--- a picture of a diamond amongst a collection of rubble.

"You win," confessed Harriet as she looked into Quinn's eyes. "I've tried to scrub your poisonous words off my skin. All I have left is scars. You broke my will, my very soul. You have drained me of my identity. Injected my veins with self-doubt. It's gotten to the point that I question my own sanity. Like my old doll, I am frazzled. Worthy of nothing and longing for redemption. Longing for the day of salvation. I've beat myself for far too long. My days of dancing with the devil are coming to an end. No more listening to your commands. No more listening to your fantasies. No more accepting your words. No more, Quinn Shanahan. No more."

"But Harriet! I'm trying to change. I admit my weaknesses I realize I've put you through an enormous amount of malice. I'm going to see Reverend Martin. He'll show me the light. He'll point out my weaknesses. I'm changing, Harriet. Just wait and see. My blame game is over. I accept that. He acknowledges my weaknesses. He guides me in my day to day actions. I try and follow him. I'm trying to reach peace with myself so that I can reach peace with you and everyone else. I no longer feel the need to fantasize with success and power, and expertise, and beauty, and perfection. My days of fabrication and lying are no more."

"Those are just words, Quinn. Just look at what you have done. I tell you what happened to me long ago and you go off the deep end and get your gun. How can you explain that?"

"I realize I'm not perfect. No one is. I make mistakes, just like everybody else. I live with my mistakes. I try to correct them. That's all that He expects me to do. It's been forty days since that bright light, that burning bush, flashed around me. I have not been the same since.

Agony in
THE GARDEN

Tell her how sorry he was for being such a fool. Ask for her forgiveness. Ask for another chance. He glanced down again at what once were beautiful flowers just as two rabbits caught his eye. They were bouncing about the yard. "No!" he shouted. "Don't be an idiot! I have to try and get her back, but it has to be under my terms."

He headed back to his bedroom and began searching, rummaging through his chest of drawers. Madly tossing his shirts, and trousers, and socks upon the floor. "Where could have I put it? I know I put it in here. Think Quinn. Think! Nothing! He sat down by the table and rubbed his chin. "Where could it be?" He began to write a letter.

Quinn pushed his chair back and read once more what he had written. He stared at the paper and then stared out the window. In deep thought he remained. Taking the toothpick out of his mouth, he grabbed the letter and threw it into his desk drawer.

Next Day.

Harriet moved back to her parents, taking with her all of her belongings, as well as a few extra 'things'. While going through Quinn's dresser, she found what she was looking for---that 38 caliber Smith & Wesson, seven - shooter, and she brought it with her. "I need a place to stay," she begged as she hugged her father. "Oh, sweetheart," soothed Stanley. "I told you it wasn't going to work out."

"It's just temporary, Father. We had a little argument about the past and we both got too upset." "I know," noted Stanley. "I don't blame him for that. What I blame him for is not taking your side. I knew from the first time that I met him that he has a problem with his ego, among other things. I'll just let him sit at home by himself for a couple of days and let him think about how stupid he's been and I'm thinking he'll not only change his ways, but he will also change his personality.

THE GARDEN

We all have faults, and I'll be the first to admit mine, but he is a different story. I don't think he realizes how self-centered he really is.

But, I think he's the kind of man that can figure out his shortcomings and straighten his life, and his thought process, out."

"Well dear. Your room is still the way you left it," noted Clare.

"I changed the sheets and did a little dusting, but everything else is the same. Welcome home," she offered as she gave her a hug. "You put things away and I'll come up later and tidy up. By the way, we're going back to Northfield to pick up the rest of our belongings. Naddy is going to come along. You are more than welcomed to come also.

We shouldn't be gone more than a week."

"That sounds like a wonderful idea. I think I could use a little time away from this town."

Soon, Clare was moving about dusting Harriet's room and she began searching for more than dust. She opened the drawer to the writing desk and fingered through the papers. Finding nothing of importance, she moved to the large chest of oaken drawers. She continued to rummage until she got to the bottom drawer. She found the gun. The gun that Harriet had just brought over from her house. She picked it up and sat down to take a closer look. "Why on Earth would she have something like this?" she asked herself as she tucked it in her apron and left the room, as snow began to fall.

Chapter 17

"THE AWAKENING"

Several months later.

The snow-covered trail was in dire straits as Dr. Quinn guided his buggy along the questionable route. The sun was shining but the heat was lacking, as the grueling trip to Dalton, about five miles southeast of Fergus Falls, was progressing slowly. Dressed in a winter wardrobe of buffalo coat and raccoon hat, with boots to match, Quinn valiantly put in the effort. On his way to a farmer friend's house t o try for a miracle.

Typhoid fever was on the loose again, running rampant in the neighborhood, and the farmer had three children with the disease. Dark clouds were forming in the west, a sure bet that they'd be heading this way in a matter of a few hours. With the thought haunting him, he tried to move along faster, but to no avail.

Down the snow-covered trail trudged Beelzebub, with Quinn in charge. Upon arrival Quinn knocked on the door. Nobody! He knocked again. Still no answer. He opened the door. "Henry!" he shouted. "You in there?"

"In here," came a moan from one of the side rooms.

Quinn entered. The house was in a shambles. Dirty dishes lying on the kitchen table, fireplace shut down, and frost covering the windows. The putrid smell of defecation hovered throughout. The hint of death lingered everywhere.

Off in a dark corner sat Henry Johnson, a tired man, in his middle thirties. He was sitting alongside the bed of his wife, Margaret, who was lying prostrate and in dire straits.

The Awakening

"*I*, I'm giving up, Doc," moaned Henry. "I, I have no willpower left. Don't worry about me. Try and save her. She just lies there, with eyes open and mouth shut. It's as if she's begging to move on, to catch the train for that house in the sky but it's the children that I'm worried about. They're very quiet."

"I'll be right back," noted Quinn as he took his bag and headed into the next room. He stopped in his tracks. His mouth fell wide open. "No!" he shouted. "No! No! No!" The scene was gruesome. Three children, two girls age 4 and 7, and one boy, all seemingly lifeless, were lying in two beds. Wiping the tears from his eyes and rubbing his forehead in disbelief, he went to each. His hopes soon vanished as no sign of life could be found for either girl. He stepped back, trying to gather his wits. Little, nine year old Johnny lie in his bed, barely hanging on. "He's got to be about the same age as William. Ah, Willie! I wonder what ever happened to him. Hope his childhood is turning out better than mine. That was one of the dumbest things I've ever done. I complain about my childhood and I threw away the chance to give him a childhood I never had. I wonder. Maybe I should contact my brother. Maybe it's not too late. He sat down next to the bed and began crying, as the skies darkened and the snow began to fall.

"Johnny! Can you hear me?" whispered Quinn. No reply. "Johnny!" Still nothing. He searched for a pulse. Nothing! "All three are gone." He went back out of the room.

"Henry," he moaned. "They're gone."

"All three?" questioned Henry as he and Margaret fell further and further down in their chair and bed.

"I feel like I failed you. I should have been out here earlier. I'll never be able to forgive myself."

"Yes, my friend. Now, you two? What do I need to do to save you? I wish I could understand this disease better.

127

The Awakening

I cannot emphasize enough that I think the main culprit is the water. It must be contaminated. Any drinking water, make sure it's boiled first."

Quinn went over to the kitchen stove and threw a few more blocks of wood in; He grabbed a small kettle and poured some water in it and placed it on the stove. "I'll make up a little batch of beef broth for you two. Try and get a little nourishment in your system."

"I'll be back tomorrow. I'll have the county coroner, Bedford, come out and take care of the children. Now, Henry. Do not try and do anything. Stay in bed. Don't go out in this weather. He looked out the window and could barely see ten feet in front of him, as the snow was coming down relentlessly.

"You better stay here," suggested Henry. "Wait for the weather to clear." "You might be right, Henry, but I think Beelzebub can find her way back to her stable. I'll just go along for the ride," continued Quinn as he poured two small cups full of hot broth and set them down by Henry.

"Henry, I want you to take this and take all of it. There's more in the kettle. Margaret! I'll help you try and get some nourishment," he continued as he took a spoon and helped her. "That's my girl. Good job. Henry! See to it that your wife eats all of this. I have another appointment to get to. From the looks of what I'm seeing out your window there it could be a problem."

Quinn put his raccoon hat back on and his buffalo gloves and headed for the outside where the weather had changed considerably. "Let's go, Beelzebub, we got work to do."

Snow was falling at a heavy clip and the wind, stronger. Bucking the wind and poor visibility, Quinn guided his wagon on an uncharted course. All in the hopes of making it back to Fergus in one piece.

The Awakening

Doubts infiltrated the ice crystals on his face as he drove forward, ever so slowly. Pushing Beelzebub to her wit's end, driving the wagon further and further into unfamiliar territory. "Oh Lord! Where are we?" he asked himself. "No time to get lost! Only a fool would be roaming around out here in this weather."

The winds were cutting, ripping through the heavy buffalo coat, riveting into his half-frozen face, penetrating into his very heart and soul. With eyes half-frozen shut, he pushed onward, whipping poor Beelzebub into a frenzy. He resisted, fighting back by raising her front legs high into the air. She let out a terrifying neigh, a magnified whinny, a cry of desperation, followed by disapproval. She bolted forward, breaking the wagon tongue and setting herself free from the wooden encumbrance. Forward she went, racing off into the distant mirage of white. The wagon, with driver in a frantic state, went tumbling down a hill, flipping over and over into an unwelcomed pile of snow, far from the snow-covered trail.

Quinn was knocked unconscious, as the wagon landed directly on top of him. The only motion being the left side buggy wheel spinning in the air. Snow continued to fall and the terrifying winds continued to blow on the desolate graveyard of the broken buggy and the unconscious doctor.

Minutes passed. Quinn returned dazed and out of focus. He rubbed his face and then his forehead and fingers. He looked around at his new surroundings. Then he noticed it. His left leg. Something was wrong with his left leg---his shorter leg. It was not only shorter, but it was broken, with the wagon resting on top of it. He tried to move the wagon, to no avail. The snow continue d to fall, placing a new coat of white on everything in sight. The trees, the bushes, the ground, the wagon, and yes, even the good doctor. Cold, wet snow clinging, absorbing, penetrating through his buffalo coat.

The Awakening

Through his coonskin hat. Through his homemade leather boots. Moisture, cold moisture, settling in the most inopportune locations of the human body, frigid and real. The blinding, wind-driven snow pummeled the weakened body and soul of Quinn. Relentless and unforgiving, as if to say: take that, you fool!

"Blanket! I need a blanket!" He looked in the back of the wagon. Nothing. "Where are the blankets?" Spread out and being painted white along the sides of the path, the cotton blankets were of no use, under the circumstances.

"Freezing! I'm freezing and there is nothing I can do about it. Oh the pain," he moaned as he tried to comfort the leg. What would he do? The chilling thought of doing nothing was constantly repeating itself to the bewildered bumpkin who now had a face fraught with redness.

The agonizing thought of freezing to death inched closer to reality as he tried to unleash his wrath upon the stubborn Mother Nature. Co-operating she was not.

The pain was becoming unbearable. Constant, throbbing, and painstaking. With a feeling of helplessness and hopelessness, he lie there unable to cast out the evils, unable to free himself from the clutches of death. His life was passing before him. His childhood years in Pennsylvania. His marriage to his LePette. Her death in childbirth. Yes, and the baby, William. His second wife, Harriet. Why didn't that work out? Was it me? What a failure! I am witnessing another collapse. My weaknesses have been overtaken. I will go down in history as a simple fraud, a do-nothing, an inconsiderate derelict, just taking up space. Change! I have to change! But, how can I? Lying here, unable to move. Unable to rid myself of past iniquities and present shortcomings. This is a rude awakening. What can I do about it? Maybe, just maybe, it's time for me to start praying.

The Awakening

With the tentacles of death hovering all around, he closed his eyes and entered into a new scenario, where it was just him and Him. A smile appeared and, suddenly, Quinn was at ease. A sense of satisfaction, a feeling of hope, a promise of things to come. All of this rolled into one complete package of deliverance.

The winds died down and the snow stopped falling, and the clouds opened up, and the sun appeared. Bright, warm, invigorating sunshine. Perfect medicine for the beleaguered doctor, but alas, it quickly returned to cold. A biting cold. A gnawing cold. A cold that took away the feelings in Quinn's fingers and toes.

He opened his eyes while wiping the frost from his face. His pain was still there but something made it bearable. And then a couple of chilling howls filled the air. "Cats!" shrieked Quinn. "That's all I need. Bobcats. Oh Beelzebub! Where have you gone?" Quinn asked. "I should have called her 'Nellie'. Not Beelzebub. Like her namesake, she abandoned me. Why would I be asking for help from the devil? He's played more than enough of a role in my life already. But where is she? Could she have made it all the way back to town? If so, someone would soon be here." Yet he kept shivering.

More cat shrills. Haunting, penetrating, nerve-wracking. Quinn knew they were coming closer. Almost sound like they were right beside him. Then, they became more and more quiet, till there was no more. "Oh, if only I could find some daffodils. I'd feel so much better."

He heard a crackling sound in the nearby brush. He focused his attention toward the noise, which was getting louder and louder. Tensions arose. Quinn was defenseless. What could be out there? A bear? A rabbit? A fox? No! It was a dog. A big old farm dog. Henry's neighborhood farm dog. Henry's half-breed, named 'Peanut Butter'. Quinn sighed a big relief as the monstrous animal took one look at Quinn and headed off to the north. "Peanut Butter! Come here!" shouted Quinn.

The Awakening

"Now what? Lie in wait? Wait for someone to pass by and find me?" he asked himself as he turned his attention back to his leg and the burdensome wagon.

With caution, the dog returned and approached Quinn. Sniffing as he got closer, not knowing what lie in front of him.
"Peanut Butter! Go get help! Look! I can't get up. Go get help!"

The dog stared at him.
"I know you can do it. Go get help!"
 Peanut Butter barked twice and took off running up the trail, while Quinn remained pinned on the ground, shivering and full of bewilderment, not knowing if survival was in the cards. He lie on the frozen ground, feeling helpless and abandoned. Unable to fix! Helpless, broken, empty, all alone. Fading! Falling into submission. It's as if he was unable to move. Paralyzed from head to toe.

Into a slumber he fell. Into unfamiliar territory. Into a dream world where Beelzebub was flying through the snowstorm with Quinn as a passenger in the buggy. He was partaking in a feast of oysters in the half shell, and Naddy was sitting beside him. She was sitting tall and erect, with a full womb and a smile of conquest on her face. It was windy and she was tossed into the atmosphere while Beelzebub stopped in mid-air and the buggy and Quinn went flying into space, joining Naddy.

Daffodils, and coyotes, and oysters, and fishing boats, and train locomotives were floating by. "I'm not ready!" shouted Quinn. "I don't want to die! God! Make this go away! Save me from eternal damnation! Give me one more chance!" he begged as he floated by Naddy.

Sweat was everywhere. He was completely drenched, not only from his own sweat but also from his own iniquities, and there was nothing he could do, as he came to."Oh Lord! Lend me your ear. I've been trying. Help me! I'm sure you know, but I want to talk to you about my family.

The Awakening

Mara and I had the most wonderful mother a person could ever ask for. She always would be there when we needed her. My father was a different story. I very seldom spent much time with him. If he wasn't out peddling his wares he would be at the local pub, bartering for something to quench his thirst. He always had such a thirst! He wasn't nice to any of us. Always seemed to be in a bad mood. He'd come home at night and I'd make sure I was in bed before that.

He'd start hollering at Mother and pretty soon you could hear him beating her. Oh! I can still hear those sounds. She was such a saint to put up with him for so many years. When I got older I made it a point to stay up until he'd come staggering home. I'd tell Mother and Mara, and Braden, that I'd protect them. I think he was a little scared of me because he'd usually end up going to bed without saying a word."

"One time we were all out by the lake, trying to enjoy a warm Sunday afternoon at a picnic. Well, he thought it would be a good time to teach me how to swim I can't tell you how much I was against that idea, but he insisted. He took me and drug me into the water and kept taking me deeper and deeper. I'm going to teach you if it's the last thing I ever do, he said, while Mother and Mara and poor little Braden watched in utter disbelief, from the shore. He lifted me up and kept going deeper and deeper. I'm going to let you go and you're going to swim back just like I showed you, he yelled. I was in panic mode. So scared I could hardly speak. My muscles were so tight! Help me! I yelled to my sister, Mara."

"Mara won't help you. You are responsible for yourself. You can never depend on anyone else for survival in this mean world, he'd say, and threw me in. Yes, the bastard wanted me to drown! I flailed and hollered and cried and went under. My legs wouldn't move. It felt like I was tied down with a load of rocks. My feet touched bottom and I tried jumping up but that didn't work. I prayed and prayed some more. Then I lunged forward and found the bottom again and stood up. I headed for the opposite shore.

The Awakening

As I got out I heard a gunshot and then I felt it. A sharp pain in my ankle. I saw blood flowing like a river. He fired a shot at me! I couldn't believe it! I fell into the water and that was the last thing I remember until I woke up, lying on the beach, and my little brother, Braden, who couldn't have been any older than three or four, was holding my hand, and waving that old yellow ribbon in the other, while my mother and Mara were standing over me. Needless to say, I didn't learn how to swim and I was afraid of the water ever since, until this past year when I was fishing with Gavin. I looked around for Pa, but he was nowhere to be seen."

"I found him the next day, though. I waited for him to come out of the bar. It took a while, but he finally appeared. He saw me and staggered over. Drooling and weaving, he came right up to me. You still around, he asked. I'm your son, I shot back. He tried raising his right fist. I have no sons, he said. Yes, you do, I bluntly replied, and a wife, and a daughter and three sons."

"Why, you, he barked as he tried swinging at me. I pushed him away. He fell on his back and hit his head. Just like when I came out here. It reminded me of that Jasper fellow. That man tried robbing me and I put up a fight. He never woke up. I had killed him. I put him in the river and laid a big rock over him. He's still buried there and haunts me every day, just like my father. When he came to he got on his horse and I never saw him again. I was told that he went back to Ireland. What a relief. I never had to worry about coming into contact with that evil man again. But still, my guilt was overwhelming and that has been gnawing at me ever since that terrible day back in Pennsylvania. Since that day I swore I would have nothing to do with children. I was afraid I'd be just like my father."

"Then you came along. I loved what I saw. You were just what I needed. Then I noticed I was blaming others for my problems, thinking that it surely wasn't my fault. I owe it all to you and Harriet for pointing out my shortcomings and having Reverend Martin come into my life. Now, look it. I need you once more."

The Awakening

As the skies cleared the temperature dropped and evening arrived. Just what the doctor didn't want. Still no rescue. Still no savior. Feelings were lost in his fingers and toes. Ice was forming on his cheeks and nose. A dismal outlook was fast approaching. Or was it dismal? The more he thought about it, the better he felt. Prepare myself for one last journey. Don't have to worry about anyone shooting at me from behind. Just keep looking forward. Forward to a just reward. Thoughts of the next world kept twirling in his mind. When all hope was rising, faith in the fellow man was reaching a higher point, he heard a dog barking. It was getting closer and louder. It was Peanut Butter. Peanut Butter and a wagon, with several heavily-bundled men aboard.

"What a sight!" exclaimed Quinn as one of the men jumped down and lifted the wagon off of Quinn.
"Careful! It's broken."
"How long you been out here?" questioned one of the other men.
"Here's a blanket," offered a third.
"Oh, I imagine it was two of three hours."
"We'll get you back to town, Doc," noted the oldest of the three as he watched the other two extricate the victim from harm and placed him on the back of their wagon. "You can thank Henry's dog. He ran down to our place, a good quarter mile away, and kept hounding us until we followed him here. If it weren't for that dog you probably would have frozen to death by now."
"Boys! Let's get to town."

Several days later.

Quinn was lying in his bed, just like he had been since his return home from his episode down near Dalton. His leg wasn't broken, but it was still messed up. He needed something to pass the time while his leg healed. He found it. He became deeply involved with the Good Book. It was a lonely time for a lonely person, yet he had his book. Quiet reigned as king, while Quinn lie in wait for rejuvenation. Many an hour was taken up by reading --- some by reading newspapers, but mostly by reading the Good Book, but some time was also spent languishing in thought of why he failed in his marriage. It was during this time that Quinn began to hit rock bottom.

The Awakening

He started to drink brandy and it wasn't long and brandy became his companion. He had no life, no wife, no business, and no friends. The only thing left was a Smith and Wesson, 32 caliber, hammerless revolver, lying on the kitchen table, in front of him. He picked it up and stared at it. While pouring himself another brandy he heard a young boy outside, crying. He staggered over to the window and saw the boy dressed in pajamas, standing in the snow. "Billy! That could be Billy," he murmured as he put on a buffalo coat and headed out. "What are you doing out here?" he asked.

"I, I, I don't know where I'm at," sniffled the young boy.

"Come on inside before you catch a cold," he suggested as he took the little boys hand. "What's your name?"

"Billy."

"Billy who?"

"Billy Robinson."

"Oh," noted the disappointed Quinn as he paced back and forth between the table and the window, whilepulling on his right ear lobe. "Robinson? Robinson? You Homer's boy?"

"Yes. Yes, Sir."

"Come on, boy. I'll take you back to your house. It's not far from here."

"But, Mister. I, I."

"Never mind," interrupted Quinn. "You can warm up in here for a few minutes and then I'll get you back. Let me warm up some milk. Are you hungry? I can make something to e at. Maybe some flapjacks, or some biscuits and gravy."

"Oh, that sounds so good, but..."

"It'll just take a moment. I had biscuits and gravy for supper and just so happen to have some left over," Quinn continued a s he headed for the pantry box and grabbed the bowl of gravy. He lit the wood stove and soon Billy was scarfing down supper.

"This is really good, Mister," offered the little boy as he continued to fill up.

"Good," laughed Quinn. "You finish that and then we'll head out into the cold."

"But you still look like you've been laid up from that accident you had a while back."

"You never mind about that. It'll do me some good to get out and about. I've been feeling sorry for myself much too long."

The Awakening

Soon, the two were on their way down the street, plunging through the snowdrifts that were vastly accruing. The winds had picked up and the visibility was getting worse, yet the twosome continued to move forward. One block, and then two blocks. Onward they moved.

"I see it! I see it!" shouted the jubilant boy. "I'm home! Oh, thank-you Mister."
"My pleasure," replied Quinn as he knocked on the door.
A short heavy-set man, in a full beard, opened the door. "Billy!" he gasped. "We've been out looking for you. Where have you been?"
"I got turned around, Pa. This man saved me," as he pointed at Quinn.
"Doctor Shanahan! Thank-you. I don't know what else to say. You truly are a lifesaver," stated Mr. Robinson as he hugged his son.
"Won't you come into our humble home?"

"No thank-you, but I better get back. This weather doesn't look like it's going to get any better. If I stayed Billy would probably have to show me the way back to my place."

"Well, thanks again," offered Mr. Thompson as he shook Quinn's hand and walked him back to the door.
While Quinn went back to his time recuperating, Harriet spent her time educating --- educating herself and many a pupil in the world of music. And doing piano concerts. She drew huge crowds, sometimes with her sisters, sometimes alone, whether it be in small towns like Perham or huge cities like Chicago and San Francisco. She would give private lessons in piano and in voice. Still, many an hour was spent languishing in the thoughts of Quinn. Always asking herself why she failed at marriage. "He needed help. Maybe I should offer my assistance?" she murmured. "No," she continued. "Only if he asks."

"FOR BRADEN'S SAKE"

Molly was skipping past the Occidental hotel, waving Braden's dirty old yellow ribbon and humming the 'Oh Susanna' tune. Quinn and Remy had just finished lunch at the hotel and were walking past the Well of Despondency, heading back to their office when Quinn noticed the ribbon. Could it be? He asked himself. It sure looks like it. They reversed course and headed in Molly's direction, staying back far enough so as not to be seen. "She's getting into a buggy. Look Remy. That's my buggy. See the two golden spokes? Go get your buckboard. Looks like she's going out of town. Hurry!"

Molly turned onto Northern Avenue and then took a right onto Mt. Faith. "Dang. We're losing her! Come on, Remy. Hurry up!" demanded Quinn as he lost his patience until Remy finally arrived. "She's heading out," noted Quinn as he jumped on board. Hopefully, we haven't lost her. Do you have your revolver?"

"No."

"Fortunately, I have mine. Come on, get up to her."

But there was no one in front of them. Past the cemetery and out into the country and not a soul to be seen. "Dang. Now what?" queried Quinn. "Hopefully, she didn't see us. Now we know that Braden is somewhere out here in the country. Let's follow the road out to Fish Lake."

Remy stopped the wagon. "I can't. I have to get back to town. I have an appointment I can't miss," he continued as he got off the wagon. You go wherever you want. I'll walk back to town."

"But, Remy?"

"No, you go ahead. Just let me know when you get back."

For Braden's
Sake

*Q*uinn grabbed the reins. Be that way. I'll find my Braden by myself. I don't need your help."

As Remy was walking down the road, heading back into town, Quinn turned around and wondered. "That's kinda funny that he would take having an appointment over helping his friend. I guess there is always a first." He continued down the rough trail going past several farmsteads and keeping a close eye out for any semblance of a buggy with two golden spokes.

"I just know I'm close," noted Quinn as his anxiety reached a high level. "I'm going to find you, Braden. I'm going to find you tonight." Meanwhile, out at the farmhouse Braden lie on his bed, ankle cuffed to the frame, looking out the window, toward the lake. "Fish! Fish Lake! That's it! There's that island. Pinafore. Yes siree. I know where I'm at."

The door opened and in came a young man, who couldn't have been any older than Braden. He was a peculiar fellow. Tall and thin, with big feet and little hands. Long, black hair flowing down past his shoulders. With thick black glasses covering a real weird pair of eyes, and a small goatee covering his jagged chin. He was the only son of the Judge and had recently celebrated his eighteenth birthday, at which time he was promoted to be his right-hand man. "Where's Molly?"

"Don't know, Lester. She told me she'd be right back. Think she's in town."

"Damn it! She wasn't to leave you out here alone. What's the matter with her?"

$\mathcal{F}or$ $\mathcal{B}raden's$
Sake

"Don't swear," shouted Braden.

"Why you little…" threatened Lester as he raised an arm up at the scared Braden.

Lester stormed out of the house and headed back to town, while Braden returned to working on his ankle lock. Molly would be back any time and he wanted to be gone. This was his chance. It's almost there. He continued to use the rasp on the chain. Desperation set in. He wiped the sweat off his forehead and rubbed his fingers. They were raw and sore and aching, but he kept on.

And then he broke through. He still had the bracelet around his ankle but he was free. He threw the rasp down, grabbed his jacket and headed out the door.

The howling of the coyotes was still going on, and that was the direction he headed for. It was in the area of the vault, his temporary destination.

Molly entered the farmhouse, still twirling the old dirty yellow ribbon. She immediately noticed that Braden had escaped. She put her hand on what was left of the chain on the bed. "How did he ever do that without me not noticing? What is Bannister going to say, or worse yet, what's he going to do when he finds out? Oh my! Am I going to be in danger? There's only one thing I can do---go tell Shanahan. That's it. He'll know what to do." She packed up her few belongings and headed out the door.

Braden was getting close to the coyotes. Maybe if I could get near to that one in the trap and set him free the others would go away, he thought. It was getting dark in the woods as he tried to paint a picture of the entire area in his mind. Got to remember to go up the hill here. That vault on Pinafore has to be in this direction. I can see the lake from here.

The yipping continued nearby. The growling, the sharp barks were closer, and all around. Braden squinted into the dark with the full moon peeking through the evening clouds.

140

For Braden's Sake

He could hear him yelping, but it was too dark. Straight ahead. He's got to be straight ahead. Just get him out of the trap and they'll all leave. That's all I have to do.

He looked to his left. He could see a pair of eyes and he could hear a continuous growl, a shrieking cry of agitation, to his right. "My God! I'm being surrounded," he gasped.

He moved forward with caution, watching and hoping. Watching for any sign of the wounded, hoping for any sign of assistance. He was shaking. He could hear the crackling of branches on all sides. He could hear snorts of contempt and a hoot owl off in the distant. He could hear his heart beating faster and faster.

He inched his way towards the wounded coyote. He was just a pup. He was caught in a trap. He growled and grunted, watching Braden every moment. The five others inched closer and closer from all sides. He could see them, all staring at him with watchful eyes---skinny, mangy, straggly, conniving, no more than 35 pounds. Gray and cinnamon in color, with erect ears, white lips, edged with black, and they had bushy tails.

All eyes seemed to be on Braden as he froze in place, waiting to see what the coyotes would do. Closer and closer they came. Louder and louder they growled. Their eyes sparkled while their teeth clattered, and the captive cheered them on.

Come on, Braden. Think! How do I get out of this mess? What would Quinn do? Huh! He'd never get himself in such a situation. He began rocking in place while rubbing his hands along his crossed arms. Sweat was rolling down his face. "Where is Quinn? I need Quinn. He take care of me. I need water. Mouth dry. Oh Lord! I'm doomed. No! I must do this."

He moved closer to the wounded. The coyotes attacked. Down went Braden. His shirt and pants were ripped. His hands were bitten and chewed. His face, clawed. He grabbed one by the back leg and threw it into the air, yelping as it went. Another attacked from behind. Back down to the ground, amongst a field of thistles. One pounced on him from the side, wrapping his jaws around Braden's neck.

141

For Braden's Sake

Blood appeared, seemingly everywhere from head to toe. Braden raised his arms over his head and grabbed the attacker and ripped into his belly. More yelps! More screams! More attacks! Two, three, four of them, each punishing, each tearing into his very soul. A slash across the left cheek, a cut on the forehead and chomping on his fingers. All hope was disappearing. The chances for survival were getting slimmer by the minute.

Then they stopped. Braden stared at the pup and the pup stared at him. Braden moved closer while the pup moved closer to his mother. "What would Quinn do? If I run, they'll come after me. He perused the pup. "His right front leg. He has a problem. Caught in a trap."

He tried to scare them off, but they kept coming back. The onslaught continued. He spotted a four foot branch, decaying and moss-covered, lying on the ground. He crawled over and picked it up. He started wildly swinging it in the air as he inched closer to the wounded pup. He swung at the pup, but missed, making the pup more scared and determined. He swung again, with the same result, as the pack regrouped. He swung a third time. This time a direct hit, knocking the pup out. He crawled over to the trap and with all of his strength he opened the claws enough to get the paw out.

The other coyotes ceased howling and watched as Braden pulled the injured pup away from the snare, and crawled away from the endangered site. They stopped, thought Braden. Amazing! All they wanted was to save their pup.

He crawled as best he could to find a safe spot along the river, dragging himself, inch by inch from somewhere to somewhere else. From one unknown to another unknown. He moved on his hands and knees, feeling nothing. Nothing in his fingers. Nothing in his knees. Nothing in his mind. He'd glance back on and off to see if any of those dogs were still in the neighborhood. He could sense their nearness, but had no feeling. He laid down at the foot of a giant oak tree, and a large patch of daffodils, right next to a huge rock protruding from the Red.

For Braden's Sake

There wasn't a single bone in his body that didn't hurt. Not a single piece of skin that didn't feel stained. Not a single series of thoughts rushing through his mind that didn't make him feel defeated, overwhelmed with negativity and hopelessness. "Oh Lord!" he yelled as loud as he could. "Just let me die!" Then he began to realize what he had just done. A smile reappeared. "Me like Quinn. I fix." Within minutes he was sleeping, as the gentle flow of the water went by and the coyotes were content.

Darkness hindered Molly's trip back to Fergus. The ruts were hard to follow under the circumstances. Molly was good at handling horses, but tonight it was more than treacherous. There was a moon barely shining and provided little light for the scared buggy driver. Her imagination was playing tricks on her, especially when she went past the cemetery.

"Oh, what's the use!" she moaned. What good is it going to do to wake the doctor up at this time of the night? What if my boss sees me before I find the doctor? Maybe I should just go back, she thought. "No. I can't do that. He'll kill me. No, I have to find the doctor and maybe even the sheriff."

She arrived in front of the doctor's house. No lights on. No sign of life. As she parked the wagon and found her way up the walk she paused and look around in wonderment at the large edifice. She inched her way up to the door and knocked. Lacking patience, she knocked again and again until the front door opened.

Quinn appeared with lantern in hand. "Who's out here?"
"Me. Molly Finnegan."
Quinn got a good look at her. "You're that girl that had that dirty old yellow ribbon, aren't you?"

"Yes sir. I, I got some news for you. It's Braden. I know where he is."

"You what? You know Braden? Where? Where is he?"

"Out by Fish Lake, I think. That's where he said he wanted to go."

143

For Braden's Sake

"Come in. Come inside. I just got back from out there. I didn't see a thing. Tell me more. How do you know Braden?"

"I, I've been taking care of him," she quietly replied.
"You have? For who?"

"I don't know his name for sure. The first time I met him he called himself Butch, then someone else called him Charlie. He calls himself Lester. He's not very nice. We've been out at the old Nelson farmhouse, not far from your resort."

"Can you take me to him?"

"I can try. He broke loose and he's been talking a lot about that vault on your island."

"You wait right here and I'll get dressed," ordered Quinn as he disappeared.

In a few moments he returned with his gun in one hand and his medical bag in the other and a toothpick in his mouth. "I'll take the reins, Molly. Don't know if you knew but this is my buggy," he continued as they boarded and headed out.

"So, how is Braden?"
"I'm not sure. There were coyotes up in that area where he wanted to go."

"Oh my! I had just about given up on ever seeing him again. Oh, you've made my day," exclaimed Quinn as he cracked the whip. "So how long you've been doing this?"

"For months. I rather enjoy it. He is such a considerate boy. When I first met him I didn't think I'd be able to do it. He was so quiet and reserved, except for when he went to bed at night. He'd start singing. Always the same song. Same poem. It had to do with daffodils, but he'd call it dilodaffs. Oh, I wandered lonely as a cloud that floats on high o'er vales and hills, when all at once I saw a crowd, a host of daffodils.

144

For Braden's
Sake

Beside the l ake, beneath the trees, fluttering and dancing in the breeze. Every night he'd go through that whole poem, all by heart. I'd end up listening from my bed and he taught me the whole thing. When I first saw him I thought there was something wrong with him. He didn't talk much, and he didn't seem to explain himself very good, but as time went by he opened up some and we were able to carry on some good conversations. The more time I spent with him, the more I realized that he has a big heart. He'd do anything for me, no matter what time of the day. He, definitely, is smart. Why, I figured I'd have to teach him everything. Well, it's just the complete opposite. He' been teaching me reading, writing, and arithmetic. Even some history. Why he would go on and on about the war, on how the Confederates got whooped, and..."

"Alright, Molly. That's enough. You made your point. I know all about my little brother."

"Why, a while back I was thanking him for making my job so much easier that he kissed me. I just know he liked it cause I sure did."

"Didn't you think it was a little peculiar that you were keeping someone locked up? Did it ever occur to you that you were an accessory to a crime?"

"Why, heavens no. A crime? I was just doing what I was told to do and getting paid a little for it."

"By who?"

"Shorty."

"Shorty who?"

"Don't know. He never told me. I was always told to respect authority."

Braden sat down in the field of daffodils and checked over all the wounds received from his battles. He knelt down next to the river and poured water over some of the wounds, but there were some that water could not wash off. He sat back up and attempted to sing.

145

For Braden's Sake

"I wandered lonely as a cloud that floats on high o'er vales and hills, when all at once I saw a crowd, a host of golden daffodils, beside the lake, beneath the trees, fluttering and dancing in the breeze."

He noticed something in the water. A big rock, partially submerged, had something under it. He looked closer. "Dear Lord! It's a hand!" He pushed the rock deeper into the river and, with a horrified look, pulled the entire skeleton up and gently laid it on the shore. "Now what?" he asked himself. "Do I tell the sheriff? Do I leave it laying right here? I better go find Quinn."

Back with Quinn and Molly, the conversation continued. "Was he treated humanely?"

"Not at first. If you can imagine he was blindfolded, his mouth, for the most part, was covered, he was shackled to the floor, his hands were tied behind his back, and he had to kneel on the floor, with hands tied behind his back, and he had to eat that way, and his bed was a little pile of straw. But as time went by, I was able to change that. We moved him out into the country and he had his own bed, although I still had to chain him to it, but he didn't have any of those other things."
"Ah, poor Braden! How could you do such a thing?"

"I didn't have much of an upbringing so I really didn't give it much thought, but that started to change as the more time I spent with him. He started teaching me things and he treated me with respect and I liked that. And I started to like him and I think he started to like me. Yeah, he and that dirty old yellow ribbon. It was as if that was his only hope."

"I could tell he and I were an awful lot alike. Neither of us had much to be proud of. Self-esteem wasn't in our vocabulary, but we started to grow on each other and I was thinking that maybe I loved him. I sure hope he didn't get tangled up with those coyotes."

146

For Braden's
Sake

"Well, we should be coming up to that area real soon. My resort is straight ahead a few miles. Look real close on your side. We'll follow the river for a bit."

"Look!" shouted Molly. "By the river, right by those daffodils, and that big oak tree."

"Ah! Dilodaffs! How fitting! But, wow, is he ever torn up!"

Quinn stopped the carriage, grabbed his medicine bag, and rushed over to his brother. "Braden! Braden! It's me, Quinn." He shouted. No reply. He checked his heart. "He's alive!"

"Oh my poor Braden," moaned Molly as she began to cry.

"Braden! Wake up! Molly! Take that bucket and fill it with water," commanded Quinn, at the first sight of Braden coming to. "What have you been doing, little brother? I have missed you so."

"Quinn! Quinn! Is that you?" weakly asked Braden. "And Molly?"

"Yes, yes, it is us," answered Quinn as he started wiping the blood off of his brother. "We have to get you to town immediately. You might have a few broken bones. Oh, little brother. You have no idea how relieved and struck with joy I am."

"Mr. Shanahan," interrupted Molly. "Look!" she ordered as she showed him the skeleton.

Quinn was in shock. He couldn't believe that his brother found the evidence.

"I was washing myself off and noticed this body under a rock. It looked like somebody got murdered and the murderer covered him up with that big rock."

147

For Braden's
Sake

"I'll take it back to the sheriff," offered Quinn as he threw the skeleton in the back of the wagon.

"My, my chest," noted Braden. "It hurts real bad."

"Here Molly! Help me get him in the back seat and you have him lay his head on your lap."

Once everyone was situated, off to Fergus Falls they went, with Braden content on Molly's lap and holding her hand, and they both were smiling, while Quinn noticed. It was still dark outside, but the relieved threesome had just received a great batch of light and a whopping package of thankfulness.

"TRAIN WRECK"

Harriet sat in the back of the Wiggins buckboard, relaxed, yet holding her stomach. Her sister, Naddy, was next to her, among a large number of wooden boxes. Their father was at the helm, with Clare and Voyance beside. Returning from a trip to Northfield with the remainder of their household goods, they were heading for their home on Lakeside Drive. Harriet was reading a telegram, explaining Quinn's situation. She couldn't help but worry about his mishap. The details were absent and she thought nothing but the worst. Would he be waiting for her? No! Impossible! He doesn't even know we're coming home. I wonder if he even missed me.

She could hear the nearby school bell ringing and a distant train whistle blowing. Just the beginning! She thought. A mother! I can't believe it. Waited so long. The eyesight has taken a turn for the worse. He didn't warn me about that. He explained what to expect, like pregnancy glow and why that occurs. He talked about the breasts changing and about morning sickness. So far, he'd been completely correct. He said my taste buds and my nose would play tricks on me, but he never said a thing about my eyes and my mood swings. Unexplainable! I can be full of joy one minute and then angry the next. Depressed, then sentimental. Powerful and then insecure seconds later. Married to a doctor, getting my musical aspirations going, settled in a new home, but now back with mother and father. What a mess!

If only he could understand what he's doing! So selfish! So me, me, me. Understanding him is impossible. It's not my fault. He's the one that doesn't trust anyone except himself.

"Harriet!" shouted Naddy. "Are you dreaming?"

"Oh, ah, yes. I guess so."

149

Train
Wreak

*Y*ou're thinking about Quinn. Aren't you?"
"I'm thinking about many things. I'm thinking about my body. What it's going to be like going through this pregnancy alone. Nobody at my side. Nobody to help. I'm wondering if maybe I should go see Remy. He'd take care of everything. I don't really have time for a baby. It's going to make me miss plenty of engagements. I'll miss out on a lot of money."

"You don't need him," shot back Naddy. "You're too good for him and you know it."

"He hasn't signed the papers yet."
"I'll remind him."
"Why are you so excited to have my marriage fail?"
"Cause I hate to see you in this state."
"You sure it isn't for you to take my place?"
"That's nonsense. Why don't you go see the judge?"
"I've thought about that. At least he gives me attention."

Yes, thought Harriet. Maybe it would be so much easier if I let him spoil me. I could use some of that now. Quit thinking so much about Quinn. There's no pleasing him.

The neighborhood was becoming quiet. Even the school had an eerie silence. A silence that haunted Harriet. Too quiet! Children were walking to school but they were not talking. It was as if they were in their own world and showed signs of being afraid of the situation.

The clouds were getting darker as Harriet looked over to the homes across from Summit Avenue. It was a nice neighborhood. Friendly people all along the street, some darting about, working in their gardens, or spending time in their vaults. There were little three and four year old boys and girls playing tag and looking for mischief. They were too young to be in school and too old to be in their mother's hair. Harriet could see some playing hide and seek and having fun. Oh, to have fun again! Be like the children.

Train
Wreak

Nothing for them to worry about. There's old man Montgomery. God bless him. He's up there in age. He's our senior. Such kind and generous person.

She glanced back at Naddy. If only Naddy knew how much I love her. She's not only my sister but my best friend. She's so much better at playing the piano, I know it, yet I'm still jealous. I put more time on those keys than anyone. Sure I'm getting the recognition now, more than Naddy or Deb, but that's going to change. I only wish she'd leave Quinn and me alone. Constantly trying to butt in.

"I sure hope Deborah hasn't messed up the house too bad," noted Clare as she looked back at the girls.

"I've missed seeing that magical little face," offered Stanley. "If it weren't for her you girls would be lost in your musical careers."

"Oh, that's nonsense," shrugged Clare. "You don't know what you're talking about."

"Harriet," continued Clare as she turned around. "How's my mother-to-be doing back there?"

"Not a worry in the world. Have a few minor jabs once in a while, but it's all going to be worth it."

"Has Quinn been helpful?"

"Yes, Mother, although I haven't seen much of him lately. Ever since I told him when we were down on our honeymoon he hasn't said much when it comes to the baby."

"My Deborah has that burning desire to be the best at whatever she does," continued Stanley, as the wagon got closer to the railroad tracks. "Especially when it has to do with men.

151

Train Wreak

She is very adept at lighting the world on fire. She always tries to find the good in people. She's always tried to impress the boys, always wanting to fit in with them so that she'd look better in the eyes of you girls, but I have to admit, she's been acting a little strange ever since she was at Dr. Oglesby's."

"Excuse me, Father," interrupted Naddy. "But it's Deborah who complains about the mosquitoes and the wood ticks and the garter snakes in the summer and the shelter-seeking field mice and the frosted windows, and the frost-bitten fingers in the winter. She calls it the Tundra."

"When we were out in Jamestown we almost got in a fight with some of the other girls in the troupe," interrupted Harriet. "Deb came to the forefront. She took charge. She may be a private in private, but she was the 'General' who led her troops with all she had. You should have seen those women back off. Ever since that day they've had nothing but good things to say about her. She commanded respect and she got it. Before that day I always thought she was too withdrawn, too shy, always unhappy and very apprehensive. She was transformed that day and hasn't looked back since."

Harriet noticed the train noise getting louder. "That must be Uncle Charlie coming back from Barnesville. He has spent his entire adult life with the railroad."
I remember Father saying that it was Uncle Charlie who convinced him to move us out here. Charlie Rush! He's my favorite. He's always nice to me. I'm sure he favored me over Naddy and Deborah. He's been working for the Manitoba Road as far back as I can remember. He's the head engineer here. He spends his days going up and down the line, moving boxcars around on the side tracks and sometimes even taking cars up to Moorhead. He loves his job. He knows everything there is about his engine. Its strengths and its weaknesses. He takes real good care of his 'Bets'. He's been showing bad signs of hearing lately and his eyesight isn't what it used to be."

Train
 Wreak

He's given us all rides on that engine. Ah, yes, good old Uncle Charlie. He knew his engine was getting up there in age and needed special attention. He loved the sound she'd make when moving a boxcar of grain. He loved the ringing of her bell, and the bellowing of her horn. "Looks like rain coming," observed Clare. "Better get those nags to move faster."

"Yes dear," replied Stanley as he shook the reins and yelled at the plugs.

"Careful when you cross the tracks."

"I'm always careful when it comes to trains," continued Stanley as he looked both ways and started across Summit Avenue.

Thunder roared and lightning flashed, and the rain clouds opened up and poured forth, and the children took cover and the dogs hid in the sheds, as the wagon creaked over the train tracks. Then, it happened. That powerful switch engine, with Charlie Rush at the controls, with whistle blowing and bell ringing, came around the bend from the northwest and smashed head on into the defenseless wagon. Charlie slammed on the brakes, to no avail. Too late! Spine-chilling screeching of metal against metal added to the cacophony of incredulous magnitude, shaking the very foundations of the nearby dwellings. Pandemonium erupted from the crushing sounds as the little engine that could obliterated the wagon, sending the occupants hurling through the air, along with the wooden boxes of things. Screams of horror added to the morning air, overtaking the deafening thunder and lightning. Shouts of anguish reverberated along the tracks and throughout the slumbering village of Fergus Falls, as the lights went out and darkness prevailed.

Flashes of her life flooded Harriet's mind as she saw her Uncle Charlie in desperation mode frantically try the impossible. Into the air she went with uncontrollable speed and landing in Duke's flower garden, amongst a cluster of thistles.

153

Train
Wreak

She lie there in a daze with blood flowing down the face and arms. Wait! There's pain in the right arm and no feeling in the left ankle. A large six-inch gash extended from the top of her forehead, down the left cheek, and to below her chin.

The pain was horrendous and gut-wrenching, while the heart was pounding, pushing blood through her veins and spurting it out onto the thistles.

Confusion reigned as she tried t o raise her right arm, but to no avail. "It's broken," she gasped. " The arm is broken. A dead arm! A useless arm! My piano days are done for. No more traveling around the country. Meeting new and wonderful people. New York! Chicago! Minneapolis! No more tours! No one deserves this. My life is ruined.

Where is everyone? She could hear voices, shrieks, and moans, while she tried wiping blood off her face.

She tried moving. Impossible! Bursting into tears, she weakly pounded the ground with her fist. Harder and harder, to no avail. "Naddy! Where are you? Can't you see me?" she asked, while crowds were gathering and the rains continued.

"Over here," replied Naddy, who was lying twenty five feet straight ahead of the crushed wagon. She was in a mud puddle, off to her right. She didn't have her glasses but was still hugging her Bible. Mired in mud, Naddy lie still. "Harriet! I can't move my legs. There's no feeling. My eyes! Oh, please God. Give me another chance. I can't see," she shouted as the crowd of onlookers continued to grow.
"Have you seen Mother?" asked Harriet.

"No. Nothing! I can't see a thing."
"Here," moaned Clare. "Look about thirty feet away from the tracks, towards the school." Her mouth was bleeding. She was holding on to her bleeding left ear. "My fingers! Some, I think, are broken. My poor Voyance is right next to me. My poor Voyance. Breathe, Voyance, Breathe.

154

Train
Wreak

You listen to me. Now is not the time. You always listened to me. She began to cry as she hugged the lifeless body of her best friend.

"Mother!" exclaimed Harriet. "Do you see Quinn?"

"No. I don't see any doctors. Are you alright?"

"Don't worry about me. Where's Father?"

"I don't know," screamed Clare. "Oh, my poor Voyance."

"I see Quinn," yelled Naddy. "Over here."

"Naddy! My God! What a mess!" blared Quinn, as he and Remy

arrived on the scene. "Have you seen Harriet?"

"She's over in that yard. In the garden," pointed Naddy.

"Remy!" blurted Quinn. "Get Naddy over to the Wiggin's house. We'll make that the central point. If possible, we must get them all in one spot, out of the rain, and away from the public eye. A place where we can work in conjunction with each other, a place where we have water, electricity, clean beds, and fresh cleaning supplies. We should be getting four more doctors here any minute now. I'm going over to find Harriet."

"Quinn? Is that you?" weakly asked Harriet. "Come here."

"Harriet!" Quinn noted, as he knelt down beside her. "I'll try and get you out of this mess." He paused to catch his breath.

"This don't look good." "Here! Take my jacket," he continued, as he wrapped it around her.

"Oh, Quinn! Thank God you're here."

155

Train
Wreak

"Her right arm is mangled," noted Remy, who came over to help. "It's not just my arm, Quinn. My left ankle. I think it's broken." "Oh Harriet! We'll get you over to your house and operate. Remy! Get her in the wagon. Put her beside Naddy. She's pregnant, so be careful. Get her to her bed. The house should be open. I think Deborah is there. I don't think we're going to be able to do much with that arm. Make sure you give her some laudanum right away. I'll be over there as soon as I can."

She was placed on a stretcher and laid her down beside Naddy in the back of Remy's buckboard.

"Where's my father?" nervously asked Harriet. "I haven't seen my father."

"We'll find him," insisted Quinn. "Don't worry! We'll get him over to your house as soon as possible."

"You can't take my arm!" cried Harriet. "I won't allow it. It'll ruin my life. I'll never be able to play the piano again."

"I'll do my best. I'll take care of you," he replied as he held her hand until Remy took off.

"Quinn!" shouted Remy. "You know I can't do the operation, right?"

"Yes," shot back Quinn. "I'll do it as soon as I get done here."

Uncle Charlie came running up to the wagon. "I didn't see them," he ranted. "Until it was too late. I blew and blew and rung the bell, but it was too late. I slammed on the brakes, but I was too close. Too darn close! My God! I hope everyone comes out fine. This has never happened to me before in all my years. Oh Lord! Please make them all well."

"Did you see anyone up there?" queried Quinn.

156

Train
Wreak

"Yes. I found Stanley way up almost to the train station. I asked him how he got up there and he didn't know other than that he held onto the reins and tried to stop the team. He was looking for his shoes. Can you believe that? He lost his shoes. Doc Edison took him over to his house. He done lost four front teeth. When I found him he was on his knees and he had a metal bar sticking in his chest. He was looking for his shoes. Can you believe that? He lost his shoes. His whole body was in a shambles. His arms were bruised and numb. He was having difficulty breathing. Blood covered his face, coming from a large gash on his forehead. His clothes were barely hanging on."

"Good! Remy! Get the girls over there. I'll be there in a few minutes," noted Quinn as he watched the wagon depart.
Neighbors came rushing out of their houses and gardens as they heard the horrendous crunch, while their children went into hiding. Students and teachers poured out of the new school and ran over to the distraught and befuddled.

The wagon was in a hundred pieces, dispersed all along the track, as far down as the old depot, just like many of the ripped wooden boxes of things, scattered far and wide. And the rains provided an encore, drenching not only the poor souls of victimhood, but also the good Samaritans. Cold, damp, miserable rain, highlighted with indiscriminating flashes of light, pummeled down upon the scene on and around Summit Avenue. Misery was everywhere as panic displayed its ugly face. Despair and gloom, fright and sorrow covered all as the monumental task of search and rescue played out. Snippets of sensationalism spread like wildfire, with each opinion varied in scope and depth. Tragedy foretold, death predicted, rumors maligned, and confusion inundated the faces of many.

More doctors arrived. "What do you want me to do?" queried Dr. Jim Benson, the young, recently-arrived surgeon from New York. He was tall and heavy set, over 6'5" and 250 pounds. Today he was somber, nervous, and scared.

157

$\mathcal{T}rain$
Wreak

"Get over to the Wiggins house. That'll be our central command."
Bedlam was on full display at the Wiggin's house. Rooms were filling
where Deborah, trying her best not to fall prey to being overwhelmed
with grief, was in full command. Harriet and Naddy arrived and were
transferred to their respective bedrooms, as the dogs and cats went
into hiding while the streets were filled with redness and wanderers
and fragments of crushed boxes of things.

Sheriff Bartelson was standing at the main entrance, directing traffic,
while Uncle Charlie wandered at the scene, looking for Stanley's boots
and Naddy's glasses.

"SAVING HARRIET"

The Wiggins home was converted into a temporary hospital. Havoc was everywhere. Cots were set up on the main floor. One for Stanley, in the parlor, and one for Clare, in the conservatory. For Harriet, a mattress was brought down and placed on the kitchen table. Four kerosene lamps were positioned and lit. White bedsheets were fitted and finally, Harriet was placed on the table. Naddy was placed in a makeshift bed in the library. Guards were posted at the two entrances, while crowds gathered by the windows.

Six doctors had arrived and plans were being made on how to handle the casualties. Leading the charge was Quinn. With all that had happened in the past several months to his health and well-being, it was beyond a doubt a most noble offer of assistance. With Braden and Molly settled into their new environment, and both on the mend thanks to Quinn, it was now his time to display his knowledge and experience with the whole group of his in-laws. Challenges, with gut-wrenching decisions as part of the daily routine, would become an everyday occurrence for the next few months.

He stood in the entrance with the other doctors and watched as the injured were brought in, designating where each was to be placed. He walked over to the table where Harriet was lying. "Hello, Harriet. I am sorry to see you in such a state. As you probably noticed, there are six doctors that have volunteered their services. If you would rather have one of them take care of you just let me know, otherwise I will try my hardest to get you back up and running."

$\mathcal{S}$*aving*
Harriet

"*U*p and running?" shouted Harriet. "With a broken ankle and a worthless arm, among other things?"

"It could have been worse. From the ravages of the site on the tracks you should consider yourself lucky."

"Lucky?" she moaned. "I don't believe in being lucky. Everything I've accomplished is because of my willpower, my determination to get what I want, regardless of the situation. There may be six doctors here but you're the only one I trust."

Deborah came rushing into the room and headed straight for Harriet. "Oh Sis! You poor thing. Is there something I can do? I feel so guilty. I should have been the one on that wagon."
"Oh Deborah! Thank-you, but it was meant to be. How's everybody else?"

Quinn interrupted. "There is something you can do, Deborah. Get a pitcher of warm water and wash her up as best you can. See if you can get rid of all that blood. Be very careful when you're near any of the wounds. Her right arm is broken very bad and her left ankle is broken, so be gentle. Harriet. I'm going to make the rounds and see how everybody else is doing, and then I'll get all the doctors together and we'll figure out how we're going to go about changing all of you."

"Changing all of you?" queried Harriet.

"Getting all of you back to working order," replied Quinn as he headed over to the door leading to Stanley's cot. "I'll be back shortly. Deborah! Come over to the parlor when you get done here."
Stanley was lying in his bed, gazing out his window, showing signs of self-blame for what just happened. With tears in his eyes and a lump in his throat, he rubbed around his mouth, showing excruciating pain. "Stanley, my dear Stanley," noted Quinn as he entered the room and walked over next to his father-in-law. "After all I've been through these past few weeks and feeling so sorry for myself, I realize the pain and insecurity you must be dealing with in your mind right now.

160

$\mathcal{S}$*aving*
Harriet

I wish there was something I could say that would whisk away all the negativism that must be tearing your insides apart, but you must not blame yourself for the accident. That engine was going entirely too fast and old Charlie Rush will pay for his negligence when this is all said and done."

"How is everyone else?" moaned Stanley as he showed discomfort from breathing.
"At first glance it looks like everyone is going to make it, but it is too early to tell. All five of you have a list of problems to deal with and it will be up to me and my doctor associates to get you all back to normal. Although, that just might be impossible when it comes to Harriet. The only fatality so far is Clare's dog, Voyance. He didn't make it, but there is hope for everyone else. I haven't talked to your brother, Charlie, but I understand he's taking it very hard and we might have to pay close attention to his behavior."

Deborah came into the room with a fresh pail of water and a new rag. "Do the same for my father?"
"Yes, please. Be very careful, especially with his chest where that little piece of metal bar is sticking in there."

"Stanley! That gash on your forehead is going to have to be sewed shut. I'll have Eisen come in and do that. As far as your teeth go, I'll see who I can get to find you some false teeth. Let me take a look inside your mouth," he continued. "I see, uh-huh. All four of them are broke off at the gum level. I'll have Eisen give you some pain medicine to relieve the pain, but don't expect to have new choppers for some time. What else? Your right leg? Is it the knee? Let's take a look.

Quinn raised Stanley's pant leg. "Oh wow! That's gotta hurt. It looks like your knee cap is partially torn off."

"I tried to move it, but it is virtually impossible, without having such a horrendous discomfort."

161

Saving
Harriet

"I'll have Remy take a look. We'll probably have to operate on your chest, too. Stanley. That's going to be very touchy. Pretty close to the heart."

"You talking operations, Quinn? I trust you. I've heard too many stories about some of Remy's work, and another thing, what about my shoes?"

"I think someone is out there looking as we speak. Deborah, when you finish here. Come on over to your mother's room, the Conservatory," suggested Quinn as he headed out the door as the thunder clamored.

"Ah, my dear Mrs. Wiggins, and how are you doing?"
"What a stupid question!" yelled back Clare. "Can't you see? Take a good look! There's so many things wrong with me, you'll never be able to fix them all. If only Stanley would've listened to me. We wouldn't be in this situation, this catastrophe. I'll never be able to forgive him."
"Now, take it easy, Clare. Don't be so hard on him. It wasn't his fault. Charlie Rush even admitted that he was going too fast. Don't say it's Stanley's fault."

"Voyance! Voyance! Where's he?"
"He didn't make it, Clare. Too big of an impact. Spat took him behind your house, by the garden. Now, let's take a look at you?"

"What about the others?"
"Oh, a few minor scrapes and bruises. Harriet has some major problems, but don't you worry. We'll get them all taken care of. Now, let's talk about you. Let me see your hands."

Quinn looked closely at each hand. Her left hand's two end fingers were swollen and red, as were the two outside fingers on her right hand.

"My God! How did that ever happen?"
"I tried to cover my face when I was flying. Oh, everything happened

Saving
Harriet

so fast! I landed face first and my hands bore the brunt of the collision and it was those four fingers that really took a hit."

"I see you have a problem with your right eye. It looks like there is something inside. Can you feel it?"

"Yes, and it's a constant pain. I need to blink on and off to keep it from getting dry. It's like a little pebble of some kind."

"Your arms have a high amount of dirt and debri in them. I'll have Deborah wash them down and I'll be back later today to take out any pieces that are still in them. Anything else?"

"Yes. My left ear. It's been bleeding, on and off. It doesn't affect my hearing, but it is really a nuisance."

"Oh, I think we'll be able to fix that. Listen Clare. After I stop to see Naddy, in the library, I and three other doctors are going to operate on Harriet. I'm almost positive that I am going to amputate her right arm. She also has a broken foot and we're going to set that. After that we'll stop and see you. So, for now, I suggest you find some sleep and we'll be back as soon as we can," noted Quinn as he departed, and the thunder clamored and the lightning zapped.

Quinn went into Naddy's room. She was sitting up in bed, unable to move any part of her lower body. "I understand your legs are giving you a problem, Naddy. Where does it start? At the hips, knees, upper chest?"

"From, from the hips down."

Quinn pulled back the blanket. "Tell me if you feel anything," he requested as he tickled her feet.

"No, Quinn. Nothing."

He moved his hand up her left leg and down her right. "Still nothing?"

163

$\mathcal{S}aving$
Harriet

"Nothing," she replied as she burst into tears. "My glasses! Where are my glasses?"

"I don't know. I'll have someone go back to the site and see if they are still laying there."

Quinn stood back and rubbed his chin as he took out his toothpick. "I'll stop back after I take care of Harriet. I'm sure you heard what happened to her. Deborah will stop by and clean you up. Mention to her about your glasses. Perhaps, she can find them. I'm going to be meeting a group of doctors in a few minutes and we will be preparing an operation on Harriet. It might be a good idea if you could say a few prayers for a successful operation. Actually, it might not be a bad idea to say a few prayers for everyone in your family. These next few days, or weeks, are going to create a lot of anxiety and turmoil."
"Have you talked to Harriet?"

"Yes, of course. She's still my wife. I do care for her. I do want her to have a musical career. I'll try and do my best to see to it that we succeed."

"But if she doesn't have a right arm, how can she play the piano?"

"There's nothing wrong with her left arm."

"But she'd have to completely relearn how to play."

"She wouldn't have much choice in the matter. I've heard of one-armed piano players. They even make music sheets for left-handed pianists, so it's not something that is totally unheard of."

"I may not have always gotten along with her during our careers. I know that of the three, I am the poorest, and I always knew that she was by far the best, not only with the piano but also her voice. I feel so sorry for what she must be thinking right now. She's the one that has made the Wiggin's Trio what they are. This could mean the end of her career, and Deborah's, and mine. Oh my God! Yes, even mine."

164

Saving
Harriet

"I'll keep you informed. I'm not sure how long this operation will be but I will stop up and let you know how it goes. If you're sleeping, should I wait till tomorrow?"

"Sleeping? How am I going to be sleeping?"
"We'll figure something out," answered Quinn as he departed, and the thunder clamored and the lightning zapped, and the rain came down.

"Good day, Harriet," greeted Quinn as he walked up beside her. "Are we ready?" he asked as he checked around the upper right arm, feeling the skin area where he would be placing the incision. "Is this area sore, or sensitive to you right now?"

"No."
"I'm going to try and accomplish two things today, Harriet. I want to set your ankle and I will be doing an amputation of your right arm. We are going to be doing both at the same time. While I'm working on the arm, Dr. Bedford will be setting your ankle. You will be given plenty of ether, plus a dose of laudanum. It shouldn't affect the baby, hopefully. Dr. Eisen will be in charge of that. Remy will be assisting me in the operation."

"This will be the area I cut," he pointed out. "When I go in I will be cleaning out any bone spurs I find. I will be removing any damaged tissue I find. I will then smooth the uneven stud. I will seal off any blood vessels and nerves that may have been severed, or damaged.

I will cut and shape muscles in the area so that you'll be able to get an artificial limb later on. Once I'm sure you are clean in there I will close you back up. Then, we'll just have to wait for you to heal up and prep you for a new arm. Hopefully, when you wake up we'll all be done with the operation. Any questions?"

"How long will it take?"
"That'll all depend on what we find in there. Shouldn't be more than an hour. You just relax here as best you can for now. Dr. Eisen! Go ahead and administer what she needs and then come over next door to the extra bedroom.

165

Saving
Harriet

We're meeting there," he commanded as he left, and the thunder roared and the lightning struck and the rains came down in sheets. Quinn headed next door to Deborah's room, where the other doctors had already gathered. Plans were devised and responsibilities accepted. The medical staff of Quinn Shanahan, Will Eisen, Remington Oglesby, William Bedford, Jim Benson, and Walter Edison, were assembled and were making progress in the planned attack upon the horrendous damages thrust upon one family in the growing town of Fergus Falls, as the thunder mounted, and the lightning flashed, and the buckets came down, to try to wipe away the remnants of the incident on Summit Avenue.

Into the house came Charlie Rush, soaked to the gill. "I found 'em. I found 'em," he shouted as he lifted up Stanley's shoes to anyone that was looking. "Now, he doesn't have to go barefooted," he continued as he bounced around the entrance.

Dr. Edison came down, took the shoes, set them on the floor, and took Charlie's arm. "That's good, Charlie. You did good. Now, how about you?"
"How about me? What are you talking about?"
"Come with me. I'd like to check you over."

"But, I have to get back to work. Need to take several cars over to Barnesville."

"That can wait. Let's find an empty room. I'd like to ask you a few questions. You can tell me your version of the story."

"But, Doc. I ain't got no time. I don't want to lose my job. I got too much work to do," he objected as he was led up the stairs.

Meanwhile, the entourage headed to work. Basins of warm water were brought in, along with soap and towels. The scrubbing down began. Anyone who would be participating in the operation needed to be as germ free as possible. Rubber gloves and a hand towel were distributed to each.

166

Saving Harriet

Quinn brought his medical bag out and placed it next to the stand. He set out the necessary medical supplies on the table. As he put each item down he would pause and temporarily stare at it. Another wooden stand was placed next to the bed and was covered with a hacksaw, a Bowie knife, a jar of ether, several bottles of pills, various sizes of scalpels, and needles, white vinegar, garlic, ground ginger, needle and thread, and gauze. A large metal pail was situated under the table, along with a pile of white towels. "There! That should be all we need," stated Quinn as he viewed the setup. "Remy! Can you think of anything that we're missing?"

"You're asking the wrong person."

"Take this knife and heat it up in the fireplace."

"Alright Harriet. I realize that you are totally against this procedure, but it is the only chance we have. If we don't, you'll end up dying from poisoning. If we operate now we'll keep you on this Earth a while longer. First, you will be given a glass of liquid medicine. This liquid will consist of ten per cent tincture of opium and ninety per cent whiskey, with a cinnamon flavor. This mixture will ease your pain. Dr. Oglesby will administer some pleasant smelling medicine by way of a rag. It is called ether. This medicine will send you off into unconsciousness. When you awake we should have successfully completed the task at hand. I will have Dr. Eisen assisting me at my left side and Dr. Oglesby on the other. We will make sure nothing happens to you."

"It looks like I have no choice, so do what you have to, Quinn. I trust you and don't forget about the baby," continued Harriet as she accepted the glass of medicine and drank it. Almost immediately the drug took effect.

Remy placed the cloth over her nose and mouth. She put up a major struggle, but the laudanum won out. Hence, began the difficult process. Her screams were silenced, but the ears of Stanley and Clare were still ringing, and then silence took over, as the group of doctors went to work.

167

Saving
Harriet

"Dr. Bedford! Are you ready?" asked Quinn.

"Ready."

"It's time."

Dr. Bedford proceeded to place a bucket of plaster of Paris, a pail of warm water and a roll of cloth right next to Harriet's left ankle. He carefully examined the swollen ankle, adjusting the position of the foot. He placed a pillow under her lower leg with the objective being for the foot to be raised an inch, or so, off the mattress. He felt where the break was and marked it with a red crayon. He took the end of the cloth roll and cut off a two foot piece. He placed that piece into the pail of water, and then into the bucket of plaster of Paris. Slowly, he unraveled the strip, making sure that it was completely covered with the white solution, and proceeded to wrap the foot in an overlapping and criss-crossing the heal and the bottom of the foot. He repeated the process of cutting, dipping, spreading and wrapping, while the other doctors began their tasks at hand.

Taking a small scalpel, Quinn cut through the skin, an inch above the breaks in her right arm. "We cut it above so as to make it easier for the skin to heal, away from the wound. Most of the time we cut muscle. We need to make sure that the cut is in the best possible location to allow the muscle to continue its job of protecting the area around the bone after surgery. Once we move the muscle to the side, we need to cut the nerve higher up from the amputation point and cauterize or sew the nerve endings within the surrounding tissue. This will help control unwanted regeneration of the nerve endings into a disorganized mess, like this," he showed. "We must make sure we keep them away from the large blood vessels. We then go about tying the large vessels off firmly to control the blood flow. Blood flow is very critical to keep the tissue healthy. Remy! Give me the knife, and go heat up the hack saw."

Time was of the essence. Quinn took the knife and cauterized the ends of the above blood vessels, slowly and meticulously, one by one, in two second bursts. Making sure that the area was clear of any infected material, as the clock slowly ticked away. Quinn took the hack saw, from the returning Remy, and meticulously proceeded to cut away at the bone, paying close attention to not disturb any of the surrounding tissue.

Saving
Harriet

Remy continued to wipe Quinn's forehead on and off during the time-consuming operation. Quinn then discarded the amputated part into the bucket under the table. He rushed to smooth any uneven area of the remaining arm bone and cleanse the infected area, pouring white vinegar on it, and wiping that off, and pouring garlic on it. After arranging the muscles properly and adjusting the location of the remaining blood vessels, he stitched together the skin flaps with a heated needle and thread, thus closing the wound. While this was going on, Dr. Bedford was finishing up on his ankle cast. Crutches were placed next to her bed and mess with the plaster was all cleaned up.

As the four doctors backed away from the operating table, Quinn continued, "We'll have to keep a close eye on this case for the next several weeks and tonight we'll need to check every hour for any sign of infection. We're also going to have to do something with that gash. That could be a real challenge. It's been a long and tedious day and I'm sure you are ready to take some time to relax, but I need each of us to take a four hour shift and monitor each of our patients, from five today to nine tomorrow morning. At that time we will decide who needs operations etc."

"I'll take the first shift," offered Remy.
"I'll follow you," offered Quinn.
"I'll take the one to four shift," volunteered Eisen.
"I guess that leaves me with five to nine shift," acknowledged Bedford.
"Good. Maybe by then we'll have it all figured out," continued Quinn. "I'd like to head back home and spend some time getting reacquainted with my brother.

With agreement reached on the watches the tired warriors went about getting cleaned up and heading out. In the hallway Quinn took Remy aside. "Remy! I think we're doing something wrong. We got ourselves in a situation here, away from the big city, and most of our clientele have empty pockets.

Saving Harriet

We're expected to cure them of their typhoid, and smallpox, diphtheria, and syphilis, and not succeed and not get paid. Then this happens. The Wiggins family may be rich and famous but we can't ruin them financially. It'll get to the point where no one could afford us."

"That's an easy one to figure out," chimed in Remy. "The railroad. We'll just inflate the bill and have Stanley file a lawsuit against the railroad, for negligence."

"Negligence on Charlie? I'm afraid he's going to not only lose his job but possibly his sanity. I don't want to be in his shoes right now.

Anyway, as I was saying, our stiffest competition is the druggist. Where we have a chance to make a living by selling medicine at retail, but we're left out of that market. The ladder for obtaining health starts with a family member, then a neighbor, then a storekeeper, then finally, us. We go to the farm to save them from disease and end up being asked to save the cow, or the pig. We write out the bills, but most of them go unpaid. We have more than our share of diseases we don't know much about. And even if we know what the disease is we probably don't have a correct procedure to cure it."

"Our profession is still in its infancy. We still have so much more to learn. We were successful with Harriet's amputation, so far, but that included a lot of luck. We have five doctors in this town right now. Five doctors and not one single hospital. Why, Remy? Why do we still do this?" "I wish I could answer that, Quinn. Perhaps, it was meant to be."

"Is it our fault trying to be helpful to society? Isn't that the way it's always been? There always seems to be people who blame us for our failures, while they sit in their almighty mansions in the sky and take credit for our successes. I sometimes think I would be so much better off if I'd just up and leave. Go someplace where I'd be appreciated for at least trying. It looks like we were successful with Harriet, but Naddy is another story. I'm going to need your help with that one. I'm not sure what it is. It looks like maybe it's her spine. She can't move her legs. We got problems with Stanley and Clare that we need to figure out too.

Saving Harriet

When you make your rounds tonight, see if you come up with any suggestions for tomorrow. I'm afraid I'm not going to get much sleep tonight. I think I'll head home for a break. Be sure to put fresh dressing on that stump. And don't forget to wrap it all up with a silk stocking. We don't need an infection. I'll be back later to take your place."

Several hours later.

Harriet awoke to the flickering of a candle, providing very little light to her room. She was in perilous territory. Lying in her makeshift operating bed, she wondered what the future held. Depression was already showing its ugly face each time she looked at her right arm, her little nub that would prevent her from ever performing again. And that darn cast on her foot! And the thought of never swimming again. And what about that ugly gash on her face? They'll never be able to hide that. My life will never be the same, she thought. What's the use? I have no purpose. No reason to continue. I'll never be able to survive!

She rubbed her stomach. She grabbed her side with her left hand, trying desperately to soothe the sharp pains. Signs of morning sickness were evident. Headaches were almost continuous, as she rubbed her forehead. She tried itching her right backside, but was unable to stretch her left arm far enough. Then she noticed her legs. `Her left one was bloating and her right foot itched, but the plaster cast blocked any attempt from her to eradicate the nuisance. "What a mess!" she moaned. "Such poor timing!"

Remy stopped by to scope out the situation and was somewhat surprised to see Harriet awake. "I hope I didn't wake you, Harriet." "Oh no," murmured Harriet. "I was just feeling sorry for myself." "Let me take your temperature and your vital signs," suggested Remy as he went about doing his medical tasks. "Your husband was at his finest today on the operating table. He is very good and precise and hard to keep up with. Ever since we've been together as partners I've noticed that he is always one or two steps ahead of the game.

Saving Harriet

I wanted to be like him. Actually, I entertained the idea that I wanted to be better than him, but after watching him perform today, my mind is changing. He is too good for a small town like Fergus Falls. He needs to be in Minneapolis, at the big hospital down on University. Well, your temperature is fine, and your vitals tell me that you're alive, so let's take a look at that bandage. It looks like I'm going to need to change it. Are you having much pain in the arm?"

"No, but I have plenty of pain in my head, just thinking about what's left of my right arm."

"That's perfectly understandable, my dear. That should subside as time goes by. You must remember that your body went through one horrendous change today, a change that will affect the rest of your life. It will be hard for you to come to grips with for a while but I know you. You have the spunk, the willpower to overcome anything that gets in your way. I only wish that Lin would have half the determination you have. My life at home would be much better. She stopped by out front earlier this evening and wanted to see you, but Sullivan told her to come back tomorrow, that it probably wouldn't be as hectic."

Remy took off the bandage and put the candle up close to the wound. "It looks fine from what I can tell. No discoloration. That's good," he carefully replaced the old bandage, and put the silk stocking back on. "I'll get out of your hair. I need to check up on the others. I'll see you again in the morning."

Quinn stopped at a bench on the way home. He seemed to be lost in another world. He'd daydream about his situation, his predicament, about Harriet's conundrum. The divorce papers were still not signed. She seemed so understanding, so friendly. Maybe there is a chance. I need to change that bitter taste in my mouth. I so want to get back to a normal life with her. Normal? What's that? I really can't remember what normal is. So many things don't make sense. Maybe there will never be another 'normal' day in my life. With the return of my brother and his 'friend' living with us, it seems a whole new world for me could be in the making. Is that possible? Perhaps, for yes, I still love her. Oh, life can be so confusing!

172

Saving
Harriet

Quinn made his way back home where he was greeted at the door by Molly. Ah yes. Molly. Who really is this mysterious Molly? With the tangled hair, and the drooping eyelashes, and those evasive, yet captivating eyes. But that is all I know about her, other than that she has been secretly taking care of Braden for the past months, and, as far as I don't know, who she was working for. She does seem to be taking good care of him. I just wonder if there is more than meets the eye. No one else, besides Mara, and maybe Remy, know that Braden is back, safe and sound. Or is he?

"Hello, Mr. Shanahan," offered Molly. "I've been anxious to hear from you on how everything is after that accident."

"Hello, Molly. Well, I think they'll all make it. There's a few questionable situations that are going to be dealt with tomorrow. Then we'll see. My wife seems to have borne the brunt of it, both physically and mentally. Where's Braden?"

"He's been sitting by the window all day, waiting for you to come home. He would stare over at that patch of daffodils, and holler 'dilodaffs, dilodaffs', and then would repeat that poem. I can't believe he knows that by heart."

"Ah yes, those dilodaffs. That's my Braden."

"Tell me, Molly. Tell me about yourself. Where did you come from? How long have you been in Fergus Falls? Who did you work for? Do you have any other family out here? There are so many unknowns when it comes to you. We're taking a gamble by both of you staying in my house. Please forgive me if you think I don't trust you but, but my main responsibility right now is my brother. I know he's 19, but that doesn't mean he's that mature. You mentioned a 'Lester' a while back. What can you tell me about him?"

"That's a lot of questions, sir," laughed Molly as she picked in her nose. "I'll try and answer them. My parents both died several years ago, from smallpox. I have two older brothers and one younger sister. The last time I saw them was right after the funeral, out in Chicago.

173

Saving
Harriet

I was approached by a young man that offered me a job as a housekeeper and caretaker for a well-to-do couple and their two year old daughter. He caught me in a very vulnerable state. Then he told me that it was going to be in a little town in west-central Minnesota, in Fergus Falls. Well, I barely left the house in Chicago, and when I did it was only to certain places in the neighborhood. The sound of Minnesota was both scary and intriguing. My siblings really didn't want to have anything to do with me, so it was up to me. I thought why not, so two months later there I was in the middle of a snowstorm out in the middle of nowhere. And it went downhill from then on. I never met the owner, nor his wife or child. Just Lester."

"Where did you live when you first got here?"
"We came in on the Manitoba line late during the night, within walking distance of the depot, but I couldn't tell you to which direction we went. It was a nice house, but I was never allowed out of the house, unless I was with Lester. They treated me well, for the most part. Except for that one young man who tried to take advantage of me, but Lester took care of him. Haven't seen him since."

"What do you want to do with your life?"
"I wish there was some way to have a choice, but I'll accept whatever happens. You'll find that I can be a very loyal person to someone I am fond of and that treats me like a lady. Like your brother."
"You do know that Braden has issues?"

"The first day that I met him I thought that there would be no way I could handle taking care of him for one minute, but the more time I spent with him, the more I realized that he is something special. Yes, he has some speech problems but he has made some big changes ever since I've been with him. Remember I told you about how he tried to block that rat hole so he wouldn't have to share his meal with him, and that he ripped pieces of material apart, tied them together, and was able to freeze the material. I'm sure it would have worked had I not caught him and showed him how to plug the hole much easier. He is smarter than most people think."

Saving Harriet

"Do you have any suggestions on what we should do in order for you two not to be found here? If your old boss finds out, how long do you think it will be before he's over here and takes care of you two?"

"Are you saying we need to leave?" asked the worried Molly.
"Only until we can take care of whoever your boss was. I am suggesting a 'Strategy of Subterfuge'. By that I mean deceiving them. We'll change you two so that you will become very unrecognizable. I'd like to see you get a haircut. Make it very short and black. We'll get you a new wardrobe---more debonair, more aristocratic. We'll find you some glasses. We'll have Braden grow a beard. I'll have Rufus fix him up with a new hair style and mustache. Get him some glasses. Teach him a new tune. Dress him up like a farm boy. We'll get you two to the point where I'll even have trouble recognizing you. At the same time, we'll move you to that little house over by the Mt. Faith cemetery. What do you think?"

"Wouldn't it be a lot easier if we just left town. Maybe move to Minneapolis?"

"No. That would be too much responsibility for you. Braden wouldn't go for it. And it would be awful hard on me, too."

"Quinn! Is that you?" came the yelling from the back room.

"Yes, Braden. I'm home only for a couple of hours."

Braden rushed out and ran straight for Quinn and gave him a hug. "You stay home now. You've been gone long enough. You stay with Molly and me and play games?"

"Oh, I wish I could. I'd like to take a short nap and then I have to go back."

$\mathcal{S}aving$
Harriet

It was very dark in the Wiggins house, with candles lit in a few choice spots in the hallways for the convenience of the doctors. Rooms with occupants were completely without light. Unfortunately. Harriet was beginning to wake up. She looked around the room. "Anybody out there?" she weakly asked.

Remy came in with candle and turned on one of the kerosene lanterns. "Mrs. Shanahan?"

Harriet glanced over at her right arm, or what was left of her right arm. Just a stud, a nubbins, a stump, and bloody bandages. She looked down at her ankle. It was leaking. "My God! What am I going to do? I'm missing so much!"

"Oh, toughen up! You're a Wiggins. At least you can walk. You can handle it. We'll get you back sitting on a piano stool. First thing we have to do is take care of your baby."

"I can walk? Can't you see this cast? I'll have to use crutches and how in the world can I use crutches with only one arm? And why would I need a piano stool? Look at this arm. Something is missing. My whole arm! My piano days are over. My career is over. My marriage is over. What else can go wrong?"

"You're just looking for sympathy. Quit feeling sorry for yourself. At least you are still alive. I can't say that for your mother's Voyance. Your folks have a lot of problems that we need to work on tomorrow. Naddy is possibly going to be unable to move her lower body. At least you have two legs. You can drag that cast to wherever you want to go. And you have a left arm. All you have to do is learn how to play left-handed."

Harriet turned away and began to pout.
"I know I may be sounding hard on you," continued Remy. "I'm not really that rough.

Saving Harriet

I know you have the gumption to succeed, even if that means relearning how to play. Your mother missed out in the chance to be a concert pianist. Naddy will probably miss out. There's just you and Deborah. Don't you see? You have to fight for everything. For everything you want in life. Nothing is free."

"Oh Remy! I know that nothing is free, but I'm trying to face reality. Reality is that if God would have wanted me to continue playing, he would have made sure that nothing would happen to my arm. There has to be a reason why we were in that accident. I realize that I'm not the only fish in the water. I know they all have injuries to put up with. I get that and I feel their pain, too. I keep asking Him why this happened and I'm not getting any answers."

"Quinn will be here any moment now. He's been figuring out how we're going to deal with tomorrow. I'm sure he'll be stopping in to check up on you as soon as he arrives. For now, I suggest that you go back to sleep."

"Sleep is about the last thing I can think about right now. I seem to have pain everywhere. Could you please give me a little dose of laudanum? Then, maybe I could fall back to sleep?"

Remy looked at his pocket watch. "It's a little early. We have to remember that you are with child. Ask Quinn when he gets here. I'm not sure it would do you much good right now."

In walked Quinn. "Time to relieve you, Remy. You can go home and get some sleep. Going to be a long day tomorrow."

"Her vitals sound alright, Quinn. No problem with the baby. She asked for some opium, but I didn't give her any. Told her to talk to you."

177

Saving
Harriet

Quinn began checking her over. "We're going to set you up on an aggressive rehab program. It'll be up to you to follow through on what we propose. I cannot stress enough how important this will be for you to get back into shape. Gradually, we'll get you to increase your commitment to good health. We want you to be able to strengthen those muscles of yours, whether it be in your arm, or in your legs. As time goes by we hope to be able to transform your self-esteem into a positive reality."

"You are asking for the impossible," shot back Harriet as she turned away from Quinn.

"I would think you would take this challenge and run with it."

"I don't believe you," continued Harriet. "How can you expect me to be so positive? You could just as well have cut off my head. I'm useless. I'm a freak. People will pay money to come see me at the circus. Oh look! They'll say. Look at that one-armed monster! The one-armed geek of the midway, the one with the ugly face. How will I be able to teach? To show my students how to play the piano? How will I be able to go out in public?"

"Slow down, Harriet. That was one of the characteristics I really loved about you. You've always adapted to what was put on your plate. I won't expect anything different this time," continued Quinn as he headed for the door. "I'll see you in the morning."

Deborah was sitting on a bench in front of the Wiggins hospital. All had quieted down from the Day of Hell, except for the minor groans, from the patients inside. She was thankful and yet guilty. She was rubbing t wo match sticks together, as she tried to make sense of the days' activities. Her feelings were numb.

$\mathcal{S}aving$
Harriet

She felt relieved that she wasn't one of those lying in the makeshift hospital, yet guilt was choking her very essence. Her spark was missing. In the doldrums of frustration, her fiery disposition was replaced by an uncommon grief, unable to come to grips with reality.

After giving off a deep sigh, she headed off into the nearby woods, adjoining Lake Alice. She sat down next to a pile of oak leaves. She stared and wondered, and stared some more at the dead and wilted leaves that once had provided such beauty.

This has to be a test, she thought. Why would He test me, of all people? There was nothing I could do. No matter what I could have done differently, the accident would still have happened. Now that they won't be able to play piano, maybe it's my time to shine. I'm good! Just as good as, if not better than, Naddy. If I'd ever get the chance, I could be just as good as Harriet. Oh! Who am I kidding? Mother would never let that happen. My father would stick up for me, but we know who has the control in this family. She always kept me at the bottom. When it came to the three of us girls I was always at the end of the line. Yes, always at the end. She lit the matches, watched them for a moment, and then threw them on the pile of leaves, and headed into the house.

Charlie followed behind with a pair of muddy boots. "I found 'em! I found 'em! Took me a long time but I found 'em," he proudly yelled as he handed the prize to Deborah. "I couldn't believe where they were. Darn near down by the freight rooms."

"Oh, I'm sure my father will be happy," noted Deborah as she slowly set the shoes next to the entrance.

"How, how is everyone?" nervously asked Charlie.

"They are alive. How about you?"

Saving
Harriet

"Not so good. I think I'll need to get a bottle to put me to sleep. I talked to my foreman and he has put me on leave without pay. I tell you I can't get that sight out of my mind, of that wagon setting right on the tracks when I came around that bend. I'll never forgive myself. I don't know what I'm going to do. I have a wife and four children. How am I going to provide for them?"

"Have you talked to anyone about this?"

"No. I don't know what to do. I've been thinking that maybe it would be best if I ended it all."

"Oh, my God. Don't do that! Think of your wife and children."

"I have. I have."

Next morning.

Quinn and Remy were standing over Naddy's bed. She was lying on her back and staring up at the ceiling. "There has to be something you can do," she begged. "I don't know how long I'll be able to put up with this. I feel so helpless."

"I know how you're feeling," consoled Quinn. "The spinal cord is a touchy piece of equipment. There is so much we don't know, or understand. It would be very easy to flip a switch and everything would be fine but the spine doesn't have a switch. As of yet we consider it a DO NOT TOUCH injury, and all we can do is hope for the best."

"You make it sound so disheartening, so hopeless. I should just lie here and accept what you say without putting up a fight?"

"Naddy, Dear Naddy. It is too early to tell. Give it a couple of days. If you don't see any movement, or feeling, in your lower parts within the next week, or so, then we can assume that you have permanent damage and will never be able to use your legs again.

Saving
Harriet

I suggest that you do a whole bunch of praying. Believe me, Remy and I would love nothing better than to be able to fix you up, but I'm afraid our hands are tied on this one. Your mother has placed a small bell here. Whenever you need something just ring it. Deborah will come at your beck and call, and remember, pray."

"Deborah? Where is she? I haven't seen her."

"She was out front. She feels very badly. She says it's hard for her to look at you and Harriet, eye to eye. That for some reason she should be the one with the problems. If you remember, it was Deborah that your father wanted to go with them to Northfield, rather than you and Harriet. I'll send her in when I see her."

"STRATEGY OF SUBTERFUGE"

The hands of Dr. Shanahan were kept busy tending and mending --- tending to his customers' needs and mending his past discrepancies. The roads to recovery for the Wiggins family, and others from Fergus Falls, were long and treacherous. Advancements were followed by setbacks, successes by failures, wishful thoughts were hampered with unexpected reversals.

The main recipient of Quinn's time was Harriet, both on and off the clock. His days were spent watching her right nub, unsure of what to expect. Hours were consumed paying close attention to her temporary companion.

Quinn and Remy were in Stanley's room, all prepped and ready to take on the task of ridding him of his extra weight that was lodged in his left mid-section. "Stanley! Stanley! Sorry it took so long to get to your little predicament here but Remy and I have been putting in a little extra time in the next room. I can't ever remember having a day like yesterday in all my years as a doctor, but I was able to get a few hours of sleep last night so I should be good for a few more hours."

"Remy will be giving you a little medicine to rid yourself of any pain that we may cause when we try to extricate. I see that the discoloration has remained the same. That's good. That means infection hasn't set in. As soon as the drug takes effect, we'll start. Till then, just relax. I realize those words are really meaningless, under the circumstance. I see that Charlie found your shoes."

Strategy of
Subterfuge

"Ah yes," weakly replied Stanley. "Deborah stopped in and woke me up. Then, Charlie stopped in. He doesn't make much sense. I think the accident has affected his head. I'd suggest you check him out. He scared me. Very confused. Something isn't right."

"Yeah, he's taking it really hard."
As Quinn was taking Stanley's pulse, he could see that Stanley was falling to sleep and it was time to go to work. From what he could tell, the 1"x3" piece of gold metal had been a piece of the Wiggins wagon axle. How it ended up in Stanley's side was impossible to know. "Have you ever seen such a thing?" gasped Quinn, as he pulled and pulled.

"Here. Let me try," suggested Remy, as he took over with the operation.

"This is very strange," continued Quinn. "He's not bleeding."

"It's coming," interrupted Remy. "Slow, but sure. It's leaking now. Be ready to stitch her up.

"That's luck on his part. I was afraid we'd have a lot of problems," continued Quinn. "The next operation is the one I'm afraid could cause irreparable damage. That knee cap! I have a feeling that it got crushed pretty bad. He's going to start coming to any moment now, so you better give him some more. Not sure how long it will take, but make sure you give him enough to last. I'll finish up here. You go start on the knee."

Remy pulled Stanley's long johns off and placed a pillow, with towels, under his right leg. "Oh my! What a mess you have here, Stanley."
"Careful, Doc. It hurts really bad."

Strategy of
Subterfuge

"You had an overabundance of swelling, but it's coming down real nicely," Remy noted as he gave Stanley another dose. "The knee cap is a small, inverted, triangle-shaped bone that sits at the front of the knee joint. It protects the knee and connects muscles in front of the thigh to shin bone. It sets inside the bottom of the quad muscle. It slides up and down in this groove to prevent it from moving sideways. This accident doesn't happen that often. About one per cent of all bone injuries are caused by direct blows to the patella and that's what this looks like."

"We'll cut in here," continued Remy, as he placed his heated knife in the designated spot. He looked over at Stanley.

"Anything I can do to help?" inquired Quinn.

"Yes. You can take over. This looks too complicated."

"Get the Tension Band wiring. I'll need that," ordered Quinn as he meticulously put the broken pieces of the knee cap back together. Such a time-consuming and pain-staking procedure! He then would place screws and pins in the appropriate places and wrapped wiring all around.

"Remy! Make up a batch for the brace. It looks like we can't do anymore for him in here."

As the cast was being set, Quinn continued. "You might as well get used to this for six to eight weeks, Stanley. We'll start you on an exercise regimen in a couple of days. We must get that swelling down. You are not to put any weight on the leg until the fracture heals. You will receive a pair of crutches as your companion. They will be part of your walking experience for at least the next two months. We'll have someone come over once a week to check up on you. Remy, or I, will stop also. After surgery you normally wear a brace to hold the knee in extension, but you can remove it to do exercises."

Strategy of
Subterfuge

"A combination of knee exercises and general strengthening exercises help reduce the pain, improve function and reduce the chance for future problems. I cannot emphasize exercising enough."

"Doc! Doc!" interrupted Chief Sullivan as he came running into the house. "Don't know if you heard, or not, but Charlie Rush committed suicide last night. He couldn't handle the guilt. Too much pressure for him."

"No! Not Charlie!" noted Stanley.

"I was a little worried about him last night. Guess I should have followed my hunch. And his family?"

"They seem to be taking it as well as can be expected."
"Remy! Can you finish up here? Make up a batch for the brace. It looks like we can't do anymore for him in here."

As the cast was being set, Quinn continued. "You might as well get used to this for six to eight weeks." I need to get home. Also, could you check up on Harriet? Make sure she is comfortable. I got a meeting with Braden and Molly."

"Braden and Molly? What for?"

"Going to get them moved to a safer place."

"Sure. I can take care of that. Don't worry."

"Let me know when the funeral will be," continued Quinn as he took off his whites.

Quinn pulled up in front of his house and went in to pick up Braden and Molly. "Are we ready?"

Strategy of
Subterfuge

There was no answer. No one to be found. No fireplace burning. No lamps lit. "That's not like them. They knew we were going out there when I got back. What could have happened? "Braden! Molly! Come on. Let's go! Rufus will be waiting. Still no answer. Quinn lit a lantern and sat down by the table, all the while playing with his toothpick.

His imagination was going full force. What if they found out that the two were here? What if they kidnapped them again? No. Nobody knew what was going on. Nobody knew they were being moved to a different hideout. Only temporary. Just until I find out who was behind this episode. No one else knew what was going on. Except. Yes. Except Remy. He knew they were here, but he was with me. Maybe it was that Lester. Oh, I really don't need this. It's been a hectic day the way it is. I don't need more problems.

Then the door opened. In came Braden and Molly, both laughing and having a good old time.

"Are you ready?" asked the disgusted Quinn.

"Oh, we forgot. Sorry Quinn."

"Let's go! The horses have been waiting," commanded Quinn as he led them out.

The Strategy of Subterfuge was underway. Roaring off into an entirely different world for Braden and Molly. The sham was put into high gear. Chicanery at its finest! A ruse of magnificent proportions. A scheme of the century began to unfold.

Both were willing participants and both were willing to attempt at outdoing the other when it came to change. The goal was to be able to fool everyone by making changes to their bodies, to their lifestyles, to their wardrobes, and to their daily activities.

186

Strategy of
Subterfuge

Everything was to be a secret. Everything was to be kept as a secret until Quinn could find out who the culprits really were that attacked them on that cool, snowy evening on the dark streets of Fergus Falls.

Their bags were packed and Braden brought them out from the bedroom. Two for him and two for Molly. New wardrobes. New outfits, never before worn. Braden had already started to grow a full beard and mustache. It was a bit uncomely but it was falling into place and Rufus would be able to fix it up. Molly's tangled web was also on the agenda for change.

They were to be a newly-married couple, fresh from Illinois. Ready and willing to put their minds and their hands to work on an recently -acquired 80 acre farm of nothing but woods and rocks and the Red running right through it. A relatively, newly-built house with two stories but very little room for movement. Only lived in for one season. It was so bad that it chased the previous owners off to California wine country. Yes, the farm was no thousand acre spread but it was outside the city limits, hidden from view from the gravel trail that led to Fish Lake, and right near Mt. Faith cemetery, in an area where nobody wanted to go after dark. This set-up would buy Quinn some time to figure out who was responsible and it would give the two young charlatans a chance to know each other better, maybe.

Quinn pulled the wagon in behind Rufus P. Jones Barber shop and the threesome entered the small, dimly-lit, dingy, smoke-filled, one chair barber shop, where the middle-aged Rufus was calmly sitting, puffing away on his crooked pipe and reading the latest Fergus Falls Journal. "Ah, good evening folks. I've been expecting you. Which one do I get to work on first?"

Strategy of Subterfuge

"Do Molly!" insisted Quinn. "See if you can get that long, straggly, acorn-colored hair changed into a real short, black hair. You might have to spend a lot of extra time with some soap and water and some shampoo, and if you got some real nice smelling toilet water. I know you can do it, my friend."

"Alright, Miss Molly. Have yourself sit down on the throne here and we'll get to work. I'm not so sure that we'v e ever met. I've heard a little about you, but have never seen ya. You look like you could be a handful."

"Never been in a barber chair before," she shot back. Never had no need. I'd just go in the river and wash up. Of course that depended on how the river was flowing. Sometimes, I had to wait for days."

"Well, you just make yourself comfortable," commanded Rufus as he put a towel around her and began combing her hair. He'd stop and heated up a pan of water and hoped that that would do the trick. "I've never failed in all my 20 some years of barbering not to get all those kinks out. We'll make that hair sparkle and shine. Where you from, Molly?"

"I thought I told you. Illinois. Down in the southern part. Pretty close to St. Louis. Real near the Mississippi River. My Pa, he tried being a farmer, but it didn't work out too well. He knew how to make a good mash and pretty soon that kinda overtook his farming time, and also his life. He ended up drowning in the river. Thought he could swim across her, but the only problem was he was too drunk."

Quinn sat back, in utter disbelief, with mouth wide open.

"How about your Mammy?" asked Rufus.
"Didn't really know her. She ran off to St. Louie and never did come back. Farming wasn't in her blood neither."

Strategy of
Subterfuge

"So, you ended up living by yourself?"

"Yes sir. Spent some time at an orphanage, but it didn't take me long to high tail it out of that swamp hole. Heard about all the possibilities of making a living up in St. Paul, Minnesota, so I hitched a freight train up and I've been in Minnesota ever since."

"How did you end up in Fergus Falls?"

"You're getting pretty nosey, don't you think?"

"Oh, I like to find out about all the people that I work on. You're one of those intriguing types that I probably could find a thousand questions to ask."

"I was working as a hotel maid. One day a young gentleman came up to me and ask if I'd be interested in going to work for him. Wouldn't have to do no cleaning, just cooking, and being friendly. He offered to pay me at what I thought was a real nice amount so I said yes."

"Well, then he tells me that it would be in Fergus Falls. They just built a new hotel, the Grand Hotel, one of the most beautiful hotels I've ever been in. Got my own little room. Didn't cost me one penny. All part of my job. Pretty soon that gentleman, well he started not being so gentle, and he figured he could do anything he wanted to do with me. I didn't care for that one bit. One night we went swimming in the river, over by the mills, by the falls. Well this man thought he was a good swimmer and he found out that you don't mess around by the falls. He got wushed away like a little fish. Got sent down the river and they never found him. Probably went all the way up to Winnipeg for all I know."

"So, then what did you do?"

"I stayed at the Grand until they ended up kicking me out for not paying rent. That's when I met Lester, and Lester took good care of me, for a while."

189

Strategy of
Subterfuge

"Well, Molly. I usually think that I'm the one that does most of the talking when I have someone in the chair, but, by gully, I think you beat me by a mile. Here now. Let me put this towel on your head and see if we can't get that hair dried enough. I have some coloring that I'll mix up. You just keep wiping your hair."

"Now, Quinn, how is everything over at the Wiggins house?"

"They're all progressing quite well. So far, so good. Stanley got his new front teeth. First time he's been able to chew since the accident. He was one happy fellow. Naddy is starting to get movement in her lower body. I thought for sure she was going to be messed up for the rest of her life, but that's not going to happen. Looks like she'll recover completely and be back playing the piano in no time. Harriet has started to learn how to play the piano with her left hand. She's not too good at it, but knowing her, she'll become an expert in no time. Clare is mostly cleared up. She's got a hearing problem in one of her ears and I don't think we're going to be able to help her. I'm trying to find a specialist that maybe can help. Of course, I'm sure you heard about poor Charlie Rush. He couldn't take the pressure. Blamed himself for the accident. Took it too serious. Had a self-inflicted wound that did him in. Such a shame! Needless to say, it's been hectic around there. And Harriet's getting close to having the baby."

"She's still staying at her folks place?"

"Yes. Deborah has been babysitting all of them. I thank God every day for her. She surely has been a God send. She's the General you know. She always seems to take control of a situation and make the best of it. I think she's Daddy's favorite. I think she has a split personality. She seems so adrift at times. It's like she's in another world. Then, she turns around and wants to be the dominant person in the room. She has a spitfire temperament. She can stoke a lot of people's fires."

Strategy of
Subterfuge

"Alright, now," continued Rufus, "Miss Molly, you're going to put your head over this here bowl and I'm going to do a little magic to your hair, but first, I'm going to get rid of that long hair. He grabbed his scissors and comb and began cutting off long clumps of hair while Molly looked in the mirror with question marks all over her eyes.

"You won't even recognize yourself when I get done with you, Missy. Why, I might even surprise myself. If what I have for a vision for you turns out I think you will be very happy."

"Why, it's even shorter than Braden's!" observed Molly. "Save some. I don't want to be bald."

"You just wait, young lady. Wait for the best barber in town to do his tricks. Now, there. Put your head over the bowl."

Braden was quietly sitting off to the side, watching every move of Rufus P. Jones, and carrying that dirty, old, yellow ribbon. The barber had a way with a scissors and boy, there was a lot of hair lying on the floor. Now he was going to put that coloring on her. "Going take some getting used to," he blurted out, with a smile.

"My, my, Braden," interrupted Rufus. "You are talking so much better."

"Molly is a good teacher. She's showing me how."

Rufus looked over at Quinn and winked.

"So, Rufus," noted Quinn. "How are things with your new gal?"

"Mighty fine, Quinn. She can be a handful sometimes, but, for the most part, I can't complain. We keep to ourselves, mostly. Don't care much to have people googling at us when we walk by or be sitting in the Silver Moon and having everyone stare. Don't get me wrong, but I sometimes think we'd be better off in Minneapolis, or St. Paul, but we're determined to prove to people that we aren't any different than them. We know it'll take time."

191

Strategy of
Subterfuge

"Alright Molly. Let's get this hair done with you so you can tell people how great a barber I am," he noted as he took a towel and began to wipe her hair dry, while Molly kept staring into the mirror.

"And what are we going to do about you there, Braden? Braden, with that mighty fine looking beard and mustache. Should I change your hair color, too?"

"If you would, Mr. Jones. I'd sure appreciate it."

"Alright then. Give me a few more minutes with Molly. Isn't she looking mighty fine?" She reminds me of a young lady I knew down in Minneapolis. She was one of my favorites. Had short black hair, sparkling teeth, always with a smile on her face. Just like you, Molly. There now. What do you think?"

Braden smiled. "Very pretty. She's a new lady," he laughed. "A very pretty new lady."

"Now, it's your turn. Get over here and sit in my butcher's chair. Let's trim that rat's nest up a bit and then we can change that color."

"I sure do appreciate what you're doing for us, Rufus," offered Quinn. "You've been a very good friend of mine ever since I moved here. I owe you so much already. As a matter of fact, I consider you not only my confidant, but also my best friend."

"Oh think nothing of it," smiled Rufus. "We came to this little piece of Heaven about the same time and I remember many a time when you helped me out. That's what friends are for. Alright Braden. You have a pretty good head of hair growing there. Beard is a little straggly, but that'll fill in just fine. What color do you want for your top?"

"How about black, just like Molly?"

"With a tint of gray?"

"Sure."

192

Strategy of
Subterfuge

"You want me to cut any?"

"No. I want to let it grow long. By the time we're done nobody will recognize me beside you, my brother, and Molly."

As Rufus went about his final adjustments on the new Braden, Molly was nothing but smiles. She knew, deep down, that she had a special feeling for him, and she knew that he was evolving into a new Braden, and life was good.

"Again, Rufus. I want to thank you for all you have done for us," noted Quinn as he led the threesome out of the shop.

The wagon, with two horses tied behind, made its way out to the House of Braden, a small, humble and limited home. It was withdrawn, far past the Mt. Faith cemetery, on a long driveway into a thick wooded area, at least a half mile back from the main road. It was situated on a small hill amongst a grove of oak trees, with a little pond nearby.

The house was little, very little. Quinn unlocked the new residence and entered, followed by the new occupants, each with their two bags of luggage. It had two bedrooms, all decked out in simple, plain furniture. An old wood stove covered a huge space around one wall and a table and four chairs filled that area. A huge fireplace, with a massive rock ledge, took up the other side of the house.

"Very nice," offered Molly. "Very nice," chimed in Braden.

Quinn took Molly to the side. "So, which story about your folks is the correct one?"

"Oh, ah, what do you mean?"

"You told Rufus a different story than what you told me."

"Oh, ah, I, ah, I...."

Strategy of Subterfuge

"Alright, I understand. I suggest you think before you speak. Don't be so loose with the mouth. Alright?"

"Ah, yes sir."

"This will be your home for the foreseeable future until we find out and get rid of the kidnappers. I'll have to bring out a wagon load of feed, and straw, and hay, and a cow, and a few chickens. Plus, I'll bring out some food supplies for you two."

"Make yourselves at home, but do not leave the premises unless you have a dire emergency. We don't want anyone, and I mean anyone, knowing where you two are. Chances are high that whoever kidnapped you, Braden, he, or they, are still in the area."

"I'll come back tomorrow after I get done with my work. Make yourselves comfortable," he suggested as he headed out.

"Bye, Quinn," offered Braden.

"Yes, Braden. Good-bye, and you take care of Molly."

"I'll take care of Molly. Molly will take care of me."

Like the coyotes, Molly was cagey and elusive. She had learned to protect the wounded, and she was beginning to show signs of falling for someone for the first time in her life. She was changing. She wallowed in a sea of sensuality and floundered in a pool of discernment, not really knowing what was really going on, while Braden indulged in unadulterated innocence.

He would display a burning desire to see her intensify as time went by. Whenever close, his arm hairs would stand on end as exciting shivers flowed through his body. Whenever together his eyes shimmered with joy. She was creating a new Braden and he loved it. He was opening her mind and heart to a new world and she loved it.

Strategy of
Subterfuge

Their innocence showed front and center. Their bodies drew closer and their minds discovered newness and their hearts transcended to new heights. Beauty was found, both outward as well as inward. Like the trumpets of yellow, shouting out a new beginning, the two were coming to accept the reality of true love, but how did they know what true love really was? Neither had ever experienced it. Never before did they participate in an experience, a transition from irrelevance to one of renowned prominence in their lives. Life had new meanings for both and they loved it. They were making music without instruments. They were experiencing something different and they loved it.

They toured each room of their new mansion. Both had visions of what could possibly happen, although neither really knew what was in store. "Take your pick," offered Braden. "Which bedroom do you want?"

"I'll take whichever one you don't want," laughed Molly.

"Then I'll take this one," replied Braden as he grabbed Molly's hand and pulled her down on the bed. Their bodies came in contact. Their minds were foggy. Life was good as their lips met and they loved it.

"THE REVEREND AT WORK"

The old wooden church on Lincoln was empty excep t for one man sitting in the front pew. He was in a deep conversation, not of this world. It was the Reverend Herald Mayes Martin. The same preacher that had married Quinn and Harriet earlier. Dressed in a worn woolen suit, tattered and frayed, he was in deep discussion. "Lord, give me the power, the courage, the necessary tools to accomplish what I am about to do. I ask for your guidance, your zeal, your patience. I feel unworthy and doubtful, but hope that my faith will pull me, and my friend, Quinn, through what we are about to undertake. I ask that you show me the way to cure my good doctor. He is truly a good man, but suffers from a disease that I'm not sure if it's curable, but if you interject yourself and show me now, I would appreciate it."

Meanwhile, Quinn entered from the back and listened as Reverend Martin continued. "You know that he is getting divorced and is dealing almost constantly with Lucifer. Give him the courage and wherewithal to face up to his imperfections and his wayward deficiencies. Grant him the ability to castigate his iniquities, to shed his weaknesses and to see and honor the Light. Oh God, I ask for your forgiveness for my own shortcomings and allow me to also enter into a bond with you. Forever at your mercy. Amen."

"Reverend?"
Reverend Martin was startled. He turned around and stood up. "Oh, ah, Mr. Shanahan. So glad you could come."

"I have my doubts after listening to you."

"How is everything at home?"

196

The Reverend At Work

"*L*onely, quiet, and scary. I sit by the window and I hear voices in her room. I shut her door and still hear her. She's haunting me. She's getting even. She always blamed me for our problems. Don't do this! Don't do that! What's the matter with you? Constant. Every day. The same thing. Always blaming, never claiming. She's such a drama queen!"

"Well now, Quinn. You need to stop playing the blame game. In order for you to have any chance of getting Harriet back, you'll need to change your outlook on life."

"What? It's my fault?"

"That's a good first step. Now, here's a Bible. We've talked about this book before. I'd like you to take it home and start on the list of readings I put inside. I want you to read the first three on that list. Then, two weeks from tonight, we will meet again at your house, at seven, and we will discuss those topics. Any questions?"

"No sir."

"Now. I'd like to talk a little about change. Change is what you're going to have to incorporate into your lifestyle. It comes with difficulty. When we need to think differently. Paul says that it comes when we are transformed by the renewing of your mind. Such renewal is revolutionary and radical. It is based on proving "what's that good and acceptable and perfect will of God." In Proverbs 3:56 we find that trust in the Lord with all your heart, and do not lean on your own understanding. In all your ways acknowledge him and He will make straight your paths. The good news is that God has a plan for your life to hope for a future, and to prosper. If we trust in God and allow the change to grow us to become more like Jesus in how we respond and act, then we are promised that all things will work together for good, for those who love Him and keep His commandments.

The Reverend
At work

Lots of admirers, yet lots of hustlers. Men looking for a good time at her expense."

"Really? She told you that?"

"No, but I believe it's true."

As the black carriage pulled up in front of the Shanahan domain, signs of anxiety remained on Lin's face. Was this really happening? She asked herself. Was this me, or the Merlot talking? Almost ten and I'm at a married man's house, alone. How did I get talked into this? Oh, maybe it was what I really wanted? Maybe, it's my fault, but this is the first chance I've ever had of being alone with him. My whole body is shaking. Is it the wine, or is it my desire?

"Here you are, ma'am," offered Quinn as he dismounted and held out his hand to her.

She was shaking more than ever, but determined. She got down and held on tightly to his arm, as they made their way to the front entry. Everything was still wet from the rain---the grass, the trees, the flowers. Even the sidewalk boards and the minds of two wandering souls. They entered the confines of Quinn's world. He lit a lantern and then the fireplace, and then he turned to Lin.

Lin could feel her presence. The smell of her lavender perfume was everywhere. Harriet was everywhere. Nothing was hidden. Pictures of her on the walls---looking and watching, and following her every move.

"Give it a few minutes and I'll have this place nice and warm. Please, have a seat by the fireplace. I'll find us a little Merlot and then we can talk."

As Quinn disappeared into the kitchen, Lin took a seat right in front of the burning fire. "I'm not sure which one, the fire or me," she murmured. Yet, there was the lavender.

"Here you are," stated Quinn as he handed her a glass of wine. "Direct from the Napa Valley."

198

The Reverend
At work

Sure you may have setbacks. You may have difficulties, but rest assured, He is beside you all the way."

"Our friend, Isaiah, describes the most compelling individual in the history of the world. This Jesus, the very Son of God, came to Earth for the very purpose of becoming one of us. We can relate with him to our struggles and hardships. He kneels alongside us to revitalize our energy, provides relief from our stress, sets us free from sin and enables us to endure life's storms. Then through His powerful Holy Spirit, he offers us a fresh start. Now, Quinn, I would l ike you to tell me what you think of Harriet."

"I know, deep down, she loves me, but she sure has a strange way of saying it. When we first started courting she would always tell me that she loved me, at least five times a day. Now, those words don't come out of her mouth. She always seems to be the one that says I blame others for my problems. I'm not so sure I have. I'll be the first to admit that I have a tendency to spout little white lies, but I see lately she has been noticing them. She's starting to question them. She can be so understanding. Why is she questioning me? Why does she act that way? And one other thing. I swear she doesn't think I'm very responsible when it comes to money matters. Maybe, I should pay more attention. I don't know. Oh, yes, and another thing. She used to be shy and quiet. Now look at her. She's competition, or is she putting up a front? I just don't know."

"Very good, my son. In changing back to what some call normal the first step is that they must feel a level of love before they can love themselves. You are in a state of confusion right now. That is good. You are open for suggestions. You are looking for answers. One of the first things you need to recognize is that you need to love others like you love yourself.

Everything you've been doing up to now has been I, I, I, You need to start thinking we, we, we, and us, you, they.

The Reverend
At work

You'll be surprised at how your relationships can transform overnight into ones that make you feel good about everyone and everything. It is a very strong sign that you are overcoming your uncomfortable traits and you begin to see the world through your reformed eyes."

"One of my favorites is Psalm 119, verses 103-105. How sweet are thy words unto my taste! Yet sweeter than honey to my mouth! Through thy precepts I get understanding, therefore I hate every false way. Thy word is a lamp unto my feet and a light unto my path. Oh, what a feeling to know that you are on a strong foundation and you have someone who will help you along the way, Quinn! I pray every day that you will find this way and you will be cleansed from all your past shortcomings."

"So, when you leave the confines of this church, I want you to walk back to your house and think of the ways you can change your lifestyle to accept the responsibilities for your actions. Try to smooth out and maintain a personal relationship with someone. You need to collaborate with other people. Get yourself away from the loneliness that has been haunting you for quite some time."

"You need to accept your potential and your level of confidence to decrease extreme reaction to criticism. You need to improve your ability to understand your own and their feelings and to tolerate issues related to self-esteem. Your self-esteem and the self-esteem of your loved ones play an important role in development. It is a person's overall sense of self-worth or personal value. It tells you how much you like yourself. It can involve many aspects of your life, such as your appearance, beliefs, emotions, and behavior. It plays a significant role in your motivation and success throughout your life.

It can help you achieve because you navigate life with a positive, assertive attitude and believe you can accomplish your goals."

"I realize this is a long list and I don't expect you to change overnight, but once you begin this process of renewal your picture of life will become much clearer and more comfortable."

200

The Reverend
At work

"I don't know, Reverend. That sounds like quite the challenge."

"I know you're up to it, Quinn. I know you always love a good challenge. Think of them as little pitchforks that continuously prod and poke until you succeed and realize your negative attitudes. By and by, those prods and pokes will become less and less until, finally, you have no more prods and pokes, and you have arrived at HAPPINESS. Just remember what the Bible says about anger. Psalm 37, verse 8. Refrain from anger, and forsake wrath. Fret not yourself, it tends only to evil, and Ecclesiastes, chapter 7, verse 9. Be not quick in your spirit to become angry, f or anger lodges in the heart of fools, and Proverbs, chapter 29, verse 11. A fool gives full vent in his spirit, but a wise man quietly holds it back."

"Quinn! FEED YOUR FAITH AND YOUR FEARS WILL STARVE TO DEATH,"

"HOUSE OF HORRORS"

After the good reverend left, Quinn went back to his big castle on Cavour. It was cold and empty. He turned on several oil lamps, and settled in his dusty chair to read the Fergus Falls Weekly Journal. On top of the paper was a letter. Quinn opened and read it. "Dearest Quinn, I'm not ready yet. Feel free to continue your doctoring of me. Come over any time, Sincerely, Harriet."

This was his room---his place to hide, his large room to contemplate, his comfort zone, his station of stability. In the middle was a life-sized statue of himself. The walls were overloaded with pictures---a picture of an optical illusion of a staircase going up, or going down; a picture of Quinn giving a speech to a cheering crowd; a picture of a Bowie knife hanging on a wall, behind the divan. This was his room of warped floors and shallow shelves. It was a green room. Green and wilted flowers; green furniture; green lampshades and green wallpaper. In one corner stood a huge vanity, obscured by worn blankets and the smell of rotten eggs, a box full of masks, a magic wand, and several mousetraps. In another corner sat a pedestal, empty and forlorn.

He set the newspaper down and perused the room some more. The pipes were plugged, the keys, lost, and the strings, cut. No chatter or song; no laughter or s mile. Total silence ruled---an eerie silence, an unwelcomed silence. "This can't go on. It makes no sense," he mumbled. "What to do?" Dirty clothes scattered about, coal bucket empty, chamber pot full. Windows smeared, cobwebs in the corners and in his mind. No supper on the stove, beds not made. No wood in the fireplace. No fresh bread, or peas and carrots. Soiled dishes on the table, smudges on the mirrors, crystal chandeliers broken, cuckoo clock, cuckoo. "Huh, and I wondered what she did all day. Everything in disarray. How did it ever get this way?"

House
Of Horrors

A knock at the front door broke the silence. Quinn jumped to his feet and made his way to the main entry. "Rufus! Please come in."

"Do you have a minute?"
"Of course. Come on in. Let's take a seat in the parlor. I'm going to get a few pieces of kindling. It's quite cold in here," noted Quinn as he disappeared. Rufus found a chair and put it to good use, as Quinn returned with the wood. "This time of year we shouldn't have to need a fireplace."

"I was wondering how everything is going with you. I was over at the Wiggins. Stanley's not too happy with your situation. You do know that Harriet is due shortly?"

"Of course I know, but she created this mess. She didn't have to tell me about that run-in. Now the whole town knows about it. You realize how embarrassing this is? It's as if I don't have any other problems to deal with. I have goals set in my life. You know that. I thought it would be great to be married to the most beautiful woman in the world. She had everything, I thought. Beauty, brains, charm, talent. But then I find out about her past. That was the last straw. How could I ever trust her after what she did?"

"That wasn't her fault."

"She could have kept it a secret. No one needed to know."

"She didn't want you finding out from someone else."

"How do you know that?"

"She just told me all about it. She wanted me to pick up her clothes satchel. She said it's in her room."

House
Of Horrors

"Well, let's go see."

"It was a small room, barren and mute. The floor was littered with eggshells and the walls held a picture of a lamb on an altar, two unraveling straw chairs, and a disheveled bed. On another wall was a portrait of a young girl drowning in a sea of despair.

"She used to call this room her 'Bastille of No'. I never did figure out what she was trying to say. Here's the satchel," noted Quinn as he pointed to the battered carpetbag.

Rufus picked up the bag and the handle broke. "This is in an awful bad shape."

"That's fitting," shot back Quinn. "Just like her."

Chapter 24

"THE OTHER HOUSE OF HORRORS"

Meanwhile, Harriet sat by her window watching the metamorphosis of Mother Nature on stage. As the doldrums of white disappeared, the Orchestra of Renewal marched forward. With trumpets blaring and drum pounding, the symphony of songs arose to the occasion. Robins were chirping; eagles, preying; ruffed grouse, strutting; geese, mating; all in unison, all with future in mind.

The chilling morning air was disappearing, being replaced by a breeze of renewed hope. A chance for her resolve. Enough with this living with her parents. Enough pretending. "I want more. I need more. I am innocent. I am wounded and I need a man. in my life. I need someone that could be a father to my child. I need a husband. Today is a new day. Today is the day I will meet with Quinn. What shall I say? What will he say? What will my family say? What will the townspeople say? Oh, I don't care what they say, except for Quinn. I've never stopped loving him," she continued, as she looked at his picture." Oh, he's as handsome as ever. How I miss him! His gentle fingers, caressing my hair, his fingers skipping along my arms. I can feel the goosebumps. I can smell his dashing perfume. I see his rich wardrobe, and long for his sense of humor."

But wait, she thought. Wait Harriet M. Shanahan! What about his problem? His disease? I've heard he's getting better. That's what Reverend Martin has been telling me and I should be able to believe a preacher. Father says there's no way I can fix him. That it's never been done. That he is too far gone, but I have to give him another chance. I have to. My life yearns for him. My heart cries for him. My mind is excited for him. Oh my! What am I thinking? Am I alright? Or am I crazy? She kept talking to herself as Quinn entered her room.

The other

House Of Horrors

"Good morning, Harriet."

"Quinn."

"Are you expecting to do some walking today?" he asked as he set his medical bag on the night stand and pulled out a knife and heavy duty scissors. He took one of her pillows and put it under her lower left leg and began cutting away at the worn cast.

"I have my fingers crossed, Harriet, that everything will be fine. It'll all depend on how well Dr. Bedford set the bones." He continued to cut and rip until he was ready to pull it apart and away from the ankle.

"There," he noted as he accomplished the task at hand.

"Now you know it will take you a while to get back to a normal walk. How does it feel?"

"It can breathe. It feels good."

"Let's give it a short try," suggested Quinn as he helped Harriet get out of the bed.

"Now, take it easy. Don't step down too heavy. Gentle, that's what we want. Careful. That's it. Keep your left hand on the bed. I know it's going to feel strange. Take your time. Don't be in a hurry. Take a few steps and then back up to where you started.

That's it.

Good job."

The other
House Of Horrors

Harriet was determined. She grimaced in pain, Sweat was rolling down her face. She was shaking and clenching the bed sheet. "Oh, I have to get back in the bed," she gasped as she almost fell over.

Quinn guided her back to her favorite spot and gently straightened out the sheets. "I know it's going to take a lot of willpower and I know that you will provide it. This is just the beginning, but it was a good beginning. From what I can tell, your nub looks like it's mending well."

Harriet grabbed Quinn's arm. "Is there anything you can do with this scar that I'm getting on my face?"

"I have sent a letter to a doctor out East that is a specialist in the field. I'm anxiously awaiting a reply. I wish I could pull off another miracle, but not yet. I will be back later. Now, I best go see your mother."

"How's Naddy?"

"I stopped in. She was sleeping. As far as I can tell, there has been no change."

"What do you think her chances of recovery are?"

"It's still too early to tell, but as each day passes the chances grow dimmer."

Harriet watched with a sharp eye as Quinn departed the room. "He's looking better and better every day that goes by."

Meanwhile, Naddy lie awake in bed, reading her little black Bible. She occasionally looked out the window in hopes of seeing the arrival of a miracle, but alas, all she saw was a squirrel gathering acorns and a little rabbit twitching its way along a row of lettuce.

No knight in shining armor to save her. No Aphrodite to drop off an extra lover. Oh what the heck, what good would that do? She asked herself. No Apollo to sweep her off her feet. That's no good, she thought. Sweeping off my feet won't work! No Artemis to drop off a bow and arrow. Nothing to shoot at here.

207

The other
House of Horrors

Oh, if only Dionysus would come with his vine of grapes and a crown of ivy. I could handle something like that. Oh, a good bottle of Merlot, or Chardonnay. That would get me out of this state of misery.

Quinn knocked and entered. "How's my little patient doing this morning? I stopped by earlier, but you were still sleeping."

"Oh Quinn! How can you be so jovial? As you can see, I haven't moved."

"We must never give up hope, dear Naddy," he continued as he pulled the sheets back and hand rubbed her calves. "We have to keep these muscles awake so when they decide to go back to being useful you'll be able to handle it."

"How long before I give up and realize I'll never walk again?"

"When the Pope becomes a Lutheran. Never give up. Think positive. You can beat this. You keep active on top and I'll keep you active below. You have your medicine in your hand. Use it to your advantage."

"If I didn't have this," she continued as she lifted the little black book, "I wouldn't be here at all."

"Oh, my sweet Naddy. You don't deserve to be put in such a predicament. It's as if you are being tested. I know how that feels. There isn't a day that goes by that I don't feel like I'm being tested. Now I'm not trying to compare my problems with yours. I just want you to know that if you look at it that way you'll keep your sanity."

"Let me see your toes," he continued as he worked on her toes. "You feel this at all?"

"No."

"I know this can be very unsettling but just bear with us. Has your sister been doing the changing for you as far as your bowel movement goes?"

208

The other
House of Horrors

"Yes. It is embarrassing but she has been stopping in almost every hour on the hour. I feel so helpless. It's so uncontrollable."

"I understand, Naddy. I'll be back tomorrow. You just keep your upper body active. Do your exercises as often as you can. It is vitally important. We don't want to go backwards. We're far enough back now."

Quinn made his way over to where Clare was sitting. "Hello Clare. Shall we get those fingers back to good use?"

"Oh, I hope we can, Doc. My gut feeling is that it's going to be a great day."

"Good," continued Quinn as he set his bag down pulled out the necessary equipment. "Let's have a look-see," he suggested as he began to carefully tear away the cast around her fingers.

"You do realize this is the easy part. Once we get rid of these casts then it's up to you to get the necessary exercise to get your fingers back to work. Here we go. Starting with the left hand he meticulously unwrapped the bandage, uncovering and opening to the air, two very white fingers. Clare was watching every move that Quinn did. He gently took her hand and felt her fingers, looking to be sure that the break had mended properly. There's one free hand and now the other," he continued as he worked away on the final cast. "There. That should do it. "So much for the casts. From now on we'll just wrap them in a heavy blanket to help so they don't move around and you don't bump them. They will be very tender for quite some time and we have to be very careful with them. Your daughter, Deborah, has volunteered to help you with your daily exercise routines. You will need to do those seven days a week. You'll start out slow and as each day passes they will get longer and longer and more difficult, but necessary."

"You should be very proud of your daughter, Deborah," continued Quinn. "She has volunteered to do the daily routine for all four victims. I don't know how long that will last, or even if she'll be able to handle it all, but we'll see."

The other
House of Horrors

"I don't know what this family would do without you," exclaimed Deborah.

"This has been a house of repugnance, where I could feel the hidden animosity. Now, I see it is changing. Now there is hope for the disappearance of all dread and deception," he noted, as he headed out the door.

Chapter 25

"ONE BIG SECRET"

Quinn sat by his desk and opened the Good Book. Without reading, he paged through the New Testament. He paused and looked out the window. It was raining. He noticed Braden arriving in a buckboard. Quinn continued to watch as Braden entered the stable. Moments later, he returned to his buckboard and was carrying the bag of bones, which he had discovered out by the river.

Quinn jumped to his feet and rushed outside. He headed for the stable as Braden headed north. What is he doing? Quinn asked himself, as he put a saddle on his horse and left in search of his brother.

Braden drove his wagon into the Mt. Faith cemetery at the edge of town, as Quinn remained far enough back not to be noticed. The rain had stopped and the sun appeared as Braden pulled up to the designated pauper area. He began digging as Quinn watched from afar. Shovel after shovel of rich black soil was removed, creating a large hole. He placed the bones in the hole and returned the soil to its original site.

Quinn's hands were shaking. His body, in a sweat. His mind overflowed with guilt. His heart, covered with shame. The sight of the Red River flowing past the field of daffodils reappeared in his mind. He pictured himself hitting that Jasper with a rock. He watched as the lifeless body fell into the water. He pictured himself placing a huge rock over the submerged body. "My God! I killed him!" he gasped.

ne
Big Secret

He rubbed his eyes, but the haunting picture remained. He shook his head and turned his horse around and left, all the while asking himself if he should tell his brother. "No. I can't. He doesn't need to know." I'll go back and check on Harriet. Nobody needs to know.

Harriet was lying in her bed, with Dr. Remy standing at her side. "It's been two weeks. I've noticed some improvements, but I need to see more. I want to be able to fit you with a prosthesis. Just think what you could do with an artificial limb?"

Harriet sat up in bed. "You mean I won't have to look at this nub of an arm much longer?"

"Let's hope so. I was talking with Quinn and he feels the same. I did notice a little discoloration around the wound, and that has me quite concerned. We don't need that. We'll have to keep an eye on that. You haven't felt any pain there, have you?"

"No. Sometimes I don't feel a thing, and then other times, I feel an imaginary pain."

"That's quite normal. Well, I'll be back again tomorrow to check up on you. By the way, your father got his brand new teeth, finally. Four shiny white teeth. He's in a much better mood now that he can chew again."

"That fake arm won't make me play piano again."

"Perhaps not, but it would do wonders to that poor image you have of yourself. Besides, I was told that there has been piano music written solely for left hand only."

"I know. I've been playing it. And another thing. In case you haven't noticed I'm getting very close to my due date. As much as I want a prosthesis, I think we better wait till after the birth. Here. Come with me. I want to show you something."

One
Big Secret

Harriet grabbed Remy's hand and they made their way over to the piano. She sat down. Took out a sheet of music and placed it in front of her. She began to play. She began to play with her left hand. It was rough and choppy but it was music. In some ways, beautiful music, considering the circumstances. She would falter on some notes but she showed a true Wiggins determination to succeed.

"Why that is amazing," offered Remy. "I can tell you have been practicing. Have your parents heard you?"

"I'm sure they have. I've been doing it practically every day. They've had to have heard it. Of course, Mother would never say if she did, especially when it's surely not up to her standards. It's so much harder to do than with two hands. Miss LaGrave has been over several times and has been helping me."

"I'm sure Quinn will be pleasantly surprised when he finds out."

"I haven't seen much of him lately."

"He's been busy with Braden. You should see what he's up to. I don't know what Quinn has been doing with him but he is really progressing. I always thought, ever since the first time that I saw him, that he was going to be a handful, but Quinn is doing something that is really changing him."

"Doctor Oglesby! Doctor Ogleby! Come quick!" commanded Deborah as she rushed into the room. "Follow me!"
Deborah grabbed his hand and they quickly made their way up to Deborah's room. To his surprise, Naddy was sitting up with her legs over the side. "Look! It's working. My whole body is moving. My legs! My toes! Everything!"

"Marvelous!" exclaimed Remy. "Unbelievable."
"It's very difficult," noted Naddy. "But, it's working. I couldn't believe it when I noticed the feeling in my legs. Haven't felt that in months. What a welcomed feeling! The world is going to see a new Naddy."

213

"THE LIVING WATER"

Quinn sat by his dining table, with Bible in front of him and an empty chair to his left, and his scratched back behind him, and ledger of losing to his right. He was staring out the window as darkness invaded the countryside and Braden and Molly were in their bedrooms, patiently waiting. It was getting close to the time where they were to be going to the new home. The transformation had already begun for the twosome. Braden was growing a full beard and mustache. Looked awful straggly, but it was doing what it was meant to do---camouflage.

Darkness was arriving, along with Reverend Martin. The tall, thin minister knocked and entered. "Are you ready?" he asked as he sat down next to Quinn.

"I don't think I'll ever be ready. I spent hours reading about that Samaritan woman at Jacob's well and can't figure out what it means."

"Well, let's see," continued the Reverend as he opened the Bible. "Here we go. John 4; 1-40. Alright. Have you figured out the connection with you?"

"No. All I see is some woman is out at a well at the hottest time of the day, which doesn't make a bit of sense to me. Along comes Jesus and he wants her to get him some water. She was kind but since she didn't draw water at the same time as the other women, they started gossiping about her, saying that she was an immoral hooker, I think."

"No. I don't believe she was a hooker. He said to the woman. You are right in saying I do not have a husband. For you have had five husbands and the man you now have is not your husband."

The Living Water

"Jesus said that he could give her some 'living water'. She couldn't understand what he was saying, I mean, me neither. Why would he ask her to get him a cup of water and then, at the same time, tell her that he could give her water?"

"Ahhhhh, now look Quinn. He wants to give her 'living water'. It's not your ordinary water."

"I have no idea."

"What does Jesus say: 'Whosoever drinketh of the water shall thirst again, but whosoever drinketh of the water that I shall give him shall never thirst, but the water that I shall give him shall be in him, a well of water springing up into everlasting life. The living water is eternal life."

"So, what does that have to do with me?"

"It's a known fact that Jews did not like Samaritans and they did not talk to female strangers. But Jesus was not afraid of talking to this outcast. He treated everybody the same. It is suggested that he is a loving and accepting God and that we should follow his example. Jesus is the One, and no one else could ever be that One. He is the only one that can offer that life everlasting. His disciples wanted him to eat something, and he said: 'I have food to eat that you know nothing about. My food is to do the will of Him who sent me and to finish his work. We have all witnessed a discovery that makes us shout: This is the One. You found your one and married her. I'm sure you said: 'This is the one."

"In our quest for notoriety, and successful careers, and the relentless desire for THINGS, we're so busy building cisterns. Cisterns that are broken even before they are used. In our search for good water many of us have unwittingly wandered away from the water elsewhere."

"Cisterns?" shouted Quinn. "What are you talking about?"

"Jeremiah has classic examples of when the people of Judah turned to making cisterns. But the cisterns were broken and they never held water.

215

The Living Water

The only thing that happens when we turn away from God's 'living water' and attempt to find spiritual fulfillment apart from the Lord will always end in failure. God is the only one that can quench our spiritual thirst."

"You have one of those broken cisterns. You have fallen to the wayside and have tried looking for and all you end up doing is feeling downtrodden and picked on, and you end up blaming others. It's time for you to return to the 'living water'. God will provide and care for you from the grasp of the devil. You will be amazed at how much better you will feel, not only about yourself, but in the people you come in contact with. This, of course, is all symbolic. When you walk down the streets of Fergus Falls, you do not see the cisterns, but they are everywhere and you can tell by the way ordinary people act as to what kind of cistern they use."

"See how foolish it is to roll the dice and try to build your own cistern, only to find out that they won't hold the necessary water. Does it not make sense to return to the 'living water'?"
Quinn sat there with a puzzled look on his face.

"We perhaps have foolishly gotten involved in building our own cisterns. Our country was founded on the premise that we were a nation under God. Our nation has turned from the fountain of 'living water' to the cisterns of secular humanism, the fake cisterns of human freedom from God. So what you need to do is realize that there never is a reason to build a cistern when God already has one for you, exactly what you need for eternal salvation."

"Now you are learning to accept your shortcomings, your weaknesses, and your shortage of empathy. The ability to understand and share the feelings of another, vicariously experiencing the feelings, thoughts, and experiences of another. Take that one step further and you have compassion. Compassion is the understanding of another's pain and the desire to somehow make that pain less severe. Be humble, thinking of others as better than yourself.

The Living Water

Don't look out only for your own interests, but take an interest in others, too. Now you need to re-find that One. Not only your wife, but also, you. Once you can say: Yes, that is the One, everything will come into focus. Study Jesus. Realize his role in your life. Open up and transform your mindset and give yourself to Jesus. Be at peace with yourself. Be at peace with Harriet. Be at peace with the world."

"I know what my problems are. I'm finally admitting my past has not been good. I'm actually surprised that our marriage lasted as long as it did. One of the toughest things I've ever had to do was to admit that I was so wrong."

"It's going to take time. You just keep reading about Paul and his trials and failures, and successes. Put your world into God's hands. Let Him help you. Follow Him. Believe in Him."

"Listen Quinn. It gives me great pleasure to absolve you of your past digressions. I am truly convinced that you have come a long way out of the depths of Hell and are progressing in the right direction, but your journey has just begun. You have recognized and admitted your sins. You now know that you are your own worst enemy. Your faces have dropped from two to one, and I admire that."

"What is he talking about when he says: Open your eyes and look at the fields? They are ripe for harvest. Even now the one who reaps draws a wage and harvests a crop for eternal life so that the sower and the reaper may be glad together."

"Understand this, my friend," noted the Reverend, "the disciples are reaping what others have sown. Souls, my friend. He's talking about saving souls. So, Quinn. Do not consider yourself a victim. The more you read and study and accept, and notice, the closer you will come to ridding yourself of the victim complex."

The
Living Water

"When you abused, and lied, and stole, and cheated, and then you noticed that they caught on. Rather than blame them, turn around and admit your weaknesses and pray that you can put them under your control. So, make sure that your paint brush is thrown away. No more painting for you in your mind. I see your color changing. I feel you're on the right path. Continue your study and let your heart grow in a positive way. I pray for you each day and each day I know that he is listening and I can see he is watching over you. It makes me smile, where once there were frowns."

"Always remember, like it is said in Ecclesiastes 10:2, a wise man's heart is at his right, but a fool's heart, at his left. Pray that you will continue to be on the right path."

"Oh Reverend, I don't know where I'd be if it weren't for you."

"Nonsense. You're doing this all by yourself. I am just along to guide. Now, tell me, my friend, what have you learned about contentment?"

"Contentment is reached when you understand that things of this world really do not satisfy. By knowing God and living for him one will get true satisfaction. When we realize this relationship with Him gives us the essential meaning and serenity, in our lives. That is contentment. Ephesians, chapter 2, verses 8 and 9, says: For by grace you have been saved through faith and that not of yourselves, it is a gift of God, not of works, lest anyone should boast. This is contentment."

"Are you content, Brother Quinn?"

"As each day passes, I feel closer to being content, but I still have the devil inside me, pushing and shoving his way to the front of my mind, telling me how terrible some people are towards me and Braden and that I need to fight back. It's a battle, a battle that sometimes overwhelms me. I need to sit back and re-draw the boundary lines. The thought of Harriet being with those men still pops up now and then. That will probably never stop appearing. I have tried forgiving them for what they did to her, but still one part of me wants revenge. Something inside tells me to get even, but I keep trying to erase that whole episode.

218

The Living Water

I do realize I treated her unfairly and for that I'm very sorry. I realize it was for selfish reasons and if I had to do it all over again things would have been different."

"But, Quinn. Is it with Harriet in mind, or for your own personal gratification? Is selfishness still filling your mind? Can't you let go of that word?"

"Yes, it's in there, and probably will always be there. It's one big tug of war."

"There is only one thing worse than a self-absorbed person and that is two of them, married to each other."

"BIRTH AND REBIRTH"

With difficulty, Harriet was going through her daily exercise routine. Her day of deliverance exercise routine. Her day of deliverance was about to occur, with so many questions and very few answers. Was she going to be able to give birth with her addiction to laudanum? Was the baby going to be addicted, too? Would she be strong enough to deliver? Would Quinn help in the delivery? How was she going to be able to handle a baby? All these questions were up in the air.

My life is going to change. I have to accept that fact. A baby will tie me down and limit my freedom. My routine would change forever. How am I going to be able to take care of a baby when I have only one arm? My days with the piano may be coming to an end. No. Mother wouldn't allow it. She'll babysit and I'll get a new arm, and I'll make the money.

I've worried so much. I worried about not knowing if I was in labor. If I had some pain, was that labor. I'd wake up during the night with cramps and I thought it was labor. Must have did this for days.

She paced the floor, walking and thinking, and holding her protruding stomach. What's going to happen to the baby? To her? She sat down by her piano and tried playing with her left hand. Oh, so difficult! Yet, she kept trying.

One thing she had was persistence. Oh, could she ever persevere! Just what she needed under the present circumstances.

Her health was good, compared to what she had been through. Her weight had increased much more than you would see in a normal pregnancy and that worried Quinn. Due to the fact that she had needed several servings of laudanum to ease the pain in her surgeries, just gave more worries for Quinn.

220

Birth
And Rebirth

Harriet laid back down in her bed, all the while holding her stomach and experiencing pain, as Clare entered the room. "Should I be getting Quinn?"

"Oh Mother. I guess it's about that time. Yes. You better."

"I'll have your father ride over and get him," noted Clare, as Deborah entered.

"Is it time?" anxiously asked Deborah.

"Getting close. Contractions are about every ten minutes. Each lasts about a minute."

"What does it feel like?"

"My lower back seems to hurt the most. Oh, ah, ugh," moaned Harriet as another contraction occurred. "That was a long one," she moaned.

"Is there anything I can do?"

"Yes. Would you rub my temples?"

"Like this?" noted Deborah as she placed her fingers right above on each side of Harriet's cheeks.

"Oh, yes, yes. That is perfect. Deb. You have no idea how good that feels."

"What's it feel like? Boy or girl?"

"I haven't the slightest idea. It's been kicking up a storm. Does that mean it's a boy? I don't know. I'll be glad when this is all over. It feels like I've been pregnant for years. I'm turning into a complete mess. My feet are all swollen. I've been so tired for so long it seems to be the only way I feel, and I swear I've been so forgetful lately, that I'm lucky if I remember my own name. And not to mention that I think my weight has more than doubled. Oh, ah," she moaned as more contractions arrived, and more pain.

Birth
And Rebirth

"Enough is enough," she screamed.

"Oh Harriet! I feel so helpless."

"Just stay with me. Here! Help me change my position."

Deborah tried helping her move, but with so much difficulty.

"That's fine. I'm set. Listen! I know I'm never going to lose all this weight.

You might as well go through my corsets and take whichever ones you want."

"You mean it, Sis?"

"I know you'll take good care of them. That's for being a good sister."

"Here comes Quinn," excitedly observed Deborah.

"Ah, how are my two favorite girls?"

"When can we get on with this?" queried Harriet.

"That's entirely up to you. I can assist you but you have to deliver the goods. Have you been checking the time between contractions?"

"No, Quinn. I was lucky enough to make it through this ordeal. I have noticed that I've been experiencing a shortness of breath."

"Let me see your fingers," he requested. "Ah, yes. Quite a bit of swelling. I noticed it in your ankles, too, and in your face. That's not really too much to worry about. As soon as you give birth a lot of changes will take place. Most of them will be returning to normalcy. I need to check your cervix and then I'll leave you alone. I have to go out on a call in Maine town, but I should be back in 4, or 5, hours. If you need me before that, Remy is at the office. So, open your legs, please. Yes, ah, ha, yes," he measured. "You are indeed getting close. I'll try and hurry. Meanwhile, it's alright, as a matter of fact, it's a good idea if you chew on some ice chips. If you get thirsty. No more water and no more food until after birth. Do you understand?"

"Yes," shrugged Harriet.

And Rebirth

"I know you've been through a lot and for most of the experiences we've used laudanum to relieve the pain and send you mentally away from the problems. We'll use it one more time in delivery, but then that's it. No more. I'm a little nervous that perhaps you're already addicted. I'm also a bit worried that our baby might also be addicted. I don't want you to go crazy on me, or worry about such an event if that happens. With all you've overcome this should be relatively easy, but we'll cross that bridge when we come to it. I'll be back as soon as I can. In the meantime, Deborah, make sure your sister has company at all times, until I get back."

"Yes sir. I will."

After Quinn departed, Deb looked at Harriet. "He sure has changed." "It's as if he has been reborn. You are witnessing a rebirth right before your own eyes."

"Yes and I think Quinn should consider himself a very lucky person."

Several hours later.

The day of deliverance had arrived. The Wiggin's household was in an uproar. Alarm bells were going off. Warning lights were flashing. Harriet was being bombarded as the time had arrived for a miracle to take place in her bed, in the House of Wiggins.

Harriet lay on her back, with knees up. Nervous, yet determined; bewildered, yet clearheaded; her body was churning as her mind held steady. Moans of relief entwined with tears of joy. With a background of piano music and a serving of trumpets and drums, the activities of birth were on full display. Sweat was rolling and Deborah was wiping, and Deborah was stoking, while Quinn lay in wait. Outside the room, Clare was floating, while Stanley was on his knees. Pandemonium evolved with bed shaking and body trembling and Naddy scared and Deborah, lit up.

Birth
And Rebirth

"Keep pushing down," ordered Quinn.

"I am! I am!" shouted Harriet.

"Go Harriet! Go!" prodded Deborah. "Keep the sparks flying."

With cramps and leaks and with backaches and bleeding, Harriet trudged forward into the minefield of children. Valiant and determined and with laudanum active, she took on the challenge before her. With water broken, the crowning would soon be there, as Deborah wiped and glowed and Naddy was scared.

"I see it," observed Quinn as he burst out with a smile, while Harriet pushed and Deborah fainted.

Groans continued as sweat poured and the end in sight was on the horizon.

"Don't stop now," demanded Quinn. "Almost there."

More grunting. A lot of groaning and a little cursing, yet Harriet continued forward.

"Yes, yes, yes," shouted Quinn as he reached down and brought out the newborn. "It's a boy, Harriet. A spanking new baby boy!"

A smile of relief was on Harriet's tired face. Does he have ten fingers and ten toes? Shouts of joy filled the air, coming from Deborah. Out in the hall, Stanley and Clara were thrilled, as they jumped for joy, and life at the Wiggin's house would never be the same.

Quinn stood back and watched with pride as Harriet was holding the baby in her arms. Pride covered her face while words of thanks filled her mind. Tired, yet determined, she knew it was all worth it as she beamed down with pleasure upon the newest Shanahan.

Quinn's smile turned to dismay. Something didn't look right. The baby was discolored. He took the baby from Harriet's arms and laid it on the table. He checked its vitals. He looked at its eyes. "Just what I feared the most. He's hooked. We're going to have to pay close attention to his reactions," he continued as he handed the baby back to Harriet.

Birth
And Rebirth

"Nothing to worry about yet. We'll try and wean him as times goes by. We must stay positive. Lots of good news today. A child was born. Our child was born. The revocation of my license has been approved and my resume is all cleaned. The accusations of me performing abortions have been proven false. And I have been offered a job as a surgeon at the University of Minnesota Medical Hospital. We are witnessing a new rebirth in the Shanahan family."

"TRANSFUSION"

Quinn was kneeling in his flower garden, observing the remnants of what once was a brilliant display of daffodils, now reduced to a garden of decay, as Reverend Martin made his appearance. Deep in thought about the upcoming trip to Bermuda, Quinn was nervous about his future, yet he tried to focus in on what the Reverend was going to be talking about.

"Congratulations," offered the Reverend. "Your young man is a beautiful addition to our family. I understand you and Harriet decided to name him Raymond Quinn Shanahan?"

"That was all Harriet's idea."

"That's good, Quinn. That means she is acknowledging you. Honoring you. Giving your name to the child. That is excellent. Today, we are going to talk about the Light and Confidence. The Light shines in the darkness, but the darkness has not understood it. And the Light shines through the darkness, and the darkness can never extinguish it. The Bible tells us that the Light equals the Word. Light is the presence of God. It brightens dark spaces, exposing evils and danger and eliminating deception and falsehood. God is Light and Son is Jesus. Whoever follows me will never walk in darkness, but will have the light of life. To walk means to make progress. It is God's plan that believers shine forth his light, becoming more like Christ every day. You are all children of the Light and children of the day. We do not belong to the night or to the darkness."

"Light exposes that which is hidden in the darkness. To walk in the Light is to know God, to understand the truth and live in righteousness." "Believers in Christ must confess any darkness within themselves. Their sins, and their transgressions and allow God to shine his light through them."

226

Transfusion

"Light is uncomfortable to those accustomed to darkness. Jesus, the sinless Son of God, is the true Light. As adopted sons of God, we are to reflect His light into a world darkened by sin. Our goal is to open their eyes and turn them from darkness to light and from the power of Satan, to God."
"If we do not have the Light, we do not know God. Those who know God, who walk with Him, are of the Light and walk in the Light. They are made partakers of God's divine nature, having escaped the corruption in the world caused by evil desires."

"The Bible says: 'but if we walk in the Light, we have fellowship with one another, and the blood of Jesus. His Son cleanses us from all sin."

"Walking in the Light, walking away that is consistent with the scriptures. Now Quinn, while you are on your little vacation to Bermuda, I don't want you losing sight of what we have been discussing for these past several months. I'll quiz you when you get back. You are progressing quite well and I don't want to fall back to your old ways. That will never work for you if you truly want to get back with Harriet."

"I know. I know," agreed Quinn. "I'm going over to see her right now."

Minutes later, Quinn appeared at the Wiggin's house, and was directed up to Harriet's room. "How's my little patient doing today?"

"Hello, Quinn. I'm still waiting."

"Waiting? For what?"

"My new arm. I'm rather tired of looking at this," she pointed.

"Lets' take a look at that," he suggested as he took the bandage off. A worried look appeared. "Oh my! It's changed quite a bit since the last time I saw it. He checked her pulse and was surprised. "It's moving awful fast. We might have to take a closer look, Harriet. I'm going to get Remy.

227

Transfusion

I'd like to get his opinion. I'll be back in a few minutes. Your skin is rather anemic. That's not good. That's a sign of a lack of hemoglobin." Harriet sat up. "What did he see? Why did he need Remy? He's always said that Remy doesn't know enough about medicine to be a doctor. Something doesn't sound right," she continued as she looked at the discolored nub.

Quinn arrived at his office. "Remy! Remy!" he yelled as he rushed to his medical supplies and began putting items in a large bag. Rubber tubing, syringes, needles, compression bandages, hand pumps, wound dressing, packages of gauze, and more bandages.

"What's going on?" yelled Remy as he appeared from his observation room. "You need to meet me at Wiggin's. First, go get Eisen and then Bedford. We have to open Harriet's wound back up. It's getting infected. I might need you to do a blood transfusion. She's going to likely need some blood."

"And where am I going to get this blood?"
"Any relative! Clare, Stanley, Deborah, Naddy. You go get the other doctors. I'll go talk to the family. Get to the Wiggin's house as soon as you can. Any questions?"

"What if they can't give?"

"Then I'll give her mine."

"Do you know what you're saying?"

"Yes. We don't have much choice. It's only blood."

"I've never done anything like this. As a matter of fact, I heard somewhere that the chances of survival in a blood transfusion, especially when we don't know if the blood will match, or not, is one in one hundred."
"I don't care if it's one in one thousand. We can't lose her."

"But we could lose both you and her."

"Dang it, Remy. Can't you just think positive just once in your life?"

228

Transfusion

"I can't help it. What's it going to look like if you both end up dying? I'd never be able to live with myself."

"Before you go jumping to any conclusions, let's find out if anyone in the family can do it. My offer is a last resort. Just think of it the other way. What if we both survive? That would be a good feather in your hat. C'mon. Be off with you. Time's awasting."

Quinn went from room to room, telling, asking and begging for volunteers, with results being the same in each instance. That is all the same except for Deborah. She was excited and willing to offer whatever it took to help her sister. Naddy, too, was wanting to help but transportation would be a challenge, until the idea of a wheel chair was offered.

Excitement and anxiety grew at the Wiggin's household as word spread of what was about to happen. Again, the sight of four doctors, preparing to operate, sent nervous apprehension and angst among all of the participants.

"We are taking every precaution we possibly can," noted Quinn. "It looks like Harriet's wound is becoming infected. We need to go in and clean it out. She's going to lose a lot of blood, so we're going to make sure that there is some at her disposal. Clare will be taking care of the baby. I gave him a small dose to settle him down for a few hours. I will donate first. Deborah and Naddy will be standing by, willing to also donate."

"That doesn't sound good," noted Clare. "I just had a gut feeling that something wasn't right. I knew it was going along too smoothly."

"Time for you to use those knees of yours," suggested Stanley.
"Yes, we're going to need all the prayers we can get," added Remy as he arrived with his equipment and the two other doctors.

"We'll need a ready supply of water, both hot and cold," noted Quinn. "I brought quite a few towels, but not sure if that'll be enough. I'm going to have the doctor's, probably Remy, take some blood samples from Deborah, Naddy, and me, and compare them with a sample from Harriet, just in case."

Transfusion

The time for doing has arrived at the Wiggin's house. The group of four doctors, after hours of consultations were ready to pull off something seldom done in the medical world---a blood transfusion.

"Once I've cleaned out the infected area and sealed the skin, if necessary that's when we'll need to do the transfusion. Be sure every piece of equipment is thoroughly sanitized, Dr. Halsted, constantly stresses that procedure no matter what. I have everything ready on the operating table. Make sure all three of you are familiar with all of them, but the main responsibility lies with you, Remy.

The chances of survival for all the participants is nothing to feel good about, but we have no choice. Dr. Halsted succeeded in a blood transfusion back in '81, giving his blood to his sister, who was in the midst of having a baby. Some people said it was all luck, but if it works who really cares?"

"Dr. Eisen, you'll be in charge of the anesthesia. Poor Harriet has had more than her share of laudanum these past few months. I only hope she doesn't become addicted."

"Dr. Bedford, you will be responsible for her. You will do the tube connections. Remy will be using a syringe to transfer the blood. He will be using a different needle each time. Possible two pints needed. We'll see. You will be monitoring her vitals. If you notice any change, whatsoever, stop and double check. One thing you must watch closely for is making sure she keeps getting enough oxygen. You know what would happen if that occurs."

"Remy! Let's get this going."

The foursome headed for the nearest bedroom to Harriet's. Into their temporary changing room. As they began scrubbing down, two men came in and took the bed out and put it near Harriet's bed. This was to be the resting spot for whoever was going to be giving blood.

"I admire what you are doing," noted Remy as he looked over at Quinn. "I'd never be able to do what you have offered. With 1 in a 100 chances of success I couldn't do it."

Transfusion

"All you have to do is think of what would happen to Harriet and the baby if she didn't get that blood. Besides, all you have to do if she is rejecting it is stop feeding the tube. Either way there really is no gamble for me. It's Harriet that we need to save."

"Have you been in contact with Dr. Halsted?"
"Yes. We've exchanged telegrams. I'm completely at ease with what my future holds. I feel like I have placed myself in God's hands and He will take care of me. I am worried about what Harriet has had to put up with. The laudanum she's been given could actually cause much harm, but that is a problem for another day."

The foursome headed to their positions. Quinn and Remy placed themselves next to Harriet's bed, while Dr. Eisen sat near Harriet's head, and Dr. Bedford stood back on the other side of Harriet's bed.

Quinn looked down at the sleeping Harriet before he began to expose the wound. It was opened with precision. A small two inch cut, slightly up from the original cut. The infection had eroded into the artery of the arm and profuse bleeding was taking place. Pulses of blood with each heartbeat were shooting out, splattering the sheets, the bed, the blankets, the floor, Quinn, and Remy. Blood everywhere! Quinn quickly clamped the artery shut.

"She's losing a lot of blood. A lot more than I envisioned," observed Quinn. "Be ready with me," he continued as he pulled up his left sleeve and laid down on the bed. "Remember! No more than a pint at a time."

Remy zeroed in on the catheter, hooked up to one of Quinn's blood vessels, and poked in a syringe and withdrew, while Dr. Bedford hooked up two catheters to Harriet's right arm blood vessel. "Ready!"

Remy stuck the syringe needle into Harriet's catheter and began to deliver its contents.

"Keep it moving," ordered Bedford. "Looks good, so far."

Transfusion

Moment of truth. The time had arrived. Will it work? Will it clot? Will Harriet's body accept it? Will there be an allergic reaction? Is her breathing changing at all? Into Harriet's arm it flowed. Wait! Something's wrong. She's having a problem. Her body is reacting. She's having a convulsion. "Stop!" shouted Dr. Bedford.

Remy froze. The flow of blood was halted. What would her reaction be? All eyes were directed toward Harriet. All fingers were crossed. Violent contractions! Harriet was asleep, yet so awake. She's running a fever! The spasmodic activity slowly settled down. Sweat pouring off of her face as Harriet shook with chills. Then, she calmed down. The convulsion stopped. She was breathing normally. "Yes!" shouted Bedford. "She's alright!" continued Remy.

Remy proceeded as directed as he poked a new needle into Quinn's arm. "Reception looks good," shouted Bedford. "Excellent! Looks like its coagulating." She was asleep, yet her body was moving. She was drooling at the mouth. She clenched her teeth and periodically bit her tongue.

"She's taking it like a champ," noted Quinn. "So proud of her."

Quinn lie in his bed, relieved, as Remy drew more blood. He so much wanted to get up and celebrate, but he knew it was too soon. A lot could still happen. A lot of things not good. He began saying a prayer, as a smile came to his face. "Keep it coming," shouted Bedford.

The transfer continued without a hitch. Too good to be true, thought Quinn. Chance of failure was still a possibility, but roses seem to be in the picture. Harriet was accepting and Quinn was delivering. A perfect match. Everything lined up. It was as if someone had it all planned out.

"That's it," shouted Doc Bedford. "Mission accomplished. Enough. Quinn. You were successful. A valuable part of you has been transferred."

"We're not out of the woods, yet," insisted Quinn. "We'll have to watch her 24/7. I really don't know what to expect. No one does."

Transfusion

"We need to keep an eye on you, too," insisted Remy. "You've given more than blood. We have to make sure you continue to provide. You just have earned the respect from every person in Fergus Falls and beyond. We are all indebted to you, my friend. You not only have saved Harriet's life, you have enlightened every human being in the vicinity. You are truly a remarkable person."

"Thank-you, Remy. "You have been a bigger help than you may think. It's been a team effort and I appreciate that."

"THE ROADS TO RECOVERY"

The transformation had begun. The roads to recovery were being laid. The road for many of the Wiggins family members varied in length and extended in many directions. It was a journey of trepidation for some and inconvenience for others. Of the five victims of the train accident, Clare came out the least damaged. She was inconvenienced the most.

"My left ear will never be of use, so I've trained my right one to make up for it," exclaimed Clare. "I have a rather incredulous view of what's going to happen to my realm. In all my years of juxtaposing I have never held the belief that nothing but roses would be the end result. My girls were going to make my final years a little bit of heaven, but somewhere along the line things took a turn for the worse. Sure, my fingers got all broken up and they'll never get back to normal, but I'm used to the pain. I've been married to a pain for over thirty years. Oh, that's true I've had to put up with a lot from that old boy, but he has been a real God-send to me. He's a real hard worker. He has been that way ever since he was little Stanley picking up rocks on his father's home farm, when there were more rocks than dirt in the fields. He's been a good provider. I've never had to worry about where the next meal would come from. He was a great farmer in his day and he'd go to work before the sun came up and wouldn't stop till after the sun set. He knew how to plant and he passed that on to his girls."

"He didn't do much educating our girls. He left that up to me and, I must admit, I did a rather outstanding job with that. All four of my girls were pointed in the right direction and were taught everything I knew. All four, I was convinced, would turn out to be expert concert pianists and outstanding sopranos. Now look where we are! Sarah ran off at seventeen with a man I despise to this day.

The roads
To Recovery

Three years of piano lessons, a complete waste. I told her what I thought of that and she ends up committing suicide. If only she would have listened to me! Four years and not one single child for me to pamper. The others paid attention and were on their way to stardom, to a world of wealth that I would be able to use for the rest of my life. What kind of fool am I?

I should have known it was not meant to be. My dreams of having a comfortable ending have gone up in smoke. Harriet is nothing more than a so-so, left-handed concert pianist. Deborah was good, but I have a hunch that she's not going to be able to continue on that path. All that's left is Naddy. She's my only hope. She loves to do those stupid horse racing events, steeple chases. Never seen such an idiotic sport, but I can only hope that she sees her correct role in the family and will get back on tour. She'll take care of her mother."

Stanley was out in his vegetable garden, putting his hoe to good use. "Oh, how I love to spend time out here, creating, producing, and gathering the harvest, providing for my family. I don't do it as much now. I can't remember what most of my tools are used for. Sometimes, I even have a problem remembering what the name is for some of them. I used to be good at remembering names. I never forgot. Now, someone tells me their name and I forget before I ever see them again."

"I haven't completely lost it all yet, but it's getting darn close. They try to tell me that I'm just getting old. Heck, I'm only 54. That's nonsense. Then, why can I remember everything that happened to me when I was growing up back in, ah, eh, back in (pause). Oh, never mind. I know I had a wonderful family. My Clare was always by my side, but the children--- they're a different story. If I could only keep them straight. They say I got knocked around pretty good from that train wreck. I sure wish I could remember how I made that mistake of crossing those tracks. All I know is that I have some pretty good looking front teeth now."

The roads
To Recovery

arriet lay in her bed, rubbing her left leg and looking confused. Her arm was itching. How could she scratch it? Impossible! Not for Harriet. She bent over and laid on her right side and rolled her upper body back and forth. So much for the itch. "I surprise myself sometimes," she noted. "What a whirlwind of events in these past few years. I'm very thankful that I've been able to resume my musical career, albeit a major adjustment. I sometimes wonder what it would have happened had Deborah taken my place on that trip back to Northfield. She almost did, you know. At the last moment she changed her mind and I took her place. A moment of change that affected the rest of my life. Everything was going pretty good. Sure, I had problems with our marriage. Don't all couples experience that? I thank God every day for having Quinn in my life. He saved me more than once. I like to think that we saved each other."

"I can hardly wait for my new arm. Should be here any day now. My ankle is fine. The transfusion I needed worked up well, thanks to Quinn. Getting my spirit and my body back up to the point where I'm ready to fulfill my obligations out in California for two weeks. Going to be in San Francisco and then in Los Angeles. I've never been out there. Can't wait. I'm hoping my addiction problems are behind me and that little Raymond will soon be cleared also."

Naddy was walking along the north shore of Lake Alice, a short distance from her home. "Exercise! That's what I need," she stated. "I can't emphasize that point enough. Ever since I had that accident and had to lay in that bed for what seemed like an eternity I promised myself that I would never take life for granted. I'm gradually getting back to playing the piano and singing. Had to put my sweet little horse to sleep. She had some disease that I couldn't pronounce. I'm never going to get another one. My dream was to do the steeplechase circuit, but reality has finally set it. Doctor Quinn said that it could probably cause damage to my lower body if I took too many hits jumping the fences.

The roads
To Recovery

All the good steeplechases are out East, which would mean staying away from Fergus Falls for the whole racing season. My folks are getting too old to be away from for so long. Also, it would mean having to get a new thoroughbred horse. With Father's deteriorating condition, buying an expensive horse really doesn't fit well. So, I can devote all my time between Harriet and my parents. We're heading out next week for California. I'm a little rusty on the keys, but I'll mainly be singing with Harriet doing the piano. You should hear her! I didn't think she could do it. I never thought a left hand only piano player could make such beautiful music. I was surprised a little, but actually it's typical for her to achieve any goal she sets out to conquer. I'm happy for her and Quinn. There will always be a special place for him in my heart, right beside Harriet."

Meanwhile, Deborah was cautious as she approached the Otter Tail County Courthouse entrance, up on the hill. "This isn't the way I wanted things to turn out, but I have to tell someone. It might as well be the sheriff".

"Deborah! Good morning!" offered Quinn as they met at the bottom of the stairs. "What are you doing here?"

"I was going to ask you the same question."

"I'm filing some land records."

"I came up to see a friend," noted Deborah as she hurried up the steps, leaving Quinn at the bottom with a surprised look.

Deborah was nervous as she wiped her forehead. "His office is on this floor, somewhere. Or is it?" She looked around. "Oh, maybe I should just leave. They'll never figure it out. Ah, but that would mean no sleep again. I don't know how long I can do that. Everybody needs sleep. I haven't slept well in I don't know how long. There it is," she noticed the sheriff's office. She entered the room ever so slowly, paying close attention to see if anyone was watching.

"May I help you?" inquired an elderly lady, standing at the counter.
  "I'd like to see the sheriff. My name is Deborah Wiggins."
  "He's busy at the moment. Please. Have a seat and we'll get to you as soon as we can."

The roads
To Recovery

Deborah took a seat, right between two younger gentlemen. She trembled. She was scared. The man on her left piqued her interest. He was handsome, suave, and debonair, with all the necessary adjectives one would hope to carry. He was freshly shaven, she thought. I could still smell his after shave. It had to be expensive, like something that Quinn would wear. His wardrobe was superb, tight fitting and clean, an exceptional statement of his demeanor. Oh, I wouldn't mind getting introduced to him. While observing him, she took her right hand and tried to cover her blotches of acne, but no matter how hard she rubbed, the acne remained. Oh, if only I could be beautiful like Harriet and Naddy! Life would be so much easier, she thought. If I could go back working with them, but that's virtually impossible. I would just be an embarrassment to them. I sure would like to get closer to them, but in reality, I'm not that good.

The young man looked at her. "Good morning, Ma'am. Daniel O'Grady here."

"Good morning."

"Nice day out there. Too bad we have to sit and wait in here. Do you have a name?"

"Deborah Wiggins."
"Mr. O'Grady!" shouted the elderly lady. "He will see you now."

Deborah watched as he went into another room. It was not the sheriff's office. It didn't have a name on the door. So, how am I going to tell the sheriff? What am I going to say? I don't think I'll be able to admit it. Maybe I should talk to Father. It has always been easier for me to spend time with him, rather than the girls. He knew how to make me feel good about myself. He always had praise for me. The more he complimented, the more I wanted to make him feel good. Oh, I love him so. I'd do anything for him. That wasn't the same with Mother.

They were so much different. Mother was always demanding. She was a user. She'd use me till she got what she wanted and then she'd spit me out. Father put me in the spotlight and I sure liked that. I loved the spotlight.

The roads
To Recovery

He hasn't been doing so well lately. I imagine that it was because of the accident. It has caused more than just physical injuries. It has affected people's minds. I should know. I'm a perfect example of one that has been harmed and I wasn't even in the accident. The guilt that I had for not going on that trip and letting my sister go instead. Oh, what a horrible feeling! I've never been able to get over that. I've tried burning it more than once, but that didn't seem to help. I was missing something. There has to be a way to wipe away that guilt! I don't know how much longer I can handle that.

Look! There's Remy, thought Deborah. What's he doing in here? I wonder if he's following me. Maybe he knows. Maybe he's going to tell the sheriff. He's the one that made me the way I am. He's the one that took away so much. Oh, what should I do?

"Miss Wiggins," interrupted the elderly lady. "The sheriff will see you now."

"Oh, ah, never mind," replied Deborah as she arose and rushed out of the room.

"ADOPTION"

Lin and Remy were patiently sitting in the office of Ebb Corliss, the most distinguished lawyer in the area. It was warm outside, but warmer inside. The Oglesby's were sitting side by side yet looking in opposite directions. Lin was focused on the large window in the front that led to nowhere. She didn't know what she was looking for but rather she was opening up to a new and different world. It's been a rather tumultuous experience in this town, she noted. A town small enough for everyone to know everyone else, yet big enough to hide lots of things. I came here back in '80 with an open mind, trying not to think about desolation and monotony, but I couldn't help it. It didn't take long and I was beginning to think that I made a mistake in agreeing to come out to what seemed like the edge of mankind. I was so open-minded when I got here, firmly convinced that I could conquer this loneliness that kept showing its ugly face. Before I knew it, I found myself with a deck of cards in my hand almost every day. I started playing solitaire and put myself in a vulnerable position.

I so much wanted to have children. We tried and tried, but nothing seemed to work. Remy blamed me. He said there was something wrong with me and that I needed to get used to the idea that I could never have children. Since he was a doctor, I figured he knew what he was talking about. This led to me spending more and more time in my room, with that deck of cards and my little doll in a cradle. After a while I started thinking that maybe it was Remy's fault. Maybe he was the one that wasn't providing the right ingredients. Lord only knows that he wasn't providing much of anything else. So, I went to see Quinn. He said as far as he could see there wasn't a thing wrong with me.

Adoption

That got me to thinking Remy never did say too much about children. I started testing him. I'd mention adoption. There were plenty of young children in the orphanages. Whenever I brought it up to him he'd change the subject.

I was so tempted to look for alternatives. That's when Quinn came in. He caught my eye and then some. He was having his own set of problems with Harriet, yet I spent many a night dreaming about what it would be like married to that man. He had so much potential. Remy was his partner, but I know how that worked. Quinn was in charge and Remy went along for the ride. I've had friends that even told me straight out that they couldn't figure why I still put up with such a man. We actually both knew. When we first got here Remy would come home and complain about how Quinn never spent enough time doctoring, that he was always looking for ways to make more money. I told him that I admired a man who was full of gumption and wasn't afraid to venture out into uncharted territory. That just got his craw. He'd gasp and go hide in his room.

No matter what our problems were, whether they were financial or personal, it always came back to having, nor not having, offspring. I started talking to Mr. Corliss about what was involved with getting a child from the orphanage. He made it sound so easy. The difficult part was getting Remy interested. Any time that I'd mention it, he'd close his ears, until just lately. He's actually started to listen to what I have to say. I think I can thank Quinn for that changeover. Maybe he finally saw the light and figured that I was getting ready to move back home, or maybe it was after he saw me and Quinn having that little meal of oysters and Merlot. Or perhaps it was that Judge Franklin Bannister. Remy seemed to spend an awful lot of time with that man. Needless to say, here we are in the office of Mr. Corliss, discussing the acquisition of three little children. It's been a long process, but I'm not giving up hope.

241

Adoption

"I'll be right back," noted Lin as she left the room. Meanwhile, Remy turned his attention to another elderly gentleman sitting to his left. Remy had his eyes fixed on the wall portrait of Ebb Corliss. "That son of a gun has the audacity to have a large portrait of himself, and it's in his office, right where he could admire it any time of the day. What an ego! I sure think he could use a shave! That beard is so big it almost covers his whole face. I wonder what it's going to cost me. Of all the things to spend money on, she wants me to spend it on children. I can think of a thousand other things I could use. But, if it means staying with me, I suppose I should at least listen to what he has to say. That doesn't mean that I'll say yes, let's do it. I'll think about it. I could say the heck with it all and let her go back with her parents. She's done that plenty of times already and she always comes back. However, this time could be different. Do I gamble, or not? Guess I'll wait and see who he has found. I believe that I should finally tell her that it was me that couldn't. I blamed it on her. What a stupid thing to do. I don't know what I was thinking."

"I'm here for the same reason. My wife wants children and I don't particularly care to."

"Ever since that accident Quinn has been a lot nicer to me. He hasn't called me a turtle, or a sloth, since then. Of course, it might have something to do with all the help I provided in getting those Wiggins back to health. If it hadn't been for Quinn a couple of those girls would never have made it. Of course, I had something to do with it too. Why, come to think of it, I've been doing a better job doctoring than even him. He'd never admit that, but I know what's true."

"I've heard all about you two."

"Where you from?"

"I live on a farm a little north of Perham. Drove my horse and buggy all the way down here just to see a lawyer. I told my wife that we could accomplish the same thing by just going to see Judge Daly, in Perham, but no, she insisted on talking with Corliss."

Adoption

"I feel a little guilty telling Harriet some little white lies about Quinn. I guess that's what'll happen when a man is pushed to the limit. I know what his real problem is. I saw it show its ugly face back when we were in New York, at medical school. He'd get so worked up. He'd blame everybody else for when something went wrong. It never seemed to be his fault, or at least in his mind. It wasn't my fault that he believed he was innocent. I got falsely accused by Harriet for rape. I was just along for the ride. That was Keegan's work and Keegan's work alone. But nobody seemed to believe me. When Quinn found out, wow did he ever get wound up!"

Harriet returned to the waiting area and quiet also returned.

"Good morning, folks," offered Mr. Corliss as he entered the room. "I have set up a meeting in Little Falls for tomorrow morning. The good Sisters will have some suggestions for you to look at. From what I've been able to gather, they do an excellent job of placing those youngsters. I gave them the list of your desired ages. I got tickets for the evening Northern Pacific. We'll go as far as Wadena and then switch to the train for Little Falls. Do you have any questions?"

"That doesn't give us much time," noted Lin.

"Be at the depot by five," ordered Ebb. "I'll meet you there."

"MEA CULPA"

Quinn stood up at the top of the "Well of Despondency" , which not only provided life, but also intrigue. It was a spiritual creation of the mind and a cacophony of discord. He was nervous and distraught, as he awaited the arrival of Harriet. He kept looking at his pocket watch, as he glanced up and down Lincoln Avenue. No sign. "What's keeping her?" he asked himself.

"She should have been here an hour ago."

I could think of a hundred other places I'd rather be right now. This place was my favorite wishing well, but it always gets me nervous. It's like I'm standing waiting for that baby to start crying. Oh, don't be so stupid. There's no one down there. Only a fool would believe that story. Just the imagination working overtime. I didn't care to meet her here, but she insisted. Why here? Why not in my office? Of all places she demanded that we meet here at the Altar of Maria. Lord knows what that means! This is the exact place where we first met. After all we've been through lately, you'd think she'd be a lot easier on me. I know this is one of her least favorite spots. Many times she told me that.

Quinn heard the creaking of the steps and turned around to look down the stairwell. It was Naddy, all decked out in her best tempting attire, and carrying an empty bucket.

"Well, imagine seeing you up here," smiled Quinn.

"I could say the same for you."

"Harriet requested that we meet here."

Mea Culpa

"That sounds rather strange. Are you two getting back together?"

"I'm not sure what she's up to. Have you talked to her lately?"

"We had lunch at the Silver Moon. Your name didn't come up. All she could talk about was that Judge Bannister. Bannister this, and Bannister that."

"Oh, is that so?"
"No. I take that back. She talked about Mother, too. How she really despised her for being so greedy when it came to our musical careers and about that if it weren't for her there wouldn't be any financial windfall for our family. Yeah, she really tore into her. Let me show you something," she continued, as she took Quinn's hand and led him directly in front of the old oaken bucket. "Take a look down that hole. There is no way that a baby could fall into that well, especially a newborn. It had to have been thrown in."

"What are you saying? Are you talking about that Maria?"

"It was murder and I know who did it."

"Who?"

"Harriet."

"What?"

"She hid the pregnancy well. She told you about what happened with Spat and Remy, but she didn't tell you about what happened after that. There were a few of us that knew she had been raped but I knew she was pregnant. She tried as hard as she could to hide it by wearing father's baggy pants and shirts. She fooled a lot of people, but not me. I knew she was going to have a baby, but then a few days later, after a visit from Remy, she was back wearing her own clothes and then the story of a baby girl drowning in the well became the talk of the town. She made that story up. I never talked to her about it, but I knew I was right."

Mea Culpa

Quinn stood there dumbfounded, while below, near the steps, stood Harriet. She began the 20-step trek up the dilapidated stairwell, as Naddy grabbed her bucket and headed down.

"Harriet! I've been waiting for you."

"And Naddy?"

"She just stopped to get a pail of water."

"I have despised this eyesore ever since the first time I came here. It constantly reminds me of a wretched sepulchral wasteland that serves very little for us progressive citizens of our fair city."

"Why did you want to meet here?"

"To tell you the truth. I am responsible for the name of the 'Wall of Despondency'. I think it's time you knew the truth. You put yourself on an island, but it is an island with a tall snow-covered mountain with cliffs, and jagged rocks, and your pool of pomposity where you stare at and adore your image of arrogance. You claim that I live in a house of mirrors, yet you wade in your pool. Yet, you search for fulfillment of your needs, but your pride gets in the way. You are changing. That I can see. You search for tranquility, like me, but fear still lingers. When things change inside you, things change around you. We will never find that tranquility until we quit creating chaos."

"You have saved my life and that I will be forever thankful. It has caused me to reflect on my own shortcomings, and I have come to the realization that we are alike. That brings me to a conclusion. I completely, with open arms, desire to welcome you back as my husband and lover and I commit to becoming a renewed Mrs. Shanahan. A good friend knows all your stories. A best friend helps you create them. I want to be that best friend."

"What made you change?"

"Solitude. Solitude is companionship with nobody. I hate being a nobody."

Mea Culpa

"Oh, Harriet. How I've wronged you. I have made so many judgement calls in this short time. I always thought that I understood what loving a person meant. Ever since that day I met you right here, I had a strange, but wonderful, feeling come over me. I knew right then that something different, something so magnificent, had invaded my mindset and tossed my world into another sphere. My mental capacity was shattered, my thought process shaken, my view of the world turned upside down. My view of myself engulfed in turmoil. My feelings for you have increased immensely, and there now is no room for anyone else. You are what I live for."

"You are on my pedestal of fantasy, but I see that pedestal is cracked and weak. My life is much better than I first believed. When I left Ireland, kicking and clawing, not wanting to leave my homeland, I thought that it would be my downfall. My belief that the whole world evolved around me and that it was going to be me that saved my fellow patriots from destruction and prison, but when I got to New York a whole new world opened up to me and at first I did not like it. I was a nobody amongst a crowd of somebodies. My acts of jealousy ran rampant and I never once apologized for my misconceived actions. My life was becoming one of jealousy of everybody, without me realizing it until much later. I now realize that I did not, and still do not, take criticism very well.

Exaggeration of my life has been so blown out of proportion. Not sure if I can ever fix that. My fantasy world of being immortal, while everyone else is purely mortal, has to change and I promise it will. My entire body has been masked to protect me from showing my feelings of emptiness and shame.

I have made it a point to rid our home of the ungodly amount of eggshells that I forced you to walk on. I've blamed you for your desire to return to the musical world, thinking how selfish you were for doing such, but I now realize you have a life too, and a baby. Our baby. And you should have control of what you say and do in your own matters of life."

"Oh, Quinn. Don't be so hard on yourself. If it weren't for you and your talents, I would not be alive. True feelings of goodness can only come from within, not from others, and now I understand."

"I'm going to have a farewell party out at the lake in a couple of weeks. I'd like nothing better than if you showed up."

247

Mea Culpa

Harriet smiled. "I'd love to."

"I'm selling everything. I'll let you know when it will be."

Chapter 32
"PINAFORE INN"

It was quiet at the Pinafore Inn. Activity on the island just wasn't happening. The usual clientele had found new and exciting spots to spend their free time. Ten Mile Lake and South Turtle Lake were two hot spots for the frolicking partygoers. Quinn had basically given up on luring the sportsmen out to his Hotel LePette. Almost the entire resort needed repairs, or replacements, things that Quinn refused to do. The only regular customer for the summer was Maggie and she spent all of her time out on the island at the Pinafore Inn. One day she had a visitor. It was Naddy. She pulled up in her little buggy. Maggie noticed and came out to greet her.

"I wasn't sure if I'd find you out here, or not," noted Naddy as she got down from the buggy.

"What a nice surprise! Come on in my little castle. What brings you out here?"

"I wanted to talk to you," replied Naddy as she glanced around the room.

"This was a great job Quinn did in building this place. I have some good memories out here. I spent some time right over here with him. Does he ever come out here?"

"No. Why do you ask?"

"I just thought it would get very lonely out here all by yourself."

"It's so nice and quiet," she mused. "Please, have a seat. This is just what I need. It's been a couple of years since I started to get serious about writing a novel. I'll be the first to admit that I really didn't know what I was getting into. Why on Earth did I think that I could do such a thing? Little old me, barely could afford a pencil and paper."

Pinafore
Inn

"It started out rather rough. I loved coming out here and having fun. It was mostly clean fun. Just a small group of fifteen or twenty. We all got along pretty good. Every once in a while somebody would get out of line, especially Spat O'Malley. Quinn bought this place and built the vault. I absolutely loved it. On the highest point of the entire island. Right smack dab in the middle of all these gorgeous cottonwoods. One of the nicest spots in the whole area around Fergus. I started coming out here by myself at first and then I met Sam. He was fresh off the farm in Wisconsin. He led a simple life and really didn't fit in with the rest of us, but that's what I liked about him. Had my eyes leaning towards Quinn before Sam came along, and then reality. There was no way Quinn would get serious with a simple hotel maid. So, I married the young man from Wisconsin."

"Things didn't go so well for Sam. He volunteered to help an acquaintance move some furniture and it cost him a normal life. He fell down a flight of stairs outside and knocked himself silly, never to regain his sensibilities, and he did this after I married him. Such luck! I tried taking care of him, but there was really something wrong in his head, something I couldn't fix. It seemed to get worse as time went by. It was so hard to put up with. I started looking around. I met some shady characters and things began to unravel. They introduced me to laudanum and pretty soon I was getting involved with some real problems that I really didn't even realize I was doing. Those were some awfully dark times. I got involved with a madam. She promised me wealth and fame. That I'd have so much money I wouldn't know what to do with it all. I figured as long as I was taking part in this activity I might as well get paid for it. I tell you what, you don't want to end up being beholding to these people. It only gets worse. I was hooked. The hole I was digging was getting so deep that there was no way out, so it seemed.

Pinafore Inn

People were calling me 'Button'. You know, Button, Button, who's got the Button. There were times when I got up in the morning and had no idea where I was. It was desperate times. So desperate, that I got myself a little pistol and was inching closer to using it, but then I would think about Sam. He needed me. It felt good knowing that somebody needed me. I'd stop in and check up on him whenever I could. I'd make sure he had food and clothes and things like that. It was a good feeling. At least there was one person that looked forward to seeing me, but that kind of situation can also eat on you. I tried as hard as I could, but then the laudanum would kick in. He's the only real close friend I ever had. Soon, I had a visit with Dr. Quinn. He told me like it was. No sugar coating. I had a nasty disease, eating away at me. It was way over time to do something. He gave me a good butt chewing and talked to me about that novel. Before that day I had almost given up on the idea. I didn't have the patience and the determination necessary to accomplish that, or anything, for that matter. Yes, if it weren't for Dr. Quinn Shanahan I wouldn't be here today. He actually saved my life."

"I was able to escape the situation and now I spend much of my time out here, when I'm not with Spat. Yes. Who would have thought I'd end up with Spat? Not sure if I'm good enough to accomplish my dream, but at least, Quinn believes in me. A person, any person, needs that. They need someone that believes in them and lets them know it. He said I could use this place for as long as it took. He even brought out some of the bare necessities for me to survive. Things that I didn't even give it a thought to bring out. This was our little secret affair. He did this for me. Not so that I'd be beholden to him, but just as a friend. Yes, a true friend."

"Spat never was good enough for you, Maggie. He's nothing more than a masher. Always looking for a good time."

"Not anymore. Spat's had a rough life."

"What? He inherited enough money to last him a lifetime."

"I'm not like you. I can't pick and choose."

Pinafore
Inn

"Sure, you can. Listen! When Quinn was out here building this monument I came out to see him. I'll never forget it. He was just finishing the building. He was tired but I got him excited. We laid down right over here and we talked and talked. Pretty soon we stopped talking and hugged each other. It felt so good knowing that I was involved with someone that he preferred over Harriet. I despise her and Quinn knows it. Yes, we made love right on this spot and he saw my mole.'

"You were taking advantage of him."

"He didn't seem to mind."

"Why are you telling me this?"

"Maybe it'll give you some ideas for your book."

"I already have everything in my outline."

There was a knock at the door. "Excuse me, ladies," noted Quinn as he entered and grabbed his side."

"What's the matter?" queried Naddy.

"Oh, it's nothing. I've been having a little trouble breathing. I needed to talk to Maggie."

"I thought you were on your way to Bermuda?" asked Maggie.

"That's what I wanted to tell you. I decided not to go. Too much on my mind."

"I was just getting ready to leave," stated Naddy as she headed for the door. She stopped and turned back toward Quinn. "And by the way I told Harriet about you and me. I told her that I made the whole story up."

"SPAT'S INFERNO"

Quinn was in his office, shuffling paperwork. In comes the Reverend Martin, for his next training session. Quinn was daydreaming, reminiscing about his wedding day. He was standing left of the Reverend, as the music began. He turned and watched his queen slowly make her way down the aisle. Adorned in a white gown, smothered with pearls and diamonds, and led by pride and followed by a 12-foot train. Her skin was as soft as the voice of an angel. When will I ever be able to spend time with her? Quinn asked himself. My medicine chest is finally taking off. They'll need more attention. I won't have time for her. It's as if I have no choice. Oh! What have I done?

"Hey! Wake up!" yelled the good Reverend.

"Oh, ah, here I am."

"Did you get your homework complete?"

"Yes. With difficulty. I saw Harriet on the street today, over by the well. I waved to her, but she just kept right on walking. I don't know if it's worth it?"

"One thing you definitely need is patience. You can't expect her to switch just like that. You must remember you were the one that asked for the divorce. You're the one that needs to straighten out first and then show her that you're a new man. Just give it some time. From what I've seen, and heard, you won't have much more time to wait. You're progressing nicely. I see Harriet every Sunday at services. She doesn't seem to be talking to any other man, as far as I can tell, so we just have to make sure you don't have a relapse."

Spat's
Inferno

"I have been sleeping much better lately. I seem to get much more done at work. I'm still having my doubts and I hold bitter feelings towards Spat. I have been getting along with Remy, and that's a miracle in itself. I have noticed that he seems to be snooping more than ever in my personal affairs. He even went so far as to make a home visit to one of my former patients. Can you believe that? Remy's like a little private detective. I've been ignoring for the most part, but I'm going to start keeping an eye on him."

"Are you sure you want to do that? What about the trust you built up with him?"

"Trust? Doesn't it work both ways?"

"Not in this case. You have to be careful. There are several points that I need to make perfectly clear. One, is don't take everything personally. See people as equals. Treat them with what? Do you remember?"

"Empathy."

"Yes. Very good. Empathy. Number two. Don't worry so much about what others think of you. Make your home in that healthy middle ground. It is not caring what most people think of you, but caring a lot about what those close to you think about you, not in your achievements and garnering praise, but in caring whether they feel respected by you; feel safe enough to be honest, open and intimate with you; feel that you sincerely care about their well-being. Number three. Focus on you. Find a healthy version for you, by putting your head down and running your own life, based on your values, having a healthy vision of a life filled with your passions, priorities, and goals. Here I'm talking about running. You see the word 'running' quite often in the Bible. I, myself, have been a runner all my life. Never content where I was at. Always looking for something, or someplace better. I used to hate running. I dreaded having to run, at school and to home afterwards. But, over the course of time, I came to realize that I had to keep running. It might hurt sometimes, but you have to keep going. Some days when you're having problems you start thinking about quitting. You feel so discouraged and feel like you let God down and you feel like quitting. But the Spirit won't allow you to quit."

254

Inferno

"You must run, understanding God's grace. You have those times when you think about quitting then you think about the love of Jesus. He kept moving through humiliation. He kept going even though the pain was excruciating. His mind was on God's great love for him. It is the love of God that will motivate me to keep pushing. When I'm moving I feel like I'm doing God's will. I feel I am transforming spiritually and physically."

"Running is a great way to let go and leave the past behind us. We run and we leave the bitterness, the regret, and our past failures behind. We move on. With running you can't look back or it will slow you down. You have to keep looking forward. Isaiah 43;18 says Remember ye not the former things, neither consider the things of old. Strip off the every weight that slows you down, especially the sin that so easily trips us up. Remember, you are not alone. Your bodies are temples of the Holy Spirit, who is in you whom you have received from God. Follow this formula: Make every effort to add to your faith goodness; to goodness, knowledge; knowledge to self-control; self-control to perseverance; perseverance to godliness; godliness to mutual affection, and mutual affection, to love."

"Number four. Truly, enjoy the company of others. There are people who are passive, or walk on eggshells. They are afraid of confrontation, are afraid to define andstate their needs and wants, and so live their lives paradoxically like narcissists, actually shaped by others. And, finally, Number five. Take responsibility for your actions. Reach the middle ground of admitting mistakes but holding firm to what is important to you."

"I realize this is a big dose of information for you to digest, and I have written a copy of it for your perusal. I know you can handle it."

Meanwhile, the little one-room hovel, towards the north end of Lake Alice, lie amongst a heavy underbrush and sickly elms. Up on a challenging hillside, in its' coat of dirty white, it told the world that was the home of Spat O'Malley. A broken window, next to a broken entry door was the greeter for anyone who dared come forth.

Spat's Inferno

The sun had already completed its' path across the sky and was replaced by a magnificent full moon. The entire neighborhood seemed to be in slumber as nary a candle was burning in sight. Except for Spat's abode. Home alone, he sat beside his bed, with cigar in one hand and a pint in the other. He rubbed his forehead, and then his stomach, as he wavered in the light of the dying flames from the fireplace. Another puff and then another swig. So went his day on this cool evening.

He held tightly to his drinking cup as he contemplated what had happened to him in the past few weeks. The answer to all his problems should have occurred when the marriage between him and Maggie took place in the spur of the moment, but no, it had only gotten worse. Even Dr. Shanahan had expressed his displeasure.

"Why didn't I listen?" Spat asked as he poured forth from the bottle. "Nothing seems to be working. Maggie's gone. No one blames her. They all blame me. How could I do anything different? Perhaps it would be best if I just ended everything right here and now. He staggered over to a small chest of drawers and pulled out a pistol, sat down on a nearby chair, and stared at the shiny weapon. It was as parkling Harrington and Richardson's Young America Self-cocker, 2 caliber, double action, rifled barrel, with control fire. Nickel-plated, rubber stock, six-shooter.

"Not a friend left in the world, except maybe JK O'Brien and old Rufus. No one really cares what happens to me. No one would even notice if I were gone," he murmured to himself as he lit his old stogie and puffed away. "I do believe my short chapter in this life is about over. What a ride it has been! Finally found what I was looking for. The most beautiful lady in Fergus Falls. The perfect bride who was going to be the mother of my children. My companion! My partner! The joy of my life! Why? Why can't I ever catch a break? What could have I done differently? How could have I talked her into staying? Why did I have to hit her? That perfect, beautiful face! I didn't mean to. It just happened. She wouldn't listen, but why should she? Nobody else does. He put down his cigar and headed for O'Brien's Saloon. He stared at the gun as he placed it in his pocket. And down the street he went.

256

Spat's
Inferno

Minutes later, the house was ablaze. Flames bursting into the air. "Sound the alarm!" Time was of the essence, but still no firemen, just a crowd of onlookers. Nervous neighbors, and one young lady standing in the background. Finally, the alarms could be heard from afar. With bell ringing and horses plodding, closer and closer they came. Straight from the City Hall fire department, through the sloppy, muddled Lakeview Drive, pulling their new Silsby fire engine, closely followed by the Wide Awakes, with JK O'Brien in charge, and the Hook and Ladder crew, led by Rufus B. Jones.

Pandemonium was everywhere as the engine wa parked and the hose dispersed, all the while with the fire doing its' consuming faster than ever. "Get closer!" ordered JK. "Get the water on there. My God! Hurry! We're going to lose her even before we begin."

"It's too late," shouted Rufus. "Gonna be a complete loss. Where's O' Malley?"

"Down at O'Brien's."

Meanwhile, Spat was sitting on a barstool in O'Brien's. He was working on a glass of beer, desperately trying to find the answers to his life's many questions. With sorrows drowning and pain disappearing, his mind led closer and closer to thoughts of the revolver. "What's the answer, Nick?"

"Never give up! You can't let it get you down. Find the inner strength and use it to your advantage. It's never too late."

All of a sudden the main entry door opened and in ran Quinn. "Spat! Get home! Your house is on fire!"

"No!" screamed Spat as he jumped up off the barstool and struggled out the door. "No, no," he continued as he staggered to his home, or to what was left of it. "Now what am I going to do?"

As the fire crew began the clean-up of the aftermath, Rufus walked up to Spat. "From what I can gather the fire started on the north side, in the kitchen. Your neighbors had buckets and tried putting it out before we got here, but it was really getting hot.

Spat's
Inferno

We had some difficulty getting the hose hooked up from Alice, but once we got that going, we at least were able to get water to your neighbors. Needless to say, I'm leaning toward the idea that the fire was started intentionally. Do you have anything to contradict that statement?"

"That's ridiculous. There wasn't anyone else at home."

The young lady was still standing off in the background. It was Deborah and she had a big smile on her face.

"FREEDOM OF OBEDIENCE"

The Quinn house was evolving again. The mission of search and destroy by the satanic invasion was reaping its' rewards, as Quinn sat in his castle on Cavour Street. His knees had been shaking; his nails, unkempt; his hands, constantly digging; his ears, plugged; his eyes, clouded; his heart of stone. He had been a builder of walls.

He sat in his favorite old lounger, puffing away on his favorite old pipe, in his favorite old room, while staring out his favorite old window, at his favorite old yard. He observed the once beautiful splendor of a landscape of green grass, turned brown; elm trees, wilting in the sun; and tainted flowers, begging for drops, reminding Quinn, of days gone by. The outhouse was in dire straits, with shingles missing, and walls decaying. He could smell the stench coming from the horse barn and the slop piles, intruding through the cracked windows. "Oh, how I miss her," he murmured as he wiped his eyes.

He looked over at the cracked mirror. "What are you doing, Dr. Quinn Shanahan? You just can't sit there and feel sorry for yourself. Just because they lie about you. It's not your fault. They have to live with themselves. Oh God! What am I saying? I should really get out and clean that mess up," he prodded himself. "Ah, no. Let it be for now. I'm too busy."

He picked up the Fergus Falls Journal and turned to the back page. There he found an article with the headline: "Harriet Shanahan, ex-wife of our beleaguered doctor, suffers a major setback in her struggle for her sanity." He desperately threw down the paper, trying to shed the burden of guilt he had acquired over the past year. Reality was beginning to take hold. "Time to rearrange. Time to wipe out the cobwebs, chop wood, fill the pedestal, invite Beethoven to return, re-paint the walls. Time to scrap the traps, erase the smudges, dispose of the masks, eliminate the egg shells, and throw me away, Replace me with a babe in swaddling clothes, or a man on a cross. Change the art.

Freedom
Of Obedience

For me, a stairway leading upward and a painting of a Bowie knife stabbing the devil. For Harriet's room, a painting of lambs entering the gates, and a sign saying: Bastille of Yes."

It was time for Reverend Martin to make his visit and he was right on schedule. "Good morning, Mr. Shanahan. Beautiful morning out there."

"Morning, Reverend."

"I was hoping that you will take center stage and talk to me about what it had been like when you two were married. You can say whatever is on your mind, and I can assure you that nothing said in our little visits gets repeated."

"I recollect the countless times in my marriage where I argued for my right to be alone and responsible to no one. There was a time when she requested my presence and I stormed out to my vault in a downpour. Once inside my haven, the rains stopped and the sun appeared to wipe away the moisture. I fell to my knees in bewilderment, unbeknownst that God was working on my behalf. He cleared my path. He opened his powers. He displayed his magnificence. Here I was, selfish and angry, being changed into humble and guilty. He showed me his heaven and filled my heart with pleasantries. He made me realize that Harriet was my true love. He showed to me, hope and kindness, and forgiveness, and I could feel that a fresh love was kindled."

"I finally realized that only the love of God lasts forever. All the earthly things, that we place so much desire in, no matter how attractive they may be, are worthless in the scheme of things. They are only temporary substitutes for God's love. Sooner or later, no matter how attractive, these idols will eventually tarnish and fade away. When we let stress take control of our lives it is time for a change. When we relinquish control of that stress to God, we leave the results in His hands because we acknowledge that we never had control over them in the first place."

260

Freedom
Of Obedience

"When the pressures of life threaten to crush us and we are called to action, begin by simply willing your mind to be still and recognizing that God is in control. (cough) This was my conversion on the Mount. I now have a Freedom of Obedience. A freedom of living a life for God, of following his will."

"It has taken me an extraordinary amount of time to realize that it was difficult for me to love. It was not till I rediscovered my need for God. He provided the inner spiritual energy to love. When he died he actually prayed for those that killed him. That is love's ultimate expression. He is the source of all love. Now, I realize that. Now I've been entertaining the idea of re-marriage, getting a decree signed in court nullifying our divorce document. God's walking with me and struggles with me through my agony and this enables me to understand."

"I found contentment when I understood that this relationship with Him also assured me of eternal life, in which even my deepest desire will be fully understood. There was an empty space inside that I've desperately tried to fill and I failed until I finally turned to God. I have you to thank for that. Only he could fill the void and provide the ultimate reward in life. Ever since my marriage fell apart I've been traveling on a road of detours. They left me disorientated. They test our confidence that we know where we're headed. They take us off track and sometimes even lost."

"There is something else I need to tell you," continued Quinn. "Something that has been gnawing at me for the past ten years. Something that has eaten away at me in a terrible way. Ten years ago my first wife, Hattie, died while giving birth to my first son. I delivered the baby and at first had felt responsible for her death, but then I started blaming God. I took it out on Him. It was so much easier for me to pass the blame. Before I came to Fergus Falls I lived out in Pennsylvania, in a little town called Bloomsburg, on the Susquehanna River. I was married and we were expecting our first child. My wife was strong and healthy and I just knew that she would have no problem delivering. I remember it as if it took place yesterday. It was in the spring and in the evening. The little snow we had was fast disappearing and I remember hearing the ghastly sound of a barking German shepherd, as my wife signaled that she was in labor."

261

Freedom
Of Obedience

"We lived in a small house in the downtown area and Hattie let all the neighbors know that she was going to have a baby. Her screams and moans and yelling were resonating throughout. She was having trouble in t he delivery. She begged for assistance from above. I tried to understand what was transpiring. The thought of her not making it scared me even more. The thought of having to raise a child without help from a wife really scared me. Surely, I couldn't take care of a newborn! How would I be able to succeed in my medical practice? Impossible, I said. I have too many things I had to do to advance my career. No one was going to mess up my plans."

"My brother, Jim, and his wife, Emma, came into the room and were of great assistance. If it weren't for them I'd a never made it. Finally, she delivered. A brand spanking new baby boy. The most beautiful thing I ever saw. Almost instantly Hattie started having chest pains and she was having trouble breathing. I handed the baby to Jim and Hattie said to him: Jim meet your new son, William Howard Shanahan. I said don't you mean nephew and she replied: I mean what I said. He's a Shanahan and will always be a Shanahan, no matter what. I tell you, Reverend, it was as if she had a premonition, as if she knew what was going to happen. A major blood vessel had erupted and she was losing an awful lot of blood and, and (bursts into tears) I couldn't stop it. Then she began having convulsions and all I could do was cry and feel sorry for myself. I tried to comfort her but she buckled under the pressure. She smiled at me then peace fell upon her bed. A calm display of acceptance took control. I kissed her lips one last time. My sweet LePette. I cried some more. I turned to Jim and Emma. All I said was that the baby was theirs. That was ten years ago and I've never seen William since. I can't get that scene out of my head. It has haunted me ever since."

"You continue to amaze me, Quinn. I could never be more proud of what you have done over these past several months. You are on your way to becoming a new man. Be satisfied at being humble. There is nothing wrong with humility. I see my work is done here. It is now up to you to carry this conversation forward with Harriet, and I feel that she will come to the same conclusion that I did."

Freedom
Of Obedience

"Thank-you for all that you've done." I will never forget you."

"Good-bye, my friend. Perhaps, I'll see you in church on Sunday."

After seeing the Reverend to the door, Quinn headed out to his hideaway in the backyard. Many an hour he'd spend in his garden of daffodils. This was his favorite time and place. Spring was coming. Time for the bright yellows to make him feel better. They gave him a sense of accomplishment, a sense of self-worth, a boost to his ego. So peaceful, yet so unsettled. A cause for contentment, yet a question of why. Why has everything closed in on me? Why hasn't my marriage worked? Why does she do this to me? Why doesn't she know that I'm the perfect man for her? Yet this was spring. The yellows were just arriving.

He knelt down and began to pull up weeds among the wavering daffodils. "Who would put these thistles in my world? Why do they want to destroy what I like? Always thorns in my side. What did I do to deserve this?"

Poor Quinn had built up his estate, and his practice, only to turn around and, unknowingly, begin to tear it down. Instead of building perfection, he was building walls, while his heart was turning to stone. But, he was determined to change all that. Enough of the old Quinn Shanahan! No more stones. A new day had arrived. A day of internal reckoning. A day to spread the good news. A day in the life of a new man, ready to accept life as it comes.

Next Day.

As Remy was sitting in the office, having a cup of coffee, Quinn entered with a large box. He set it down on the table. "Are you about ready?"

"As soon as I finish this cup."

"Good! I can hardly wait to see her reaction."

"Is that what's in the box?"

"Yes. It looks gorgeous as far as those things go. I hope she thinks the same. I told Clare that we'd be over shortly. She didn't seem to be too interested."

263

Freedom
Of Obedience

As the two doctors arrived at the Wiggins house, they could hear piano music coming from upstairs. It was Harriet, masterfully handling the keys with her left hand, with little Raymond lying in his basket, wide awake, but quiet. It was outstanding. So beautiful! So unbelievable! Into Harriet's room they went. "Bravo!" commented Remy. "Mighty fine!" added Quinn as Harriet stopped and went back over to her bed.

"Look what I found," suggested Quinn as he set the large box down on the bed and pulled out a prosthetic arm. Harriet looked at it and then glanced at her nub. And she smiled.

"Isn't it just absolutely marvelous?"

"Yes, Quinn. Yes. Put it on!"

"It's not that easy. We have to prep your stub. It's a very precise procedure. Now, you do understand that you really won't get much use of this arm. It's mainly for looks. You wear long sleeves and no one will know the difference. This elastic band will wrap around your stump and hook on to this pin. I wish I could supply you with one that would make your fingers work, but maybe next year."
As the doctors emptied their medical bags with the necessary items, Harriet got back into bed and watched the doctors every move. "Your son isn't as fussy anymore as he had been," noted Harriet as she looked at Quinn.

"Good! Maybe we succeeded in weaning him off that stuff. How about you?"

"I haven't had any urge to take it. As far as I can tell, I'm cured too."
"That's music to my ears. I couldn't be happier for you. It's been a long trial for you and now we can celebrate out at Pinafore Island, just as soon as I perform this prosthesis," he noted as he began the process of putting Harriet back together again, albeit not the real item. It took several hours to get each meticulous piece of equipment set in the exact spot. With minor adjustments here and there, with the help of several other doctors, he had soon Finished. The task was complete and Harriet had two arms.

Freedom
Of Obedience

Preparations were underway for the final Shanahan party to be held on Fish Lake. Quinn wanted to go out in style, having decided to rid himself from the losing proposition of the tourism trade. "Oh, I hope everything turns out just right," he mused as he finished hanging the Japanese lanterns, which were placed all along the trail from the campsite to the Pinafore Inn.

Someone approached the inn from the underbrush. Quinn noticed. It was that Dan O'Grady. "Well, who do we have here?" queried Dan as he stood in front of Quinn. "I've been watching you, Doc. You could be a big help for me. I want to go out west, but I need some money. I think you could pay for my train ticket." "What are you talking about? You're the one that ran off with all my belongings and money a few years back."

"But, Mr. Shanahan. I know where Jasper is. The sheriff would probably like to know that. I need, oh, around $400. Yeah. That would get me out to California and get me set up."

"You don't know where Jasper is. You actually think that I would do something that stupid? You can just go to hell," shouted Quinn as he sent a left hook into Dan's jaw and knocked him down.

Quinn ran for it, heading for the shoreline. Get off the island, but, wait, the boats are all gone. Where are the boats? Dang. That means I have to swim. Don't think about the 8-ft depth. Don't get nervous. Do as Harriet had taught me. Don't get excited. 500 yards. 1500 feet. I'll never make it that far. No time to waste. He entered the water. He began to flounder. Relax. Don't think about how deep it is. Float on my back. Put arms out at right angles so the body is in a 'Y' shape. Don't panic. Don't flail. Don't start breathing quickly. Just lie on my back as flat as I can. Float. That's not working.

Try a whip kick. Keep legs tight from hips to knees and from knees to ankles. Bend my knees so that my shins… Ahk! That won't work. Just swim. Left arm extended, right arm extend. Kick. That's it. Keep relaxed. It's working. Yes, I can swim. Stay calm. Keep moving. I'm running out of breath. Tread water. Catch my breath. Eggbeater kit. Use my hands to keep my balance. Yes. That's it.

265

Freedom
Of Obedience

Keep my forceps flat on the surface. Move one arm in a clockwise circle and the other counter clockwise. Almost there. Surprise! Looks like I'm going to make it. I can touch the bottom. I can stand up and my mouth is above the water line. Hurry, get to my wagon. Hide under it. I got my gun. Did the water mess it up? I'll just wait for that Dan to come. Yes. I'll finally get rid of him. He's been a pest ever since that day back on the river. Wait! What am I saying? That's murder. That's not right. There's got to be a better way. What would He have me do? Turn the other cheek? I hear him. He's talking to someone."

"You see anything?" yelled Dan.

"Nothing."

"What?" thought Quinn. "That's Johnny! What's that all about? Now, I really need to be quiet."

"Let's get out of here before his friends get here," suggested Johnny.

"Yeah. You're probably right. Maybe we can still catch the train to Fargo."

"ON THE RUN"

A spring storm was rumbling through Otter Tail County. Strong winds and a heavy downpour rattled the little house of Braden and Molly's, as they sat at the kitchen table, enjoying Molly's special goulash. "I can't wait for my brother to get back," noted Braden. "It seems like he's been gone forever."

After finishing up, they moved over to the lounge and sat down beside each other. "Me very lucky man," exclaimed Braden. "Before you came along all I had was Quinn. Don't get me wrong, but I needed more than a big brother. He took real good care of me, always making sure that I had the necessities, but he was a very busy man, so I spent a lot of time alone just wondering how my life could get better. Then, you came along. When I first saw you I wasn't very happy with the situation. I thought you were a snob and thought only of yourself, but as time went by I began seeing the real you. You are a very caring person and the more time I spent with you the more I felt comfortable being around you, and when you weren't there I was starting to worry about you, and started missing you. You have changed my life. Everything is so different. One day I didn't want to live and now all I think of is you. What do you think my brother would say if we got married?"

"That is interesting," noted Molly as she laughed. "The first day that I met you I didn't think I'd be able to make it all day. I thought you were so different and I'd never be able to handle your outbursts, or your periods of depression, but the more time I spent with you, the more I began to like what I saw. I not only noticed your outer actions but I began to understand your inside, your mind, your thoughts, and I liked what I saw."

"Oh Molly! I do so love you. If only I'd be able to provide for you. When I'm beside you I feel so different. Like never before. It's as if you have a magic spell over me and I get these tingling feeling throughout my body, and things happen to me that have never happened to me before and I just want to hug you and kiss you and, and you have made me a new man."

267

On The Run

Let's go to Minneapolis and I'll find a job and we can go get married and have a family of our own."

"Oh Braden! How can I answer you if you don't ask me?"

"Molly? Will you marry me?"

"Yes. Yes. But not till the right time."
Then, suddenly, the door burst open and in came Bannister, with his sidekick, Lester, right behind. Braden jumped to reach for his gun but he was cut off by Lester. "Bet you thought I forgot all about you," snidely laughed Bannister. "I knew your brother was gone and I finally found out where you were staying. Won't your brother be surprised when he gets back and finds this house empty?"

"Lester! Take Molly and get in the wagon. I have a little unfinished business to do."

As Lester grabbed Molly and drug her out into the rain, Braden hollered. Bannister pulled out his pistol. "I hate to do this but it's the only choice I have."

"What are you going to do?"

"We're going on a trip," replied Bannister. "By 'we' I mean Molly and I. This will be my way of getting back at your brother," he continued as he fired two shots at Braden, hitting him in the chest.

Braden fell to the floor. "My God! You shot me," he gasped.

Bannister rushed out the door, joining the other two in the awaiting wagon.

"Braden? What did you do with Braden?" cried Molly.

On The Run

"Let's go, Lester. You know what to do," noted Bannister as he jumped in the front seat.

Braden lie on the floor, trying desperately to stop the bleeding coming from his left side. He was weakening fast and finally he passed out. Meanwhile, Quinn arrived at the Fergus Falls train depot, expecting to be met by Braden and Molly, but there was no one to be seen. After spending several minutes looking in each direction, he got into one of the hacks.

"Take me out to my other house past Mt. Faith."

On the way out, all Quinn could think about was why they weren't there to meet him. "I sent them a telegram when I was in St. Paul."

Upon arrival at Braden's house, Quinn hurried inside. There, lying on the floor was the unconscious Braden, with blood everywhere. He ran over and knelt down. "Braden! Braden! It's me! Your brother!"

Braden opened his eyes and smiled. "Quinn! Help me!"

"I'll get you to my office," suggested Quinn as he carried Braden out to the awaiting wagon. "You hang in there, brother."

On to the office they went, where he carried him up the outside stairs, and placed him on his operating table. "Remy! Are you in there?" he shouted in the direction of Remy's office.

"Yes, yes. What do you want?"

"Need your help. Bannister put a couple of bullets in Braden's side. He's lost a lot of blood, but he's tough. I need you to help me get the bullets out."

"How do you know it was Bannister?"

"He said so."

269

On The Run

"What do you want me to do?"

"Need a couple pails of water. One, warm. One, boiling," commanded Quinn as he was preparing the patient. He tore off Braden's shirt and pants and wrapped them around so that the two bullets were noticeable.

"I think he was lucky. Neither bullet went in too deep, I don't see any internal damage."

"Here's your water," stated Remy as he set the two pails on the night stand, next to Braden.

Quinn placed several surgical items in the hot water including his forceps and scalpel. Next , he poured hydrogen peroxide on the wounds. He carefully used the forceps and went in to find the bullet. "Get the bandage ready, and the suture and thread. I've got the first one," he noted as he plunked it into a tin pan. "One down. One to go."

While Quinn went searching for the second bullet, Remy sutured the wound and wrapped it in a bandage.

"Ah, Braden. You were lucky. This second bullet was real close to doing some major damage," noted Quinn as he put it in the metal pan.

"I knew you'd take care of me," smiled Braden. "Now find Molly."

"I should have known better."

"You can't blame yourself for this," insisted Remy. "I've dealt with that conniver. He's had it in for you ever since he came here. It's amazing what jealousy will do to a person."

"Do you have any idea where he might have taken Molly?"

"No. I haven't had any dealings with him for quite some time.

On The Run

I have to confess, Quinn. I was working with him on getting you in trouble. I haven't had a good night sleep since."

Quinn stared at Remy. "Why?" he asked after a long pause. "Why?"

"I'm so sorry," cried Remy.

"That doesn't matter now. All that's important is that I get Bannister before he does any more damage."

"He does own a place up by Perham."

"You know where?"

"Never been up there myself, but he mentioned several times that it was on the north side of the tracks."

"As soon as I get Braden back to the house, I need to talk to Harriet. Could I have you stay with him till I get back? I think I'll need to pay a little visit to Perham."

Bannister, in his uniform of black, was on the move. Shanahan was on the move. Both heading in the same direction. Both determined. Both filled with hatred and revenge. Bannister in a buggy with Molly tied in back. Quinn on his horse with revolver in front. Bannister overflowing with fright, while Quinn dashed with rage, on his way to see Harriet. Molly, with mouth gagged, lie silent as Bannister worked the two horses into a lather. Going past Fish Lake, through Maine town, alongside Dead Lake, through the rural St. Joe area, and into the bustling little town on the prairie, Perham. Houses, spread out here and there, on both sides of the Northern Pacific Railroad, a mish-mash of retail establishments were located along Front Street and 7th Street.

On The Run

Bannister rushed right by all of this and headed straight across the tracks to his house on Elk Street. Scared and nervous, he hid his wagon and took Molly into his one-room shack.

"Sit here," he commanded as he shoved her on to a wooden chair and tied her up and took off her mouth gag.

"You won't get away with this," screamed Molly.

"We'll see about that. Nobody messes with Judge Franklin Bannister and gets away with it. I'll be ready."

Quinn was not far behind. He was riding along Dead Lake, admiring the scenery but concentrating on the task at hand and worried also about Harriet. She hadn't returned from her performances in St. Louis. No word on the delay, which only led Quinn to expect the worst. He reached his destination and checked in to the two-story Merchant's Hotel, on Front Street.
"Welcome, Sir. May I help you?"

"I need a room for tonight. Just me."

"Here you are. Sign right here," noted the night clerk as he showed him the guest book. "That'll be three dollars."

As Quinn paid, he continued. "Do you happen to know of a Judge Franklin Bannister?"

Bannister? Ah, no, can't say that I do."

"I heard he owns a house on the north side. That's all I know, but I have to find him."

"That's funny. I thought I knew everybody in this town."

On The Run

Quinn went up to his room and settled in for the night. He lie in bed, wondering. I'll go house to house, tomorrow. There can't be more than ten houses over there. They have to be in one of them. Wait! They might not even be in this town.

There was a knock on the door. It was the owner of the hotel, 40 year old Martin Shea. "Doc. I understand that you are looking for Bannister. I saw him just a little while ago. He was getting on the east bound train along with a young lady."

"Did you talk to him?"

"No. He came from St. Paul. Maybe that's where he was headed. That's all I know."

Quinn gave up for the night. Next morning he was up bright and early and out reconnoitering the north side of Perham. Not much in the way of houses of elegance. Mainly one story huts of poverty and love. No way would Bannister live in any of those, thought Quinn. Much beneath him. Nevertheless, Quinn stopped at each house with getting the same results at each, until he came up to the very last building, a two-story affair. It was rundown with cracked windows, and unpainted walls. He knocked but there was no answer. He knocked again. Still no answer. And then a muffled noise. An almost silent scream, coming from the rear of the building. He busted in the door as he held on to his pistol. More muffled screams. "Molly? Is that you?" he yelled as he rushed into the back bedroom. There, lying on the bed, tied to each corner post, was sweet Molly.

Quinn jubilantly entered and untied the excited and relieved Molly. "We have to hurry before that bastard gets back. My horse is all I came up on. Hope that is alright with you. Hugs continued as they made their way to the door. "Oh Molly, you have no idea how Braden is going to act when he sees you."

"Is he alright?"
 "He's been doing a lot of moping since you were abruptly taken away from him. You've been the only thing on his mind since.

On The Run

I can't wait to see what he has to say to you when you meet," Quinn continued as he led the way out of the house and to the awaiting horse. Off to Fergus Falls they went, non-stop and usually at a full gallop. "The sale of my resort is in a few days and I've been planning a 'Last Hurrah' on Saturday. Getting you back with Braden will be one more reason to celebrate."

Braden was sitting in Quinn's chair, in Quinn's room, in Quinn's house, looking out the window with hopes of seeing Molly come up the steps and back into his life. He kept one hand on his side where he had been shot. Oh, how he missed her. Oh, how he thought about her every moment of every day. Oh how he couldn't wait till they could get married.

The daffodil trumpets were blowing as Quinn and Molly arrived on Cavour. Braden had a feeling that she'd be showing up any time now. He rushed over to the window and saw his brother and Molly pulling up to the main entrance. He headed straight for the door, while Quinn and Molly dismounted and Quinn watched as Molly headed straight for the on-coming Braden. The church bells were ringing. The firetrucks were clanging. The dogs were barking, and the geese were honking, while Molly and Braden became as one. Quinn stood tall and proud while his brother showed his love and while Miss Molly returned the feeling. Their minds were flooded. Their hearts ecstatic.

"There is something I need to take care of," exclaimed Quinn as he prepared to depart. I have some unfinished business that needs fixing. I have received some very important information that I need to check out. Hopefully, this won't take long," he continued as he headed for the door. "I should be back before nightfall."

"Be, be careful, Quinn," warned Braden. "You find him."
 "Going to try, brother. Going to get even."

Quinn got in his buggy and headed out into the country. With gun safely tucked away in his vest pocket, he approached a run-down shack in the middle of a small woods. He stopped the wagon and cautiously walked up to toward the house.

274

On The Run

He took out his pistol and made sure it was cocked and loaded, as he crawled his way up to the target. He could see in the front window that his prey was inside. He hid behind a bush to see if there was anyone else inside. Once he decided that there was no one else, he snuck up to the front door, got up off of his knees, and burst into the house, catching Bannister off-guard. "Finally!" shouted Quinn. "I got you, you bastard. I should blow your head right off. Put your hands behind your back."

Quinn grabbed his rope and tied Bannister's hands behind him. He pulled out a rag and plugged Bannister's mouth. "There. Now we're going to go pay a visit to a place you'll never forget. Let's go!"

Quinn led him out to his wagon, tied him to the wagon backseat, and headed for Pinafore Island. "By the time I get done with you, you'll wish that you had never messed with me and my brother."

"You have no right doing this!" shouted the scared Bannister.

"You just shut up and start praying."
The trip out to Fish Lake took only a few minutes, and a few more minutes to get out to the Pinafore Inn. Quinn threw a blanket over his captive. The storage room door squeaked as Quinn entered. He knew Maggie was there, since her horse and buggy were out front. "Maggie!" he called out. "It's me, Quinn."

"Over here," she replied, with excitement, as she came out from behind a writing desk. "What a nice surprise."

"I hope I'm not interrupting. I came out to check on how everything is coming along for this weekend's shindig. How are you doing?"

"It's slowly coming together. I've been waiting to see my first copy. They sent it from New York, so I don't know how long it's going to take."

"Isn't it just absolutely marvelous out here? I'm going to miss this place. As a matter of fact, I'm going to miss Fergus Falls. I accepted that position down in Minneapolis."

275

On The Run

"Good for you. I'm just finishing up. Have to get back to town and work."
"You amaze me," offered Quinn. "Always doing something. I admire you for what you're doing out here, but I'm not sure about your evening work. I wish I could help you. I still hope that you will be here this weekend. I want it to be a time of reminiscing about all of the wonderful times we've had out here."

"I'll be there, Quinn. I'm not so sure why you want to get rid of this structure. It has helped me immensely, not only in my writing, but giving me a chance to understand life and personal responsibility and the actual meaning of our life here on this Earth."

"Good. We'll see you this weekend, then. Good day."

"Good-bye, Quinn."

Once Maggie was gone Quinn drug Bannister into the store room. He was placed in a large wooden box. With Bannister's mouth gagged, and hands tied behind his back, and legs tied, Quinn closed the lid and placed a padlock on it. "There you are. Nobody will know what ever happened to you," Quinn noted as he departed.

Chapter 36
"NO VAULT OF HIS OWN"

Fish Lake was calm on the surface as preparations were being completed for the Shanahan Party on Pinafore Island. What was happening beneath the surface was another story. The row boats lie in wait to transfer the partygoers out to the island and the island was set up with pitched tents, waiting for occupants, and campfires waiting to be lit. This was to be Shanahan's last hurrah at his Hotel LePette, a final farewell to a piece of property that had so much potential, yet wreaked havoc with his financial world, in large part due to the competition from Judge Bannister. Time for change was fast approaching for the Shanahan family. Wedding bells were soon to be heard for Braden and Molly. A new job was awaiting Quinn down at the University of Minnesota. Harriet was still doing her thing on the world stage, and her sisters were side kicks.

Quinn made his way to the island and up the hill to his Pinafore Inn. He walked around the long, wooden building, the pride of his 'carpenter' career. However, it was not pride that showed on his face. It was more like guilt. Guilt in the belief that this shrine of domination; this refuge, begging to relieve; this retreat for necessity, was no more than an outhouse, with crooked dimensions and clusters of flaws; a vault of volatility, easily changed in a whim.

"Clare never did take kindly to this castle of contempt. The first day she laid her eyes on it she shook in utter disbelief. Nothing more than a sanctuary for mosquitoes. Nothing good will ever come of that four-room prison," he mused. "This was a symbol of my dreams, a product of my failures, a reminder of my shortcomings. Just a 'john', Remy said. Nothing more. Nothing less. I can't believe I built this with Spat's help."

Quinn chuckled as he went toward the trail. He stopped one more time beside the edifice of deception and watched as a yellow cabbage butterfly, nonchalantly, fluttered past the ill-fated hideaway for previous mistakes, and landed on a small patch of pansies. "Ah yes. Those beautiful purple and yellow pansies that Maggie had planted from seed.

277

No Vault Of His Own

He opened the door and entered the storage room. He looked on the floor and spotted a used deck of playing cards. He went back outside and noticed that the butterfly had not left. "Not a worry in the world," shrugged Quinn. "Oh, how lucky!" He looked over in the underbrush and noticed a cadre of mosquitoes preparing for battle. "Now I see why Deborah wanted to burn it down. Ah, and Naddy. She had dreams of us being together in this little hideaway. Our whole group had a role in this creation. This place will get interesting this evening."

Quinn took out a box of matches and began lighting the Japanese lanterns that he had placed along the trail. They ran from the Inn to the campsite which would soon be abuzz with a select group of close friends. He made his way down the hill and rowed back to shore where the guests began appearing, all prepared for a day of basking in the sun and an evening of diabolical devilment, whether it be inane or mean. The first to arrive was Spat, dressed in a swimsuit of disarray and carrying a whiskey bottle in one hand and an umbrella in the other, he approached Quinn with a precautionary laughter and an eye full of question marks.

"Welcome," offered Quinn, now dressed in a white and black swimsuit. "Glad you could make it."

"I wouldn't miss this for anything in the world. Ever since you invited me and the Mrs., all I could think of was how this day would be a most memorable time in my life. I truly believe something important will happen to me today. Maggie will be coming out later. You know how she is. She takes her time getting all fixed up. How about Harriet? I heard a rumor that she was coming."

"That's not a rumor. She asked if she could come so, of course. I said yes." "So, is there still a little spark in there?"

"Of course. There always was. She is a wonderful woman. Much too good for me.

No Vault
Of His Own

There just wasn't a good mix between her and my job, but that's all going to change. You'll see. I'm a changed man."

"Do you have any regrets?"

"My only regret is that it took me so long to figure things out. We're looking at getting re-married. I've given it a lot of thought these past few days. We'll see what happens."

"Good for you. I wish you nothing but the best."

"Feel free to take one of the boats over as soon as at least three people go over with you. All the necessities of a picnic at the lake are set up on the island. We'll have croquet, Quoits and Skittles, lawn tennis, and horseshoes. The vault is ready for occupancy."

"I figured you'd go out in style," complimented Spat as he took a swig from his bottle.

"Don't ever let it be said that Doc Shanahan was a miser when it came to putting on a party. My only hope is that no one gets hurt, or too obnoxious, or, for that matter, dead."

"Ah, I'm sure we all will have a good time."

"Remy," greeted Quinn as he spotted his partner approaching. "Where's your wife? I thought she'd be back by now."

"Nope. Still at her folks."

Well, welcome. I have a tent set up for you and one for you, Spat. I also have identification tags for each. Just in case you forget who you are."

No Vault
Of His Own

The Wiggins family was next to arrive. Stanley, Clare, and the two girls. All were excited as the girls jumped off the wagon and plunged into the water. All dressed in homemade swim suits, all ready for a day of excitement and turmoil. "Good to see you, Stanley. Welcome to my home away from home, for at least one more day. The island is waiting. Take a boat and head on out."

"Here's the main course," noted Clare as she pointed to the large basket in Naddy's hand. "Should be more than enough for everyone to have their fill."

"Ah, oysters! Fresh from the East coast," noted Quinn. "I can hardly wait. The delicate oyster began his life being thrust onto the scene and had fallen into the abyss, through no fault of his own. Trapped in his precarious shell he spent his time dreaming and hoping that someone would could along and rescue him. Loneliness prevailed. Bitterness ensued. Surrounded by angels and devils, cats and dogs, parrots and clowns, amongst the various fish to a new purpose in life. They can be deadly, especially if baited. It all depended on who takes the bait. Oh, how I can relate."

"They're still in the shell. We'll have to shuck them shortly, but they'll be as fresh as possible," added Naddy.

"Oh," shouted Deborah as she came running up to her mother. "That water sure is cold!"

"Get yourself wiped off and head for that boat. Time to get to Pinafore, girls," ordered Stanley as he walked up to an awaiting boat.

The next carriage to arrive was that of three women and baby Raymond, Harriet, Maggie, and Lin. "I'll see you out there in a little while," added Quinn as he turned his attention to Harriet. "It was nice that were able to make it. Hope you have a wonderful time. Let me see Raymond? How's the arm?"

Harriet lifted the basket and showed Quinn the beautiful newborn. It's amazing how calm he's been. I really think the medicine is doing its' job.

No Vault
Of His Own

The arm is taking quite a bit of getting used to. It really feels weird. I could have sworn I felt my fingers in that arm," she continued as she followed her parents to the rowboat.

"I hope to spend a lot of time with you this weekend," noted Quinn as he held her hand and watched his arm hair stand. "I'll be out there shortly."

Next, Quinn turned to Maggie. "Maggie! What's that that you have in your hand?"

Maggie showed him a book, a beautiful hard-covered book.

Quinn looked at it. 'I'm Starving, A Novel by Margaret O'Malley.' "What an interesting title. Well, I'll be Maggie! You did it. Oh, I'm so proud of you."

"I owe it all to you, Quinn. Without your help I'd have been gone a long time ago. You believed in me. That meant the world to me. That was my driving force. I found that place where I could concentrate without any interruption. It was ideal. I made real good use of the Inn. Thank-you very much."

"We have another reason to celebrate, everyone. Maggie is an author."

The rest of the crowd made their way to the awaiting rowboats and soon were all out on the island. Those included Rufus and Sophie, and the main characters, Braden and Molly. The party was soon in full swing. Games were being played. Refreshments were disappearing. Laughter and frolic filled the air. Tables were set near the campsite and filled with a variety of foodstuffs.

The towering cottonwoods shivered with fear as clouds covered the full moon and the rabbits hid in the underbrush. The waters of Fish Lake showed calm as the exuberance of the young partygoers evolved around the camp. The lonely barking of a German shepherd sounded the alarm for things to come. Clare set out her large basket of oysters and her girls were shucking away. "I want all of these shucked," she ordered. "If you find a cracked one, throw it away."

Of His Own

"It's probably a bad one, and we all know what to do with the bad ones. Save as much of the natural liquor juice as you can. It'll make the stew that much better. Deborah! Light the fires and prepare the pots."

"When can we go swimming?" queried Deborah.

"As soon as the oysters are prepared."

Nearby, Spat and Maggie were in a deep discussion. "I told you to leave that at home," shouted Spat as he took a swig from his bottle.

"You have your liquor, I have mine," shot back Maggie.

"You don't know what that does to you."

"It makes me feel good. That's more than I can say for you."

"I've been trying, Maggie. I've been trying."

Quinn was talking with his sister. "I recognize my shortcomings," noted Quinn. "I realize what kind of fool I've been when it came to family. Reverend Martin pointed it out many a time. It was the mountaintop experience of Peter, James, and John, where they witnessed the Transfiguration. They reacted by showing fear. I realized I showed fear when it came to responsibility to family. I took it out on Harriet. I wanted nothing to do with little Raymond. I have realized how wrong I was. I needed to listen to Jesus' word, to trust him, and to follow him. He will guide us through whatever challenge or difficulty, we face in our everyday life and in our short time on this Earth."

"My! My!" exclaimed Mara. "You sound like a different man."

"I am, Sis. I've been freed I am at peace with Him and, finally, with myself. Into his hands I have put myself."

"Oh Quinn," continued Mara as she gave him a hug. "I have been praying for you for so long that you'd finally see the light and change your ways. My prayers have been answered."

No Vault
Of His Own

"It seems that our whole group has been subjected to changes, one way or another," noted Quinn as he began coughing. He couldn't stop. Something wasn't right.

"Is there something I can do?" asked Mara.

"No. It's just a tickle that I can't seem to get rid of. My throat gets so dry."

"You better have Remy take a look. I've heard that you've been coughing a lot, lately."

"Ah, it's nothing to be worried about. Come on. I'll get Harriet and we can play a little croquet while the shucking takes place."

Speaking of shucking, it was already in full swing, thanks to Clare. Naddy, Deborah, and Maggie. There were oysters everywhere. Good one, bad ones, big ones, and little ones. Real ones and fake ones. Over the watchful eye of Clare, the trio of experts grabbed their knives and began to shuck. "These, for the most part," noted Clare. "Look like a very good batch. I can't wait to get them in the stew."

"Mother," noted Deborah. "Did you hear that right after we eat, Quinn is taking us all on a boat ride around Fish Lake? On the Pinafore."

"Yes. I heard he had to sell it. It's going over to Battle Lake. So, this'll be the last chance for us."

"Have you noticed how much he has changed in the past few weeks?"

"Yes, if it weren't for his Medicine kit, he'd be living at the Poor Farm. I never see any roses in my thoughts when I think of Quinn. The poor guy is due for some good luck. If people would only quit taking advantage of him when it comes to his medical practice. I've heard that terrible cough that he has. I'm worried."

No Vault
Of His Own

With campfires lit and lawn games completed, and pints emptied, the crowd gathered in anxiety and impatience for the upcoming oyster stew extravaganza. Into the pots went the oysters. The stew was heating and so were a few minds. In a matter of minutes the delicacies would be ready---ready for all to partake, although some getting more than they bargained for.

"Make sure they don't boil too long," commanded Clare. "We don't want to try and eat sponges. No more than two minutes. Take them off the fire and put them on this table. Maggie, Lin, Naddy, and Deborah, you do the serving. Make sure everyone gets as much as they want. There should be enough for seconds, if so desired by anyone. Lin! This plate of stew is especially for Spat, and Spat alone. Make sure he gets this. Any questions?"

The feast was on as everyone received a helping of Clare's fantastic oyster stew, with fresh shallots and celery and cayenne pepper. "Here you go," offered Lin to Spat. "I was told that these were especially made for you, for being such a big help. You just holler when you need more."

Spat staggered to a table and sat down. "I, I'll take care of this in no time."

"Here," interrupted Maggie. "Take this plate. "I made it especially for you."

"But I just got a plate from Lin."

"I'll trade you," insisted Maggie as she switched plates."

"Very well. It all looks the same to me," noted Spat as he took another swig.

The stomachs were being filled as everyone devoured as fast as they were fed. Second servings were soon being begged for. "Here's another helping," noted Naddy as she handed the plate to Quinn. "Here's some more," noted Deborah as she gave seconds to Braden and Molly.

No Vault
Of His Own

"May I have everyone's attention," shouted Quinn as he knocked on the table. "I want to thank everyone for coming out here this evening. As you know, (cough) it is a special occasion that we have Braden and Molly back with us and Harriet and I would love to tell everyone that the young couple will be getting married in three weeks and that Harriet and I are getting re-married tomorrow. I hope everyone was able to find their tents for the night. Have fun and be careful. Thanks again."

As contentment spread on the island, so too, did resentment. Alcoholic beverages became abundant, bringing with it bruised feelings and ideas of pomposity. Spat led the charge with imbibing since early morning beginning to show results. "Hey Shanahan," he shouted. "When we going for that ride?"

"Patience, my friend. The Bible often connects waiting with faith. While you might not like it, waiting serves an important role in our life. The work God does within us while we wait is just as important as whatever it is we are waiting for. Waiting demands patience and exacts a price. God proves himself faithful again and again. It is up to us simply to wait, with a confident, disciplined and patient assurance that He will keep his promises. He will come through."

"What? All I asked for was a boat ride."

"And I'm telling you to wait until I and my captain are ready to navigate."

"Are you preaching? I thought you were a doctor."

"Ah, my friend, call it what you want. Just pay attention to what I have to say. I am a new man. My guilt caused both mental and physical illness. I turned to Him--- the real physician. A real man can do nothing more courageous than falling on his knees before God. Confess his sins and ask relief from the deep grief. The boat should be ready in about 15 minutes. So, if any of you plan on going swimming you better make it quick."

No Vault
Of His Own

"Huh, I don't feel good," complained Spat as he sat down on the ground and rubbed his stomach. "Something isn't right."

"Probably too much of that bottle," suggested Quinn as the ominous sound of two barking German shepherds filled the distant air.

"No. I don't think so. I need to go check out your new outhouse," continued Spat as he staggered up the hill.

"Maggie! You might want to go check on him."

"He can fend for himself," stated Maggie as she grabbed a towel and headed over to the nearby beach where the other girls had congregated.

"Maggie! Where did your husband go?" asked Lin.

"He didn't feel so good. Needed to go to the vault. I think the liquor and beer has been getting to him."

"I just don't see what you see in that man. He's evil. Always has been and always will be."

"He treats me well when he's sober. Yesterday was a bad day for both of us. He got fired from a painting job and he came back home and took it out on me, but that was an exception. He has been a good husband, for the most part, since after the fire."

"I need to go there," noted Maggie. "I'll check on him."

"He's pretty blistered," continued Naddy. "Maybe, it is best if we just let him be."

"Well, I have to go no matter what."

"Be careful."

"I have this," replied Maggie as she pulled out a 44 caliber, Colt Double Action army revolver. "He won't argue with that."

286

No Vault
Of His Own

"My God! We don't need no murdering out here," gasped Naddy.

"Make it quick," nervously ordered Lin. "Captain Quinn says the boat leaves in 15 minutes."

"Yes Lin. I will. Don't worry."

On the way up the hill, Maggie met Rufus. "Did you see Spat?"

"No. I can't say that I did. I just came from the vault. Mighty fine building. Best Inn around. Great place to hide. My friend was smart enough to put s ome fresh flowers in there. Sure helped make it bearable. Listen. He might have went all the way over to the west end, down in the grove. I didn't go that far."

"May I have your attention, everyone," yelled Quinn. "Time to board the USS Pinafore. Fill the rowboats and head for shore. My pride and joy is waiting to explore the vast area of this marvelous lake for one last time."

Meanwhile, Maggie was already exploring. Looking for Spat. She approached the magnificent little Pinafore Inn. She made use of the female room and then went over to the men's room. She knocked. "Is there anyone in there?"
Taking small steps she inched her way forward. With the fresh smell of lilacs soothing her wits, she entered. Nothing and nobody. Failing to achieve, she returned to the gathering storm, only to find out as the rowboats were being filled that Lin and Naddy had both disappeared also.

Quinn paced back and forth in front of the helm of the huge sailboat. "Where did they go? Why?" he kept asking himself. "Did something happen to Spat? Lord knows his list of enemies was long. Virtually everyone out here has had some kind of run-in with the poor chap. If there was anyone out here that really had cause to get even with him, it would be Quinn.

The two girls returned and got aboard the Pinafore. "We were beginning to worry," noted Quinn as he glanced over at the girls. "This'll be a short trip around the lake just to show you all of the changes that have taken place over the past year.

Of His Own

Lift anchor, Rufus, and we'll be on our way. I have to be back before sunset and before this nice breeze decides to stop."

"What about Spat?" yelled Maggie.

"He's probably sleeping it off on the other end," suggested Quinn.

"I better stay behind," noted Maggie as she disembarked.

Maggie stood back on shore and watched as the Pinafore departed with crew and baggage. Once out of sight she turned her attention to the Temple on the Hill. She made her way out to the island, but rather than landing at the normal spot she went around to the dangerous west side, where she had to dodge dead trees hidden right below the water line. With precision, she disembarked and made her way through the underbrush and upward to the top of the hill, all the while looking for any sign of Spat. She approached the vault. With caution, she entered the male side. She turned on the kerosene lantern. Nothing inside. "What a nice building," she whispered as she headed over to the women's side. Again she entered. Again, she lit a kerosene lamp. Again, she found nothing.

As the Pinafore made its' way around the lake, some of the excess baggage were expressing their feelings to the public. "I don't care what you say, that O'Malley doesn't deserve Maggie. She could have had her choice of husbands so much better than him," observed Deborah.

"I agree," noted Harriet. "He still hasn't paid for his past indiscretions."

"He'll get his just reward," chimed in Lin.

As the Pinafore returned to its' starting point, darkness began to cover the area. The passengers transferred to the rowboats and returned to the island, where they were welcomed by Stanley.

"Didn't Maggie come back?"

"No," replied Stanley. "Haven't seen her, nor her husband."

Of His Own

"Look over there," pointed Lin. "Here comes Maggie."

"Did you see anyone up there?" asked Deborah.

"Not a thing. I think he went back to town," replied Maggie as she got out of the rowboat.

Maggie felt a sudden pain in her chest. She fell to her knees and winced in agony. "My God! What a horrible feeling! I better go back to the vault."

"Do you want me to come along?" asked Quinn.

"No. I'm sure it's just an upset stomach. Probably too many oysters," she replied as she moved out, placing her hands on her stomach.

Darkness was in full force. The Japanese lanterns were lit up by Deborah and Maggie found her way up to the vault. She cautiously entered the female side. The kerosene lamp painted a picture of uneasiness, while the cool northerly breeze invaded from the outside. The creaking of the floor boards added to the uncertainty as she sat down. She took off her glasses and placed them in her bag as she continued to peruse the site. She lit a cigarette. Rubbing her stomach, she tried desperately to relieve the pain. She heard a noise outside. She reached in her pocket and pulled out her gun. The pain was increasing. She curled up on the floor and the haunting sound of a barking German shepherd could be heard.

Outside, there was more activity. Spat had appeared from the underbrush. Still half asleep he could hear moans coming from the female side. He staggered up to the entrance. Slowly, he opened the door. "Maggie! What are you doing?"

"Spat!" she screamed. "Help me! Something is wrong. My stomach is---Spat, tell them that I saw someone... There was a gasp and then silence. "Maggie! Maggie! Don't! I'll get a doctor."

Spat headed out the door, only to be confronted by a knife-wielding person, standing in the shadow, away from the entrance. The stranger made him go into the men's room where he lunged the Bowie knife right into the chest of Spat.

No Vault
Of His Own

"Who are you?" moaned Spat as he fell to his knees, holding the knife in his chest. Blood flowed profusely as he fell to the ground.

The adult figure, dressed in black and wearing a red hat, stood back and waited while Spat struggled to maintain life-support. In agony, he cried out. "Help me! Save me! I don't want to die." He continued to cry out as the culprit continued to silently wait.

Back at camp, Harriet was talking to Quinn. "I need to toilet," she noted as she headed towards the hill.

"You be careful up there," warned Quinn.
Spat tried to crawl back towards the campsite. Blood was everywhere. On him. On the ground and on the perpetrator. Inch by inch Spat moved, grinding his teeth and crying out. "Lord! Forgive me!"

The stalker pulled out a pistol, aimed, and fired at Spat. Bullseye. Desperation set in. Futility disappeared. His eyes widened. He looked up and gasped his last.

The shot was heard down at camp. "No!" shouted Quinn. "Harriet."
The stalker made his move. He went over to Spat and started dragging him back into the men's room. He took the knife and placed it in Maggie's hand. All the while another person was standing in the background, hiding behind one of the cottonwoods.

Back at the campsite, people were scared. "Something is just not right," observed Quinn. "We have too many people missing all of a sudden. Clare! Where's Clare?"

"She went back to town," answered Stanley.

"So, we know that Spat, Maggie, and maybe Harriet are up the hill. Clare is in town. Rufus! Let's go up there and check it out. Remy! You're in charge back here. Make sure nobody leaves. Braden, and Molly! That means you two, also."

No Vault
Of His Own

Quinn pulled out his brand new, never been fired, Hopkin's and Allen, 32 caliber, double action, 5-shot, revolver with blued, rubber stock. With guns cocked, the two men headed up the hill. They made their way to the men's side. Other than a burning kerosene lantern, nothing seemed out of the ordinary. But, wait. Blood on the floor, leading over to a large piece of canvas, in the corner. Quinn pulled at the canvas. There, lying face down, was Spat. Quinn checked his pulse. Nothing. "His body is still warm. From the looks of things, he was placed in here. Let's go see what's in the other room."

They headed over to the woman's room. "It's Maggie," gasped Rufus as he shined the lantern on the lifeless body. "She's got a knife in her hand. That don't make sense. There's no blood on her. If she had done the stabbing there would have been blood everywhere."

So what do we have? Spat stabbed to death and shot. What happened to Maggie? This seems so peculiar. From the looks of the blood trail, I think he was stabbed first and he tried to make an escape, to get back to camp and was shot and drug back to the vault. Our perpetrator is still on the loose."

"Where's Harriet?" asked Quinn, in desperation. "Can you go back to town and get the sheriff out here? Don't say anything down there to the others."

"Why, ah, sure," replied Rufus as he headed back to the campsite.

Quinn went outside and walked over towards the underbrush. As he perused the area he noticed something red, lying in the brush. He made his way down and picked it up. A red hat. Then, something dawned on him. What if the killer is still in the area? What if he is lurking in the background, waiting to pounce? That red hat? I've seen one like that before. Maybe, our shooter is a woman? Or, maybe, the hat was a plant, to make it look like a woman did it.

No Vault
Of His Own

Quinn walked over to a large bush and sat down behind it, and began waiting for the culprit to return to the scene of the crime. He didn't have long to wait. Someone was coming up from the underbrush. Could it be the murderer, or maybe, it was Harriet? He waited. The silence was deafening, except for the eerie sound of someone breathing. He squinted, trying desperately to identify. It was Harriet. What was she doing? Why would she stay around the scene of the crime? Quinn pulled out his revolver in anticipation, as Harriet walked towards the Inn. A person, dressed in black, and wearing a mask, came out from behind a tree and was preparing to shoot at Harriet. Quinn jumped up from behind the bush and rushed toward Harriet. "Watch out! Harriet!" he shouted as he pushed her to the ground. A shot rang out. Quinn fell to the ground while the attacker took off running toward the underbrush.

Harriet arose and went to check on Quinn. "Quinn! Quinn!" she hollered. Blood was flowing down his arm as he opened his eyes. "Harriet! Are you alright?"

"Oh Quinn! Yes! Yes! I am," she replied as she tore off her sleeve and wrapped Quinn's arm wound.

"Where did he go?"

"He headed for the underbrush."

Quinn stood up. "You stay here. I'll be right back."

While observing the area he took a look at his revolver. He heard a branch crack. He looked around. Nothing. The light was disappearing as he continued to search. Squinting into a large clump of brush, he spotted something. He aimed. He fired. Direct hit. It was a body. The body fell to the ground.

No Vault
Of His Own

Quinn rushed down to the fallen corpse. Cautiously, he made his way up to him. He lifted the mask. "My God!" he gasped. "No one will believe it."

"Did you get him?" asked Harriet. "Who was it?"

Quinn paused for a moment. "It's Bannister. Lester Bannister."

Quinn gave her a hug, as Rufus and Sheriff Bartelson appeared on horseback. "What's the latest?" queried the sheriff.

It's all over," mused Quinn. "The murderer is over there in the underbrush. It's Lester Bannister. I think he's still alive, but he won't be going anywhere. His wound looks bad. Take him to my office. Have Remy go with you. Have him patch him up .I want to have a talk with him first chance I get. There's a body in each of the vault rooms, Spat in one and Maggie in the other, and I'm wounded. Rufus. Could you go down to camp and let everyone know the situation?"

"Yes sir, Mista Shanahan. Right away, sir," excitedly noted Rufus as he headed back down the hill, while the sheriff went over to check the bodies in the Inn. "By the way, Harriet," he continued. "We arrested your sister, Deborah. She admitted setting the O'Malley fire."

"What are you saying? Impossible! Not my sister!" gasped Harriet. "We have to get Remy to take care of your wound."

"Don't worry about me. It's just a nick. You just take care of yourself."

"Quinn. I have had some time to ponder what has happened to me since the accident. I realize now that I spent much of that time feeling sorry for myself, and not even thinking about what you have been going through. It has finally donned on me that at every turn of events you were there for me---the amputation, the infection, the blood transfusion, the birth, and the drug addiction problems. All the while I was thinking 'poor me', Please forgive me for being so selfish. I now realize I need to forgive you for your past discretions."

293

No Vault
Of His Own

"I have always loved you, Quinn, even when you allowed your other self to control. I see that you have conquered the weakness and I admire you for that. You were willing to give up your life in order to save mine. That is a sign of someone who really cares for me. I will forever, hold you in the highest regards. I forgive you and I would just like to say that I would consider it an honor to be your wife again. I love you, Quinn."

"Oh Harriet!" exclaimed Quinn as they hugged. "I know I don't deserve to have such a woman for my wife, but I will promise to put you on my pedestal.""I thought I'd never be able to forgive you, but now I realize that you had no choice. You didn't know. My whole family has fallen apart. Deborah will probably be spending years in prison. My father has been auditioning for a trip to St. Peter's Insane Asylum. Sarah committed suicide. Mother has accepted defeat. Naddy is the only one that perhaps came out unscathed."

How could all of this happen to one family in such a short amount of time?"

"It's not just your family, Harriet. It's also our whole group. Gavin, Maggie, Spat, God rest their souls!"

Chapter 37

" THE TOMB OF ENTANGLEMENT "

Next Day.

The decree was annulled and the vows renewed. With the weaknesses absolved and egos repaired, unity returned to its' rightful place in the Shanahan abode. Fish Lake was silent except for the Shanahan threesome of Quinn, Harriet, and little Raymond, who was lying in a cradle on the shores of Pinafore Island, while his parents were swimming in eight feet of water. The time had arrived for the cleansing.

Every day was to be a day of sunshine, a day of responsibility, a day of equals. The daffodils were part of the scenery twelve months out of the year, even though they only bloomed for a couple of weeks. Clusters of love versus bushes of blame. Samples of understanding versus units of abuse. The ankles of the Shanahan's were unfettered; their hands, caressing; their knees, worn; their nails, polished; their eyes, clear. They were creators, builders of success, as their ears listened to the soft romantic music from the waters of Fish Lake. And then little Raymond began to cry. Louder and louder.

They got out of the water and went to Raymond. Harriet knelt down and changed the diaper, all the while trying desperately to stop the crying, but to no avail. "What is the matter with him?" she screamed.

"It looks like he's reacting to the lack of laudanum."

"Well, give him some."

"I can't. I don't have any with me."

Harriet picked up Raymond and tried rocking him, yet he continued to cry. "Let's get back to town."

"We can't leave now. Everybody will be here soon. I'm afraid we've had a bad oyster, or two," exclaimed Quinn.

295

The Tomb
Of Entanglement

"The stew at our party was more than a few could handle. Maggie and Spat had 'Rough on Rats' rat poison in their stomach. It had to have been in the stew."

"Do they know who did it?"

"I think the sheriff knows but he can't prove it. All I know is that Spat was shot by Lester."

"They'll never be able to prove it," insisted Harriet. "Blemishes that besmirch our very soul. Stains of imperfection that haunt us. Whoever was responsible will pay for their misdeeds, if not in this world, in the next. God will forgive if we follow Him."

Quinn watched as Remy and Lin pulled up in a carriage. With them were three young children, two boys and one girl, no more than seven years old. All dressed in their Sunday best and wearing a smile from ear to ear and carrying the name of Oglesby.

What a surprise, thought Quinn. Remy gave in, yet the bitterness still showed. He has changed and all is forgiven for what he has done in the past. The resentment was so unnecessary. Maybe now he will put a smile on that face, like he did back in medical school. Maybe this is a sign that he has rid himself of Bannister's stranglehold. No more jealousy. No more hiding. Such a good feeling, he thought, as he began to cough. Lin should be happy and content.

Braden and Molly arrived in their surrey. After getting down, Braden was holding his dirty, old, yellow ribbon and gently placed it in the middle of his Bible. Oh, what a change! So proud of him. They're getting married and they're going on their honeymoon to Lake Minnetonka. Hope they enjoy it as much as we did. Molly will be a welcomed addition to the Shanahan family. She's perfect for Braden. He has learned so much from her.

The Tomb
Of Entanglement

There's Mara. Poor girl. She hasn't been the same since Gavin passed. For that matter, maybe none of us have. Who's that young man with her? Could it be? No. That would be asking for too much. That's her brother-in-law, Jim, with her. Maybe. Just maybe.

Mara arrived with her brother, Jim. She was noticeably much thinner and was holding the hand of a young boy. They walked up beside Quinn. "Quinn!" she stated. "I'd like for you to meet someone. This is William Howard Shanahan."

Quinn turned and looked at the young man. The boy stared at Quinn. Both stared at each other. "Oh Lord!" Quinn shouted as he burst into tears and fell to his knees. "My son! Please forgive me. I never thought I'd ever get to see you. It brings such joy to my heart. Welcome. Welcome. Leaving you was the hardest thing I've ever done. I can now see you for who you really are, not who I imagined you to be. Even walk around with a toothpick in your mouth. Sharply dressed. Very handsome. Very impressionable. It's amazing you look so much like me."

"Pleased to meet you, Sir."

"I hope you give us a chance to be your real parents."

Quinn turned momentarily to his brother. "Jim! Hello! Where's your Emma?"

"Hello Quinn. Emma is no longer with us. She passed away several weeks ago. She got very sick and the doctors could not save her. It's just me and Willy. That was the main reason we came to see you. I'm having trouble taking care of him. He needs a mother. I was never any good at raising children. That was Emma's skill."

Harriet and Quinn were both surprised. Harriet looked up and down at Willy and then she turned to Quinn. "I would consider it an honor to have him become part of our family. Raymond could use a big brother."

Willy was nothing but smiles from ear to ear as he glanced over at Jim, and then over at his new parents.

297

The Tomb
Of Entanglement

Quinn looked at Harriet. "Oh darling. That is asking a lot from you. You have no idea how much that means to me."

"Willy!" continued Quinn as he turned his attention away from Harriet. "We have so much to talk about. We are about ready to burn this vault down. It is time for a cleansing for all of us. As he continued to cough."

Next to arrive were the Wiggins family, with Stanley driving and Clare guiding. In the back seat of their surrey sat Naddy and Deborah. Deborah with her fiery eyes, looking for a thrill, and Naddy with her conniving manipulations and short blond hair. Both had searching eyes, one for Quinn and one for impulse.

Reverend Martin and Rufus P. Jones arrived. Everyone that was invited was now present and ready to participate. Quinn grabbed two kerosene cans. "Alright everyone. Gather around the Inn. I am about ready to start dousing the kerosene. I am hoping that you all will get a chance to pour. I am also hoping that you realize the purpose of this symbolism and necessary destruction. It represents a cleansing---a necessary purging of our iniquities. I don't want you to get too close. Those cottonwood timbers will throw off big flames and lots of heat."

Quinn began to spread kerosene on the trembling edifice. With one eye on thekerosene and the other on the participants, the change could be seen.

Amazing! Everyone stopped in their tracks and dropped open their mouths. All were fixated on the works of Quinn. Stanley sat down and wiped tears away, as he spit out his chewing tobacco. He glanced over at Clare and they both trembled with a smile.

Naddy placed her hands on each side of her head and slid her fingers down her cheeks. Her face lit up with smiles.

All participants stepped forward with caution and trepidation. Quinn noticed. "Stay back!" he shouted.

The Tomb
Of Entanglement

"Too dangerous! I want each of you to do some spreading. Harriet! I'd like for you to take over, It's all yours," noted Quinn as he handed the can to his wife. "Try and get some on every spot. I'll have Remy replace you in a few minutes."

As Harriet was preparing to pass it to Remy, a short, heavy-set man approached. "Doc! Do you have a moment?"
"Ah, Johnson. What a surprise! I was wondering if I'd ever hear from you. Did you find out anything?"

"Yes Sir. Took some digging but I came up with an answer to your puzzle. Found out your Molly is the actual daughter of Bannister."

Quinn stood with mouth wide open and in utter disbelief.

"It turns out his wife left him shortly after Molly was born and she was put in an orphanage. She was in there till she was around ten and she ran away. She knew that her real father had gone west. Turns out she ended up here in Fergus Falls and Bannister took a liking for her. As far as I can tell she doesn't know her birth name and the guilty Bannister doesn't know it either."

Quinn looked for a place to sit down. "Stanley! Take Braden and Molly over to Mara. Johnson, do you know what you're telling me?" he asked as he fell to his knees. "Molly! Molly Bannister! Her father is Judge Franklin Bannister, Molly Shannon will be my brother's wife. He'll be my brother-in-law and Braden's father-in-law. Good Lord! I have to do something before Deborah lights the match."

Quinn arose and tried to stop his legs from trembling. He looked over at Harriet. "I'll be right back."

He slowly limped over to the Inn's storage room. Before entering, he looked back at Molly and Braden. "I have to do this," he said convincingly as he entered, while everyone else watched in wonderment.

The Tomb
Of Entanglement

He made his way to the store room entrance and nervously entered. There it was. In the corner. The box. The box that held his arch-enemy. The man that tried to destroy him. The man who tried to get his wife. The man that he despised to the utmost. The man he wanted to get rid of more than anything else in the whole world. He rubbed his eyes and then his chest. The pains were getting worse with each passing day. "Oh Lord! What have I done? What must I do to make things right? Oh, dear Lord, help me. I beg of you."

He unlocked the latch and lifted the cover. There lie Bannister, unconscious. Was it too late? Quinn shook his arm. Bannister opened his eyes and stared at his captor, as Quinn opened his eyes and stared at Bannister. Tears came to his eyes as he fell to his knees. "I can't believe what I've done. Dear Lord, forgive me."

The Judge sat up.

"It's time for you to meet someone," Quinn noted as he began coughing again while helping Bannister out of the Inn.

Quinn led Bannister over to the surprised group. "Has everyone had a chance with the kerosene?"

"I haven't," replied Rufus.

"Go ahead. Finish up. Deborah! Get ready."

The crowd worked themselves into a frenzy as the special moment was about to take place.

Alright Deborah," noted Quinn. "Light it up!"

Shouts of joy, cheers of relief, roars of approval, howls of pleasure were heard throughout the township of Aurdal and the people of Fish Lake. Tension disappeared. Replaced by jubilation.

The Tomb
Of Entanglement

Hugs were given. Pumping of fists. Release of stress. Hearts pounding with pride.

Quinn held Harriet's hand tightly as he surveyed the situation. He watched almost everyone enjoying an intense pleasure and well-being, with unbridled laughter and sheer joy. People were holding their arms high above their heads in a "v" shape, as they watched the flames devour the Pinafore Inn.

Everyone except Remy. He sat beside his wife and three children and moped away in somber dismay. Constantly turning away from the dancing embers, as guilt covered his face.

The gathering moved further back as Deborah approached. She took out a wooden match, scratched it on the cover, and lit it. She glanced back at each of the others as they showed their approval. She turned around and threw it on to the kerosene-soaked edifice.

POOF! The vault was torched. Smoke transcended high into the sky as the faces of the participants showed signs of relief and satisfaction. The crackling of the timbers, the dancing of the flames, filled the air. The charred cottonwood structure was quickly disappearing. The cleansing had been completed. The sins were lifted. The site of death had been burned away.

Absolution was accomplished, almost. Normalcy, perhaps now would return to those remaining in the Shanahan party.

Quinn watched the crowd as the flames roared upwards. He could feel his tense body relaxing. This cleansing will be good for everyone. I'm having a feeling of invincibility. My enemies have scattered. No more need to worry. No more pain to endure. I feel stimulated. Anxious to explore, willing to accept more responsibility. My heart is racing, as serenity is replacing turmoil; tranquility erasing pandemonium. No more apprehension, only peace. Peace with nature, peace with everyone, and peace with myself.

The Tomb
Of Entanglement

My soul is at ease. I feel like being lifted into the air. Such an awesome feeling of power! I am being mesmerized by the moment. I feel comfort when thinking of my adversaries. I feel strengthened in my resolve to move forward and upward to new heights on my journey to redemption. I accept and acknowledge that my weaknesses have been strengthened.

I am shivering with pleasure, as I watch my friends enjoying the moment. No more danger lurking in the distant. No more fears clouding my perceptions. Everyone except for one.

They're all raising their arms in praise and celebration, as their minds accepted and their pains, relieved. Into the vineyard of life we joyfully enter and we feel like we're floating on the waters of Fish Lake, except for one.

We are watching as the heavens open. The dark clouds part ways and the Light presents itself and all accept, except for one. Where once was quiet, now there is verbosity. Where once there was desert, now there is lush. Where once there was emptiness, now there is fulfillment, except for one.

The shackles of depression were unleashed and freedom is ringing out. We are enjoying the verdant pastures as the fateful edifice is consumed by fire. We are all relieved, except for one, and that one is Judge Bannister, for his day of reckoning had not yet arrived.

Lin matched the smiles. Her wish had come true. No more solitaire. No more need for Merlot. No more fantasies to chase. Contentment had arrived at part of the Oglesby household, although Remy was putting up a big fight, still holding bitterness in both hands.

Next Day.

Quinn was sitting in his favorite chair amongst his field of daffodils, and in deep thought about how everything had turned out these past few days.

The Tomb
Of Entanglement

Everything happens for a reason, he thought. That's what Harriet always said. What was the reason for Willy showing up after ten years of not knowing what ever happened? Jim says he never told him the truth, yet he brought him all the way out here from Pennsylvania. Am I to tell him? He does look like the spitting image of myself when I was that age, except I don't think he has a satchel.

What am I going to say to him when he comes out any minute now? What does a father say to a ten year old son? Should I tell him that I abandoned him at a time when he needed me the most? Should I tell him I had no choice? Would he even believe me? Oh, sweet Jesus! What should I do? He's going back home and I haven't said much of anything to my own flesh and blood. How can I make it up to him for all those ten years? I've been so wrapped up in my own little world, not giving a single thought of how he must be feeling about his past. I got a smile out of him when I asked for forgiveness, but that's about all. I was hoping for a big hug, but that's probably asking for too much. He maybe even didn't understand. I can't blame him if he cared less about me, after all, I've been a lot like my father. I haven't treated Willy any better. Ten years! Ten long years and I never found the time to see how he was doing.

Willy made his way up the walk and over to where Quinn was seated. "Mr. Shanahan."

"Oh, call me Father," he insisted. "Come! Won't you sit down? It's a gorgeous time to be alive. This spot is my ideal home each spring, when the trumpets are blowing their horns, symbolizing a rebirth and new beginnings that come to the forefront. How appropriate that you should come and make an appearance at this time! There was a time in my life when I preferred that these beauties went by another name. Narcissus, the name for the son of the Greek river God. He was celebrated for his beauty, but he had a major problem. He was arrogant. The goddess, Nemesis, noticed and lured him to a small body of water where he fell in love with his own reflection. Some people believed that he drowned while attempting to capture his reflection. There are others that say that the nodding heads of the daffodil flowers actually are Narcissus bending down and gazing at his reflection. For many years I had back problems, but since I stopped bending over to gaze, the back pains have gone away. It has been tempting, even now, to bend but I have changed."

"I'm familiar with that story."

"So, how has your little trip to Fergus Falls been so far?"

"Fine."

"Tell me, has your uncle Jim told you much about when you were born?"

"Not really. He said my mother died giving birth and that you had done all you could to save her."

"Is that about all? Had Jim and Emma been good parents?"

"Yes. They've taken good care of me, but there is one thing that bothers me to this day. I really never got a good answer for why you couldn't have taken care of me."

"Ah, Willy. That question has haunted me every day of my life. If there is one thing that I regret having done in my past, it was that. I hope that over time we can become good friends."

"I would like that very much, Father."

Quinn was caught off-guard as a tear came rolling down his cheek and he gave Willy a big hug. "There will always be a place in my heart for you. You get all of your possessions and come back as soon as you can, knowing that there will be a place for you right here in Fergus Falls."

Jim came over carrying a piece of luggage and joined Quinn and Willy. "It's that time," he noted. "Got to catch the train for Minneapolis."

"Thank-you for all you have done, Jim," offered Quinn. "This has been a very special time for the Shanahan family," as they shook hands and hugged each other. "I shall forever be indebted to you and Emma for what you have done for me. Please send me a telegram when you arrive back home, and we must make it a point to stay in contact, and you are welcomed anytime at our home."

Quinn watched as the twosome headed down the path. "Now, all I need to do is take care of my unfinished business with Bannister."

"FORGIVENESS"

Quinn made his way to the bedside of his main nemesis, all the while with intermittent coughing. Bannister slowly turned around and faced Quinn. "I don't know how you did it but you sure had me going. The more you outsmarted me, the more I hated you. I convinced myself of that. One way or another I would get even with you. You always seemed to be one step ahead. I heard about you back in Pennsylvania. You being a well-respected doctor, and all. A fancy man with the woman of your choice. You thinking that just because you were a doctor you commanded respect. Well, I saw through you. You're not any better than the rest of us."

"So did that give you the right to kidnap my brother?"
"I didn't harm him."

"You have raised hell with my family for the past couple of years, ever since you came to Fergus. You have no idea how many times I have fancied the notion of putting a bullet between your eyes. I know how you're feeling right now. I know your kind of people. I was one once upon a time. It took some hard decision making and countless hours of talking to the preacher and the Man above. In my mind I've killed you a hundred times, but that's not the way I'm going to do it. You made me a bitter pill and that pill made me angry. Even angrier than when I think about my father and how he treated me."

"You not only made the life of my little brother miserable, you forced it upon me too. When I was chasing you, all I could think about was revenge. Going to make you pay real bad for the anger you created and the sleepless nights, and all the worry of not knowing. Then something struck me. What good would it do for me to kill you? Sure, it would put you out of your misery much quicker, but what would happen to me? I'd end up in Stillwater prison for life.

Forgiveness

That wouldn't be too smart on my part. No sir, Judge. That would have been too easy."

"Aren't you going to fix my wound?"

"I've been taught about forgiveness. I've had so many things happen to me over the course of my life that most people would never believe, but I know better. There isn't a night that goes by that I don't think about my childhood and what my father put me through. I gradually came to the conclusion that I deserved whatever he would do to me cause I was a no good, worthless, human being, but while you had Braden locked up and me not knowing where he was, or even if he were still alive, that gave me a lot of time to think about what I'd do. You'll be glad to know that Molly has been a God-send for him. He has changed 180 degrees and now is even talking about going to college. She's been so much of an influence on him that I can't thank her enough."

"I learned that there are four steps in forgiveness. You have to corral that anger, that hatred, that has built up inside. You must decide to forgive. It's human nature to want to hold that grudge. To keep the target in full view, but one must rid himself of the old emotions. Let the anger disappear. Holding onto that anger only hurts you, not the other person. Why would I want to hurt myself? It makes no sense. Undue stress arises. I am convinced that forgiveness is for me. You must work on the forgiveness. Perhaps my father treated me the way he did because that's all he knew. He maybe didn't think it was unnatural. Maybe that's the way most fathers were back then. I do know his life was not full of joy. It was really bad in the home country, and didn't get much better for him when he got to Pennsylvania. It seemed that he didn't have the time for family. Maybe he tried, but didn't have the wherewithal to handle family problems. He more than likely didn't realize he was hurting me and didn't think he was doing anything wrong. Yet, I loved him. No matter how often he would knock me down, and beat me, and swear at me, I resisted. I was more determined than ever to show him."

Forgiveness

"I was determined to release myself from that prison he put me in, release me from my emotional journey of disillusionment and resentment. Lord, help me. Guide me down the path of righteousness and give me the hope I so desperately need. I am making a conscientious effort to let go of my grudge. I want to be set free, free so that I can move forward in my own life. Forgiveness is giving up all hope of having had a different past, accepting reality and promoting a new vitality for the future. I have said my good-byes to my past and that includes you, Mr. Bannister. I have blocked you out of my life, but I want to feel empathy towards you, regardless of what you have done to me and my family in the past."

Quinn paused and looked straight at Bannister. He could feel a sharp pain in his chest. He was having difficulty swallowing, while holding back tears, as he again pulled out his revolver. "This was going to be my answer. All the while I was hunting you down, that was all I could think of, but now that chapter comes to a close and so does this one," he remarked as he placed the revolver back into his pocket. "And now I feel the weight of the whole world departing from my back. I have forgiven you and, finally, I have forgiven myself."

Bannister sat up, holding his side, speechless and dumbfounded. Surprised at what was just said, he stared at Quinn, with jaw wide open. He glanced out the window where the bright sunshine was flooding in. "I have no words. I never expected to hear this." He paused and wiped his eyes. "I have something to say to you. Ever since the day my father passed away from heart disease, back in Pennsylvania, while under your medical care, I blamed you for his death. I always said that I would search you out and get revenge. The thought gnawed at me for all these years. It was consuming me. I was destroying my insides and I didn't care. But the truth is that I caused his death. We got in a big argument and I caused him to have that heart attack. I could not handle the fact that I killed my own father, so I blamed you. All these years you were innocent but I refused to believe the truth. Please forgive me," he moaned as he closed his eyes. "As of yesterday I am no longer a judge. I have been stripped of all judicial power and I am in complete disgrace," he continued as he left the scene.

Quinn arose and quietly went back to where Harriet was standing. "Another chapter (cough) has come to an end," he exclaimed as he hugged his wife.

307

"No, Quinn. There is one more chapter," noted Harriet. "I want you to meet this elderly gentleman that has been waiting to see you. That's him there on the bench."

Quinn suspiciously looked over to where sat a man, in his middle sixties, short, with a receding head of white, with overflowing eyebrows and a nose of granite, and eyes with shades of bewilderment, and a back all hunched out of shape. He was carrying a cane in his right hand and tugging on his ear with his left hand, while biting his lower lip. All Quinn could hear was gunshots and splashing water, as a rush of adrenaline filled his body. All he could feel was a huge lump in his throat, as sweat rolled down his forehead, while his hands were shaking. He put his right hand in his pocket and clutched his 32 caliber pistol. Do I, or don't I?" he asked himself. With head spinning and legs wobbling, and stomach churning, he could smell the foul odor of whiskey, and then...then his body and mind erupted. A huge dose of reality slapped his face. "Yes! It is time!" he shouted, as Harriet led him over to the bench. They stopped about ten feet away.

The old man was unshaven and crudely dressed in a suitcoat much too large for his little shaking body, as Quinn stepped forward by himself. Each looked the other over from top to bottom, without saying a word. Silence filled the air. Question marks were floating in their minds. Apprehension was running rampant as a dog barked and a cat meowed and Fergus Falls slept while these two souls inched closer together, each waiting for the others to speak. But silence continued.

Quinn stepped in front of the old man. "You have changed considerably since the last time I saw you."

"And so have you," answered the old man.

"I swore that I would never forgive you, for what you have done to me and my family, but as I walked toward you I realized that I must let go of my bitter hatred and move on with a clean slate. Harriet! I'd like you to meet my father, Desmond. Desmond! I'd like you to meet my wife, Harriet.

Father! Please forgive me!" Quinn noted as he gave him a strong and meaningful hug as Desmond began to cry.

Quinn turned and looked at Harriet. "FORGIVENESS IS HARD TO GIVE, BUT IT IS EVEN HARDER NOT TO."

"NEARING THE END"

Angels hovered over the Shanahan house as a German shepherd barked and the eerie sound of silence spread throughout the neighborhood. Raymond spent the night shedding tears and begging for relief, while Quinn lie awake from a night of coughing.

Help me, dear Lord, I begged. My skin is shivering with goose bumps and I can detect wheezing in my throat. A warning that something is not right. I'm now in my favorite chair, next to my bed, knowing that my lungs are filling with mucus, at half past ten in the evening---a thick gray mucus, a rubbery substance that clings to everything, especially my lungs. Pressure is building. I could feel it. It's like there's no place for my breath to escape. Hurry! Get down in bed and lie on my stomach. Try to spread my arms off to the sides. Be as comfortable as you can considering the circumstances, and hope for the best.

My head is beginning to spin and pound, with tears coming to my eyes, as the hacking once again began. Right on schedule. Heavy and loud the coughing returned. Oh, how to stop it? Show me a way! The pain in the chest is almost unbearable. My heart feels like it's ready to burst. There's a sharp ping and then it would disappear only to return minutes later.

My nose is running full speed with the loose, white mucus trying to escape. I blew and blew, desperately trying to rid myself of the unwanted phlegm. But, what happened? Blood came pouring out of the right nose and splattered across the bed sheet. Oh no! Blood splotches all over where I lay.

I checked my nose again. It was oh so sore, but the blood stopped. Whew! But the coughing continued. The pile of used and abused rags was getting larger as I continued my attempt to stop the flow. My chest felt much better as I positioned myself in a different location in the bed.

309

Nearing
The End

Relief was in sight. My head quit pounding. My nose quit running. My heart slowed down. Maybe now I could fall back to sleep?

Into bed I returned. Tried laying on my right side. Wrong! The itching in the chest immediately began, with the loud coughing following. Pressure was so strong I began to flatulate and to piddle, with no control. What a predicament! So embarrassing! What will people say? Have to make sure they don't find out.

Oh, my throat f eels so rough, so torn, so defenseless. Somehow I need to stop this barrage of pain over my entire body. I need sleep, better yet, I need a miracle. Get something cold to drink, to coat the insides of the throat. To help the lungs do the job that it supposed to do. Yes! A cold glass of refreshing lemonade.

I grabbed a glass and moved to the ice chest, and poured a serving of ice cold lemonade. Ahhhh! Did it ever feel soothing! The only thing better would have been if Harriet showed up, but it's going on one in the morning and this would be the last place she'd show up.

How am I going to get some much needed sleep? Got some warm merlot, some warm Pig's Eye, some more lemonade. Maybe a little goat's milk? I'll try some more lemonade. That seems to be working.

Remy says I need to do more exercise. Go for more walks. Build up my system. It's so hard to do when the coughing begins as soon as I think about going to bed. Here I am a doctor and I don't even know how to take care of myself. A fine doctor I turned out to be! Do more walking, he says, but little does he know that my left heel is in such pain when I step on it, I try to figure out other ways to exercise. He thinks I'm' fibbing.

When I had my last bad episode one of the first nights I heard something crack in my muscles in my left leg. I told Remy that something broke and that my whole left leg went numb from my hip to my ankle.

Nearing
The End

For the most part it didn't hurt but under certain circumstances I would get a darting pain halfway between my left knee and my left hip. It was punishing and stalking and constant, but no one believed me. It has gotten better over time, but there are still times it lets me know that something is haywire.

I slept the night from after two with very little coughing. It is now 6:15 am, and I feel quite relaxed, just waiting for the process to repeat itself. I'm not looking for sympathy. I just want people to know that I'm not imagining things out of the ordinary. I just want everyone to believe me.

Harriet was at her wits end having run out of patience with the only two people she ever really loved. She was holding Raymond on her lap rocking and singing to him in hopes of calming him down. She rubbed her forehead as she heard the coughing coming from the room next door.

Remy was standing beside Quinn's bed, taking several items out of his medical bag. "That was a rough night," he exclaimed. "I don't think I'm telling you anything that you don't already know, but you do have pleurisy. About the only thing I can do is withdraw some blood from you and hope that it relieves your lungs. I realize you don't think I have the knowledge or expertise on this topic, but I'm willing to try. Your blood in the pleura around your lungs has become viscous, a thick honey-like substance that is causing your pleura sacs to rub against each other. I'm going to draw out 10 ounces today and 10 tomorrow. No guarantee. If this procedure doesn't work we don't have any other alternatives."

As Remy began the procedure he continued. "I was with Harriet and the baby. I gave him a small dose of laudanum. I'm afraid he is getting worse. He hasn't shown any improvement."

"I wish there was something I could do."

$\mathcal{N}earing$
The End

"You just concentrate on getting your health back. Rest now and I'll be back tomorrow. I'll have my wife come over."

Friends and neighbors were put on alert to watch for changes in the health and welfare of the Shanahan clan. Prayers were dispensed and sympathies acknowledged as the return to normalcy faded, while the Wiggins entourage cancelled engagements and laid in wait, hoping for the best, yet expecting the worse. Harriet would rotate from one room to the other, praying for a miracle. She would sit beside Raymond and stare at him as guilt covered her face. It was a display of simplicity invaded by powerful demons and a revelation of intricacies being surrendered by a weakened immunity. She would move over and sit by Quinn and tremble with doubt, yet she could see an improvement. Remy's procedure was working, so she thought. Change is what's needed, but what kind of change would there be?

She returned to Quinn's bedside. Quinn noticed. "Oh Harriet. The pains are hard to bear. The gasping is still difficult. The precious air is still in short supply. I need it more and more with each passing day."

"Give Remy's procedure time to work."

"What will happen when the time comes?"

"Don't ask such foolishness. You'll get better. Just you wait and see."

"I'm at ease with the man above. I pray that he will accept me into his realm. I pray that I've been following his rules to his satisfaction, and that he will allow me to be with my mother."

"Remy has been such a big help. So much different (cough) than when we first met back in medical school. Ah, yes. Those were the days. He was my best friend, but I really didn't know him that well. I didn't have many friends back then. Huh! I wondered why. Was it me, or was it everyone else? I thought there was nothing wrong with me. It must have been them. How could they not like my personality? I thought I was a normal person, even if I was so much smarter than all the others. Even if I was being eyed up by all the girls in the neighborhood. Even if they were all jealous of me. Oh well, I thought. It was their loss."

312

 Nearing
The End

"Now I've changed. No more exaggerations. No more manipulation. No more eggshells. No more control. It was hard to admit my weaknesses, but I now see where I've been wrong. I'd like to think that I'll be prepared for whatever decision he makes, but I'm a bit hesitant about being sent down. I hate fires. I hate the heat. I hate the thought of who I would meet down there, and I really hate the idea of being 'forever'."

"Oh, Harriet. What if no one shows up for my funeral?"

"I don't want to hear such nonsense. You're going to recover and you'll see Raymond recover, and we'll all be one big happy family."

"I sure hope you are right. Now, I think I'll go to sleep."

"Good night, dear," offered Harriet as she arose and left the room.

Time slowed down as minutes passed into hours. The only sound heard during the night was the monotonous ticking of the wall clock and the intermittent squeaking of Harriet's rocking chair. Yes, Quinn and little Raymond were sleeping. If only that would continue!

"THE GATHERING"

Quinn lay on his back, in bed, with hands folded and eyes closed, as he departed the present and entered a realm of uncertainty. His throat was parched and his shortness of breath remained obstinate, as the sound of a lonely church bell rang out along Lincoln Avenue, while somber men and women, dressed in black gathered, some in sorrow, some in pain. He saw them walking past. What were they doing? Why were they going ever so slowly? Saying not a word. Just staring at me! My head! I can't move it! I have no choice but to see these people! My hands! I can't move them! They're holding beads! Why am I holding beads? My feet are getting cold. I need my shoes!

The skies were cleared. Blue. Never before have I seen such blue. What beauty! Oh, how I long for such joy and peace. Wait! What's that I see coming right at me? It's getting bigger and bigger. A huge black square. Looks like a rock. No, it can't be. It's a large glob of dark chocolate, begging for me to enter. It's tempting, but no thank-you. I smell smoke. I see fire. I don't like smoke and fire. It looks dreary and gloomy and desperate, repugnant and forbidding. Oh, such putrid odor! The stench is inflaming. I don't want anything to do with that woeful sweltering.

Wait! Look over there! Another glob, but it's white and shiny, and sparkling. It's moving closer and closer. Is that white chocolate? Oh, I've always wanted white chocolate. Some people say it's awfully hard to earn white chocolate. I'd give anything to have white chocolate, with its enchanting fragrance and its perception of purity.

The glob, with its sound of trumpets filling the air, came closer and stopped. Take me, I shouted.

"It's not your time," came a thunderous voice from within. And the glob disappeared.

314

The Gathering

The fragrance of incense is growing stronger and stronger, overwhelming the scent of pine while darkness invades. Tighter and tighter came the walls. I can feel the pressure. I don't like the darkness, but no one is listening. What is happening? I am alone in the dark. I don't want to be alone. I hate loneliness. I despise the dark. Lord! Help me!

I feel movement. Up and down! Why am I moving? Where am I going? I feel trapped. No way out! No way of knowing what lie ahead!

The petrified pine grew stronger as my willpower faded, while in the distance candles flickered and organ music began. Yes! Music! I hear music! Loud music! Organs! Drums! Opera! Sounds like Mozart!

"Yes! The Light! That's what I want. That's what I need. Oh Lord, open your arms and welcome me. Let me be free of all my transgressions. Let me arise and be with You, and with my poor mother and all my relatives. Take me away from this darkness."

Water! I feel drops of water! It can't be rain. There's not a cloud in the sky. Wait! I don't see the sky! I see boys placing something beside me. What are they doing? They're putting three long, black candle holders on each side of me.

The sound of someone shoveling dirt on top of me appeared. Thump! Thump! Thump! Heavy was the burden as the organ music grew weaker, and a German shepherd barked, and I shivered with fright. I began scratching and clawing, albeit to no avail, and then an eerie silence suffocated all. I could feel sweat all over my body. I could see flames! I could feel the heat! I don't like fire! I don't like the heat!

Angels gathered around me. They began playing harps. Then it happened. A brilliant light covered the sky. The blast of trumpets joined the harps.

"Quinn! Quinn!" shouted a deep voice. "I am the Light of the world. Whoever follows me will never walk in darkness, but will have the light of life. Quinn! You are free from your affliction."

The Gathering

I was relieved, as the trembling disappeared and calmness arrived, and then the angels began singing Alleluia. Louder and louder their voices rang out and thunder joined in, and I began to cry.

"Quinn! Quinn!" shouted Remy. "Wake up!"

I opened my eyes. What a welcome sight! There was no pine, no organ music, no lit candles, and no incense; no trumpets and no harps. Just Remy. And I began breathing easier.

"Remy! I need to go to the office," shouted Quinn, as he arose and got dressed.

"But you're too sick," suggested Remy.

"No. I feel much better. Tell Harriet I'll be right back."

Quinn headed out the door. While walking towards his office he passed a new well and it had a sign next to it which read: 'The Fountain of Life.' He continued onward and soon passed the Well of Despondency. He noticed a large sign that read: 'Contaminated, Water Unfit For Use.'

The End

CPSIA information can be obtained
at www.ICGtesting.com
Printed in the USA
BVHW032311030722
641252BV00003B/4

9 781956 349306